Dedicat

To my wonderful children Thomas and Emily,

for their massive support, love and

encouragement.

'The Gower peninsula...a secret that people hug to themselves'
Wynford Vaughan Thomas

Chapter One

'I've found the girl,' shouted Catrin in panic, her hands shaking as she shone her torch down on the crumpled body. She stepped over the soaking headland grass, reached down and touched the girl's frozen hand.

'Gareth' she called, but her words were drowned by the rain and the sound of the waves crashing on the rocks of Rhossili Bay far below. To the left of the headland path was a fence and fields, but the girl lay on the other side of the path where a grassy area led to the treacherous unprotected cliff edge.

'Come over here!' She screamed to Gareth. To her relief she saw him turn his torch her way. He left the path and came slowly towards her. Gareth knelt down beside the girl, feeling for a pulse. He pushed her long wet hair away from her face.

'She's unconscious,' he shouted to Catrin. The sodden, thin, white, smock dress clung to the girl. As Gareth shone his torch down her body, Catrin saw the neat bump, which had been disguised earlier at the party.

'We must get an ambulance, and quickly,' said Gareth. 'Where the hell is your brother? Where's Aled?'

'I don't know,' Catrin cried, tears now mingling with the rain on her face.

Out of the darkness, a calm detached voice asked, 'Something up?'

Catrin shone her torch beam up and wiped the rain out of her eyes. She saw a man clothed in waterproofs, carrying fishing tackle. He was walking along the path from the direction of the causeway which linked the headland to the island of Worm's Head. Catrin assumed he had been fishing off the rocks by the causeway.

'This girl has fallen,' Gareth shouted. 'She needs an ambulance.'

'Oh, right,' said the man, almost casually. 'I could go and call for one from the hotel up there.'

'Great. Tell them it's urgent. The girl is heavily pregnant.'

Catrin stood up. 'Did you see anyone on your way back here?'

'Yeah. A fellow ran past me. He seemed to be heading to the causeway. I shouted to come back. It's getting bloody dangerous out there tonight. I don't know whether heard me, but he didn't stop.'

'Is the causeway covered by the sea at the moment?'

'Not yet, but the tide will be coming in soon.'

'Catrin, this girl needs an ambulance,' interrupted Gareth. He looked up at the fisherman. 'Please, can you go now?'

'Right, I'm off,' said the fisherman, and he disappeared into the darkness.

At that moment, Catrin heard a feeble voice from the girl. She leant down.

'It's alright. We're here to help you.'

'Where's Aled?' The girl started to cry quietly.

'I don't know,' said Catrin. She stared through the darkness in the direction of the causeway and looked down at the girl. 'Don't worry, I'll go and find him.'

Gareth grabbed her arm. 'You're not to go anywhere. It's treacherous out here. Aled's not a child. He won't do anything stupid.'

2

'I have to go. Maybe he's lost his sense of direction. It's so confusing out here in the pitch black. Anything could happen.'

'That's why you shouldn't go.'

'Don't worry, I've got a torch, and I'll keep close to the fence,' Catrin said, adding, 'You're the doctor; you have to stay with the girl.' Before Gareth could stop her, Catrin left.

She clung to the fence to stop herself from wandering towards the cliff edge. She was soaked through and shivering now. The rain felt like sharp pins. It was hurting her face. Eventually she reached the coastguard's hut situated at the top of the steep incline which led down to the causeway. In the distance she could make out specks of angry white foam on the peaks of the waves. She pointed her torch down towards the muddy, stony path, then further on to the causeway. She could just make out some rocks, but the sea was slowly devouring the crossing. Catrin screamed out for Aled. There was no reply, so she started to clamber down the slippery path. Catrin managed a few steps but, as she looked up to scream Aled's name again, she lost her footing, fell forwards, and started to tumble out of control down the bank. She dropped the torch, which smashed on to a rock. Catrin tried desperately to grab at wet tufts of grass, but kept tumbling down, until she crashed into a large boulder which saved her from falling into the gathering torrent below. Petrified, she clung to the rock. She pulled herself up to a sitting position, but continued to hold on. She daren't move for fear of falling again. She knew that the strong currents of the sea covering the causeway would claim even the strongest swimmer. Her right arm, which had caught the main force of the collision with the rock, was throbbing. The pain was excruciating. Catrin just stayed there, hanging

3

on desperately, waiting. She was just starting to despair of anyone coming when she heard her name, and recognised Gareth's voice shouting through the darkness.

'I'm here,' she shouted back. 'Be careful: it's really slippery.'

A powerful light blinded her, and a man in a reflective jacket came and pulled her up the slope. Gareth was waiting, grabbed hold of her and held her close.

'What the hell are you doing? You could have been killed,' he exclaimed.

'I can't find him.' Catrin pulled away from his grasp and shouted hysterically. 'I kept calling. I don't know where he is.'

'You have to come away. It's not safe.'

'I can't. I can't go back without him.'

'This man is with the search and rescue. They'll take over now,' said Gareth.

'No. I can't go back. Not without Aled. My parents will never forgive me.'

'Don't be stupid. The people here have enough to do looking for Aled, without worrying about you,' responded Gareth sharply.

Catrin had to give in, and allowed Gareth and the man to take her back along the headland, through the gate, into the car park. She saw a police car. A police officer walked towards her

'Where's the girl?' she asked Gareth.

'She's gone in an ambulance,' he said. 'I couldn't tell them anything about her. I gave them your parents' phone number.'

The policeman shone his torch on the gash on her right arm. Catrin saw for the first time that her coat was torn and that her arm was covered in blood.

'You look cold,' said the police officer. 'What's the matter with that arm?'

'It's nothing. I'll sort it out.'

'That needs stitching,' said Gareth.

'No. I have to get back to The Dragon House, to Mum and Dad; tell them what is happening.' Catrin heard a helicopter. She saw the spotlights on the surface of the water, which only emphasised the vast area of black unsearched sea surrounding them. Where was her Aled? Nothing made sense. The one thing she knew was that they had to find him.

Chapter Two

Whoever said time heals all wounds is a liar, thought Catrin. Eighteen years: wasn't that long enough? She thought she had recovered well, but actually being forced to return to Gower was like tearing off the plaster and finding that nothing had healed.

When her father Lloyd had told her he was planning to sell The Dragon House she had been hugely relieved. The house had been abandoned since Aled's accident. No-one had visited it, but she had known it was there: empty and looking resentful. Then her father had asked Bethan, her daughter, to go for two weeks to help sort the house out ready for it to be sold. Catrin had been shocked. She had assumed her father would get in house clearance. No-one wanted to go back there. However, her father had been determined to sort it out himself and do some decorating. He said that no way would he get the asking price otherwise. Again, Catrin had been dumbfounded that her father, who was comfortable financially, was prepared to go back just to make money. Bethan, who was determined to go, had been excited. Knowing her mother's reluctance, she had said that as she was nearly eighteen she would go alone. This was difficult. There would be some very sensitive conversations to be had down there. Catrin was sure that her father did not have the ability to handle them, and in a sense, there was no logical reason for Catrin not to go. She had a long summer off work ahead of her, with no major commitments. Maybe she should help her father?

She was starting to weaken, when her father told her that he was planning to hold a memorial service for Aled at Rhossili Church during those weeks and that he was having a bench placed in the churchyard in his memory. At this point, Catrin finally relented: her visit to Gower was unavoidable. It was decided that they would travel down on the Saturday before the memorial.

And so it happened that Catrin and Bethan were stuck in holiday traffic heading out of Cardiff towards Gower. The sun was burning Catrin's right arm through the cotton sleeve which covered the long white scar on her arm. On the back seat lay folded cardboard boxes and empty cases and bin bags. Glancing in the mirror, Catrin could see a woman in the car behind tapping her fingers on the steering wheel in time to some music, while her children on the back seat were looking down at screens. Catrin envied their calm, their normality. Bethan touched Catrin gently on the arm and Catrin turned to face her.

They communicated together using speech and signs. Bethan had been born Deaf. She had some residual hearing and, with the best hearing aids and speech teaching, she had learned to speak. Gareth and Catrin also believed that Bethan should grow up feeling part of the Deaf community. The family learned to sign, albeit they only signed in the order of spoken language. Bethan was fluent in British Sign Language, which had its own grammar and syntax. She loved to use it when she was socialising with her local Deaf friends. Bethan chose always to describe herself as being Deaf with a capital D.

'I know you don't want to go to Gower,' Bethan said, her signing as well as her voice reflecting her conviction. 'I know that you hate it there, but I think it will be good for us to go.'

'It's not that I hate it–' Catrin started to answer.

'For God's sake, Mum. Why haven't you been back before, then?'

'It's complicated.'

'That's what you always say. It doesn't make sense. The accident was years ago. Anyway, I'm really excited. I'll finally see The Dragon House, the beach, and, of course,' she paused, 'Worm's Head.'

Catrin bit her lip hard and Bethan, seeing her, tutted in irritation. 'Honestly, Mum, you should have moved on by now.'

Catrin looked away. What did people expect? She had carried on with her life, hadn't she? In fact, in the past eighteen years she had brought up her two beautiful girls and it had been the most fulfilling time of her life. It was just that, somehow, the ghosts of that night never went away. They were always there whispering over her shoulder.

'It's not that easy,' she said.

'Well, you only have to go this once. The Dragon House will be sold soon and you'll never have to come again. Is the house in a real state? No-one has been there to stay since the accident have they?'

'Grandad has had cleaners going in. I don't think it's too bad. I just wish he'd sold it sooner.'

'He said he knew it would increase in value if he waited.'

'Yes, he told me that, but it's not like he's short of money. I understood why he couldn't sell straight after Aled died. None of us could think straight then. My mother would have found it hard to let go of the house. After all, it might have just been a holiday home for them by then, but it was where she was brought up. I did think Dad would have sold it after she died, but he kept insisting it would go up in value.'

'And he was right.'

8

'He was in a sense. It's worth a lot now, apparently.'

'He thinks this is finally the right moment to sell then?'

'Well, you know, he has decided to move to New York permanently. I think he's decided it's time.'

'He's very old to be moving all that way, isn't he?'

Catrin grinned. 'Don't say that to Grandad. He's always telling me seventy is the new, I don't know, fifty or something. Anyway, he's spent so much time there over the years I guess it's not such a big thing. He has a lot of friends over there and a flat. In some ways I'm surprised he's waited so long to move out there.'

'What will he do with his proper home in Cardiff?'

'I don't know. Your Grandad doesn't tell me much. We'll have to ask him, won't we?'

'You used to have holidays at The Dragon House before Aled's accident, didn't you?'

'Oh yes. When I was little, when my Mother's Mum, my Nana Beth, was alive, we had wonderful holidays there. Rhossili Bay is an amazing place. It's been voted one of the most beautiful beaches in the world, but it's so much more than that. Everywhere is stuffed with ancient history. You know, they found a skeleton in a cave close to Rhossili which is something like thirty three thousand years old. Can you imagine that? On the beach there are old wrecks sticking up through the sand. There are standing stones on the downs, and there are all these stories of ghosts, pirates and smugglers. It's an extraordinary place.'

'And there's Worm's Head,' interrupted Bethan.

Catrin stopped speaking.

'I want to see it. Go there, you know,' said Bethan.

Catrin glanced at Bethan and saw that screwed-up, determined look she had seen on her daughter's face so many times. That determination had sparked plenty of family rows but had also played an important part in Bethan's ability to cope so well with life. A teacher had said to Catrin when Bethan was still at preschool, 'Never limit what Bethan can do. She can achieve anything she wants.' The years since had been a journey with many tears as well as triumphs, but it had been Bethan's determination that had been one of the most important factors in her thriving. Bethan loved music and tried to explain to people that music was so much more that just an auditory experience. She had amazed teachers by not only learning to play the flute but attaining distinction in her exams. She had been offered an unconditional place to study music at Cardiff University in September.

The car in front moved. Catrin inched forward. She and Bethan didn't tend to attempt to converse while Catrin was driving. It was usually an easy silence. However, today Catrin could not relax, and instead was trying desperately to stay calm. 'Two weeks, and the visit will be over,' she kept repeating to herself like a mantra.

The car ground to a halt again. Catrin breathed slowly and started to feel her pounding heart slow down.

Oblivious to her mother's discomfort, Bethan started chatting again, her voice calmer, and signing more relaxed.

'Sabrina and I were watching the opening of the Olympic Games last night.'

'Oh really? I'm sorry I missed it. Was it good?' Catrin answered, thinking the conversation had moved on. But, of course, it hadn't.

'They showed Rhossili Bay.'

'Really? Are you sure it was Rhossili?'

'Oh yes. I read it on the subtitles.'

'How come it was in the ceremony?'

'They had a film of these kids in T shirts singing on the beach. You and Dad should have seen it.'

'I was busy trying to write this article about Aled for Grandad.'

'What's that for then?'

'He wants me to write something for the firm's website about Aled, to put up after the memorial. It's difficult. I'm not sure how many people will even remember him. I guess if it's for the website I need to write about Aled as an architect. I know he was meant to be outstanding at his work, but I don't know any details. It makes me realise how little I actually know about Aled in the years before he died, most of which he spent working in America. We hardly ever communicated then whether by letter or phone. He didn't even come over to my wedding. The night of his accident was the first time I'd seen him for about three years. It's a chapter of his life I know very little about.'

'Well, anyway,' continued Bethan, not interested in her mother's dilemma, 'about Worm's Head. I said we saw it on TV. Sabrina said it didn't look anything like a worm. What is it like there? Why's it called that?'

Despite the heat in the car, Catrin shivered. She was there. She could feel the wind burning her cheeks as she peered into pitch blackness, the driving rain mingled with tears on her face.

As she sat in the car, Catrin suddenly felt her heart start to pound. Oh God, not now, not a panic attack. She consciously slowed her breathing, counted silently, then she tried to notice the things around her: the hot sticky steering wheel clenched by her fingers; the sweat running down her back; the heat of the sun on her arm; and, out there, a buzzard hovering just at the edge of the motorway.

'You alright, Mum?'

11

'Yes, I'm fine.'

'So why is it called Worm's Head?'

'Let me think. Yes, the name comes from a very old Viking word, w-u-r-m (she finger spelled), which actually means Dragon. The story goes that Vikings were invading Rhossili on a foggy night and they thought Worm's Head was a dragon.'

'So really it should be called Dragon's Head? Wow. Is that why Grandad's house is called The Dragon House?'

'That's right. The Dragon House is actually in a tiny village called Bryn Draig. It's up from Rhossili on the side of the downs. You can see Worm's Head from there.'

'And it was on Worm's Head that Aled fell? On TV I saw it was an island, so how did he get there? Was he in a boat or something?'

Catrin gritted her teeth. This was one of the reasons going back was such a mistake, and particularly to go with Bethan. She was bound to be full of questions, questions Catrin couldn't answer, talk that would stir up memories best forgotten. If it had been simply her and her father it would have been easier. They both knew the boundaries of what they would talk about. Bethan was like a small child running around a silent church picking up sacred things and shouting out questions. Even the way she said Aled's name was all wrong. The correct way to say it was in solemn, reverend tones. Also, the accident was not something to be glibly talked about. If it had to be mentioned, you skirted tactfully around it, spoke hesitantly, embarrassed to have brought it up. However, Bethan had no idea of this unspoken etiquette. Catrin coughed and tried to answer her.

'Worm's Head is not always cut off. There's a strip of land, a causeway that links Worm's Head to the

12

mainland. Most of the time it is covered with sea, but for a few hours each day it is clear.'

'Do you mean like that place we went in France where the monastery was?'

'M-o-n-t-S-a-i-n-t-M-i-c-h-e-l?' Catrin finger spelled.

'That's it.'

'Yes, something like that, but there is no man-made path. It's a very rough causeway, and on Worm's Head there are no buildings. No-one lives there, well, apart from sheep. People do visit via the causeway when it's open.'

'So Aled went over the causeway? It sounds an exciting place. It must have been fun going over when you were younger. You know, when you went to stay at The Dragon House when you were little.'

'Actually, I've never been to Worm's Head. My mother, your Grandma Isabel, was adamant we should never go there, so we never did.'

'But Aled went on the night of his party?'

Catrin nodded. 'Yes, but no-one knows why.'

'It wasn't a birthday party for Aled, was it? I mean, he was pretty old by then?'

'Aled was only twenty seven, but, no. It wasn't a birthday party. My parents were celebrating him coming to work in Grandad's practice. Aled had been out in New York for about three years working in an associated office. Grandad was very excited he was coming back.'

'I'd have thought it was a bit of a come down to come back to the UK from America.'

Catrin fiddled with her bracelet. 'Aled was going to head up some big project here. He was an outstanding architect.'

'Grandad is always telling me that.'

'Aled was very special.' The car in front made a move and Catrin turned away to concentrate on driving.

Eventually they were able to leave the motorway and turn off towards Swansea. Catrin saw the first brown sign to Gower. She really was going there. Soon it will all be over, she reminded herself and, as a further distraction, she started to try and plan the things she would do after the visit. The garden: that's what she would do. She would have a go at the border; pull out the bindweed that was taking over.

Then she gripped the steering wheel. That was exactly what she had been thinking eighteen years ago as she and Gareth had driven to Gower for Aled's party. She had been nervous about going then, though, on reflection, the reasons seemed relatively trivial. The thing was that she had not been married long then, and had hated leaving her first child Lowri. It was their first night apart. She remembered giving Gareth's parents numerous lists, clothes and equipment for every possible eventuality, but still she had been worried. But, of course, there had been no question of them not going: the party was for Aled. However, she had been dreading the whole thing. Socialising with her father's trendy architect friends always made her feel so inadequate. Also, of course, her mother would be there. Catrin always worried about her at social occasions. She remembered sitting in the car next to Gareth on the way to the party her hands clasped together, thinking, 'Get through tonight; we can leave straight after breakfast. I can go home and have a good go at the garden.'

But that's not what had happened. She had sleepwalked into one of the most momentous, life-changing moments of her life. Back in Cardiff in those days she had an enormous family calendar on which she kept meticulous record of all the events coming up. It had made her feel in control of her life. But that night things had happened which demonstrated that that was a complete illusion. The calendar had been torn up on her return. Nothing had been the same since the night of the thirtieth of July nineteen-ninety-four.

As she drove now to Gower with Bethan, and planned her time after the visit, she reassured herself that fate would never do that to her again: lightning never strikes in the same place twice. She sat back and tried to relax, tried to silence the voices that nagged away, telling her that she was wrong. Because, of course, deep down she knew that lightning can strike more than once in the same place and, if that could happen, surely fate could catch her again, could once more set in motion events for which she was totally unprepared. Once again, events could occur that would change her life and the lives of those around her, for ever.

Chapter Three

Catrin pulled into a petrol station. As she got out of the car to fill it up Bethan said, 'I'm going to buy a drink.'

'OK. Take some money. Could you get me a coke?'

Bethan took a five pound note from Catrin's purse and walked to the kiosk.

As Catrin awkwardly lifted the petrol pump from its stand, she watched as Bethan, tall, slim, in denim shorts and white T shirt, her long straight black hair falling down her back, walked confidently ahead of her. Catrin felt that familiar mixture of pride and panic familiar to many parents. People talked about your 'birds leaving the nest' but, far from wanting to push her chicks out, as she had seen many birds do on Spring Watch, Catrin's natural instinct was to pull them back, to protect them from a world of predators. She admitted to being even more protective of Bethan. Out in the world, there were so many things that Catrin could not control, and it was impossible to protect Bethan from them all. Of course, this is where Bethan's inner strength and confidence came in. It was Bethan who picked herself up after being teased, ignored, or told she could not achieve a dream. Things that broke Catrin's heart seemed, often miraculously, to make Bethan stronger. But not always, and there had been plenty of tears and hurt to wipe away.

As she watched Bethan going over to the kiosk, Catrin was aware that even in this simple act of buying some drinks there were things that could happen that could embarrass or hurt Bethan. The man serving might mumble or look away so that Bethan couldn't lip read him or, if he saw her hearing aids, and actually realised she was Deaf, he might over-enunciate in some kind of pantomime, making lip reading impossible. Of course, he might be the kind of person who refused to even try to communicate, who would stare at her blankly, and claim that he could not understand her simply because her intonation was a bit flat and nasal. Catrin's fears were not groundless. These were all things that had happened to Bethan a number of times. Fortunately Bethan returned, smiling, holding the drinks.

'It was OK, Mum,' said Bethan, laughing, knowing exactly what her mother was thinking. 'It was easy. Do you know I ordered a round of drinks in the pub the other night? Orange juice for me, of course,' Bethan added, grinning in a way that did nothing to reassure her mother. 'Anyway, this woman behind the bar kept saying 'What?' to me, and looking at Sabrina to ask her what I was saying. Sabrina, of course, refused to play. In the end, the woman gave me a piece of paper and a pen, and told me to write down my order, so I wrote, 'You're a stupid cow,' and handed it back to her.'

'Honestly, Bethan,' said Catrin, shocked.

Bethan laughed. 'It was OK. There was a good-looking guy behind the bar who came over and took the order no problem.'

Catrin finished filling the car and went to pay. Then she drove to a space away from the queues where she and Bethan could have a drink.

'Someone at school told me Gower is cool now. Katherine Jenkins has a house there.'

'I heard that. Of course, Dylan Thomas spent his childhood there.'

'Who?'

'He's a Welsh poet, famous.'

'Hang on. Under Milk Wood.'

'That's right. I think he got stranded on Worm's Head once.'

'So, who do you think will buy the Dragon House?'

'I've no idea. Grandad is doing this sealed bid thing.'

'What's that?'

'Well, the house is put up for sale as usual, but then people put in their bids in sealed envelopes by a certain day. Grandad can then choose who he sells the house to.'

'Ah, the person who offers the most, I suppose.'

'Maybe, but also whoever is in the best position to buy and all that kind of thing. Anyway, I have no idea who will buy it. It'll be odd to think of strangers living there, but it should be lived in properly. It should be a family home.'

'What's the actual house like, then?' asked Bethan.

Catrin relaxed. 'The house is lovely, big, and rambling. The gardens were always pretty wild. I suppose inside will look very old-fashioned now: patterned carpets, and the kitchen was all odds and sods.'

'It doesn't sound like Grandad's kind of house. The houses he designs, like his Cardiff house, are all ultra-modern. I love them.'

'They are certainly different.'

'I don't see why you and Dad are so down on Grandad's house. I mean, you live in a modern house.'

'Ours is an estate house; nothing like the kind of thing Grandad designs. He despises houses like ours.'

'It is a bit boring. Why don't you move?'

'I don't know. Dad wanted to, but it was always handy being close to my Mum, your Grandma Isabel. You know, I could look after her.'

18

'But Grandma died years ago when I was just a baby.'

'I know.' Time was a weird thing, thought Catrin. Eighteen years since losing Aled; sixteen since losing her mother; so long ago, and yet it felt like no time at all.

'So is the Dragon House very old?'

'Oh yes, very. I think it was a farmhouse originally. That was long before my Nana Beth lived there, though.'

'It must have been a fantastic place to grow up for Grandma Isabel.'

'It was. For her and her sister, my Aunty Angela. I think it must have been wonderful.'

'And then your Mum took you and Aled to stay for holidays?'

'That's right. Every summer we all went to stay with Nana Beth. I would count down the days until we went. I loved my Nana Beth. She would take me down to the beach with my red metal bucket and spade and we would build enormous princess castles. There's a lot of shells on the beach. We would collect them to decorate the castles. Aled, of course, would be running around. He was five years younger than me and didn't have the patience to build. He'd dash back and forth getting the water for the moat, spilling most of it on the way–' Catrin could see him running, his thick blonde curls blown about in the wind.

'I like hearing normal things about Aled,' said Bethan.

'What do you mean?'

'The thing is, when you and Grandad talk about him, it's like he was some kind of god. Well, that's not possible, is it? He must have been human. No-one is perfect, are they?'

19

Catrin bit her lip hard. 'Aled was exceptional: very clever, good looking, sporty, everything. To die young, to die in that way, well, you know, was unthinkable. I still imagine I'll wake up and find it was some dreadful nightmare.'

Catrin heard Bethan's phone vibrating, and saw her reading a text.

'Ah, my big sister,' Bethan said.

'What does Lowri say?'

'She says she's bringing her boyfriend, Mark, tomorrow.'

'Really?'

'I'm glad she's coming. I never get to see her now she has this man.'

'I was surprised when she asked to come to Gower. Of course, she's never been there either. I guess she's curious. I was just relieved she was finally taking a break from her studies.'

'I wish she was coming on her own. Still, I'm curious about this bloke. I mean, none of us have met him, have we?'

'No. It's odd. They've been together since, ooh, it must be about February. I've kept asking her to bring Mark round. I know he's not a medic. She told me he's a lecturer at Cardiff University.'

'He owns his own flat. Not bad, eh?'

'Lowri always stays there. She texts a lot. What does she tell you about him?'

'Nothing, Mum. You know Lowri, very secretive. She did text me a week or two ago about your birthday. Are you excited about it?'

'Excited about tomorrow? No, not really. I don't really worry about birthdays at my age.'

'Well, I expect Grandad will be pleased to see you on it. And now you have Lowri as well. Dad will come, won't he?'

'I hope so.'

'Even Dad wouldn't miss your birthday. It'll be quite a family get together. And we all get to meet this Mark. Lowri won't answer any of my questions about him. She's hopeless at putting things on Facebook. I've not even seen a photo of him. Do you think he has hundreds of tattoos and piercings, or maybe he's a married man having an affair?'

'That doesn't sound like Lowri.'

'You never know. It could be a new side of her we know nothing about. I can't believe it's only three years now until she'll be a doctor.'

'Well, there's a foundation for two years after that. It all takes so long.'

Bethan fiddled with her hair. Then said, 'Talking of university, Mum–'

'Yes?'

'I've been thinking again about not living at home, but going into halls. There are rooms, you know, that have been adapted for Deaf students; flashing alarms, the lot.'

'We discussed it. Not in the first year.'

'Lowri did.'

'She was only up at the hospital, and she came home a lot in her first year.'

'But –'

'No. We have it all arranged.'

Bethan shrugged, but Catrin knew it was a gesture of postponement rather than surrender.

Bethan took a long swig of her drink, then said, 'Grandad wants me to play my flute at Aled's memorial.'

21

'Really?'

'Yes. You know how impressed he is that I can play the flute. He thinks it's some kind of miracle,'

'It is impressive.'

'But I love playing the flute. It was a good choice of instrument for me. I've tried to explain to him that there are lots of keys that allow me to make the correct note more precisely, and with my aids I can hear some sounds. I also told him that there is so much more to playing than sound. It's like me and the flute become one. It's wonderful. I know I find performance difficult, but I can express feelings I can't express in any other way.'

Catrin smiled. She understood why her father found Bethan's love of music hard to understand, but it was very real and all they could do was support her and stand in awe.

'You don't mind playing at the memorial, then?'

'No. I feel I owe it to Grandad. He paid for a lot of extra tutorials, and summer schools at conservatoires. All that one to one teaching with people who understood made so much difference. It's my way of saying thank you.'

'He has been very generous, I know, but you must only play if you are comfortable.'

'I'll be fine. It will be good for me, and it's in honour of Aled really–'

'Well, see how you feel, Right, we'd better drive on.'

Their route took them along the busy seafront of Swansea, past people playing pitch and putt, families eating ice-cream. Then they turned off towards Uplands, driving up the long steep roads until eventually they arrived at the Gower commons. Catrin loved it up here: the sense of space, the seascape of heather and gorse.

'Look,' shouted Bethan.

Catrin pulled in. They sat and watched a scruffy group of brown and white ponies eating the brambles and tough grass. 'When I was little, Nana Beth used to tell me they turned into unicorns and would fly at night. They're beautiful, aren't they? You know they say a Viking king is buried up here. I think he was called S-w-e-y-ne-s-e-y, (she finger spelled) or something. They say Swansea is named after him.'

'How do you know all this stuff?'

'It was Nana Beth and my Mum. They both loved history, particularly the history around here.'

Catrin looked ahead, at the sea sparkling on a distant horizon. It looked much further away than it really was. Nothing was what it seemed here.

Bethan's phone vibrated again. Catrin heard her laughing at a text.

'What's up?'

'Oh, it's Sabrina trying to get everyone organised for my birthday do in Cardiff when I get back. She's planning it for the Monday after my birthday. We'll be back by then, won't we?'

'Gosh, yes. Definitely. We have this week for the memorial and sorting out the house. Then the following week, I think the sealed bids are due in on the Tuesday or Wednesday. Then Grandad has to accept one of them. He wanted us to stay down there until the Saturday, your birthday, but the next day, the Sunday, we definitely leave.'

'Good. Sabrina is doing a lot of organising. It's so complicated, where to have pre's and then which clubs to go to.'

'Pre's?'

'You know: pre-drinks.'

'You drink before you go out?'

'Of course. No-one can get really pissed on club prices.'

'Bethan, you know what your Dad thinks about drink—'

'I know. Don't worry. We won't hold it at our house.'

'That's not the point.'

'Mum, everybody drinks. It's only you and Dad who are so funny about it.'

'At least, don't go drinking excessively.'

Bethan laughed. 'Of course not, Mum. We'll go for a coffee, home in bed by eleven.'

Catrin sighed. Lowri had never been interested in any of this. For her eighteenth, Lowri had had a group of friends around to the house. They had ordered in a takeaway, watched films. She could see that Bethan's night was going to involve a lot more stress and little sleep on her part, as she lay at home worrying. Gareth would be very upset if Bethan got drunk. Years ago, he had lost a friend who was killed by a drunk driver and he was ardently anti-alcohol.

Catrin re-started the car and began to drive down the hill, towards Rhossili.

'Oh that's it: Worm's Head. I can see it,' Bethan shouted, looking out to sea.

Catrin kept her eyes on the road and tried to calm the growing nausea. All too soon they reached the sign post pointing right to 'Bryn Draig'.

'Down there is Rhossili village. It's in that church there that the memorial will be held. Bryn Draig doesn't have its own church. In fact, most people don't even know Bryn Draig exists. Catrin turned on to the rough road. Soon they were at the edge of the village. As she drove through it she was aware how small it was, but it looked very content, basking in the sunshine like a cat. It seemed oblivious of its past. She knew there were a few new houses further down, but essentially it had remained the same. They passed the newsagent: still there, she was pleased to see. She was amazed that such a business could survive, but it did, with old-fashioned buckets, spades and fishing nets outside. Catrin had had a brief fling with Harri, the boy who had lived there. She wondered where he was now. A bright, ambitious boy: she couldn't imagine he was serving behind the counter in the shop. They passed the pub, then the house which had belonged to her mother's sister, her Aunt Angela. It looked scruffier, the hanging baskets sad with dead geraniums.

'That's where my cousin, your Uncle David lives now with Anwen. Aunty Angela, his mother, has a bungalow further down the road.'

'Oh, right. I hope we see Uncle David and Anwen. They're both really good fun.'

'I expect they'll come to the memorial on Monday.'

'How far to The Dragon House then?' asked Bethan, looking intently ahead.

'We're along here, hidden away on the left,' Catrin said. It was then that she could feel her stomach clenching. 'Here, it is: Ty Draig, The Dragon House,' she said as she pulled the car on to the driveway. Then she gasped.

Bethan grabbed her arm. 'What's the matter?'

'It's the stones. It used to be a lawn. What has your Grandad done?'

Catrin looked horrified at the mass of sharp white stones that had replaced the gentle scruffy lawn. The glare from them hurt her eyes. Next to the old wooden front door, incongruously, stood two enormous aluminium pots with spiky plants sticking out. Her mother and Nana Beth would have hated it all.

Bethan, obviously deciding that her mother was making a fuss about nothing, excitedly got out of the car. The smells of the sea, mingled with the gorse and heather, forced their way into the car. Catrin sat back and closed her eyes so that she couldn't see the stones. She had read somewhere that smell was the first sense to develop and she could believe it. It was a very primitive sense. She breathed in deeply. Then it came to her: a picture of Nana Beth coming out of the house, arms open, waiting for her. It was one of those special times when she had felt warm and loved.

Suddenly she was jolted back to the present, hearing Bethan shouting 'Grandad.' Catrin saw her father: tall, dark, looking younger than seventy. She reached for her handbag to find her brush, glanced in her mirror, and sighed. There was little point in trying to look acceptable for her father. She knew she had failed before she even started.

Chapter Four

Catrin watched as Bethan ran towards open arms that hugged her. She tried to think of a time when her father had greeted her like that, even before Aled's accident, but failed. She saw him looking down and talking to Bethan. He adored Bethan, and at least communicated that very well.

Catrin looked over at the "For Sale" sign, which made the house look disowned and unwanted. She struggled inelegantly out of the car. She was wearing an unflattering cotton skirt and a blouse. Finding clothes that hid the scar on her right arm was even more difficult in the summer, but her father was right: it was ugly and needed covering up. Anyway, she didn't want to be made to talk about it. If she was forced to wear one of the short-sleeved dresses or tops that the shops seemed to be full of, she would always wear a cardigan, whatever the weather.

The stones dug into Catrin's feet. As she walked, she could feel the tiny bits of gravel working their way into her flat sandals. She walked awkwardly, trying to kick them out as she went. Bethan went into the house but Catrin's father started to walk towards her.

'You came,' her father said. His voice was strained. It was as if he found it difficult to talk to her. He avoided eye contact.

'I see you've done the front garden already.'

'Looks tidier, doesn't it?'

'How is the house inside?'

'They've kept it clean. Better than I expected. Still, I paid them good money. I've started painting the hallway–'

'Has there been a lot of interest?'

'Pretty good. The agent tells me there have been a few bids handed in already.'

'When is the final day?'

'Tuesday next week. I'm doing an open house on Monday as well, but, of course, those people won't have time for surveys and things. I had one done when the house was valued. It's all pretty sound. Nothing major, anyway.'

'What will you do with your house in Cardiff?'

'I'm selling that as well.'

'So, no coming back?'

'That's right. It's why I wanted to have the seat put here: a permanent reminder of Aled. The vicar will bless it, or whatever they do, at the service.'

'It's down there already?'

'Oh yes, finally. It's taken a lot of emails. Had to use a few contacts. Getting permission was a nightmare; then having the concrete laid and settled.'

'You've been planning it for a while, then?'

'The seat, yes. The service idea came later.'

'I shall look forward to it, Dad,' Catrin said but, not for the first time, she felt a visitor in her father's life.

Oblivious to her hurt, her father continued, 'So, I want to make this house look good for the open day, final push–'

'Prices around here seem to have shot up.'

'I knew they would. Rhossili, well it's highly sought after. There are so many building restrictions–'

'That's understandable. You wouldn't want people throwing up buildings all over the place.'

'It adds to the value of the house. We have a busy couple of weeks ahead of us. I thought you could concentrate on some of the rooms upstairs. Not Aled's room, though. I'll do that.'

'OK. By the way, Lowri is coming to stay with her boyfriend Mark. I hope that's OK. They can help out.'

'Oh. Are they coming for long?'

'Well, I said for the two weeks. Lowri could do with a holiday.'

'God knows why she has gone into medicine after she's seen what it's done to her father. He'll be here for the service on Monday, I hope?'

'I'm sure. Actually, he said he'd try to come tomorrow, it being my birthday.'

'What's that?'

'My birthday, Dad. I'll be fifty.'

'Oh yes, of course.'

There was a silence that was marginally more awkward than the conversation had been.

'How are the plans for the memorial?' asked Catrin.

'It's a celebration, Catrin,' he replied sternly. 'The plans are going well. I want the world to celebrate what a remarkable young man Aled was. I don't think anyone ever really appreciated just how brilliant and exceptional he was and what we lost when he died. How are you getting on with that piece for the website?'

'Not well. Why don't you do it?'

'Firstly, you should be proud to write about him and, secondly, it can't always be me. We need to show the family are proud of his memory.'

'I suppose so, but I'm finding it difficult to write. I don't know that much about his time as an architect, particularly his time in America.'

'I'm sure you can manage.'

Catrin looked down and noticed a long thin shell on the ground, a perfect razor shell. She used to collect them on the beach here with her Nana Beth. The sun glinted on its smooth surface. She wondered how it had got there. She bent down to move it somewhere safe but, as she did so, her father turned and, without realising it, stepped on the shell. She pulled her hand away quickly but, as her father walked away, she looked down at the delicate shell, now cracked and splintered into hundreds of tiny pieces. Oblivious, her father continued to walk to the house. Catrin bent down and tried to pick up the fragments, but they were tiny and sharp.

Catrin stood up. Suddenly, she became aware of the seagulls screeching overhead, the fresh sea air calling for attention. She turned and looked up for the first time since she had arrived. As the house was on a slope of Rhossili Downs it was possible, even from the driveway, to look down at a wide strip of sea. The sea air stroked her face and the sea reflected the brilliant blue sky, the sun glistening on its surface like stars. She closed her eyes, and the stifling heat of the car and her father's harsh words were briefly blown away. She could smell the salt, the gorse, the heather. The air was filled with an undercurrent of sound, the shushing of the waves washing the line of pebbles and shells at the water's edge way down on the beach.

For a brief, wonderful, spellbinding, moment the place hugged her. It became real; she saw it in colour. She really had forgotten how spellbinding and extraordinary it was here. She breathed in deeply and slowly opened her eyes. She looked down at the sea and the stretch of beach just visible. But then she looked further into the distance, and saw it. Stretching out, cold and solitary: 'the dragon'. She shuddered. It would always be there, silently haunting her.

Catrin determinedly crunched back over the stones to her car. She had to take the bags to the porch in two shifts. She had brought food and basics for the kitchen, not sure what her father would have brought with him. She went back, fetched their cases and took them into the house.

'So what's that husband of yours doing today?' her father asked. His voice startled her. He had come back to the front door.

'Gareth is working. They have a Saturday surgery now.'

'When did he last have a day off?'

'Oh, he's involved in some very big research project they asked him to head. Something to do with the changing role of the G P. He's very highly thought of, you know. They place students from the hospital with him all the time.'

'So when does he take time off? Hasn't he got any hobbies?'

'Not really. He always loved cricket, playing and watching it, but he hasn't done that for years now.' Catrin quickly added, 'So, you look well.'

'I look after myself. That's why.'

She felt his eyes inspect her disapprovingly.

'Of course. That's great.'

'Time Gareth replaced that old banger,' he said.

'It goes, which is the main thing.'

'It's a thankless job being a G P. I told him years ago to go to America. That's where the money is. He'd have some time to be with his family then. If he is coming on Monday he can stay the week. He can help decorating. I expect to get over the asking price for this house. It needs to look like its been cared for.'

'Maybe he'll arrive early enough tomorrow to do some painting.'

Without speaking, her father turned and walked into the house. Catrin followed him, carrying her bags.

The first thing that struck Catrin when she went inside was the smell of paint. The photographs, and her Nana's crucifix that had hung on the wall, had been taken down. The mellow cream paint had been replaced with startling bright white. She couldn't see the familiar stone floor as it was covered in dust sheets. In the corner she saw, peeping out from under a cloth, the old cream push button telephone. Catrin thought how seldom their landline at home was used nowadays. She peeped in the front living room. The television was on for the Olympics. The old television looked large, but not the screen, which was relatively small. It stuck out so far from the wall. Underneath it was an enormous video recorder. On shelves beside it were piles of old video cassettes: her father's favourite James Bond films, and her mother's musicals. On one shelf was a pile of small cassettes, mainly classical music which her mother had liked.

Bethan was curled up on a red velvet armchair texting. Catrin's father was now staring at the TV. Bethan looked up and Catrin silently signed 'drink' to her. Bethan shook her head, but her father glanced at her. 'A cup of coffee would be nice.'

Catrin left the cases in the hallway and carried the shopping into the kitchen. She had forgotten how much she used to love this room. The walls of the kitchen were light sunshine yellow and, like the smells outside, the room enabled the feelings of light and warmth to push their way through the darkness of more recent memories. It was an odd, dated, mix of furniture: the same old 'New World' gas cooker and long wooden table, with a variety of chairs, an old-fashioned fridge, and a washing machine. The white painted cupboards looked chipped

32

and dated. The only thing of real beauty was the large Welsh dresser which had been made years ago by her Grandad Hugh. Of course, this room was also the room the policeman had talked to them in. It was strange that one room could have such a mixture of memories, but maybe life was like that. The main thing was that she could feel her Nana Beth here. Catrin hadn't expected to, and she was grateful.

The back door was open, so Catrin went outside and into the large garden, which was to the side of the house. It was the same scruffy lawn and, in the borders, random poppies and dwarf sunflowers grew. The perimeter was a low dry stone wall so that you could sit on the old metal chairs and look straight out to sea. After breathing in the salty air Catrin returned to the kitchen. She checked the cupboards, which were still full of crockery, all of which had been kept clean. She noticed the original striped glasses, and remembered her Nana pouring lemonade into them. She took out some brown patterned Wedgewood mugs. They seemed heavy, and the rims thick compared to the bone china she had at home.

Catrin put the kettle on. She had started to unpack the shopping bags when her father came in. He took an opened bottle of white wine from the fridge, and poured himself a glass.

'I think I'll have this instead,' he said.

'How was your last visit to New York, then?' she asked, aware of speaking over-brightly.

'Good. Yes, very good. I've always loved New York, and working with the practice we're associated with out there. So much excitement. I love the people, so much more optimistic than over here.'

'It's a big move, Dad. You know, at your age.'

'I'm not that old. I'm fit. There are plenty of people still working at seventy out there. And, as I say, I feel I have more friends out there now than over here.'

'Aled loved it out there, didn't he?'

Her father took a large gulp of his wine. 'He did very well.'

'But you persuaded him to come back?' Catrin spoke quietly. It was something she had often wondered about but somehow never liked to ask.

'It was for the best. There was a major project over here I wanted him to head.'

'And he was pleased to come back?' Catrin was aware that she was pushing her father.

'Of course.' He turned away. The subject was closed.

'By the way, how is the trust thing going in America?' she asked, to try and make amends.

'It's going well. I'm getting backers together. You know, there aren't many people out there now who even remember Aled, but they are very supportive.'

'And it's for young architects?'

'That's right. Bright, promising students. I shall call it The Aled Foundation.'

'That's lovely, Dad.' Catrin fiddled with her necklace and looked away.

Her father took another long swig of his wine and then looked more closely at Catrin's necklace. 'That's a good sapphire.'

'Thank you. I've had it for years. Gareth gave it to me. Actually, he gave it to me the night of Aled's party.'

'I hadn't noticed it before.'

'I didn't wear it for ages. Then I decided that I've got so little jewellery, I might as well get on and wear it. How do you know about sapphires then?'

'My mother had a beautiful ring. My father had brought it back for her from Ceylon, for her fortieth birthday, I think. I remember her telling me about it. It was nearly a five carat sapphire: royal blue; not too dark, not too light. And the clarity was meant to be fantastic. My mother had it insured for at least five thousand pounds. She left it, with some other things, to your mother, you know, and then, of course, your mother gave it all to you.'

Catrin frowned. 'Mum never gave me any jewellery.'

'Of course she did. She told me.'

'No, really. She never gave me anything.'

'Well, where is it all then?' Catrin realised that there was a hint of accusation in his voice.

'I don't know.'

'You haven't sold it, have you?'

'Of course not. Honestly I haven't had anything.'

Catrin felt herself going very red. She felt that her father didn't believe her, but why should she be lying? 'I haven't got any of it, Dad.' She changed the subject. 'The service on Monday– Did you say people will be coming back here?'

'That's right. I've booked caterers. By the way, your cousin David and his wife Anwen will be coming.'

'Oh, good.' She smiled.

'Anwen brought a cake down this morning, actually. Said she knew you were coming.'

'Gosh. That's kind.'

'She talks non-stop. Don't know how David puts up with it.'

'She's very different to Sian,' said Catrin. David's ex had been a severe, cold, grey day sort of person. Catrin had never understood why David had married her.

'She certainly is.'

35

'David was telling me that he's changed his job now. He seems a lot happier.'

'Madness. He gave up a perfectly safe job in the civil service, good pension and everything, to go and work with a load of drop-outs. No wonder Sian left him. This new woman, though, doesn't seem to mind supporting her husband.'

'She's a solicitor, a bright woman.'

'I don't know why Angela just gave them that house, you know. Just gave it to them.'

'She insisted, Dad. She has her new bungalow, and she wanted to do it.'

'But to just give them the house. Madness. No-one appreciates something for nothing.' Catrin sighed at one of her father's most over-used lines. Everything had to be earned with her father.

'I must go and visit her,' said Catrin. 'She doesn't travel because of her arthritis, so I'm out of touch with her. Though we do write occasionally. Who else is coming for the service on Monday?'

'A few architect friends. I told them about it in the New York practice where Aled worked, but I don't expect anyone to travel from there. No, they are doing their part with the trust fund, but I'm hoping some people come from Cardiff. I emailed a few people, you know.'

'It's a long time ago, Dad. A lot of people who knew Aled will have moved on by now,' she said gently.

'But not all. No, there are still people who remember what a remarkable young man he was. Of course, there'll be some people from the village coming as well.'

'It's a busy week, sorting out the house and the, um, the celebration.'

'There's Bethan's birthday as well a week next Saturday.'

'Of course. I thought we'd go all go out for a meal. She's going out with her friends in Cardiff when we go back.'

Her father grinned. 'Ah, I have a few birthday surprises planned for Bethan.'

Catrin frowned. 'What do you mean?'

'You'll have to wait and see.'

'If it's to do with Bethan I should be told.'

'You make such a fuss over every little thing. Bethan has huge potential, and I intend to see it's not wasted.'

Catrin was shocked by the intensity with which he spoke. 'What's going on, Dad?'

Her father took a long swig of his wine, but abruptly changed the subject. 'I hope you are following the London Olympics.'

'Of course,' she said, but instantly regretted it.

'So, what are you going to be following in particular?'

'Swimming?'

'What stroke?'

'All of it,' she said, and immediately saw from her father's face that she had failed the test.

'You know Aled would have loved all this. Having the Olympics here. Bet he'd have gone up to London. God, maybe he'd have been competing. Well, not now, but in the past.' He sighed. 'So many wasted years. Don't suppose you bothered to even apply for tickets.'

'No. Gareth wouldn't have the time, and I suppose I'm not really that interested,' Catrin said awkwardly, and, for some reason, she felt terribly guilty.

'And where are you working at the moment?'

She looked away. 'At the university, in the canteen. I get the holidays off.'

'Really, Catrin. You've never had a proper job, have you? It's such a shame you never settled at school. I dreaded your school reports: always late with your homework, missing lessons.'

'It was difficult.'

'Don't see why.'

'You were away a lot. There was Mum–'

'That's no excuse.'

'Shame you never went to college,' he continued.

'Well, remember, the school lost all my work that I'd prepared for the interviews and, of course, Mum–'

'Never mind. It would have been a waste of time. By the way, I noticed you signing to Bethan. Surely she doesn't need it now?'

'Dad, I've told you. Bethan actually sees it as her first language. If I was better we'd use it properly, the correct grammar and syntax. As it is, she accommodates me. At Deaf Club she uses BSL properly.'

'My God. She still goes to Deaf Club?'

'Of course.'

'She doesn't need that.'

'She loves going. It's hard work talking and trying to lip-read, using her hearing aids all the time. When you think about it, she has to do all the hard work. When she goes there she says she can relax, be herself.'

'It all seems very odd to me. She speaks well and, honestly, sometimes you wouldn't know she was Deaf.'

'I know, but the thing is, Dad, she is, and she's not ashamed of it. I admire that.'

'You should have let me pay for that operation. Then, at least, she wouldn't have to wear hearing aids.'

'I told you: we asked about it. We were told a cochlear implant isn't suitable for her, even if she

38

wanted to go through the operation. And I'm not sure she would.'

'It's a shame. It would make her better, wouldn't it?'

Catrin sighed. She had explained it so many times to her father.

'No, Dad. She would have a transmitter attached to her head, a microphone and processor that looks like a hearing aid behind her ear, and when she took it off she would still be Deaf. As for making her better, well, in one sense I don't think she can be better. She doesn't need fixing. She's lovely as she is. People have to accept Bethan as Bethan.' Catrin could feel herself getting redder, her voice shaking. She was in full protection mode and would fight anyone who she felt was attacking her daughter.

Her father shook his head, poured himself another a glass of wine, crossly said 'I'm going to watch the games,' and left the kitchen.

Catrin had just finished putting the food away when Bethan came in. 'Dad sent me a text.'

'Oh when did he send that?'

'Ages ago. I forgot to tell you. He said he'd be out of signal for the rest of the day. He'll catch up with you in the morning.'

'OK. Well, I hope he finds the lasagne in the fridge.'

Bethan wandered around the kitchen.

'This place is so old fashioned,' Bethan said.

'I rather like it.'

Bethan went over to the dresser.

'This is cool, though.'

'My Grandfather Hugh, Nana Beth's husband, made it. The carving is very good, isn't it? It's strange. Although he was a real hero, he died in the Second

World War, you see, but there are no photos of him anywhere, and Nana Beth didn't talk about him much. He did some carvings in the church as well. In fact, we must look for them on Monday when we go to the memorial, sorry, the celebration.'

Bethan stood fiddling with the shells and stones on the dresser. Then she opened one of the drawers and pulled out a very old newspaper. It was headed 'The Gower Times'. Catrin could see a faded photograph of Worm's Head on the front page. Bethan started to read.

'Early this morning the body of a young man, Aled Merrick, was found.' She looked at Catrin quizzically. Catrin stepped quickly towards her.

'Stop.'

'Aled Merrick?'

'Yes, but–' Catrin took hold of the newspaper, but Bethan didn't let go. Catrin gripped it tighter, but Bethan pulled it away and read. 'His body was washed up on Rhossili Bay, but it is believed he fell off Worm's Head the previous evening–'

Catrin managed to pull the paper away.

'Mum, it says he drowned–'

'That's right.'

'You said he fell on Worm's Head'

'I didn't want to tell you he drowned. I thought it would upset you.'

'You lied about how he died?'

'I was trying to protect you.'

'You should have told me the truth. I have a right to know how my own father died.'

Chapter Five

Catrin suggested to Bethan that they go for a walk. Somehow it seemed easier to talk outside. They began by walking down through the back garden. Catrin was pleased to see the sunflowers, poppies and geranium were still growing. She remembered going to her Nana Beth, telling her that they had to grow the dwarf sunflowers because the tall ones would never have survived the sea winds. In the same way there were few trees on this part of the Gower. As she looked down at the flowers and the poppies she noticed a patch where the flowers were less dense. They were covering a patch, but there used to be something there. She screwed her eyes tight trying to remember, but couldn't picture what had been there.

Catrin and Bethan crossed the road and made their way down through the heather, so beautiful at this time of year: a sea of pinks, purples and white, with occasional bursts of sunshine yellow gorse. They reached a ledge which looked down on to the beach.

'Shit, it's huge,' said Bethan.

Catrin looked down at the miles of white sand, the sheer scale that could never be captured on a photograph. She remembered Harri taking photographs down here. He had had some posh Olympus camera. She was still using her pocket Kodak Instamatic. Their 'fling,' when they had been sixteen, had been one of the fast burning, intense relationships that you have at that age. They had sat here at the top of the beach. She would sketch the pebbles and the shells, and they would make plans.

41

Catrin started picking up pebbles. She had forgotten how beautiful they were here. They ranged in colour from reds and pinks, orange and yellows, to buffs and greys, many blue-greys with patterns in and on the stones that included stripes, layers, lines, and abstract designs. Catrin blinked, looked up and saw that there were small groups of people scattered over the vast expanse of beach. Even on a sunny Saturday in July it wasn't crowded. The walk down from the car park was long and steep. Rhossili made few concessions to visitors. Most families would have gone to Oxwich or Caswell.

'That must be a cool place to live,' said Bethan, pointing along the ledge to a solitary white house.

'It's owned by the National Trust now. Many years ago it was a rectory. The vicar would ride his horse along the beach between the parish churches at either end.'

Bethan laughed. 'Really?'

Catrin smiled. 'They say that his ghost still rides at night. Apparently Dylan Thomas, you know, the poet I mentioned, he was going to buy it, but he said it was too far from the nearest pub.'

'You can't see Bryn Draig from here.'

'No, it's tucked away. Weird. You wouldn't even know it was there.'

They clambered down the last bit of cliffside, on to the beach. Bethan took off her sandals and pulled off her sweatshirt. As she did, Catrin automatically glanced at the neat hearing aids tucked behind her tiny pixie ears, to check they were switched on. She always looked. She couldn't help it. Even in shops, she would glance at strangers' aids to check they were switched on. Not, of course, that she would say anything if they were off; it was just a habit. A young man with long blonde hair, carrying a surf board ran past. He glanced over at Bethan and seemed to run faster and more upright.

'This place is OK,' said Bethan, grinning.

Catrin started picking up shells, but Bethan touched her on the arm. 'You said you'd tell me. What really happened?'

Catrin took in a deep breath, and bit her lip hard. Where was she to start? They sat down on the warm sand. She noticed that Bethan had started to wind a strand of hair around her forefinger. Catrin thought carefully; nothing about this was easy.

'OK.' Catrin adopted a matter of fact tone. 'You want to know how Aled died.' She swallowed hard. 'Aled died two weeks before you were born.'

'I know that,' said Bethan, impatiently. 'I know he died. I was born in a hospital near here. He fell, well, he drowned by the sound of it, and my mother was taken to the hospital where I was born. She then gave me to you, and now she is dead too.'

Catrin flinched at the cold anger hidden behind the harsh synopsis.

'We adopted you, yes. We wanted to. We loved you very much.'

'The thing is, what happened to Aled?'

Catrin looked over at Worm's Head, at that moment cut off from the headland. Bethan followed her gaze and asked 'He went over there? Did he swim there?'

'Oh, no. He couldn't have done that. There are lethal currents in the water around the causeway. I think the causeway must have been clear when he started, but it was still an extremely dangerous thing to do. It was dark, raining, and, of course, it wouldn't be long until the tide came in.'

'How do you know he got to Worm's Head?'

'They found his jumper there. He definitely got there.'

'So he fell into the sea from Worm's Head?'

Catrin cringed. 'Yes, that's what they assumed. I'm so sorry.'

'What a horrible way to die. So, it was just an accident?'

Catrin took a deep breath. 'Yes. I'm sorry. I don't understand it–'

'Why did he go there?'

Catrin looked at Bethan's anxious face. 'Nobody knows. Listen, I think I'll have to start at the beginning of the evening. Your Grandma and your Grandad were giving a party for Aled, as I said. I remembered wondering why my parents hadn't held the party in their main house in Cardiff, which was far smarter. However, apparently Aled wanted a barbeque at the Dragon House, and what Aled wanted he got.'

'Grandad told me Aled was going to be a great. He said he was as good as someone called Frank something or other.'

'Frank Lloyd Wright. Yes, he often said that. Anyway, Dad and I drove up from Cardiff. We came up in the early evening. It was so hot, like today, and we had Lady with us.'

'Lady?'

'Our cocker spaniel, Lady. Do you remember her?'

'Sort of. There are photos around of her.'

'She was gorgeous. Mad, of course. I loved her so much.' Catrin smiled, momentarily distracted at the thought of Lady, and then continued.

'Did you have Lowri then?'

'Oh yes. She was two. We left her with Dad's parents. We came down here to the beach before the party. Dad had never been to Rhossili before, and I had

44

been excited to show him a place that was so special to me. I'd been so relieved that Dad had loved it as much as me. He described it perfectly, saying, 'It's like reaching the end of the world.' To make the visit even more special he'd given me this beautiful sapphire necklace.' Catrin stopped, savouring the memory of that feeling that all was right with the world when for once she had believed that fate wasn't out to get her.

'I'm impressed that Dad gave you a present. A long time since he's done that.'

'I suppose so. Anyway, we arrived at the Dragon House. I walked across the scruffy brown lawn that was there then and into the house. Lots of people had already arrived. My Mum was in a bit of a state. She worried a lot, but her sister, Angela, was trying to calm her down. Grandad was really excited and, of course, Aled was centre stage.'

'What did he look like that evening?'

Catrin knew exactly how he had looked, but chose her words carefully. 'He was excited, bit on edge, but of course he was very good-looking, very blonde, and had deep ocean-blue eyes. You know, when he was happy, when he smiled, his eyes shone and sparkled like the sea on a sunny day.' She stopped. It hurt so much. Her darling brother: that had been the last time they had talked.

'What was he wearing?'

'He had on jeans and a white shirt. Everyone was looking at him as though he was a film star. When Grandad made the speech I kept thinking 'Wow, this is my brother. I was so proud of him.'

'A speech?'

'Oh, yes. Grandad made one all about how wonderful and gifted Aled was, most promising architect of his generation. That it was his dream to have Aled come to work with him in his firm.'

'That was heavy.'

'Well, it's what he genuinely thought: 'We have somehow given birth to a saint. We are rightly humbled and feel very blessed.''

Bethan's eyebrows shot up. 'Bloody hell. That was laying it on pretty thick, wasn't it? Didn't you mind?'

'No. It's how we all thought of him.'

'But didn't you feel a bit put out, him being the favourite like that?'

'No, I never minded. Aled, you see, was one of those grade A students. He excelled at everything.'

'Well, I'd have been pretty pissed off, being overshadowed like that.'

Catrin grinned at the idea of anyone overshadowing Bethan.

'And then what happened?'

'I remember there was a rumble of thunder and spots of rain. The caterers were quietly moving stuff inside. A lot of the cooking was finished. Grandad said we'd better all go inside. Then, I remember looking over and seeing Aled. He was talking to a pretty young girl. I remembered I'd seen her earlier down on the beach, collecting shells, and had wondered what she was doing there. She wore a white, smocked, baby doll dress and huge Doc Martin boots. I think it was the fashion then. They were talking really intensely.'

'Who was the girl?'

'Oh–' Catrin looked away. She had got carried away. Damn.

Bethan grabbed her arm. 'Who was it?'

'Just some girl.'

'Who, Mum? Tell me.'

'Um, I don't know, a friend of his.'

46

'Mum, you've gone all red. Who was it?'

'Well, actually, it was–'

'My birth mother?'

Catrin nodded.

Bethan stared. 'She was at the party the night my father died? You saw her? You never said. You've never told me you'd met her.'

'No–' Catrin cringed. Oh God, she never thought Bethan would find out.

'Why? Why didn't you tell me?'

'I thought it would hurt you. You never asked.'

'Because I didn't think you'd ever seen her.'

'I thought it would be easier for you. I didn't want her to become too real.'

Catrin felt she was drowning in a sea of words. Looking at Bethan, the words that had always seemed to her so logical and reasonable suddenly sounded all wrong.

'Didn't you think I ever wondered, you know, what she looked like?'

'No, I didn't. You never asked.'

'Because I never saw the point. You said you'd never seen her. I asked Grandad, but he refused to talk about anything. I guessed he couldn't cope because of Aled. He told me she wasn't Deaf. That's all he's ever told me. He said he couldn't even remember what colour her hair was. If I'd known you'd seen her–'

'I'm sorry.'

'So what did she look like?'

'I didn't see her very well, but she was tall, slim, long dark hair.'

'Like me. I look like my mother?'

Catrin looked at Bethan, seeing for the first time the likeness. Of course, she must have been, what,

47

twenty, nearly the same age as Bethan now. She had been so young.

'Yes, you do. You look very like her.'

'Oh, Mum. All these years I've been hoping that. I felt like the odd one out in our family. You and Lowri all tiny, and fair. Even Dad is short. I'm like some giant among you. It was obvious I didn't belong.'

'Don't say that.'

'But, Mum, you can't pretend I was your baby like Lowri. I'm not, and anyone looking at our family could tell. If I'd known I looked like my mother it would have helped me. You know, for me it's like reading a book, but the first chapter is missing. I have to try and imagine it, make it up. You should have told me.'

Bethan looked away, and crossed her arms tightly. Catrin touched her shoulder. As Bethan turned to face her Catrin saw Bethan's lips pressed firmly together and very white. She was holding in some very strong emotions.

'I thought I was protecting you,' Catrin said. 'I am so sorry.'

Bethan stepped forward into her arms, and started to shake and cry. Catrin held her tightly, but soon Bethan stepped back and wiped her eyes with the back of her hand.

'I'm so sorry' repeated Catrin. 'I never realised you felt like this.'

Bethan sat down exhausted. Catrin sat next to her.

'So my birth mother was tall and dark,' said Bethan quietly. 'I've been trying to imagine her. I was hoping maybe I looked like her, but she's been like some ghost. I can see a shape, hear a voice, but I can't make any of it out. At least now I know something.'

'I didn't know much. I'm sorry. I never even had a photograph.'

'But you knew something. You should have told me. It's part of my story. I had a right to know.'

'I'm sorry. When I heard she'd died, well, there seemed no point–'

Catrin sat staring ahead. The story had somehow gone into free fall and she had no idea where it would land.

Chapter Six

The London air was thick with dust and fumes which had accumulated throughout the hot day. In her air conditioned house, Elizabeth held a cold glass of spring water to her cheek and closed her eyes, trying to wish away her hangover. She was ploughing thorough the emails related to the art galleries which she owned in London and New York. Occasionally, she tutted with frustration at someone's inefficiency. Her replies were blunt and to the point. She heard a knock at the front door, and answered it.

'You need to tell me the code to this door sometime. It's silly me always having to knock. The chaps on the gate all greet me like an old friend now,' said Richard, as he walked in.

'One day—'

'If you want me to come in and water your plants, you'll have to give it to me.'

'Of course.'

'It's manic out there because of the Games.' Richard was red-faced and sweating, wearing an old T shirt and shorts, refusing to join the fad for designer running gear. Elizabeth grinned. She still couldn't believe she was with someone like Richard, after years of dating a string of rich and eligible young men. From the first time she had seen Richard she had known this was something different. Slowly, he had become part of her life. Instead of becoming increasingly irritated and feeling relieved when someone left she found that her life seemed empty when Richard wasn't with her. Well it was just better doing things together than apart.

'Bloody tourists,' Elizabeth said vaguely.

'Still, have to get rid of all the toxins,' Richard said, laying a sweaty hand on her perfectly groomed black hair. 'We celebrated in style. Didn't we?'

'We did, but some of us were still up at six this morning doing a proper run.'

'Well, you're just a fanatic. I was thinking, that cake they gave you last night. That was weird. Who has a cake that looks like a handbag?'

Elizabeth laughed. 'That cake cost a fortune. The people at the gallery paid for it. It was a life-sized replica of my Hermes Birkin handbag.'

Elizabeth could see Richard looking at her blankly. He had no idea what that meant, or the cost involved.

'The Centre Point building was a great venue for your birthday party, though. The views were incredible. I dread to think how much you paid for it.'

'A lot.'

'It must have been hard, so close on losing you mother.'

'In some ways. To be honest, though, although my birthday was always in the school holiday, I was often on a camp or at summer school. My parents weren't there for most of my birthdays.'

'You spent a lot of time away from your parents. Did you mind? '

'No, not at all. I knew my parents loved me. They were settled in New York with Dad's work but Mum wanted me to go to her old school back in London. It was a great place, very close community. I just didn't see that much of them. Mum didn't have me until she was in her late forties; really old for those days. And Dad, he must have been in his fifties. I was a wonderful surprise for them. They were so proud of me, and they wanted me to have the best of everything.'

'It all seems very odd to me: sending your children off.'

'I know, but I survived. Thrived even.' She smiled 'So, you didn't find last night too bad then? Being stuck with a load of artists and journalists?'

'Fortunately, none of them seemed to know what I do.'

'I always say you're an accountant. Seems to put people off.'

He laughed. Richard worked for a music agency. It had one or two notable musicians but was not a rich company. Richard himself was back living in rented accommodation following a costly divorce.

Elizabeth sat back and groaned. 'I can't take the late nights like I used to, you know. I'm getting old.'

'Don't be stupid. You don't look a day over, well–' Elizabeth saw Richard hesitate, regretting embarking on the sentence. She could see the panic in his eyes: what age was he going to pluck out of thin air?

Elizabeth waited. She didn't try to rescue him.

'Oh I don't know,' he said, retreating. 'Anyway, I dream of regretting being thirty seven.'

'Poor old man.'

Elizabeth picked up her phone at the sound of a text.

'That's Lucy,' she said, naming an art journalist. 'Listen to this. 'Don't ever have kids. I was out at eight this morning driving to an art thing at the Hayward. God I have a terrible hangover. Thanks for last night.' Elizabeth shook her head. 'I don't know why all these parents wear themselves into the ground for their children.'

'Your parents didn't take you to things? I mean before you went off to school?'

'No, I had a nanny and went to prep school.'

'I loved doing all that with my kids,' said Richard earnestly. 'It's hard to explain, but, you know, it physically hurt me when I left my children to go to work, even after a terrible night's sleep or after they'd had a tantrum. I still wanted to be with them.'

'You were some kind of martyr, then.'

Richard's phone sounded an alert. He read the text, and said, 'I'd just better ring Justin.'

Elizabeth found it difficult, the way he dropped everything, including her, for his children. They were both in their early twenties, and shouldn't be so needy. She thought Richard spoiled them. Elizabeth heard him talking quietly, reassuringly, to his son. 'Don't worry. Look, I'm travelling up to Edinburgh by train tonight to see Rosie, staying a couple of days. I could stop off at York on the way back. We could go for a drink.'

Elizabeth fiddled with the delicate gold brooch that Richard had given her for her birthday. It was an antique rose gold, with tiny diamond flower clusters. She loved it. She had one or two special pieces of Cartier from her parents, and a Tiffany bracelet she had bought herself, but she wore little jewellery. After the phone call Richard explained. 'Poor Justin's been dumped by his latest. I feel sorry for him. It hurts at that age.'

'I don't see why you have to break your journey. He's into cricket. Get him some tickets for that or something.'

'I want to see him, talk to him. He'd been with this girl since he started uni. That's about two years now. He'd got a job in York so they could have the summer together.'

'So they've been together the same length of time as us,' Elizabeth said, laughing.

'Exactly.' She saw his face turn serious. Elizabeth had caught Richard looking at her a few times like that lately.

'I think you'd better go and shower. Don't want you sweating on my leather suite.'

Richard nodded but didn't smile. Elizabeth knew he didn't miss the 'my' and wished she hadn't said it. Elizabeth watched the wooden stairs shudder as Richard ran up them. There was no hand rail: the stairs were meant to give the illusion that they were floating in mid air. Everything was square, neat, spotless, each item carefully, purposefully, in its place.

She could hear him turning on Radio Three in the shower, and felt a twinge of irritation that she would have to change the settings when she went up. It felt so strange to have a whole week off coming up. She didn't know when she had last done this. It felt very odd.

Elizabeth walked barefoot into the kitchen area, which was tiled and had glossy white fittings. On the cupboard, she saw her cards piled up, and scowled.

She thought 'Why are so many cards for women my age about weight, shopping or getting drunk? For God's sake is this as far as we've come?' Elizabeth picked them up and put them straight in the recycling. Green tea: that would help. She ignored the awful, 'Keep calm and drink vodka' mug Fiona had given her, found her favourite fine bone china mug, and turned on the kettle. She soon heard the gentle clunk behind her of Poppy arriving through the cat flap.

In contrast to the surroundings, there was nothing sleek or designer about Poppy. She was of very mixed parentage, mainly tortoiseshell. She was semi-feral, came in for meals, and sometimes if it was raining. Elizabeth had bought her the best white cat bed, but it had never been slept on. She leant down and stroked

54

Poppy, who tolerated rather than enjoyed it. Elizabeth grinned. 'You want food, don't you? Sensible girl, no fuss.'

She put down some expensive organic cat food: shrimp and cod today, and at the same time wondered why you never saw cat food labelled mouse, rat or shrew. Now that Poppy really would get excited about but, of course, it would never sell. Poppy ate quickly and very neatly, washed her paws, then let herself out through the cat flap with a minimum of fuss.

After a few minutes, Elizabeth heard Richard thumping back down the stairs. He was not particularly good looking. Tall, but with a definite tummy. He had kept his hair, which he was very proud of. He had terrible taste in clothes. As if reading her mind, Richard asked, 'How on earth did you and I end up together? We really couldn't be more different.'

'I don't know. Opposites attract and all that.'

'You're young and rich. I'm middle aged and poor, you mean.'

Actually, that is partly what she had meant, but she said, 'No, of course not. It was bit like a film, wasn't it? I mean, you catching me when I nearly fell in front of a car. Your Rosie would think that was very romantic.'

'She would,' said Richard, laughing. 'I must admit I wasn't being completely altruistic when I took you for a coffee. I mean, you were pretty shaken up, but that wasn't my only motive.'

Richard found a mug. 'You drinking that muck? Decaffeinated green tea smells ghastly. Anyway, some of us need caffeine.' He made himself coffee. 'Shall we take these in the garden?' He opened the back door. Immediately, London entered her house. The smell of fumes and junk food; the sound of traffic: all were again part of her world. She picked up her tea, followed him into the back garden, or garden room as her designer had called it. It was very secluded. The grey slate floor was already warm, the air still and heavy. The garden was meant to be her calm haven from the chaos of London, but today Elizabeth felt more like she was under siege. She sat down on integral furniture, moulded from stone but with expensive padded leather seats. At night, the cleverly planned lighting lit up the garden in a range of warm blues and greens. She liked it best then. Lying in the shade of one of the pots she saw Poppy.

'She'll be alright while you're away, then?'

'Of course. I've booked her into the best cattery in London. You know, I can look her up online, see her in her room.'

'My God. It's madness.'

'I know, but there we are.'

'So I come in on Thursday evening. Is that right?'

'Yes, just water the pots, and also can you make sure this is kept clean? You know the birds mess it up or it gets dusty from the traffic. I like it to be kept in this pattern exactly.'

Elizabeth pointed to a Welsh slate bird bath. In it were carefully arranged shells and pebbles. On the edge was engraved 'August 11th 1994' and the words 'May you be filled with loving kindness. May you be well'.

'That's unusual. The eleventh. That's a week Saturday. What does it commemorate?'

'Oh, just a date.'

Richard smiled, used to Elizabeth's evasions.

'Well, I shall keep it tidy while you are away. Give me the key code now while we think of it. Fancy the new exhibition at the National this afternoon? It'll be nice and quiet. Most people in watching the Olympics.'

'Your train is early evening, isn't it?'

'I know, but we could squeeze something in.'

Elizabeth recoiled at the thought of being 'squeezed into' someone's schedule. 'No, it's OK. I have things to do as well.'

'I'm really looking forward to seeing Rosie. She and Zac are renting in the centre, and I don't know Edinburgh at all. You know I wish you were coming–'

'No, not my kind of thing. They'd rather see you on your own, anyway.'

'Nonsense. I reckon they think I'm making you up. You'll have to meet them some time. Still, I'm glad you're having a break from the gallery. You work ridiculous hours. It's doing well. You could ease off, you know.'

'No. My father set me up, and I will never let him down. I could lose it a lot more quickly than I have made it.'

'You need this break. Your flight to New York tomorrow, what time is it?'

Elizabeth took a deep breath. 'Actually, I've changed my plans.'

'Oh. I thought you wanted to go and sort out the sale of your parents' house?'

'I realised that the estate agent out there can do all that. There isn't anything for me to do.'

'Don't tell me you're not taking the week off, then?'

'Actually, I am. I'm going to the Gower peninsula in Wales.'

'Why there? I've had friends go walking there, but it's not your sort of place. Really, why are you going there?'

'I'm going to a service there, a kind of memorial to be held in the church at Rhossili.'

'Who's that for, then?'

'It's quite complicated. Someone I knew a long time ago. I did three months in my father's office in New York after I left school. I was trying to decide what to do. I met this chap there. He was the son of Lloyd Merrick, founder of a big firm over here. Anyway, we saw each other a few times out there. I returned to the UK. Then he came back. It was then he had this awful accident.' Elizabeth stopped.

'What happened?'

'He died on Gower, at Rhossili Bay.'

'This was all years ago?'

'Eighteen. Yes, a long time ago.' Elizabeth started to twist a long black strand of hair around her finger, tighter and tighter.

'And you are going to this service?'

Elizabeth could see Richard looking totally mystified. She guessed it did sound pretty strange.

'I keep in touch with a girl I met when I was doing my work experience out in America. You know, if I'm over there we meet for coffee or a drink. Lloyd still goes over there a lot and he had told people about the memorial service. Obviously, he didn't expect people to come from the States. Most of them would never have met Aled anyway, but I think he is setting up some kind of trust. Anyway, this girl: she knew me and Aled had been together for a while, so she emailed me the details, and I decided that I would go.'

'It was a long time ago.'

'I know, but I need to go. Let's call it unfinished business.'

'That sounds even odder. What's this all about?'

Elizabeth looked deep into Richard's eyes. For a spilt second she was tempted to tell him, just spill it all out. She imagined the relief. She saw the tenderness and compassion in his eyes, but then she remembered the

58

way he had spoken about the bond with his children. No, he would never understand, and she couldn't bear for him to hate her.

She looked away. 'I can't talk about it, but it ended in a dark place. I need to go and make peace.'

'Sounds heavy, as Jason would say.'

'It is, so I need to sort it out.'

'Where will you stay?'

'Just a B & B. It's in a tiny village up the road from Rhossili called Bryn Draig'.

'Eh? You'd never stay less than five stars–'

'The only hotel said they were booked up. I found a list of places to stay, and rang round to find a vacancy. I haven't had time to research it, and it's not on Tripadvisor. There's no website but, if it's not up to much, I'll just find somewhere else once I'm down there.'

'That's taking a bit of a chance.'

'Not really. They are all boutique now: plasma TV, en suite, wifi. I didn't ask. There was just a number, but I'm sure it will be fine.'

Suddenly Richard looked serious, nervous. 'You will think about what we talked about, won't you?'

Elizabeth's mug started to shake so violently that she thought the tea would spill. Carefully, she placed it on the coffee table.

'Of course. But you know why I'm worried–'

'I know you're frightened of commitment. Heaven knows, you've told me enough times, but we've been together quite a while now.'

Elizabeth shook her head. 'It's not that, really. If I knew you would definitely never want children–'

'You know I can't say that. I may be old, but I can't promise never to want more. You'd be a great mother.'

'No. No, I wouldn't. You don't understand. I shall never have children, never had–' Elizabeth sighed. 'Why can't we stay as we are?'

'Because we have to move forward. I don't like living on my own, and I don't think you do either. We can't just stay still.'

'So, really, it's an ultimatum.'

'I'm sorry. I think it might be. Go away and think about it this week. OK? Then we can talk again.'

Elizabeth twisted the strand of hair tighter and tighter, then said, 'I think you'd better go and pack.'

Richard stood up, and kissed her gently on the cheek. His lips felt like butterfly wings brushing her cheek. Elizabeth's heart fluttered. What was the matter with her?

'OK,' he said. 'You have my number. I'll be back in London on Thursday. When do you plan to get back?'

'I expect I'll come back a week Sunday. I'll just be gone for a few days. Maybe I'll go on to Bath, somewhere like that, have a look around.'

'Maybe I could come down and join you?'

'Oh, no. No, don't come. I don't know how long I will be anywhere.' Elizabeth panicked.

'OK. Well, I hope you resolve what ever you need to.'

Richard stood up and went inside to pack his things. Elizabeth sat, knowing that some people would be chasing in after him, crying, saying sorry. Well, that was not her way. She looked over at Poppy lying alone in the sun and thought maybe that was the way it had to be for her: lying alone in the sun.

Richard came back, his face strained. He kissed Elizabeth gently on the forehead. 'Take care. Do you still want me to come and water the plants?'

Elizabeth nodded, and wrote down the key code. 'Thank you' she said, giving it to him. He didn't say anything. He just left.

Elizabeth heard the front door shut, and went back inside. It seemed quiet, empty. She went upstairs to have a shower. In the bathroom she tutted as she picked up the wet towel from the floor, then retuned the radio to Radio Four. She had never liked music, preferred people talking. She showered, and realised how tired she was. Maybe yoga at home tonight instead of the gym?

Back in the bedroom, she sat wrapped in her towel and started to blow dry her long black hair. She scowled as she saw a white hair, and pulled it out quickly.

Then she opened her dressing table drawer. Hidden under a pile of art catalogues, she found, wrapped in tissue paper, a small white wooden box made to look like a plain white book. She had had it for years, but it was immaculate. On three edges were gold etchings to look like pages, and on the fourth a white decorated spine. The lid was the 'cover', which opened on gold hinges. She stroked it, but couldn't bear to look at the contents. Instead, she looked at a photograph she had also hidden under the catalogues. It had been taken the week before Aled's party. She saw the secretive, barely hidden excitement in the eyes of the girl posing: a girl whose head was full of Disney endings. But she hadn't had her fairytale, far from it. That smock dress hid a secret. Lucky that it had been in fashion: like those ridiculous, heavy boots.

Suddenly, Elizabeth knew she couldn't sit there on her own and wait another night. Why not go now?

She telephoned the cattery: yes, she could bring Poppy early. She realised that booking her into one of the most expensive catteries meant that at least they had vacancies, even at the height of the summer season. She found the number for the B & B. The quiet Welsh voice of the woman on reception sounded flustered, chatty.

'You want to come tonight, not tomorrow?'

'That's right. I wondered if you had a spare room?'

'Oh, yes. That would be fine.'

'Right, good. So I can come tonight?'

'Of course. But where are you now?'

'London.'

'Oh, my goodness. What ever time will you arrive?'

'It should only take me about four to five hours. If I leave now, I hope to be with you by ten. Would that be alright?'

'Of course. You won't be much later, though?'

'No, unless there are hold ups. If there's a problem I'll ring, find somewhere else en route.'

'Oh, good. That's fine.'

'Yes, right. I'd better go and get organised.'

'Of course. I'll see you later, then.'

Elizabeth thought it all sounded rather informal. Still, they could give her a room: that's what mattered.

Elizabeth got out her paisley Stella McCartney jumpsuit. She thought this would be the right kind of casual wear for her visit. She had bought a few from the ready to wear collection, and packed them with some lace-lined slip dresses. To these, she added a pair of Calvin Klein jeans, a few T shirts and a cashmere jumper, in case it was cold. She also packed silk lingerie, her Clinique make-up collection, Miu Miu pink-tinted sunglasses, and, of course, her jewellery wrap. Then she looked in her drawer and took out two long rectangular documents. She would take them: best be prepared. Carefully, she folded them and zipped them into her handbag.

Elizabeth heard the cat flap clunk, went and found the cat basket, but left it upstairs. She tried to go back down nonchalantly. Was she imagining the suspicious look on Poppy's face? Quickly, she picked her up, took her upstairs, and posted poor Poppy into her cat basket. With a background racket of loud cat protest she packed, checked the house, and then went out to load the car.

After that, Elizabeth checked around, set the alarm, and looked again at her home. She gave a satisfied smile. All safe, organised, like her life. She realised how nervous she was now, going back, revisiting the past. Still, she had decided to go and, just think, soon it would all be over.

Chapter Seven

'Tell me the rest of what happened that night,' said Bethan, wiping the tears away with the back of her hand.

Catrin swallowed hard. She was frightened to speak now.

'We went into the house. I noticed the girl was standing on her own. I went to the bathroom. Then I heard shouting from the study. I went in and–'

'What happened?'

'Grandma, my Mum, was having a row with Aled.'

'What about?'

Catrin started to scratch her wrist. She said, 'I don't know. They stopped when I went in. It seemed unbelievable: they never argued. He was in a right state. Mum was as white as a sheet. Aled then shouted out that he was going to Worm's Head and left the room. I though he was joking. I mean, it was such a ridiculous thing to say. I thought he was just trying to wind Mum up for some reason. I didn't seriously think he would go out in the pitch black and rain and go anywhere, let alone there. It was all so odd. Aled never lost his temper. Mum, your Grandma, was upset, so I settled her down and then I went to find your Grandad. He said he'd seen Aled leave with the girl, and that I had to go and get him back. Well, it was dark and raining heavily. Your dad didn't want me to go anywhere.'

'I'm not surprised. Aled was twenty seven. He wasn't a child, and he certainly wouldn't want his sister coming after him if he'd gone off with a girl.'

'Grandad seemed really worried about him. He was very insistent that I go. I didn't understand that, either, but he was very upset.'

'But why? Aled was just having a tantrum by the sound of it.'

Catrin cringed. 'I don't know. I don't understand, but I knew it was serious. Anyway, Grandad persuaded us to go. It was pitch black, no stars or moon even, just sheets of black. We pulled into the car park, next to Aled's car. I shone my torch though the window but there was nobody in it. Your dad said they might have gone to the hotel, for a drink. I didn't think so, but we ran over. We looked around, but they obviously weren't there. The rain was really heavy by then, and your Dad wanted to go back, but I persuaded him to go on to the headland, even though it was very dangerous. We went though the gate and started to walk along. It was awful. Then I spotted the girl lying on the ground, near to the cliff edge. Your father looked at her, said she was unconscious. We could see that she was pregnant. She obviously needed an ambulance. Of course, we didn't have mobiles then, but luckily a fisherman came over and went to phone for help.'

'But where was Aled?'

'The fisherman said he'd passed someone heading towards the causeway, and that it would be covered over very soon. I was really worried about Aled, that he would try to get to Worm's Head.'

'But why would he go there that night? It was a really dangerous thing to do.'

Catrin bit her lip. 'I don't know, but I was very frightened he might. So, despite your father trying to stop me, I made my way towards the causeway.'

'In the dark?'

'Yes, I was so scared. I held on to the fence. Well I got to the top of the path down to the causeway. The sea was coming in and starting to cover the causeway. There was no sign of Aled. I fell down. I realised I couldn't go any further, so I just clung on to some rocks until your Dad and a policeman came and found me.'

'And what about the girl?'

'She'd gone off in an ambulance. I didn't see her again.

'We drove straight back to the house. Grandad was in the hallway waiting. He was very worried. He knew something was seriously wrong. I told him that search and rescue had been called, that the girl had gone to hospital.'

'And Grandma, what did she do?'

'Oh she was in the kitchen, obviously very upset. She crossed herself. I remember that. I'd never seen her do it before.'

Catrin sat back on the sand. She ran the dry warm sand though her fingertips. She was exhausted. It was as if she'd lived through the night all over again. The warm sand was soothing, but she knew Bethan was waiting.

'Aled's body was found the next day, washed up on the beach.'

'That's awful. To be out there alone in the dark and rain. Why ever did he go there? It should have been a wonderful night, a party in his honour. He was coming home to a good job. I don't understand why he went off and did something so stupid.'

'It is very difficult to understand.'

'And my birth mother?'

'Grandad went to see her. He talked to her.'

'But you didn't?'

'No. I went back to Cardiff to look after Lowri. You were born soon after. It was then that your Dad and

I were asked about adopting you. Grandad had originally suggested it to Elizabeth in the hospital. Elizabeth talked it over with her aunt and the social worker, and agreed. Then the social worker came to speak to us. It was all done properly. We had to be approved as adopters. All the papers were signed. Then it was the social worker who brought you to us.'

'I would like to have met my birth mother.' Bethan looked up, her face pale but determined.

'I know.'

Bethan looked over towards the causeway thoughtfully. 'I really need to visit Worm's Head now.'

Catrin shuddered at the thought of going to Worm's Head: no way would she go there. However, she said, 'Maybe. If there is time.'

'It's important to me, Mum. I need to.'

Bethan screwed up her eyes, put her head to one side.

'Why did Aled run off?'

'I'm not sure. Maybe he was trying to get help for Elizabeth or something.'

'But the fisherman said he was running towards the causeway not back to the village.'

'Well, yes.' Catrin stopped and bit her lip. 'I don't know. We'll never know what happened out there. It was just a terrible accident. He did know that she was pregnant. Grandad told me that. He knew, and was really pleased.'

'He wanted me?'

'I'm sure of it.'

'So why did he run away?'

'I don't know. We'll never know that.'

Bethan leant down and started to pick up shells. When she spoke, her voice was hard.

'But my birth mother just wanted to get rid of me?'

'It was so hard, love. She was young, nineteen.'

'That's older than me.'

'I know, but she was young in her ways as well. Her life had been pretty sheltered, I think. I'm sure she thought she was doing the best she could for you. Grandad spent a lot of time with her in the hospital. It was obviously the best thing for you to come to us.'

'Why was that?'

'Elizabeth's parents were older and lived abroad. She'd been to boarding school I think and she didn't want them to know she'd had a baby. They were very religious, I think. Anyway, she was young. She didn't feel ready to raise a child. I'm sure she was trying to do the best thing for you.'

'And how did she die?'

'An accident skiing abroad, I think. The most important thing is that your father and I love you very much. You are our daughter. You and I bonded quickly, and you were beautiful. I remember the first time I held you. You had lots of black hair even then. Lowri was so excited to be having a little sister.'

Bethan stood looking out to sea, then over at Worm's Head. I'm sure both your birth mother and Aled would be very proud of you and all you've done,' said Catrin.

Bethan didn't reply.

'Are you alright, love?'

Bethan gave a sad half-smile. 'Yes, Mum. I wish you'd told me the truth before, though.'

Catrin didn't comment, but it didn't mean she agreed with Bethan. In her experience, people often preferred a sweet lie to a difficult truth. Throughout her teens she had told lies, lies to protect, lies to sooth people. We all want a happy ending. She remembered once when the art teacher had asked her if everything was alright at home. She had nearly told the truth. She had liked him, trusted him. For a moment she wondered if he was different. Then she had noticed him anxiously holding his breath, and realised that he was no different. 'It's all fine,' she had replied. His sigh of relief told her all that she needed to know. The teacher had not wanted the truth. Even he wanted it easy.

Catrin looked at Bethan. She had told her far more of the difficult stuff of life than she would have wanted. That was enough for today.

'Now, let's get Grandad some supper, or he'll be really grumpy.'

They climbed back up off the beach. It was tough going. Catrin suddenly felt exhausted. But that was over. Just the memorial, the week and whatever that ridiculous surprise her father had planned. Soon the house would be sold and the past could be finally packed away for ever.

Chapter Eight

Elizabeth pulled into Rhossili car park, and rested back on the leather headrest. It had been her first decent drive in her new blue Audi and, once she had crawled through the London traffic and had broken free on to the M4 she had enjoyed it.

Of course, it had been hard leaving poor Poppy incarcerated in the cattery. It may be the best 'Cat Hotel' in London, with her 'room' equipped with chairs and a sofa, and meals of fresh fish and liver provided, but they couldn't provide Poppy with what she really wanted, which was her own territory in which to hunt and kill.

Elizabeth switched off the air conditioning and opened the windows. The stop at the services for much needed coffee had been horrendous. She had found herself having to sit outside. She had been surrounded by fractious children, tired at the end of a busy day, with equally stressed parents. On the next table a woman had lit a cigarette. Elizabeth had scowled at her, amazed that there was anyone left smoking.

She had enjoyed the drive over the Severn Bridge, and had glanced over at the old bridge, looking like a dinosaur, sad and neglected. The journey to Swansea from there had been slow. It was a few hours later that she finally found herself driving up from the seafront at Swansea to Gower.

She had seen nothing of the Gower commons before. Previously, she had taken a taxi from Swansea station, and missed all this. To Elizabeth it all looked rather scruffy and unkempt. She checked her satnav, and started down the road towards Rhossili. She could see the turning off to Bryn Draig, but decided to carry on down the road and have a walk around before going to her B & B.

On the night of the party she had arrived earlier than this and she remembered asking the taxi driver to drop her down at the car park so that she could see the beach first. She hadn't realised how far the walk down would be, but she had enjoyed collecting pebbles and shells, and putting them in her large shoulder bag. It had been weeks later that she had found them in there, and then years after that that she had used them in her bird bath. She remembered staying down on the beach for ages and then, of course, being heavily pregnant, having to face the climb back up, which was really hard. She had underestimated how far it was. She had been exhausted by the time she got to the church, but had been lucky that a couple, seeing her walking, had given her a lift to the Dragon House.

All seemed very benign this evening. Elizabeth glanced at her watch: it was just after nine. The younger families had all left long ago. Now the surfers were out in force with their dilapidated campervans. The only building open was the hotel, with groups of people standing around drinking and others eating. It was all very unsophisticated. She suddenly felt rather over-dressed. She put on her sunglasses, and reluctantly left the safety of her car. The fresh air was soft but, as the scent of the salt air seeped into her senses, she shuddered, thinking how a smell can be more unnerving than a sight or sound. It can bring back remembrance of a memory which you can't quite tie down, but you know makes you feel uncomfortable.

Elizabeth started to walk across the car park. She was nervous as she approached the headland. She wondered what memories would return. Her feet hurt.

She realised that her cream leather sandals with four inch high wedges were impractical here. She stood by the gate. In front of her was the headland, to her right in the distance the steep path down to miles of sandy beach and the tiny black spots of surfers that speckled the sea. She waited for a memory, a panic, to grip her, but it never came. It was as if she had never been here before. It was just that the smell unsettled her, but nothing else. It was very strange. She was not a great fan of the sea, but even she could see that was staggeringly beautiful. London seemed light years, rather than miles, away.

Elizabeth returned to her car, reset her satnav, drove back up the road, and turned into the road to Bryn Draig. She kept following the satnav until she reached a small modern bungalow. Surely this couldn't be 'The Sea View'? However, there was the sign, boasting bed and breakfast. Oh God, where had she come? It was getting late to find anywhere else that night. Maybe it would be better inside? The front at least looked well cared for and tidy. She parked the car, which looked far too flashy to be parked on the concrete run-in, got out, and wheeled her case up to the front door.

'Evening.'

She looked around and realised that an old man in next door's front garden was talking to her.

'That car, it's the altered Audi isn't it? Bet that was good to drive. You come a long way, then?'

Elizabeth scowled at him. 'Not really.'

'So, were you able to give her a good run on the motorway?'

'Mmm, yes,' she replied and turned away. For God's sake, why was he talking to her?

'She's good with the garden. I'll say that for her,' she heard the man say. 'I've asked her to help with mine, but she's always too busy.'

Elizabeth went quickly to the porch, and was less than impressed to find a discarded trug with gloves, trowel, and a pair of wellington boots covered in dry mud there. There didn't appear to be a doorbell, so Elizabeth knocked on the door, which swung open. She peeped inside at what appeared to be a normal bungalow. She couldn't see a reception desk or any of the normal trappings of a hotel. It really was just somebody's home. She had never been anywhere like it in her life. The light was on. She could see green patterned carpet and rather hideous china ornaments of cats and dogs grinning at her from shelves in the racks on the wall. She could hear a television, and was just about to turn and make her getaway when a short, round woman with tight grey-brown curls and an apron came along the hallway.

'Hello, come on in. You must be Elizabeth,' she said. 'I'm Angela. Come in, come in. Had a good journey?'

Elizabeth found the informality unnerving. It was very odd, disconcerting, to be walking into someone's home.

Angela was saying 'I'll show you your room, and then you must come and have a nice cup of tea and some scones. I know it's late, and you've probably eaten, but I'm sure you'd like something.'

'Well not really–'

Angela flung open a bedroom door. Elizabeth was horrified to notice that there was no key. The room was small. There were more horrible ornaments, and a very bad print of some dying flowers in a vase. There was a tiny portable television the likes of which Elizabeth hadn't seen for a least twenty years. Next to it, a small table with a tray. On this were a cup and saucer, a small kettle, some tea bags, coffee sachets and mini cartons of long-life milk.

'Now, I hope you're comfortable. The bathroom's across the hall.'

Elizabeth tried to hide her horror.

'Do you have many guests?' she asked faintly.

'Oh no, you're my only one. You see, I just let out the one room. Right. You settle in, and come into the living room when you're ready.'

Elizabeth looked again around her room. She opened drawers, pulled back the duvet cover. At least it was clean.

After she had unpacked she would have been glad to get into bed, but thought she ought to at least go and say goodnight. It seemed very strange to be walking around someone else's house so freely. The woman seemed to be very trusting.

Angela had put scones, cream, jam, butter, and chocolate cake on the coffee table. It was a long time since Elizabeth had been presented with such food.

'Oh, thank you, but I was just going to go to bed actually.'

'Oh, you must have something' insisted Angela.

Elizabeth sat on the edge of the floral armchair, took a cup of tea, and one scone, which she cut into quarters.

'No jam, cream, butter?' asked Angela, looking concerned.

'No, no thanks.'

'Are you ill?'

'No, just watching the calories.'

Angela shrugged and sat down, liberally spreading her own scones with butter, jam and cream.

'So you've driven down from London today?'

'It's not too far, actually' said Elizabeth. 'The roads were better than I expected.'

'Still, it's a long way.'

'I was talking to your neighbour just now. Or rather, he was talking to me.'

'Oh, Bill? He's so nosey.'

'He liked my car. Obviously knows about them.'

'He used to run the garage here. That's why. Never to be trusted, though. No, my husband said he wouldn't trust him to fix an old bucket, let alone a car. Always on the fiddle, Bill.'

'Well, he admired your garden.'

'Bet he said I was a mean old bugger for not doing his.'

'Well, not quite.'

'Bone lazy, he is. You know, his wife left him a few years ago. Not sure why she didn't leave before that. I reckon he'd been playing around–'

Elizabeth was astounded at the gossip Angela seemed to be prepared to share with a total stranger.

'So what brings you here?' asked Angela

'I'm just having a break.'

Angela immediately looked interested. 'Oh, really? What from?'

'I own art galleries.'

'In London?'

'Yes, and one in New York. I buy and sell works of art.'

'Now, that is interesting. Is it like paintings, sculpture, or a bit of everything?'

Elizabeth smiled. 'Paintings, watercolours mainly.'

'Oh, do you like this?' Elizabeth looked at a small oil painting of heather, of the downs: blazing reds, yellow, like the downs were on fire. It took her breath away. 'It's striking. Who painted this?'

'Oh, Catrin. My niece. Years ago now. It's the heather here up on the downs. I love it. You know her father, Lloyd, gave it to me. I remember one day seeing his car arrive. He and my sister Isabel owned the Dragon House then. Well, I was wondering why he had come. It wasn't long after my mother had died. Anyway, I went up to check everything was alright, and he had this pile of paintings. I admired them. I thought maybe they'd been done by Aled, his son. He was the clever one, you see. I was very surprised when he said Catrin had done them. I hadn't realised she was good at anything really. Anyway, he offered me this one. It's lovely, isn't it?'

'You know the family in the Dragon House?'

'Yes, I said it was owned by my sister and her husband. I was raised there, you know. I lost my sister, Isabel, sadly. You look interested. Do you know them?'

'No, not at all, but it's very good,' Elizabeth said, quickly.

'She had great potential, looking back. It's a shame she never went to college. But, well, my sister Isabel, she was very clingy. You know, poor Catrin spent half her life looking after her. But then, that's Catrin. Always looking after everyone.'

'Catrin sounds a very good kind of person.'

'Oh, she is. I never felt her parents appreciated her like they should. It was all Aled this and Aled that with them.'

'Aled?' Elizabeth tried to still her voice as she said his name.

'Oh, that was their son, my nephew. Terrible it was. He died here, you know, out on Worm's Head. He was twenty seven. Tragic. They worshipped that boy, and to lose him like that, well, it was devastating.'

'What happened?'

'Oh, it was a terrible accident. So sad. I was at the party. That night, there was a girl Aled went off with. It turned out the girl was pregnant, but she didn't want the baby. Catrin and Gareth took the baby on.'

76

'What about the girl, the mother of the baby?'

Elizabeth knew she was taking a chance asking. After all, why should she want to know? But Angela, in full flood telling a good story, didn't seem to think it was odd.

'As I say, she wanted nothing to do with the baby. Still, it was as well Catrin and Gareth took the baby on in the light of what happened to the girl.'

'What was that?'

'The girl, the baby's mother: she died in an accident a few years later. It was so sad. Still, the little girl, Bethan her name is, she's had a wonderful upbringing with Catrin and Gareth. Now, you really should have another scone.'

In the whirl of chatter, the words nearly washed over Elizabeth, but she grabbed hold of them.

'Hang on. You said the mother of this baby died?'

'Oh yes. My sister Isabel told me. She said the girl had been in an accident.'

'What kind of accident? Do they all think the mother is dead?'

Angela frowned at her. 'Well, yes, of course. I can't remember now how she died.'

'Are you sure she died?'

'Oh, yes. Someone told my brother in law, and he told Isabel. She was upset, but then, well, that's life, isn't it? You look upset. Are you sure you don't know them?'

Elizabeth realised that she needed to backtrack quickly. 'No, of course not. Sorry, I'm tired. It's been a long day.'

'Of course, and here I am keeping you up gossiping about people you know nothing about. Now, there are towels at the end of your bed, and we just sort of take it in turns for the bathroom. What time would you like breakfast?'

'Oh, don't worry. I'll pick something up.'

'Oh don't you want a full Welsh? That's what I call it. I do lava bread; buy it from Swansea market, and Glamorgan sausages, the lot. It's very good.'

'Oh no, really. I usually just have fruit and toast.'

'If you're sure. I'll make sure they are set out ready for you.'

'Thank you, and good night.'

Elizabeth returned to her room, and threw her case on the bed. She was very angry. She was sure her aunt would never have told such a lie. Her aunt, like her parents, was deeply religious. She had come to the hospital the night of the accident and had obviously been very shocked that her niece was pregnant. She had been as determined as Elizabeth that her parents should not be told, and had been relieved that Elizabeth wanted the baby to be adopted. To her, the solution of the baby going to Catrin and Gareth was ideal. When her aunt had collected just Elizabeth, taken her home to recover, she had said firmly that the matter would never be referred to again, and Elizabeth was sure she would have kept to that. No, the lie had not come from her aunt. Where had it come from, then?

Elizabeth felt like going at that moment up to the house and telling them the truth. She stopped herself. She had come here simply to see Bethan and know she was well, know she had done the right thing all those years ago. Why do anything else? She looked out of the window, into the blackness and knew she couldn't just ignore what she had been told. Bethan had a right to know her birth mother was alive and if one day she wanted to contact her it would be her choice. Elizabeth decided that on Monday she would speak to Lloyd on his own, get his assurance that Bethan would be told the truth. Yes, that would be the right thing to do, she would do that and then she could return to London knowing she had done the right thing.

Having worked out a plan of action Elizabeth felt better. She needed to get ready for bed, calm down and then think. She put on her silk pyjamas and gown. She picked up her soap bag and towel.

'Honestly this feels like staying in a bloody youth hostel,' she grumbled to herself, cringing at the memory of a terrible school trip.

She opened the door gingerly, went to the bathroom, and tried the bathroom door. She assumed this room at least would have a lock. The door opened easily and she went in. Although basic, this was fortunately also very clean.

Back in her own room she went through her rather involved skin cleansing and moisturising routine, squinting in an inadequate dressing table mirror. Then she took off her gown, turned off the main light and looked out of the window. So black. There were a few lights on in houses but they were surrounded by blackness. It was never like this in London. She opened the window and fresh, clean, air blew in. Then she heard the sea. It was louder and more threatening than she expected. She remembered that she was in a bungalow. Of course, anyone could creep out of the darkness and get in. What was she thinking? Quickly, she closed her window. She was horrified to see that there were no locks on it. It was so different to her gated house, no protection from the outside world: no walls, and no security guards; there were no burglar alarms. Elizabeth got into bed, nervously lay down, and eventually fell into an uneasy sleep.

Chapter Nine

Sunday 29th July 2012

Catrin woke very early the next morning. 'Happy birthday,' she said to herself. She looked around the room. Even though the yellow sunflowers on the wallpaper were faded now, she still loved them. Her Nana Beth had decorated the room especially for her. It was much prettier than her room in Cardiff had ever been. Her Nana had also put the little white dressing table and chair in here. Catrin smiled at the photograph which stood proudly on her dressing table of her with her Nana Beth on the beach.

She had actually celebrated some of her previous birthdays here. They had been wonderful. She had had a cake and candles and Nana Beth had made a pass-the-parcel. Back in Cardiff her birthdays had always been a bit fraught, and she had stopped asking for parties when she was quite young.

Her phone pinged. She picked it up: a text from Lowri.

'Happy birthday Mum. So excited to see you later. Just wait until you see your present. Make sure you are in at 11. Mark is coming. Be great for you to meet him. We are coming ahead of Dad. Lots of love Lowri xxx'

Catrin loved the excitement she could read in Lowri's words. She sounded so happy. One of the great things about being a mother was the warmth you felt when you saw that in your children. Conversely, of course, their tears and heartache could, as quickly, eclipse the sun, leaving you bereft and miserable.

Catrin started to flick through the photographs on her phone, and found one of her favourite photos of Lowri. She had long curly fair hair like she herself used to have. Her face was pale with freckles and she had serious grey eyes: a thoughtful studious, undemanding child, frequently over-shadowed by Bethan's exuberance or tantrums. It would be good to see her.

Catrin dressed and went downstairs. She went out though the back door. It was a beautiful morning. She remembered how, when she was little, her Nana Beth used to make a picnic breakfast just for the two of them. They would eat it in the garden or sometimes go down to the beach.

She saw no reason not to go out. She walked down through the heather, birds rustling in the hedges, a robin singing. It was idyllic. It warmed Catrin. She walked until she reached the climb down on to the beach. The sand lay before her, virgin clean. She took off her sandals, excited to make the first foot prints in the sand. The wonderful thing about the beach was that every day started fresh and new. She walked down until she reached the sea, and stood in the shallows, the sea lapping over her feet. The sound of the ripples got louder, the ebb and flow over the shells and pebbles at the edge. Catrin had read that the sound of the waves altered patterns in your brain, lulling you into a state of relaxation. Maybe that is why people meditated to the sound of waves; she knew she felt calmer. The sea was cold, but she could feel the heat from the early morning sun on her. It seemed so peaceful and serene. Despite the cold, she longed to go deeper, even wished she had brought a swimsuit, not that she had swum for years. As it was, she decided to be daring, to take off her blouse, as she had a T shirt underneath, and tuck her skirt into her knickers. She walked out further, going deeper and deeper, and the sea water seemed to get warmer. It was a wonderful feeling of leaving the world behind. She shut her eyes and lifted her head to the sun, bathing in its warmth. Suddenly the spell was broken.

'Hey,' a voice shouted behind her. She ignored it, but again it shouted, this time her name, 'Catrin.'

She turned. She recognised the voice, but who was it?

'Catrin. It's Harri,' the voice shouted. Harri took off his sunglasses, and then she knew.

'Good heavens,' she said.

She recognised his voice now, but he looked quite different. He stood confidently, wore fitted navy shorts just below the knee, a white T shirt and cream blazer. His hair was still thick and fair.

Painfully aware of the mess she must look, Catrin made her way back out of the sea, and quickly undocked her skirt.

'My father told me you were staying here. You're up early,' he said, grinning.

'My God, Harri. It must be over thirty years since I've seen you.'

'I came to stay with Dad, catch up, you know.'

'Right.' She looked around. 'It doesn't change, does it?'

Harri grinned. 'No, not a bit.' He added, more seriously, 'I was so sorry about what happened to Aled.'

'Thank you. It was awful. I've not come back, you know, until yesterday.'

'I can understand that.'

'So what happened to you? Didn't you go to France or something?'

'Yes. I went to university over there. Now I live in a lovely seaside town, Collioure; gorgeous harbour front, good restaurants, wine. Wonderful place.'

'Sounds incredible. What do you do there?'

'My wife's family own a vineyard up on the hillside there. I've turned their business around over the years.'

'That's impressive.'

'It is. Not sure they appreciate it but, yes, it's done well. It's lovely living out there. I have to say this place looks pretty primitive and derelict after there.'

Catrin look at the vast expanse of beach, the steep downs behind.

'I wouldn't use the word derelict. It's stunning.'

'But so, well, uncivilised. I mean, where can you sit and drink a decent glass of rosé, eat fine food?'

'I don't think people come here for that. And there is the hotel at the top.'

'But it's so hard to get back up there. There should be facilities further down, or at least put in some easier means of getting up and down to the beach.'

'But that would ruin it. You do know that at one time they were going to build a Butlins down here? Can you imagine it?'

Harri laughed. 'That's not quite what I had in mind. Anyway, you didn't come for a lecture. I must admit we had some good times when we were in our teens, younger more innocent times. I used to sit beside you on the beach watching you sketch. I hope you're still painting.'

'Oh, no. Not any more.'

'But you were really good. I still have a picture of shells you painted. It's a watercolour: a collection of beautiful shells, blues, pinks and creams. I got it framed. You know, people in Collioure have offered me money for it, but I said nothing would make me part with it. To me, it's priceless.'

He looked at her intently. 'We had that wonderful summer, but you never kept in touch when you went back to Cardiff. Very hard on a young man's ego.'

She smiled. 'I'm sorry. Everything went a bit haywire when I got back.'

'I heard you never went to Art College.'

'I never even finished my A levels.'

'Why ever not?'

'Well, the first thing that happened was that my Nana Beth died in the September. Mum was in an awful state. Then all the work I had in a portfolio I was putting together for my interview for college got lost.'

'How?'

'It was the school. Mum or Dad took it up to them because I was ill. I was sure it had been given to the head of art. He was meant to be looking at it.   Anyway, I went back to school and they denied ever having it, which was ridiculous. I was very upset, so was Mum. She went up, creating a fuss, but it never turned up. I started again but I never had the time to build up the work I needed. Mum was poorly a lot and I just never had the time I needed to complete things. It was frustrating, with my art teacher nagging me all the time. In the end I decided to leave school and I started casual work.'

'And you've never gone back to it?'

'No. I was happy working in shops and things. It suited everyone.'

'Seems a waste.'

'Not really. I got married when I was twenty seven, and then I had Lowri. Time just sort of goes, doesn't it?'

'It can. Do you remember the plans we made that summer before you went into the sixth form? We would both do our A levels. You were going to do your foundation year, while I was going to get a year's experience in France. Then you I would travel the world.'

'Ah, you dream when you're young. Still, you went to France.'

'I did, and I met Francine.'

They walked along the beach together.

'I hear Lloyd is selling the house now.'

'That's right. Sealed bids have to be in by a week Tuesday.'

'Do you mind him selling?'

'God, no. I'll be glad to see the back of it. So how is your wife? Is she over with you?'

'Francine is actually back in France. We have a boy, Marc. He's at university now, and, actually, me and Francine: we're on a bit of a break.'

'I'm sorry—'

'It's OK. We might still work it out. Dad said you're married to a doctor.'

'That's right. Gareth and I live in Cardiff.'

'So is he having a lie-in?'

'Oh no. He's working. I'll be impressed if he even gets down today.'

'Dad said there is some kind of memorial for Aled tomorrow. Is he coming for that?'

'Yes, but it would be nice if he came today. It's my birthday.'

'Really? Happy birthday.'

She smiled. 'Thank you.'

'I was fifty earlier this year. Is it the same for you?'

'That's right. I have to say, you have worn better than me.'

'You still look beautiful.' He touched her fair hair very gently.

85

'Oh Harri, that's very kind, but nonsense.'

He didn't laugh. 'You fit here, you know. Always have.'

'What do you mean?'

'I don't know. You just look at home. Why don't you and Gareth buy the house from Lloyd?'

'I couldn't now. Not after all that has happened here.'

'Right. Well, I might as well tell you what I'm thinking of doing, then.'

'What's that?'

'Actually, I am thinking of putting in a bid.'

'Really?'

'Mm.'

'You want to buy it? Why?'

'I have ideas. It's on a large plot. I was thinking of some kind of spa hotel.'

'You would knock down the Dragon House?'

'You just said you'd be glad to see the back of the place.'

'That's true.'

'It would give much-needed work for the locals as well. Put the village on the tourist map.'

'I suppose so, yes. But it would cost a fortune wouldn't it?'

'A lot, but then I have capital. Who knows? Your father may be interested in coming in on the deal.'

They were walking along the warm sand, Catrin tuning her breathing to the calm shushing of the incoming waves on the beach. It was heavenly, peaceful.

Harri's next words crashed in. 'Dad told me you adopted Aled's child.'

'Um, you mean–'

'The girl. Dad said you and your husband adopted the girl.'

'Yes, that's right. To be honest, I didn't know it was quite so widely known.'

'Oh, gosh. You can't imagine keeping secrets in a place like this, can you?'

'I suppose not.'

'Is she like Aled? I remember him when we were young. Sickening. He could do everything, couldn't he?'

'He was exceptional, yes. Bethan is not that much like him to look at. She is dark and musical. Aled was all sports.'

'I can remember him running the length of this beach. I was five years older than him, but he could always beat me easily. Dad told me the girl is, what do they call it now? Hearing impaired. Is that right?'

'Actually, Bethan prefers to say she is Deaf. There are people you see that say the word impairment means something needs to be fixed. She was born Deaf.'

'Do they know why?'

'No. No idea, but it happens that way sometimes.'

'So does she sign?'

'Yes. She is also very musical.'

'Really? I'd have thought that was impossible.'

'Don't say that to Bethan. And don't mention Beethoven. She's going to university to study music in September. She wants to specialise in composition.'

'Gosh, sounds amazing. You must have worked very hard with her.'

'I fought for her to do things, but there is something in Bethan that drives her. I think she will be playing her flute tomorrow at the memorial for Aled. Are you coming?'

'Oh yes. I want to speak to your father. So, if you never went to college, what have you been doing?'

'When I left school I just did casual work, you know, various different jobs. Mum needed help. I was fine. Then I met Gareth at the hospital. It was wonderful.'

'Were you nursing?'

Catrin cringed. 'No. I was only working in the shop at the hospital, by the entrance. He stopped by each day to buy his paper. We got talking, you know, about politics and things. Then he asked me out. I couldn't believe it. I still can't sometimes. We had Lowri and then, of course, Bethan.'

'Do you have a really nice house? I mean, Gareth being a doctor and all that. I bet you spend your life going on exotic holidays and things.'

'Hardly. We live in a very ordinary house on an estate. We never go out for a meal, let alone a holiday.'

'Why ever not?'

'Gareth's always working.'

'And you?'

'I've had some wonderful times bringing up the girls. Being a Mum has been the best thing I've ever done.'

'Really? I'm not sure Francine would agree.'

'Everyone's different. I had lots of friends who have gone back to follow really interesting careers, and that's fine. Thank God, actually. I mean, some went on to be head teachers, run their own businesses, all sorts.'

'But not you?'

'Oh, no. I never had the qualifications anyway.'

'But your girls are getting older now. Surely you have dreams?'

Catrin looked out at the sea. 'Dreams? Do people our age have dreams?'

'Of course they do.'

'I don't think I do. Maybe I'm not the dreaming kind.'

'You used to be. Think about it: you always wanted to travel. You and Gareth could do that now. Maybe he'll surprise you for your birthday: take you on a cruise or something.'

'The biggest surprise will be if he remembers my birthday at all.'

'I'm sure Gareth has something up his sleeve.'

'He really won't have. Look, I know it sounds odd to you, but I don't need lots of presents and things from Gareth. He's a good man and he works very hard.'

'Well, I know a great restaurant Gareth can take you to, if you need a heads up. You can get a table, even tonight, if you mention my name.'

'We don't do things like that, and I really don't mind. I shall cook for us. We will have a lovely family meal.'

'Well in case you change your mind, the name is Ffrwyth Y Môr, Fruits of the Sea. Wonderful place. Been open about a year. Already has Michelin stars.'

'Sounds pricey, but thank you.'

'You deserve it, deserve to be looked after.'

Harri reached out, and touched the long scar on her arm. She pulled her arm away, and quickly put on her blouse.

'I'm fine, very lucky. I have a good husband, two lovely girls, food and clothing. I have people who need me, who I can help, and for those things I thank God. I am very fortunate,' she said, defiantly.

'Then why do you sound so miserable?'

She frowned. 'I'm not miserable. Why do you say that?'

'Look, you don't have to listen to me, but I reckon it's time you started looking after yourself. And Gareth, well, it's time he started to appreciate you.'

'I have my girls. I have my health. I'm very lucky. Stop trying to make me feel so, I don't know, discontent.'

Harri smiled apologetically. 'I'm sorry. Not fair on your birthday, is it?'

She looked up at the downs. 'I suppose I ought to get back to the house, face the family.'

They started to walk back up the beach and clambered up on to the path.

'Right, I'm going down to the hotel. I shall, sit and drink decent coffee and read the papers,' said Harri, grinning.

'Sounds very relaxing.'

'I'll see you tomorrow then?'

'Yes of course, see you then.'

Catrin walked up through the down land and came into the village. Talking to Harri had upset her, and she wasn't sure why. She felt confused, and lonely. She looked down the street, and then she thought of something she could do to cheer herself up, something she hadn't done for years.

Chapter Ten

Catrin looked around, feeling guilty, and went to the general store. She walked around the shop. Bethan had said something about going gluten free, so she picked up a few bags of rice and oats. It all seemed very heavy. She was glad Harri's father didn't appear to be in the shop.

As she paid for her shopping she said to the woman behind the counter, 'A packet of Benson and Hedges, and a lighter, please.' Although she was speaking quietly she felt she was shouting the words. The woman looked quite bored, though. Catrin quickly stuffed the cigarettes in her handbag and left the shop. She crossed the road, and found a discrete bench looking over the downs. This is crazy, part of her was saying. She was acting like a school child hiding behind the bike sheds. Gareth and Lowri would go spare.

When Catrin had been very young, her mother would send her to the shops to buy cigarettes for her. They would sell them to children in those days. Her mother never wanted anyone to know that she smoked. She was always very grateful to Catrin for going to get them. It was one of the few times her mother would smile at her and tell her that she was a good kid.

Catrin had first smoked in her early teens down at the park. It had made her part of a group for the first time. She had impressed them all by not coughing and spluttering but, standing in what she believed to be a sophisticated way, she had nonchalantly inhaled the smoke, even blown rings of smoke. Of course, she had her mother to thank for the performance. All those years, she had been unconsciously teaching her daughter how to smoke. It had been easy.

Catrin had only smoked with friends for a few years, and once after Aled's accident. She had been desperate to do something, and she remembered that look of sheer bliss her mother had when she smoked. Maybe it would help. She had just had the one. Gareth had found the packet. A huge row ensued. That had been the last time.

Well, until today. Deep down, maybe it was a rebellion against Gareth, who hadn't even sent her a text to wish her happy birthday. She really tried not to care, but there was one tiny part which did. As she stood looking over to the sea, Catrin took a long drag on the cigarette. She realised that she still didn't like the taste. In fact, it seemed to take an awful long time to finish. She grinned at her foolishness as she put the packet in her bag. She would throw them away later. She quickly crunched on a mint and walked back to the house.

Catrin entered the quiet house and went upstairs, further along the hallway. Bethan's room was dark and silent. From her father's room she could hear snoring. To her left was her mother's old room. She suddenly realised that all her life her parents had had separate rooms, here and in the Cardiff house. She had always just accepted it, but today she did think that maybe it had been a bit strange. Catrin glanced at the door to her mother's room and tried to remember how many years it had been since she had been in there. She hadn't been in there since the night of Aled's accident, so it was more than eighteen years. Gosh, it must be nearly twenty five years.

Tentatively, Catrin pushed open the door, wondering if she would be faced with a load of boxes. The yellow curtains were drawn but still allowed sunshine to filter in. When she opened them, the room looked light and pleasant. It had been cleaned and dusted but, apart from that, appeared to have been left totally untouched.

She tried to open the wardrobe, but was surprised to find it locked. She went to the dressing table. There, she found a number of photographs. There were a few of Aled, but they weren't like the ones down in Cardiff. They all showed him gaining awards and prizes. These showed a little boy with blond curls in home knitted jumpers, and grubby knees. Catrin smiled. It was lovely to push past the older Aled and see the innocence of his early years. There were similar pictures of her, her blond hair clipped back in a plastic slide, and wearing that cotton dress she had liked, with daisies on it. Next to these was one of her mother. She was in the library in Cardiff where she worked. What struck Catrin was how upright and confident her mother looked. She had been a pretty woman, sure of herself. Tucked behind the larger ones was a small wedding photograph. She was struck again by both how glamorous her mother looked, but also how much older she had been than her father. Of course, she knew there was twenty years between her mother and her father. However, in the photograph, the age difference was very marked. She wondered if that was part of the reason her parents had no wedding photographs on display in their house in Cardiff. In fact, she had never known her parents celebrate their wedding anniversary. She picked up the photo and looked at the back. There was the date of their wedding. She blinked, and looked again. December 1961. For the first time, she realised that at the time of the wedding her mother must have been pregnant.

Catrin sat back. It had never crossed her mind that her parents 'had to get married'. An ambitious, talented, young man had married this glamorous but older woman. Had he loved her? Well, he'd never left her. Catrin remembered her mother tidying the house before her father came home from another trip to America. 'We have to make it look decent, you know. We don't want him leaving us, do we?' She would say it smiling, but there was no laughter in her voice. The more Catrin thought about it, the more she realised how much her mother's life was dominated by this fear of losing her father.

Catrin looked down at the drawers, and wondered if they had been emptied. She opened one. It was full of underwear. Another was locked. She couldn't see a key. She tried another, but this was obviously locked as well. She pulled it hard in exasperation, and realised that the lock must have been faulty because it fell open. When she looked inside she just saw a pile of scarves. She rummaged among them. Wrapped in one, she found an old used cheque book. She saw that it was for an account solely in her mother's name. That surprised her, as she remembered her mother being very cross that her father had insisted that all their money was in a joint account. There had been times when her mother had borrowed money from Catrin because she said she wanted to buy something without her father knowing. Her mother had said that because all her work was of a voluntary or charitable nature and she had no income she didn't feel she could argue with him. Looking at this, it seemed that her mother had kept a separate account. Where the money had come from to set this up, Catrin had no idea. The branch of the bank was in Swansea which, again, was odd, as all the family banking was done in Cardiff. She glanced at the stubs of the used cheques. They did not record who the money was given to, but there was a record of the amounts. Some were for a few thousand pounds, others hundreds. They were dated 1993. It was all very mysterious.

Catrin was just replacing the cheque book when she felt a cold hard object at the bottom of the drawer. A deep familiar sense of nausea washed over her. She knew exactly what that was.

Elizabeth had also woken early that morning. The curtains were thin. The sun was streaming in, and she was hot. It was so quiet here. She suddenly felt very alone. In London there was always noise, something happening. She could at least pretend she was part of something. But here, there were no voices, no cars or ambulances, nothing. She got out of bed and opened the window that she had been too frightened to leave open in the night. The fresh air wafted in, and she felt it, silky against her skin. She could hear the sea, the seagulls, and tried to remember the last time she had been to the seaside. She had often gone on holiday with her parents to stay in the north of Corsica, high up in a small medieval village among the mountains. At this time of day the villagers would have been out shopping, getting their chores done before the searing heat took a grip later. Then only tourists and lizards would venture out, and locals would retreat indoors. They seldom went to the beach unless it was to sit beside it at some restaurant in the evening, looking out over the sea. Her only proper seaside holidays had been with her aunt in Cardiff, when she stayed with her in the summer. She was taken to Barry Island. Her aunt bought her a bucket and spade. They jostled for space on the crowded beach full of Welsh people. They built sandcastles, paddled in the sea, and ate ice creams. Elizabeth had enjoyed it, but felt rather hitched on to her aunt's family, always having to be that bit more polite than her cousins. They had gone to the fair, but Elizabeth didn't like it there. It seemed so rough and noisy. The people running the rides seemed uncouth, and she wondered if the rides were safe. Here was so different: hot, but not stifling; wilder, remote. She was thinking of showering, but heard the sound of the shower being used. She would have to wait. Then she thought of Richard. He would like it here, she was sure. He had probably had years of normal summer holidays with his family.

And then she remembered the startling revelations of the night before. She had to think today what she was going to do. It would help to talk to Richard, but of course he knew nothing about Bethan or what she was doing. Somehow, talking to him could be reassuring, though, simply to hear his voice. She phoned him.

'Morning, how are things?' asked Richard.

'I'm here, in Wales.'

'What?'

'I came last night.'

'Gosh. So what is it like?'

'Ghastly. Honestly, it's a crummy little bungalow. I haven't got my own bathroom, and the woman who owns it keeps force-feeding me scones.'

She heard Richard laughing. 'It will be good for you.'

'Thanks! How are Rosie and all?'

'Great. Most exciting news: she's expecting. I'm going to be a grandad. I can't believe it.'

'What?'

'I know. Crazy, isn't it? But I'm so pleased. Just think, if you and I were married you'd be a step-granny.'

'That is not funny.'

'Don't worry. Seriously though, I am just so made up.'

'I'm pleased for you.'

'So, what are you going to do with your day?'

'I'm not sure. Sunday, isn't it? I'll think of something. There are no galleries or anything. It is odd not being in London.'

'I give you twenty four hours there and you'll be back in work.'

'No. I can manage.'

'We'll see. Anyway, I'm off for a run. Later we're going to the Royal Botanic Gardens. We'll have some lunch there. It's a lovely day here.'

'Right. Well, have a good day,' she said, briskly. Elizabeth felt put out that Richard didn't seem to be missing her. Suppose now that he was going to have a grandchild he wouldn't be bothered about living with her? Maybe he would move to Edinburgh?

Elizabeth could hear that Angela had finished in the shower, so she put on her dressing gown, picked up her soap bag and towel, and went to see if the bathroom was free. 'Honestly, it's like being a French exchange student. What am I doing here? Maybe the hotel has vacancies,' she thought, as she made her way across the hallway. The door was ajar. She pushed it nervously, and looked inside. To her relief, it was empty.

The shower was better than expected, although she felt stupid walking along the hallway in her towel.

Elizabeth returned to her room, and chose her clothes carefully. She put on a white, loose, jumpsuit, found the basic hairdryer provided, and dried her hair. She put on her necklace. It was the exquisite Cartier eighteen carat white gold necklace with a lovebird motif, diamond pendant set with emerald eyes and onyx beak which her parents had given to her for her twenty-first birthday. She knew that many people would have put it straight into a safe, frightened to ever wear something so valuable. Elizabeth thought that was ridiculous. She wore it frequently. It gave her a wonderful feeling of confidence, and she loved to see the envious looks from people in the know.

She carefully applied her make up and decided that she could face going to the kitchen for coffee. She was surprised to find Angela cooking, with a fresh cafetiere of coffee waiting for her. Croissants and freshly cut whole grain bread were set out by the toaster.

'I've laid up in the garden for you,' Angela said. 'It's a beautiful morning. You go out, and I'll bring these out to you. Now, are you sure you don't want a cooked breakfast? I'm cooking for myself.'

'No, really. Toast will be fine.'

Elizabeth went outside, relieved to find that she was alone, until Angela came out with the toast and joined her.

'So, Elizabeth. Have you plans? If you go to the church the service will be at nine. I'll be going, if you want to come with me.'

'No. No, thanks. I don't go to church,' replied Elizabeth, rather shocked that anyone still thought it was a normal thing to do on a Sunday.

'Oh, of course. Lots of people don't now, do they? I was just mentioning it.'

Elizabeth ate her dry toast.

Angela sat with a cup of coffee. 'So, do you think you will swim today?'

'God, no,' said Elizabeth. 'I can't stand the sea.'

'It seems an odd choice of holiday destination then,' said Angela, smiling.

'I'll enjoy walking,' said Elizabeth, vaguely aware that she looked like anything but a walker.

'Well, don't feel you have to rush off anywhere. Treat this place like your home. I leave a key under the mat. You can always let yourself in. Now, would you like a meal this evening?'

'Oh, no. I'll go to a pub or something.'

'Right, that's fine,' said Angela, standing up. 'Enough chatting. I'd better get off to church. I hope you have a good morning.'

Elizabeth went to her room and brushed her hair. She wondered about the pub in the village, wondered if it would be a better place to stay than here. It must be more private. She picked up her handbag, left the house, and walked up the road. As she walked along, she saw a large house to her right. Surely that must be it? The house where the party had been? There were no other houses as big. She remembered walking down that driveway. There were cars parked. She guessed Lloyd and the family were there. Strange to think that Bethan could be in that house, right now. It was tempting to go and knock on the door but, no, she would bide her time, wait until the memorial. She could control it then. After all, she hadn't come to see Bethan, only Lloyd. She continued along the street.

There were inviting smells of cooked breakfasts coming from the pub. Elizabeth went straight to reception. A young girl looked up and smiled.

'Good morning, can I help you?'

'I need a room.'

The girl looked rather blankly at her. 'Sorry?'

'You do rooms? I am asking if you have any vacancies.'

'Oh no, sorry. We're completely full. You could try Angela. She has a bungalow here. Number twelve. Just along on the left. She only takes one or two guests, though.'

'Actually, I've tried there.'

'She only has one room. I know she told me she had some woman from London coming to stay. Still, you might be lucky and she hasn't turned up. Otherwise, you could try the hotel down in Rhossili. Much bigger than us.'

'Oh, right. Thanks.'

'You have to drive up the road. Turn right.'

'Thank you.'

'I can draw you a map.'

'No, I'll be fine.'

Elizabeth returned to the bungalow and climbed into her car. She opened the windows. It was already hot in there. She drove out of the village, turned right, and followed the road to the car park at Rhossili. It was filling up quickly.

She crossed the road, and walked down to the hotel. The distant sea looked lovely, sparkling blue. There were already a few people making their way to the beach: families with young children. Probably been up since six.

She went into the reception of the hotel. However, it was obviously the wrong time. They, too, were full.

'Sorry,' said the receptionist. 'Nothing all week. It's the school holidays, you see.'

'I realised that.'

'Yes. Well, everything round here will be booked up. You could try the caravan park. They let out some of them. Might be lucky. You need to go to Llanmadog for that. You can get there by walking along the beach.'

Elizabeth shuddered. Not a caravan. Even the B & B was better than that. She would just have to stay out a lot.

'It's OK. Tell me, could I have coffee here?'

'Of course.'

'Thank you. I'll sit outside.'

Elizabeth found an empty table. There were a number of people having breakfast. She looked over at Worm's Head. It all looked so innocent here on a sunny morning. The girl came out with her coffee. As she drank it, she wondered when she was going to let Lloyd know she was there. Not yet.

She saw a notice saying that there was wifi. Maybe check the papers first? She took out her iphone and started to look at the Sunday papers. They were talking about a programme ITV wanted to make about Jimmy Saville, and the accusations of child abuse. The man had always given her the creeps, but she was shocked at the accusations being made.

Elizabeth sat back and looked over again at Worm's Head. She realised that nearby, maybe down there on the beach, her daughter could be walking. She wondered what she looked like, what she would be wearing. That dark baby hair: maybe it would have turned blonde. Would she be tall like Aled? Thoughts like that slipped in and out of her head most days, but she always quickly pushed them aside. She looked over and noticed a good-looking older man sitting drinking black coffee. He was dressed better than most of the British men, held himself with more confidence. He seemed to sense her looking at him and glanced over. She noticed the look of appreciation. He didn't look away too quickly. Elizabeth wondered who he was.

Chapter Eleven

Catrin was still in her mother's room when she heard some shouting from outside.

'Hey, is anyone up yet?'

Wrenched back into the present, Catrin quickly shut the drawer, went downstairs, and opened the door.

'Lowri, you're early.'

Lowri had parked further down the drive was out of the car, and came running towards her.

'Happy birthday, Mum,' she said, and hugged Catrin.

'Darling, you look wonderful.' Catrin was so pleased. She had never seen Lowri so happy. She was glowing, as if there was a rainbow around her.

She saw that a young man who must be Mark had got out of the car and was looking out at the view. He was short like Lowri, with spiky red hair. He looked vaguely familiar.

'Welcome, Mark,' said Catrin.

Mark turned and grinned at her, then at Lowri. Even from a distance, Catrin could see that he looked at Lowri as if she was a precious jewel. He confidently walked forward. Closer too, Catrin could see that he was older than Lowri, maybe late twenties.

'You must be Catrin.'

'It's good to meet you at last. Lowri has been hiding you from us.'

'No, I haven't,' insisted Lowri.

'Come on in, then.'

Catrin was about to go inside when Lowri shouted to her. 'Stop, Mum.'

She saw Lowri gesture to Mark as they shared some private joke.

'Hang on, Mum. You can't go in yet. We have your birthday present here in the car, so turn around, and close your eyes.'

Catrin hesitantly did as she was told, and waited. She tried to imagine what it was going to be, guessed it was something large. Maybe it was a painting, or something more practical, possibly a sun lounger? She had been hinting that she wanted one for years.

'Turn around, Mum.' Lowri's voice was quiet, but trembling with excitement.

Catrin turned, and was amazed to see Lowri leading a cocker spaniel towards her. Lowri looked nervous.

'He's for you, Mum. You are pleased, aren't you?'

Catrin could not find words. She just stared at the little dog which was looking back at her. He had deep brown eyes and soft, black, silky ears.

'Oh Lowri,' she whispered.

'He's beautiful, isn't he? He's a blue roan. Guess what his name is?'

Catrin shook her head.

'He's called Sapphire, Safi for short. Mum, as soon as I heard that, I knew he was meant for you.'

'But where does he come from?'

'A friend of mine breeds cocker spaniels. She only has one breeding pair. They live in the house. The parents are just gorgeous. This little one was bought from them but the owners split up. They asked the breeder to re-home him. He's two years old. Mum, you are pleased, aren't you? If you don't want him, the breeder is very happy to have him back. There are a few people who would love to give him a home.'

Catrin felt a warm tear run down her cheek as she held out her arms. Safi walked towards her, wagging his tail. She crouched down to stroke him. He looked up and licked her chin. She held him close.

'Lowri, he's beautiful, perfect. Of course, I would love to keep him, but I ought to check with Dad.'

'Oh, he knows. He's fine with it. To be honest, you're the one who will have all the work.'

'I know that. It'll do me good. I could do with getting out walking again. Actually, I've seen a group of people walking their dogs together in the park by us. I could get to know them. Thank you both very much.'

'We've got some stuff. You know, a bed, and some food, bowls and things.'

'Well, that's lovely. You know, back when we lost Lady I thought about getting another dog but, well, the time never seemed right. Now it's perfect.'

Catrin took Lowri and Mark through the house into the back garden. Safi started to sniff around the grass. They all stood, enchanted, watching him.

Bethan came into the garden. She was wearing short denim shorts and a white crop-top T shirt.

'Hiya,' she shouted. She hugged Lowri, then looked down at Safi.

'Oh gosh, he's even more gorgeous in real life.'

'He is. I'm finding it really hard giving him away,' signed Lowri.

'You knew?' asked Catrin.

'Oh, yes. Lowri told me two weeks ago. Sent me photos. It's been really hard keeping the secret.'

Bethan sat crossed-legged on the grass. Safi came and sat on her. She looked over at Catrin. 'Happy birthday, Mum.'

'Bethan, this is Mark,' she said.

'Hiya.' Bethan grinned flirtatiously. 'I'm the pretty one.'

Catrin watched as Lowri signed something to Bethan. It was obviously a funny and rude retort. She saw Bethan laugh but she could not work out what exactly Lowri had said. Since the girls had been very young they had developed their own language of signs and gestures.

Mark nodded. 'Good to meet you, Bethan' he said, turning to Lowri, and putting his arm around her protectively. Bethan looked put out. She wasn't used to her sister being the centre of attention. 'I'm Deaf, by the way,' she said.

'Yes, Lowri told me. She said you sign?' asked Mark.

'Yes, but I can lip read pretty well.'

'I have a friend who is Deaf. He keeps telling me to learn sign language.'

'Well, you should,' responded Bethan.

'You're right, I know. I can do a bit.'

'Well, use it then.'

'OK, but I'm pretty rubbish. I can't do the whole BSL thing. You know, the grammar and things. Just the odd word.'

'That's better than nothing.'

'Lowri tells me you do music. How does that work? Is it all done by vibration?'

Bethan tutted. 'It's far more complicated than that. Hearing is only a small part of enjoying music. It's multi-sensory, a physical thing. Music is a feeling, an emotion. A deaf person feels music within the vibrations in the same part of the brain that hearing people use when the melodies you love get caught in your head.'

Catrin watched. She was impressed at the level of passion with which Bethan spoke. It was a side of her she seldom saw.

Mark was looking very serious now. 'That is so interesting. Lowri told me you play the flute?'

'Yes, but it is composition I want to do at university. It's exciting. There are some brilliant Deaf rappers and Deaf people composing now. I even read it could be the next big genre in music.'

Mark nodded. Catrin was struck by how well he listened. So often, people asked questions not really wanting the answer. You could see they were busy thinking what they would say next. But Mark was really concentrating, genuinely interested in what Bethan was saying.

Safi started to get restless. Bethan tickled his tummy.

'Shall we go and get our stuff from the car?' Lowri asked Mark.

They left together, walking very close, their footsteps in sync.

'Well, he seems alright. Bit intense, but that would suit Lowri,' said Bethan. 'Right. I need to put this monster down and go and get your present.'

Catrin sat down on the ground and picked up Safi. He nestled in close to her as she stroked under his chin. She had the feeling he would stay there all day. It was wonderful to have a dog back in her life. She had forgotten how much having one meant to her.

Catrin could hear Bethan running through the house. Soon she returned with a pretty paper carrier bag covered in pink roses.

Catrin took out a box, inside which was a small fine bone china bud vase. It was white with delicate blue flowers. Impractical, but lovely.

'It's beautiful,' she said holding it gently. 'Thank you so much.'

'You like it?'

'Of course. Could you put it up on the table safe, away from Safi? I'd hate anything to happen to it.'

'Good. Here's your card.'

Catrin opened the envelope. The card was rectangular, with flowers framing it. In the centre was a black and white photograph of Catrin and Bethan, heads touching, and the words, 'To the best Mum in the world.'

Catrin smiled.

'Oh, and one more thing.'

Bethan handed her a book-shaped present. Catrin opened it, and found a large journal. She already had a pile at home. It had seemed to be the in-present the Christmas before. It struck her as strange that in an age of computers, people should feel the need to hark back to such an old-fashioned, Victorian idea. Catrin could see that Bethan was watching her anxiously.

'It's lovely. Thank you,' she said, but secretly she wondered what she was going to write about. Her life barely justified a few pages in a note pad from Poundland at the moment.

'Lowri looks pretty smitten, I must say,' said Bethan.

'You think she's happy?'

'God, yes. It's a bit much, though, isn't? Like they only have eyes for each other. Lowri hardly spoke to me.'

Catrin smiled. She guessed that Bethan was feeling a bit jealous. 'It's bound to be pretty intense at this stage, love.'

'Suppose so. Anyway, when's Dad coming?'

'I'm not sure.'

Before they could talk further, Catrin's father joined them.

'A dog!' he exclaimed.

'This is Safi, Dad. He's my present from Lowri and Mark.'

To her surprise, her father seemed to soften. He knelt down and called Safi, who went running to him.

'He's a fine little chap,' her father said. 'Oh, happy birthday, Catrin.'

'Thanks, Dad.'

Lowri and Mark returned.

'Hi Grandad,' Lowri said, stiffly. They eyed each other.

'Glad you could come.'

'It's lovely here, Grandad.'

'Your mother should have brought you before.'

'She had her reasons,' said Lowri. Catrin cringed. Lowri and her father had never got on. However, she had to admit that it was a relief to have someone on her side.

'You haven't introduced your new boyfriend,' said Lloyd.

'Haven't had a chance. Grandad, this is Mark.'

Mark stretched out his hand, formally. 'Pleased to meet you, Lloyd. Lowri was showing me some photographs of your work. I loved the library you designed. It was in an American university?'

Her father looked pleasantly surprised. 'Oh, good. Thank you. So what do you do?'

'I lecture at the university, marine biology.'

'Really?' Lloyd looked impressed.

Catrin felt herself going red. Of course, that was where she had seen him. She worked in the kitchen at the university. Fortunately, he hadn't recognised her. She guessed Lowri hadn't said anything because she was too embarrassed about it.

'Let me go and make coffee,' said Catrin, and I need to get a drink for Safi. You'll have to tell me his meal times, Lowri.'

'He has two meals a day, usually after his morning and afternoon walks. He has dried food. Good quality. You know, the one we gave Lady. I brought a bag. I gave him a drink in the car, but you're right. He needs another. I put his bowl down in the kitchen.'

Catrin called Safi. She was impressed that he came straight to her. He seemed calmer than Lady had been. She was glad he had a different personality and colour. She would never have wanted to feel that she was trying to replace Lady, even after all these years.

Lowri had already put water in the bowl. Safi drank thirstily. For all his quiet ways, he was a very noisy and messy drinker. Lady had always drunk neatly. Safi had splashed water everywhere. His ears were soaking wet. Lowri had put a dog bed in the kitchen. Catrin took Safi to it. He circled around in it and then, with a sigh, seemed pleased to have a rest.

Catrin organised the drinks and biscuits. As she left the kitchen, Safi jumped up and followed her into the garden.

'I think you have a new shadow,' said Lowri.

'So Mark, what do your parents do?' asked Lloyd.

'Mum is a teacher. Dad is a jeweller.'

'His father owns a chain of jewellery shops, actually,' said Lowri.

Catrin put her coffee down and sat on the grass with Safi.

She saw Mark give Lowri a nod, as if encouraging her to say something, but Lowri gave a quick shake of her head. Catrin wondered what they were keeping from her. It hurt. She and Lowri had always been so close.

Catrin sipped her coffee. It was Mark who spoke next.

'So, how are you celebrating your birthday?' he asked.

'I expect I shall cook us something tonight.'

'When is Dad coming?' asked Lowri.

'Later today, I hope. Though I haven't heard from him yet.'

'God, he is hopeless.'

'He's just busy, love.'

Lowri sat forward, grinning.

'You know, Mum. I've just had a great idea.'

Chapter Twelve

Catrin could see the excitement in Lowri's eyes.

'What's your idea, then?'

'Why don't we all go out Mum, for a change?'

'I don't know.'

'Come on, our treat,' Lowri said, smiling at Mark.

'No. You can't do that. You've spent far too much already.'

'It doesn't matter. We could go to the pub here. It looks OK.'

Lloyd interrupted. To Catrin's surprise, he said, 'Good idea, Lowri. I'll pay. I haven't bought Catrin a present. This can be it.'

Catrin looked at her father. 'Well, thank you, Dad. That would be really nice.'

'Good. I'll go and ring and book us a decent table.'

'I'll send Gareth a text: make sure he's here in time.'

Gareth replied by text: 'Still tied up but will be there by six.'

Catrin, relieved to find he was still coming, went to make lunch.

After they had eaten, Catrin sat out in the garden with Safi sat at her feet. It had cooled down. There was a refreshing breeze coming off the sea. Everyone else was inside watching the Olympics. Safi was in the shade under the table, apparently content to be with Catrin.

Lowri came out. 'Fancy a walk?'

Catrin looked up, pleasantly surprised. 'Of course. Is Mark coming?' She tried to sound bright.

'He wants to watch the sport. No, it's just me. Want to talk with you, Mum, and I've something exciting to tell you.'

'Fine. Well I'll pack up some water and a bowl for Safi.'

Catrin and Lowri plastered themselves with sun cream, found hats and sun glasses and took water for themselves as well. Catrin was struck with how much work hot sunny days could be, and even more so now that she had a dog again. However, she didn't mind; it felt normal. They walked at a gentle pace.

'Which way then, Mum?'

'We cross the road, then down through the fields.'

'It's great here. Shame Grandad is selling the house. I'd have liked to come here more.'

'I'm sorry I didn't bring you here as a child.'

'That's alright. It must have been hard coming back, and you and Dad took us on lots of lovely holidays.'

Catrin felt herself relaxing. It was lovely to have some time with Lowri like this. Safi had obviously been walked on a lead before and was happy smelling the heather.

'How are you then? What's the news?'

Catrin saw Lowri hesitate.

'What is it? Tell me.'

'Before I do, Mum, is everything all right with Dad?'

'He works too much but, apart from that, yes. Why?'

'It's just I bumped into him at the hospital. I tried to chat, but he seemed to be in a rush to get away. It was all a bit odd. He was with that nurse, Carol, from the surgery.'

'Oh, they're doing the research together. She's very bright, hoping to qualify as a doctor eventually.'

'She's very pretty.'

'I suppose she is. This research has really pushed Dad, though. You know how conscientious he is. I don't know when he was last home before nine. He's off before six each morning. You know, he fell asleep at the surgery the other day.'

'Mum, that's awful.'

'I know, but you know your father. If I nag him he seems to get even more stressed.'

'He's a perfectionist. I know that.'

'He's always been like that. It's good for his patients though. You know, the ones registered with the other doctors in the surgery always ask to see him if they can.'

'I met someone at the hospital who knew him, a consultant. He spoke ever so highly of Dad. He said he was that rare combination of a doctor who was very clever but who also had great compassion.'

'He is quite something, isn't he? I'm very proud of him.'

'But you never see him, Mum.'

'I know, but I don't expect him to put me before his work. It wouldn't be right.'

'Really?'

'I've always thought that.'

'I guess you have. Well, tell me, what do you think of Mark?'

Catrin smiled, pleased that her opinion still mattered.

'He seems very fond of you, which is what matters to me.'

'He is, Mum. I've never known anyone so caring, and he's always asking me what I want to do, if I'm comfortable, happy. We both come home shattered, yet he usually cooks.'

'You stay there a lot. You ought to bring him round. He can stay any time.'

'I know, Mum, but he owns the flat. He bought it last year when he was promoted.'

'That's great. So how old is he?'

Lowri grinned. 'He's thirty.'

'Really?'

'It's only a few years older than me.'

'Has he been married?'

'God, no. Too busy peering at things under microscopes or traipsing along beaches counting things.'

'So how did you meet?'

'At a party. You know, I'm hopeless at them. I went out into the garden and saw this chap picking up stones and looking at insects. Our first conversation was about woodlice. Very interesting, actually.'

'Well, I'm really pleased for you. By the way, he didn't seem to recognise me. That was lucky.'

'What do you mean?'

'I see him at work. He comes into the staff canteen.'

'Oh, right. You know, it never crossed my mind. You change jobs so often. Anyway, I lose track.'

'I do something for a while, and then I get bored. I applied. It's less hours, and you know I can go to all sorts there. I go to odd open lectures, use the library. It's fun. I'm teaching myself about the Tudors at the moment.'

'Really?'

'Yes, it's interesting.'

'And the work?'

'It's alright. Some nice people there. I'm sorry Jo is leaving, though. We had a do for her the other night.

Her marriage has broken down. She'd been married thirty years. Anyway, she's moving to Spain to live by her daughter, start again. It's a shame. She was doing an Open University degree, but she said she can't afford to do it now.'

'Dad used to say you should do some kind of degree or something.'

'I expect he'd like to be able to tell all his clever friends I was doing something like that. I'm sure it's why he turns down all the social things. I mean, most of the doctors are married to other doctors or lawyers or something.'

'Well, I know you're clever, Mum. You've always been able to help me with my homework, tell me about things. Remember, you always took me and Bethan to the museum and art galleries.'

'We had some great trips, didn't we? So, you and Mark: you think that could last? Is this what the news is about?'

'We're not getting married, if that's what you're thinking.'

'Oh, right.'

'Mind you, his mother would like that. She understands, though, we're not ready. In fact she's very excited about our plans. She said they'd help.'

'Hang on. You've met his mother?'

'Oh, just a few times.'

'But he hasn't been to us?'

'Sorry, Mum. I know what things have been like with Bethan: A levels, applying for uni. Well, you know.'

'It would still be nice to see you sometimes.'

'OK. Well, he's come today. Give us all time to get to know each other.'

'So, do you get on with his parents?' Catrin asked, still feeling hurt.

'Great. We've been out for a few meals. They gave Mark a holiday in Paris for his birthday. It was wonderful.'

'You've been away. When?' Catrin was shocked. She had never felt so out of touch with her daughter.

Lowri looked embarrassed. 'It was nothing, Mum. Just a few days at Easter.'

'But you said you were working over Easter.'

'I didn't want you to worry. Anyway, Mark's Mum is so lovely. You know, she only has sons, so she likes having another woman around.'

'Is she my age?'

'Bit younger. She married young. She's very successful at her work. She's a head teacher.'

'Gosh. That's impressive: clever woman.'

'She is. Mind you, she can be a bit bossy.' Lowri linked her arm through her mother's. Catrin knew it was a silent way of affirming her.

'And Mark's Dad? What does he do?'

'He owns a chain of jewellery shops.' Lowri looked closely at her mother. 'Are you alright, Mum, you look a bit stressed.'

'Oh, it's coming back here. It's not easy. I had a long talk with Bethan. She wanted to know what happened to her father, to Aled.'

'He fell, out on Worm's Head, didn't he?'

'He did go to Worm's Head. They know that, but he fell into the sea, so actually he drowned.'

'God, that's awful. You told Bethan? Is she OK?'

'She took it well, actually.'

'Why ever hadn't you told her before?'

'I don't know. I thought she'd get upset.'

'Sometimes it's better to tell people the truth, Mum.'

'Maybe. Bethan has mentioned about wanting to walk out to Worm's Head, see where Aled died.'

'That might be a good thing for her.'

'But why? Why go there? It will be so hard to see where he was the night he died, imagine things–'

'I think it might be harder for you than for Bethan, Mum.'

Catrin shrugged. 'Maybe. I try not to think about it, you see.'

'That's not always the best way to handle things you know–'

Catrin felt herself go red. 'I didn't tell Bethan I'd seen her mother either. I hadn't spoken to her, but I did see her at the party that night.'

'Oh, Mum. You should have told her.'

Catrin looked away. 'I just wanted to protect her.'

Lowri sighed. 'I know, but I guess she has been trying to imagine her mother. I know I would.'

'I didn't mean to upset her.'

'I'm not saying you did it on purpose, but you don't like to talk about things, do you? I see the way you veer off from anything difficult.'

'I suppose it's the way I've always been.'

'But why, Mum?'

'I don't know–'

Lowri looked over at Worm's Head.

'Mark was saying he'd like to cross the causeway soon. He's been there before on field trips. He's fascinated by it.'

'Oh, well. I suppose you could go with him, but you need to be careful, you know.'

'Of course. You could come too.'

Catrin looked away. 'Did you know Grandad is going to move to America permanently?'

'Really?'

'Yes, he told me. It's why he's selling the Dragon House and the Cardiff house.'

'I'm surprised.'

'Well, he spends most of his time in New York. He's getting on, mind you.'

'It's not that. I'm surprised he's leaving Bethan.'

'They don't see that much of each other.'

'I know, but he always keeps a hold, and when he comes back he always organises things for her. He went to a lot of her concerts and things.'

'I suppose so. Maybe now she's going to university he feels she's moving on.'

'Maybe. Hard to imagine, though.'

'Actually, he did say something about not wanting to see her talent wasted. I think he has something up his sleeve.'

'That sounds more like him.'

'You've never really got on with your Grandad, have you? I'm sorry he's always made such a fuss of Bethan.'

'He's bound to with her being Aled's daughter. To be honest, I don't mind. Well, maybe I did when I was younger but, well, I know he's your Dad and my Grandad, but I'm sorry to say I don't like him that much.'

'Oh, Lowri. You mustn't say that.'

'Well, it's true. You know, the main reason is I hate the way he treats you.'

'Oh, come on. We hardly even see him.'

'But when we do, he runs you down. It's always Aled this and Aled that.'

Catrin flinched. 'Aled was very special. He was lucky. Everyone thought he was wonderful.'

'But it was pressure as well. When you are very bright, people have an expectation of you–'

Catrin looked carefully at Lowri. 'Have you found it stressful? You know, being so bright?'

'God, no. You and Dad have left me be, let me do what I want, never pushed me.'

Although the words were light, Catrin was concerned at the hurt that lay deep below them.

'I'm sorry. I was aware that somehow you got left out. Bethan and all her needs, well, they took so much of my time and emotional energy. I was also aware, with her being adopted, I never wanted her to feel I loved her any less than you. Maybe I over-compensated. I did worry there wasn't enough left for you as well. I should have given you more time, more encouragement–'

'Hey, Mum. Stop. You and Dad have been great parents. You know you gave the most important thing.'

'And what was that?'

'Unconditional love. I knew that whatever happened, whatever I did, you would always love me. Now, that is the most important thing I think a parent can ever give their child.'

Catrin smiled. 'That is so lovely. Thank you.'

They crossed the rough path and started to clamber down to the beach.

Once they were on the sand they sat down, and drank their water. Safi gulped his. Catrin watched a mother trying to put sun cream on her wriggling children, couples basking, groups of teenagers, the self-conscious ones sitting on their beach towels, the confident ones running around flirting.

'It is beautiful here,' said Lowri. 'I don't know how you have stayed away so long.'

Catrin looked over at Worm's Head, today surrounded by a flat blue sheet of sea.

'It is beautiful. I'd forgotten, you know. All I could remember was the loss we'd suffered here, nothing else. It hurt so much to even think about it, so I tried to push it out of my mind.'

'I read this article in the paper about this man who makes these incredible sand sculptures, you know like the Taj Mahal, or huge palaces, on the beach.'

'On the beach?'

'Yes. So each night they get washed away by the incoming tide.'

'Oh, how sad.'

'You would think so, wouldn't you, but he said that it was good to face loss and get used to living with it.'

'He's a brave man. Facing loss is very hard. Take you girls, I have to face losing you, both making your own lives. Sorry to be so miserable, but it is a big adjustment.'

'Well it's a time for you and Dad to live your own dreams now.'

'Someone else said that, but I'm not sure people like me have dreams any more.'

'Well, you should.'

'I can't do it, can't think what to dream. As soon as I start I think of the things that could go wrong. You know, I tried to go to a meditation class once. They told us to imagine we were lying on a beach. Well, I tried, but then I started to worry about the tide coming in, whether I'd put on enough sun cream, if I had anything in for tea later.' Catrin laughed but Lowri looked serious. 'Poor Mum. Sometimes you look so sad and stressed.'

'Hey, you mustn't worry about me. Please don't. It's a burden I would hate you to have to bear.'

'Mum, it's not a burden. I care about you.'

'I know, but I'm aware I lean on you. You were such a quiet little thing and I know I assumed you were alright.'

'And I was most of the time, Mum.'

'But not all of it?'

'Sometimes you look unhappy, stressed. I don't know what the matter is, but it worried me, that's all.'

'Look Lowri, I'm fine. I grew up worrying about Grandma.'

'What about?'

'Oh, she was never that strong. But I never wanted that for you. Now, tell me what this exciting piece of news is.'

'You know, Mum, it doesn't matter.'

'Don't be silly.'

'No, I've changed my mind. You are not to worry about me and Bethan. We had a wonderful childhood. I tell you, the more I hear in lectures and from other doctors, the more I appreciate the start I was given in life. And now Bethan and I are growing up. You should be proud, Mum. You did a good job.'

They walked along the beach and came to some old wooden remains protruding through the sand.

'What's that?' asked Lowri.

'It's the wreck of a ship, the Helvetia, from the eighteenth century. It has a rather sad story. Apparently a Norwegian sailor from the ship who survived the wreck fell in love with a local Rhossili girl, but her father refused permission for her to marry. Heartbroken, she remained a spinster until she died, when she was eighty.'

'Ah, how romantic.' Lowri touched the wood protruding from the sand. 'You wouldn't have thought wood would have survived this long, would you?'

'The past doesn't just slip away silently does it?' Catrin sighed, and then said 'Right, we ought to get back. Hopefully, Dad will have arrived and we can all go out and celebrate.'

'Wonder if he's got round to buying you anything for your birthday? I did remind him—'

'It really doesn't matter. Anyway, I have this little chap,' said Catrin, and she leant down to stroke Safi. 'Come on, then. Let's get back.'

'Well, I hope Dad makes it.'

'We'll soon find out.'

They walked back up through the dunes. Catrin wondered what the news had been. For some reason Lowri had changed her mind, but she was sure it was something important. Some day soon she must find out what it was.

Chapter Thirteen

When they arrived back at the house Gareth had still not appeared. The table was booked for seven, and it was now quarter to. Catrin was thinking about what Lowri had said. Somehow, she had always assumed that Lowri would be alright. She never dreamt she had felt neglected. Maybe that was why she liked Mark's mother so much? Maybe she was giving Lowri the attention she had secretly been craving? Was this how she was to lose Lowri? She would marry Mark, spend all her time with his family. The grandchildren would always go there for Christmas day. Catrin stopped her mind running on. This was ridiculous.

She looked in her case. There was the new dress she had bought only last week. Gareth hadn't seen it. She had bought it really for what she thought was to be Bethan's birthday meal. It must be a couple of years since she'd bought a new dress, and she was quite excited. She felt it actually fitted, even looked quite nice. It was a long, loose, silk dress, cobalt blue with silver imprint. She loved the feel of it, but the sleeves were short, so she put her navy cardigan on top. She took her blonde hair out of its tie and brushed it. It was fine, getting thinner now, but curly, which helped. She even found an old pink lipstick and put a smudge of grey eye shadow on her eyelids. She stood back and looked at herself briefly. Well, not too bad. The dress was very pretty. The dark blue sapphire stone in her necklace glinted and matched it perfectly. She hoped Gareth would like it. Just then, she heard the sound of a car pulling up, looked out of the window, and saw Gareth.

She went downstairs to open the front door, and greeted him nervously.

'Hi,' she said. He walked towards her with his usual quick, purposeful stride. He only had whips of hair at the side of his head now, and was still wearing the same style of frames, plain metal rectangles, that he had worn twenty years ago. She noticed he was still in his short-sleeved shirt and work trousers. He had obviously come straight from work.

'God, the traffic was a bloody nightmare. I'm sorry I'm so late.'

'That's OK.'

He stopped, and seemed to notice her for the first time. 'Oh, happy birthday,' he said and gave her that kind and thoughtful smile that had first attracted her to him.

'Thank you.'

'I should have got a present–'

'It's alright. I'm wearing it.'

'Oh, the dress.' He looked at her and nodded. 'Nice colour.'

'Thanks.'

'Right, good. How are the girls?'

'Oh, they're fine.'

'Lowri here?'

'Yes, I've received my present. Apparently you know about it.'

He grinned. 'Of course.'

Lowri came running down the stairs. 'Dad, you made it.'

'Only just.'

'Well done.' Catrin saw the look between them: they could communicate a sentence in a glance. Lowri might look like Catrin, but she knew there was a special connection between Lowri and her father.

'Oh, Mum you look beautiful. Doesn't she Dad?'

Gareth blinked at Catrin, peered at her. 'Oh, yes. So where's the dog?'

Catrin took Gareth into the kitchen. Safi was fast asleep in his bed.

Gareth knelt by Safi to stroke him. 'He's gorgeous.' He crouched down, talking quietly to Safi, who looked up adoringly at him. That was the 'bedside manner' kicking in, when time stood still and Gareth had all the time in the world. It reminded Catrin that Gareth was not just a conscientious doctor, but also kind.

'We need to take him out for a wee before we go,' she said, unwilling to break the spell. They went out into the garden and Gareth praised Safi for urinating to order.

'He's two. It's not like when we had Lady as a puppy.'

Bethan came running out into the garden, and up to Gareth.

Gareth hugged her.

'Mum has been talking to me about Aled,' she said.

Gareth glanced over at Catrin. 'Good. I'm glad. You OK?'

'Yes. It's horrible that he drowned, but it's better to know.'

'I suppose so.'

Catrin watched them talking. Gareth's signing was very basic. It didn't mean he wasn't close to Bethan, but there had been times when misunderstanding arose between them, and it was Catrin who had to iron out the problems.

'So what do you think of Safi?' asked Bethan.

'He seems a very good natured dog.'

'Lowri chose well,' said Catrin.

'Oh, and Mark's here isn't he?' said Gareth, suddenly remembering.

'Yes, seems a good chap.'

'Let's go and meet him.'

They went inside, settled Safi, and waited in the hallway. Introductions were made, until Lloyd urged everyone to get moving.

Bethan, of course, was fussing; losing her phone, then her bag, then her phone again. Catrin could see her father getting exasperated. He hated being late. Eventually they all got out of the house.

The pub was busy. It didn't look like it was struggling, whatever Harri said. The owner gave the family a warm welcome, and Catrin watched her father. He seemed excited.

'Where are we seated?' he asked.

'Good evening. I've reserved a table over by the window. You can enjoy the views there.'

'Hi,' said a voice behind Catrin. She turned to see her cousin sitting at the bar with a pint in his hand.

'David,' she said, and grinned, delighted to see him. David was a few years younger than her, but enjoyed a relaxed, middle-aged look. His tummy was rounder than she remembered, and he had grown a scruffy beard.

'This looks like a gathering of the clans,' he said, scratching his beard in a characteristic way.

'It's my birthday.'

'Oh, happy birthday.'

'How are you? Is Anwen with you?'

'No, she's out. Hi, Gareth. How're things?

'Hectic.'

'That means exhausting. Crazy what they're expecting of you doctors now. You're never in when I go down to Cardiff.'

'Catrin tells me you've changed jobs?' asked Gareth.

'Working with people with addiction. Interesting project, multi-disciplinary team. Partly charity and partly NHS-funded. There are three of us therapists. We actually have a doctor three days a week. It's going well.'

'I'd be really interested to hear about that.'

'I think we ought to be seated,' Lloyd said, adding, 'Of course, David, you must need to get back to Anwen.'

'She's down at her daughter's for the day. No, I'm all alone.'

'Oh. Well, would you like to join us?' said Lloyd. Catrin heard the reluctance in her father's voice, but David didn't take any notice.

'I'd love that, Lloyd. Yes, thanks. That would be great.'

'I'll ask for an extra chair.'

'Lowri, how's the medicine? Killed any patients yet?' asked David

'Hi, Uncle David. This is Mark, he lectures in marine biology.'

'Really? How interesting. Are you at the university in Cardiff?'

'That's right.'

Lloyd coughed.

David turned. 'Sorry, Lloyd. Of course. Well I'd like to sit next to the birthday girl.'

Catrin glanced over to see where Bethan was sitting. The sun shining in through the bay window was lovely, but it would be better for Bethan to have her back to it for lip-reading. Catrin automatically removed the vase of flowers in the centre of the table to allow Bethan to see people easily, pleased that Lowri had gone to sit next to Bethan. Noisy places and groups of people could be harder for Bethan, and to have Lowri, who could sign, sitting next to her would be a help. Catrin gestured 'OK?' to Bethan, who nodded back. Gareth sat one side of Catrin, with David the other.

A group of people roared with laughter just as David said across the table to Bethan, 'So were you fourteen or fifteen when I last saw you?'

Catrin recognised the glazed look on Bethan's face and she signed, 'David asked if you were fourteen or fifteen when he last saw you.'

'Oh, it's the beard–'

Catrin smiled in comprehension. She turned to David. 'Sorry, you shouldn't have grown a beard! It makes it much harder for Bethan to lip-read.'

'I never realised, sorry,' he said, winking at Bethan.

'Don't worry,' replied Bethan. 'Maybe you could shave it off for next time you see me? She turned back to Lowri. Catrin was pleased to see them chatting to each other. It meant a lot to her to see the girls getting on. They were so different, but she really believed that there was a strong bond. They got on well, as long as they didn't have to spend too much time together.

'You know, Bethan is so good at communicating, I forget that she's deaf,' said David, embarrassed.

'She's done well, hasn't she? We're so proud of her. It's been a lot of hard work. People don't realise how much effort she puts in. Take lip-reading. Actually, only about thirty per cent of English is visible on the lips, and she needs lots of other cues to really follow what you are saying. It's why they call it speech reading now. Bethan is watching teeth, cheeks, eyes, facial expressions, and body language to piece together what you're saying.'

'That sounds well-rehearsed.'

'I do lots of explaining.'

'Well, I can see why you sign with her.'

'Yes, although now she goes to Deaf club, she is getting much better than me. I try, though.'

'I should learn some time.'

'It would be a good idea. The main thing, though, is to keep trying. The worst thing is when people give up half way through a conversation, and say things like 'I'll explain later', or 'never mind'. It's really frustrating for Bethan.'

'I can imagine.'

They all ordered their meals, and then the waiter, instructed by Lloyd brought champagne.

Lloyd opened it with aplomb, and poured it into the glasses.

'I'm impressed,' said David, aside to Catrin. 'Not like your father to push the boat out for you.'

Catrin could see her father looked excited. She wondered why. He chinked the side of his glass with his spoon, obviously ready to make a speech.

They all waited. Catrin felt uneasy.

'It is wonderful for us all to be here. I shall start by saying happy birthday to Catrin.'

Catrin acknowledged this shyly and felt herself blushing. Her father continued. 'Of course, this year Aled would have been forty-five. It is hard not to try to imagine what he would have achieved in that time. I've no doubt his immense talent would have been recognised worldwide by now. Tomorrow is an important day, and it's good to have family together this evening. To Aled.' He raised his glass. Everybody looked at each other self-consciously, half-raised their glasses, and sipped the champagne.

David then raised his glass. 'And, of course, a happy birthday to Catrin.'

They all toasted her, and seemed to relax.

Catrin blushed. 'You didn't have to do that,' she said to David.

'I think I did. So, the girls look fine. How are you?'

Their meals arrived. Catrin had chosen salmon salad. David had pasta.

'I should be having that,' he joked. 'Lucky Anwen doesn't mind about the spread.' He tapped his stomach.

'So, how are you now? Anwen is lovely, I really like her. Do you ever hear from Sian?' asked Catrin.

'She's settled back in Carmarthen. She's seeing someone now. Divorced, older man. Suits her. I'm glad.'

Catrin was temporarily distracted by Gareth, who asked 'Can I borrow your phone? I've left mine in the car, and I need to remind someone of something.'

She handed him her handbag, and turned back to David.

'And your Mum, Aunty Angela, is living in a bungalow now?'

'Down the road here. It's lovely, all new. She's happier there than I've ever known her. It's been good living by her. I feel we've got closer again.'

'That's great.'

'Oh, and guess what? While we were sorting out the house, I found something, and Mum ended up telling me this big family secret.'

'Really? What was that?' Catrin sat forward, waiting.

Chapter Fourteen

David leant forward. 'It's about your mother's father, Nana Beth's husband.'

'Grandad Hugh?'

'That's right.'

'I was showing Bethan the dresser that he made. He was a wonderful man, wasn't he? I know he was some kind of war hero. Funny, but no-one ever talked about him. There were no photos of him.'

'Ah, and now I know the reason.'

'What's that?'

'We were sorting though the house, and we found some photos my mother had left behind. I asked her about them, and she told me.'

'Told you what?'

'Apparently, Grandad Hugh didn't die fighting. He came back from the war. He'd met another woman out there, a nurse. He went to live with her. He never came back to Nana Beth and the girls.'

'My God. Are you sure?'

'Yes. Nana Beth never told them. They found out from the kids in the village, who'd heard it from their parents.'

'It must have been devastating.'

'It was. Nana Beth refused to talk about it, said it was all lies, that he had died a hero in the war.'

'She kept lying to them?'

'Yes. I guess she thought it was easier for them, but kids know when they are being lied to, don't they? My Mum says she doesn't think your mother ever got over it. She was twelve when Grandad Hugh went to war. He was her hero. You know, they used to go over the causeway to Worm's Head together. It was their special place. He would tell her about the flowers and the seabirds, and they would watch for seals.'

'It sounds wonderful.'

'It was. My Mum never went. She didn't want to do the crossing. It's a hard clamber over the rocks. But your mother loved to go with Grandad Hugh.'

'That must be why she would never let us go. She said it was a sad place, and we must never go there. I never understood why, of course, because she never explained.'

'You know, your mother once told my Mum that she thought it was her fault that their father left them.'

'Why ever did she think that?'

'Well, she remembered some row she'd had with her father not long before he'd gone off to war. She thought he didn't want to come back because of that.'

'But that's nonsense.'

'Of course. But she needed to be told about things properly, and Nana Beth wouldn't do it.'

'That's so sad,' said Catrin. 'I wish I'd known. It would have helped me understand.'

She noticed David watching her, and quickly added, 'Anyway, so tell me about your work.'

'I enjoy it. It's worthwhile. You know it's hard to imagine what some people have been through. They turn to drugs or whatever to try and cover the pain. If they become addicted, well, it's desperate.'

'Not just for them–'

David looked at Catrin carefully. 'Of course.'

'It's sometimes hard for people around them to understand why they don't stop.'

'I know, but it's a disease, and for some it is a chronic condition. If people don't understand that, they can put it down to lack of will power–'

'You think of it like an illness?'

'Yes. I believe it's important to understand that addiction is a disorder that changes the brain. Otherwise, people feel guilt and shame, and don't ask for support.'

Catrin looked down.

David spoke gently. 'If the addict dies, the family may still not feel able to tell anyone how they died. If things have been covered up, they find they can't talk about the person's life properly, either. They end up doing a lot of the grieving on their own, feeling very isolated. It's so sad, because they need support.'

Catrin stared at her food, her hands shaking. She was aware of Gareth returning with her bag and sitting down next to her.

'Are you alright?' She was aware David was speaking. It was like watching him through a two way mirror, but no sound could get through. She had to get out. Her heart was thumping. She was going to be sick. She needed fresh air. She stood up. Without speaking, she grabbed her bag and ran outside. The cool air outside hit her face. She tried to slow down her breathing. People around her were drinking and laughing. Suddenly, David was by her side.

'Catrin what's the matter? What is it?'

She shook her head. Her eyes filled with tears.

'Hey, tell me.'

She shook her head again.

David took her in his bear-like hug. He just held her. She swallowed really hard. She must not cry. Whatever happened, she must not cry.

David looked at her.

'Talk to me, or someone, soon, eh?'

'I'm sorry.' She tried to smile. 'God, being fifty is a bugger.'

He put his head to one side. 'I know.'

Catrin shrugged. 'We ought to go back in.'

Nobody seemed to have noticed that they had been missing.

Catrin felt Lowri's hand on her arm. 'So, Mum, you are pleased about Safi, then?'

Catrin realised that Gareth and Mark were deep in discussion. Lowri opposite her was rather alone, as Bethan was also deep in conversation.

'Of course. Thank you so much. He's very special.'

'Are you alright, Mum? You look upset.'

'I'm fine.' Then, seeing her daughter's anxious expression, Catrin said, 'I was thinking. Do you remember Lady?'

Lowri grinned. They continued chatting inconsequentially, comparing Lady and Safi.

Desserts came, then Lloyd coughed. They looked at him. 'Oh God, not another speech,' thought Catrin. She really had had enough for one day. However, she watched him glance over his shoulder, and she saw the waiter coming towards them. He was carrying some cards and two presents: a box of chocolates and a large present wrapped in gold paper. Her father glanced over at her and smiled. Her heart started to beat faster with excitement. A present from her father! He hadn't given her as much as a card since the accident.

She smiled nervously, at Gareth, but he looked at her coldly. She felt herself blushing. Everyone was watching her. Lloyd coughed again awkwardly.

'First, Catrin.' From the waiter he took a card and the chocolates.

'Thank you, Dad.'

Catrin opened the card: rather old fashioned, decorated with flowers. Inside it simply said 'To Catrin, Love from Dad'. She guessed the card and chocolates had been bought in the local newsagent's.

'That's great, lovely,' she said, and looked excitedly at the large gold wrapped present, wondering what it was.

Then her father grinned at Bethan. 'I know it's a bit early but, Bethan, I wanted you to have time to get used to it.'

Bethan shot a confused look at Catrin. The smile on Catrin's face froze, trying to hide the mixture of embarrassment and disappointment as she realised that that beautiful package might not be for her. Lloyd handed the present to Bethan, who was still looking over at Catrin.

'The present is for you,' Catrin signed to Bethan.

'Are you sure?'

'Yes. Grandad wants you to open it.'

With trembling hands, Bethan started to tear off the heavy gold paper, to reveal a rectangular, black leather case, with her name inscribed in gold. Catrin was trying to smile, but she was confused. She knew what must be inside the case, but why had her father bought it for Bethan? Only last year she and Gareth had given Bethan a beautiful new flute for her birthday. Why get her another one?

Bethan opened the case and gasped, 'Shit.'

Everyone looked at her, waiting. 'Oh, shit,' repeated Bethan. 'Grandad, it must have cost a fortune.'

She lifted out one part of the flute. A shaft of sunlight from the window behind her caught it, and the light bounced off its gold surface.

'Hand crafted, gold,' said Lloyd. He seemed almost as in awe of it as Bethan.

135

'I don't know what to say,' said Bethan, as she lovingly caressed the flute.

Catrin stared at it, desperately trying to be pleased for Bethan. She tried not to think of the extra shifts she had done to pay for the flute they had given her. It had been a new model of the open-holed flute Bethan had always used, which was better at allowing her to feel vibrations from different sounds. Catrin glanced at Lowri, who was forcing a smile, and thinking about the cheque for a hundred pounds she had received from her grandfather on her eighteenth. It wasn't fair. Catrin knew that but, looking at the joy on Bethan's face, she had no idea what she was meant to do about it.

Bethan was glowing. She kissed her grandfather. 'Thank you so much. It's amazing. Hang on; I need to take a photo.' Bethan put the flute together, took out her phone, and shot photographs of herself with her grandfather and the flute. In a matter of minutes, Catrin knew that the news of this fabulous gift would be all over Twitter and Facebook. She glanced at Gareth, who was not even trying to smile. She hoped he wouldn't say anything to spoil the moment for Bethan.

'I hope you will play it tomorrow at the celebration,' said Lloyd.

'Yes, of course, Grandad.' Before she sat down, Lowri took a photo of her standing in the bay holding the flute to her lips. Bethan looked stunning.

'The girl with the golden flute,' said Lloyd.

David frowned at Catrin. 'What does he mean?'

'He's referring to James Galway. Remember, the Irish flautist. He was known as the man with the golden flute.'

'Oh, right.'

Then she saw her father pull an envelope from his pocket and hand it to Bethan.

As Bethan read the contents of the envelope, her eyes widened.

'My God, Grandad!' Bethan handed the letter to Catrin, who read it quickly, then passed it to Gareth.

He read it quickly, and looked up, his face very red.

'This is ridiculous.'

Bethan looked at her. 'Mum, it's a fantastic opportunity.'

'What does it say?' asked Lowri.

Lloyd spoke. 'It's an opportunity of a lifetime for your sister. I have persuaded Zac Freestone to hear Bethan play next Friday morning. He is over here seeing various locations around the UK and happens to be in Swansea for a few hours. He'll be at the Grand Theatre. He has agreed, as a special concession to me, to audition Bethan after his meeting.'

'Who is he? What's the point?' asked Gareth.

'It's Zac Freestone,' said Bethan to Lowri.

'Oh, God.'

'Who's that?' enquired David.

'He's like Simon Cowell,' explained Lowri. 'He's on a huge American talent show, called 'Stars and Stripes,' I think.'

Catrin screwed up her eyes. 'What's this all about, Dad?'

'This is the most amazing opportunity. I've met Zac a few times. He's a patron of the library in New York. I worked with the main architect on the job. We got talking about things, and he said he was looking to find the next big classical music star. You know, like Katherine Jenkins, Nigel Kennedy. I showed him a video on my phone of Bethan playing. He was very excited.'

'Hang on. Did you say Zac Freestone heard me playing?'

Lloyd turned to Bethan. 'I showed him a video on my phone.'

'Oh God, Grandad. How embarrassing.'

'No. No, he thought you were wonderful.'

'Really?'

'Honestly '

'He liked my playing?'

'Yes, that and, of course, you are so beautiful and, well, you being deaf. Well, it all makes you something very exciting. If he likes what he sees on Friday, he will take you to the States. You would be based in New York City which, of course, is where I will be living.'

Bethan's eyes were shining. 'Wow, Grandad. That's fantastic.'

Suddenly, Gareth thumped his fist on the table. Everybody looked at him.

'Enough. This is not going to happen. For Christ's sake, Lloyd. What the hell do you think you're doing? How dare you arrange this without talking to me and Catrin?'

Catrin saw her father glare at Gareth.

'You have no idea what I had to do to arrange this for Bethan. Someone has to have dreams for the girl.'

'She has her own dreams, Lloyd. She is going to university to study composition: that is what she wants to do.'

'That is what you want her to do: stay at home doing a useless degree, come out and work in supermarkets like her mother, and hope she marries someone who can support her. That may be enough for you, but it's not what I want for Aled's daughter.'

Catrin sat, with clenched fists, looking over at Bethan. She had gone very pale, and seemed close to tears. Catrin felt very sorry for her. Gareth and Lloyd

138

were so locked in the battle that they had forgotten her. Bethan looked over at Catrin.

'What's the matter with Dad?' she signed, without speaking.

'He's upset, doesn't want you to go to America.' Catrin signed back.

'But why?'

'You should be going to university.'

'But I really want to do the audition–'

Catrin stopped. She realised that the table had gone quiet. She stared at Gareth now. She had never seen him look so angry. He was very red, sweating, and his hands were shaking.

'Gareth, calm down.'

'That's what you always say, isn't it? Calm down. Don't rock the boat with your father. Well, I tell you, I have had enough of him and his interference in our lives. I'm fed up with him using his money to control our lives and our daughter.'

Bethan burst into tears. She sat sobbing at the table.

'Gareth, stop it,' pleaded Catrin. 'We can talk about this later. Everyone is looking at us, and Bethan is getting very upset.'

'No. No, I will not leave it. Are you for once going to back me up, Catrin?'

Catrin felt very sick. She hated confrontation of any kind. This was a nightmare.

'The thing is, Gareth. Bethan says she wants to try the audition.'

Gareth turned to Bethan. 'This is ridiculous. You are not going to do it, Bethan.'

'I am not ridiculous. I can do anything I want.'

'No, you can't.'

'It's because I'm Deaf, isn't it? You think I can't do it. Well, I can.'

Catrin cringed. Gareth and Bethan were getting themselves entrenched. She knew neither would give way.

'Gareth, we should talk about this later.'

'No, we will talk about it now. You have to be stronger. It can't always be me saying 'no'.'

'Mum, please, let me at least try,' pleaded Bethan.

'I don't know –' Catrin responded.

'Catrin, you have to support me on this,' demanded Gareth.

She looked back at Bethan. 'What do you want to do?'

'I want to try Mum. I really do.'

Catrin glanced at her father, and swallowed hard.

Bethan reached over and touched her mother's hand. 'Mum, please.'

Gareth glared at Catrin. 'This is crazy. Obviously my opinion, as usual, means nothing. Catrin, your father, as always, is going to get his way. Good God, you are fifty and you act like a child. Well, I've had enough. I have important work in the real world. I'm leaving.'

Everyone sat silently at the table, watching Gareth storm towards the front door of the pub. He stopped abruptly. Catrin thought he was coming back, but after a few seconds he continued out of the door.

Catrin was close to tears. Bethan clasped her letter. Lowri looked over at Catrin's hand. 'Are you OK, Mum?'

She tried to give Lowri a reassuring smile, but couldn't speak.

'Well I think it's time we made our way home,' Lloyd announced. He held his head high: the victor. He pulled out a couple of ten pound notes and put them on the table, then went and paid for the meal. As everybody shuffled on to the street, Catrin saw Gareth's car's lights disappearing.

Chapter Fifteen

Catrin stood watching the car disappear. She couldn't really believe he had actually left. Gareth never did dramatic things like this. To storm out just wasn't him. And to shout at her in front of people: it had been so hurtful and embarrassing. She looked over at Bethan, laughing with her father; Mark, chatting to David. She was glad that no-one was talking about it. As the embarrassment faded, though, she started to feel angry. How could Gareth go off like that, leaving her to sort out this mess with her father? What was she going to do with Bethan? The only other person who seemed to sense her distress was Lowri, who came over to her.

'Oh Mum, I'm so sorry. What the hell is Grandad playing at? And Dad, well, I've never seen him like this.'

'I don't know what to do,' Catrin said, rubbing her forehead, blinking fast. 'Bethan can't go to America. I'm caught in the middle of it all. Oh, Lowri, what a mess.'

'This audition sounds a bit far fetched, Mum. I think this is just Grandad trying to get Bethan to go to America with him.'

'But what if this man, Zac whatever, what if he likes Bethan?'

'You know, Bethan isn't stupid. I'm not sure she would want to go.'

'You could be right. I know the more you confront her, the more she digs her heals in. Your Dad knows that. I don't know why he went so mad.'

'What's up with him? He went so red. Did you see the sweat on his forehead? What ever is the matter with him?'

'He's very angry with Grandad…and me.'

'It's not like him to be so hurtful.'

Catrin looked over at the downs. They looked so much more inviting than going back to the house.

'Lowri, love. Do you mind if I go for a walk? I won't be long.'

'Of course. Shall I come?'

'It's alright. Could you check on Safi, though?'

'Of course. And, Mum, try not to worry. Honestly, Grandad can be such a bastard.'

'Lowri!'

'Well, it's true.'

'Look, I'll be back soon.'

'Good, or I'll be out to look for you.'

Catrin left Lowri, and started walking. When she was sure that she was alone, she sat down on a bench, lit a cigarette, and took long hard drags.

'So, this is what you get up to in private,' she heard someone say behind her. She glanced up guiltily, to see David, who sat down beside her. She stubbed out the cigarette.

'It's alright. I won't tell.'

'It's just sometimes–'

'I know. It's alright. God, what a night. Not a good end to your birthday.'

'The best part was Safi. Lowri tells me he's a blue roan cocker spaniel. You'll have to meet him soon. He's gorgeous.'

'Lowri is a great kid. She'll be a really good doctor, like her Dad.'

'I'm sure. You know, they gave me a basket and all sorts for Safi. Bless them. They spent a lot of money.'

'Gareth seems rather stressed, didn't he?'

'Just taken on too much, I suppose.'

143

Catrin was suddenly aware of the sky approaching that special pre-sunset glow, which only lasted a few minutes. There were myriad shades of reds and yellows; the sea in the distance molten gold. Even the strip of sand Catrin could see was tinted red and gold. For the first time she realised that it was an extraordinarily beautiful evening. The only sound was the waves in the distance. The seagulls were silent, in awe. Catrin and David watched those magical few moments when the sun suddenly drops below the horizon. The final flash of glory was brief and easily missed. It was the kind of image which drew photographers, but which they never quite captured. Catrin was glad: some things should be kept for those who are there to experience them. The sky slowly became darker blues and purple. The change was awesome.

'This place is magnificent,' whispered David. 'Every day is different. Even in the winter, the thick sea fog is stunning. I can't believe sometimes that I actually live here.'

'When I arrived yesterday, the beauty of the place took my breath away. It seems all wrong that such an awful thing should happen somewhere so lovely.'

'That's life, though, I suppose.' They sat for another minute quietly. Then David spoke more firmly, 'Why does Lloyd do these things? This audition, he never should have arranged it without talking to you and Gareth.'

'She's all he has left of Aled.'

'But Bethan is your child.'

'Dad has never quite grasped that.'

'What will happen with the audition?'

'I don't know. I wish Gareth had stayed. Him and Bethan may clash, but he can also reason with her in a way I can't. I don't know what got into him tonight.'

'I noticed his mannerisms: his hands are never still, and he's always looking around, like he's on edge, waiting for something to happen.'

'He is, isn't he? I thought I was imaging it.'

'No, something's up. Did he say something about some research?'

'Yes. I don't know why he took it on. He's changed, you know. I have to admit he's touchy at home now. He never used to be like that. Lately, I can't do anything right–'

David put his arm around Catrin. 'I'm sure Gareth loves you and his family very much.'

Catrin shrugged off his arm in frustration. 'You don't know that. He never says anything. In fact, he's never home long enough to talk to me any more. Maybe he stays at work because he prefers it there, prefers to be with someone clever and pretty, like that Carol.'

'Don't run yourself down. Gareth knows how bright you are. He understands why you never got to go to college.'

Catrin looked away.

David frowned. 'Catrin, you have told him. Haven't you?'

'I don't know what you're talking about.'

'My mother told me. She and your mother were quite close, you know.'

'What did she tell you?'

'She told me that your mother was an alcoholic.'

Catrin looked down, the beauty of the evening suddenly ruined. She thought of the cold, empty vodka bottle she had found in the drawer in her mother's bedroom earlier. Hidden away all these years, but still there, waiting to remind her of a past she tried so hard to forget.

'It's alright,' said David. 'It's alright to talk to me about it.'

Catrin sighed, and sat back in the seat. It was almost a relief not to have to deny it.

'I didn't think anyone, apart from Dad, knew. When I met Gareth, she had just gone into rehab. She was much better. There was no need to tell him. She managed to stay sober for the first two years we were married. Then, of course, Aled had his accident. She hid away, drank in secret. Gareth didn't see her much. I went round on my own to look after her. Then, suddenly, she had a heart attack. Just like that: she was gone.' Catrin swallowed hard. 'My lovely Mum had gone. To tell people that she'd died of a heart attack was so much easier than anything else. I wanted Gareth and my children to remember her as the bright, intelligent woman that she was.'

'What was it like for you, growing up?'

Catrin looked at David. Suddenly, she longed to talk.

'She didn't drink so much when I was little. It was more in my teens. Even then, she didn't ever appear drunk when she was out. She was on loads of charity committees, went to church. She only drank heavily at home. She used to say, 'Let's make the sun come out'.' Catrin could feel her lip trembling.

'I remember the first time I was really scared by it. Dad was away. It was my first day at high school. I came home so excited to tell her all about it, show her my timetable, and tell her whose form I was in. And then I found her. She was unconscious. I was really scared. There was an empty bottle of vodka on the table. I kept shaking her until she came round. She started crying. It was awful. You know, you think your Mum is meant to look after you. She kept saying not to tell Dad, or he

146

might leave her. Anyway, she was sick. I sorted her out. The next day she said sorry: it would never happen again.'

'But–'

'But it did. The only time she was nasty was when she ran out. She would insist I go to the shops and buy it for her.'

'But you were under age.'

'There was a local shop that would serve me. As I got older, I went to supermarkets because it was cheaper. I lied about my age. I remember once or twice being turned down. It was really embarrassing. I knew they assumed it was for me, but actually I preferred that than anyone knowing it was for my Mum.'

'You must have been worried a lot of the time–'

'Yes. I would get up in the night, check on her. I was anxious a lot, and, of course, there was Aled. I would put him in front of the television and sort Mum out. I kept as much as I could from him.'

'And your Dad?'

'He went away a lot, even more once Aled was in boarding school. Before he came home, Mum would make me get rid of any bottles or cigarettes. She was scared he would leave her if he knew what she was doing.'

'But he must have known.'

'Oh, yes. I mean, she'd try much harder to hide her drinking when he was home, but he saw her unconscious a few times. It's why he sent Aled to boarding school '

'But didn't he help you or your Mum?'

'He paid for her to go to rehab. She went a few times. It would be better for a time. I did get to do my O levels but that was all. When I met Gareth, she knew it was serious. She was pleased for me, went to rehab again, and said she was going to be a good grandmother.

147

She was sober when we had Lowri. If only Aled hadn't died–'

'So, your mother's drinking has affected your whole life?'

'Yes. I was always watching, waiting, for something to go wrong. She was better when we came here to stay with my Nana Beth, but back in Cardiff it was awful. I called an ambulance a few times–'

'Really?'

'I was scared, you know. I would plead with her to stop. She would cry, but then she always started again. That really hurt: it was like the drink was more important to her than I was.'

'In a sense it must have felt like that. It can become as important as oxygen to an addict.'

'But I so wanted her to stop. You know, I'd go home with other girls after school. Their mothers would be there, making the tea, chatting. I never took anyone back to mine. I was too frightened of what I'd find. Of course, they never understood, thought I was being unfriendly. Like, when I suddenly couldn't go out. I couldn't tell them it was because my mother was drunk, could I?'

'What did the school do?'

'They didn't know. I lied, said I was ill; all sorts really. So I got rubbish reports. They just labelled me as a lazy kid. The only one who asked was my art teacher, but even he didn't really want to know.'

'So, you've gone all this time without talking about it?'

'It's better that way.'

'Listen. Some parts of our past are painful, and it's natural to want to hide them, but they don't go away. You should be able to talk to people, at least those you trust about them. You know, own your own story, as they say.'

Catrin took a cigarette out of her bag and lit it.

'How long have you been smoking?'

'I only bought these today. I haven't smoked in years. You mustn't tell Gareth. He'd be furious. I shouldn't, should I? I mean, it's bad for me. I know that.'

Catrin sighed. 'There are too many ghosts and memories here. I'll be glad to get away.'

'But the past will travel with you. It won't leave you alone. The ghosts won't rest. They'll follow you around, whispering over your shoulder, nagging you.'

Catrin shrugged and stood up. 'I don't know about that, but there are living people back at the house who need me, so I think I'd better get back.'

They stood up and started to walk back towards the house.

As they walked, a tall, sophisticated-looking woman passed them. She was wearing a long, flowing, white jumpsuit. She gave Catrin quite a shock. She told herself it was obviously not some kind of ghost, but wondered why a woman was going out, dressed like that, in the dark, on her own. She noticed her going and sitting on the bench they had just vacated. Catrin dismissed her. She was nothing to do with her and her family.

Chapter Sixteen

Monday 30th July 2012

Catrin woke up to a quiet house again the next morning. She checked her phone: nothing from Gareth. She was pretty sure he wasn't coming to the memorial but she wished so much that he was. She was dreading it. Having him next to her would have made so much difference. Also, Bethan needed him there. He should at least come for her. Catrin hoped he would have a change of heart and come.

She felt Safi snuggled on her feet. Last night, Safi had come up with her. She had been too tired to go back and get the dog bed from downstairs. As she moved, Safi's eyes opened and his tail began to wag. Wonderfully oblivious to the human troubles in the house, Safi was raring to go for another day.

'Come on, then,' Catrin said. 'Let's get on.'

She put her dressing gown on and went downstairs. Safi went straight out into the garden. It was heating up for another sunny day, but still fresh with a breeze. She made a drink and toast, and sat in the garden with Safi, watching him sniffing the perimeter of the garden.

Catrin was tired. She hadn't slept well. So many worries spinning around in her head: why had Gareth gone off like that? She had never known him do such a thing. Was her marriage really in trouble? And Bethan: what was she to do about that?

She took a deep breath of the fresh morning air. In the summer, this was her favourite time of day. She tried to play 'fetch' with Safi, but he was just like Lady had been. He wanted to chew and bury the ball rather than return it. After he had run off some energy, she sat down on the grass and he cuddled up on her lap. She stroked his ears, long and soft. He licked her hand.

'You really are beautiful,' she said to him. He turned over for her to tickle his tummy.

She took him in and gave him his breakfast, then went up to shower.

Catrin started to think about the day ahead, wondered if many people would come to the service. Eighteen years on was a long time to most people. This was hardly the most accessible place to come to. Holding it on a Monday would mean some people would need to take time off work to attend, so maybe it wouldn't be that many after all.

She sent a quick text to Gareth, just saying good morning, and put on some old clothes. As she walked along the passage she looked at the closed door to Aled's room. She was curious as to what it looked like now. She pushed open the door, and was rather shocked to find the room was completely untouched. It had an almost shrine-like feel to it. It had been dusted, but nothing had been moved or put away, she guessed, since Aled had last stayed here. There were things in there from his childhood and teens. The walls were plastered with pictures in a way his room in Cardiff had never been. There were intricate sketches of Worm's Head, mostly just pencil drawings. One, though, was an incredible picture, showing the shape of Worm's Head in the fog, very dragon-like. Most of the walls, however, were covered in large posters of Welsh rugby players. Catrin knew that Aled had loved to watch and play rugby, but he had never had posters on his walls in Cardiff. Aled had made his own headings: '1977 Wales win the Triple Crown…again!' Catrin recognised some of the players.

151

At the time, everyone talked about the Welsh team, particularly Phil Bennett and Gareth Edwards. He even had a red Welsh rugby shirt pinned on the wall, now very faded. Then she looked more carefully: there were letters pinned up. Catrin read them. Some were dated in the 1970s when Aled had been at prep school. They were asking him to go for trials for the Welsh junior teams. Catrin had never known about this. However, there was one letter written when Aled must have been about fourteen. It was his headmaster saying that he had been approached for Aled to go training with the younger Welsh squad. Catrin was surprised. She had not realised that there had actually been a prospect of Aled doing that much with sport. As she looked around, the whole room was full of rugby memorabilia. She thought how strange it was that it was all here. None of it had been in Cardiff. She wandered around the room, and was about to open a drawer when a voice startled her.

'What are you up to?' her father asked.

For some reason, Catrin felt really guilty for going into the room. 'I, um, I came in to see what needed sorting out. Nothing has been touched.'

She noticed that her father had averted his eyes from the room.

'I asked you not to go in there.'

'Aled had a lot of rugby stuff here, didn't he?'

'He was good. You know, he could have played for Wales.' Catrin could detect her father's voice shaking.

'There was a letter about him going for trials. I hadn't realised. How did he get on?'

'He never went in the end. Anyway, he was destined for architecture.'

Catrin saw the raw sadness in her father's face.

'He would have been great, wouldn't he?'

'Yes. He had everything needed to be an outstanding architect. He was very good at sketching, drawing, the technical side. He was good at maths. He was made for architecture. He really had it all.'

She saw her father swallow hard. It was so difficult to see how much it all still hurt.

'I'm so sorry, Dad.'

'Yes. Well, today is a good day to remember. Do you think Gareth will be back?'

'I don't know. I'm sorry.' Catrin coughed awkwardly, then said, 'We have to talk about this business with Bethan. You've put me and Gareth in a very difficult position.'

'I hadn't expected Gareth to over-react like that. I never realised he had such a temper.'

'He hasn't usually. He's very tired. But, Dad, I don't want Bethan to go to America either, particularly on the talent thing. It's not right for her.'

'You shelter her too much.'

'She wants to do composition.'

'There's no money in that, is there? This way, she could really get rich. Her future would be secure.'

'It's not all about money, though. Is it?'

'It matters, you know that. Just because you've never had any dreams, any ambitions–'

'I did once, you know, have dreams.'

'You?' Lloyd looked genuinely surprised.

'Yes, me. But we're talking about Bethan. I don't want her to go.'

'I think she will have to decide that, don't you?' He turned away. 'Now, today we must focus on Aled. OK?'

Her father shut the door and walked away. Catrin glanced again in Aled's room: a place of faded posters, of faded dreams.

The morning passed slowly in the way it can when you are just waiting for one thing. Eventually, it was time to go to the service. Lloyd drove down to Rhossili church ahead of everyone else. Bethan appeared remarkably unaffected by the events of the night before, apart from a momentary fret about Gareth.

'Dad will be alright, won't he?'

'Of course, but he's very stressed at the moment.'

'He's never shouted like that before. What do you think I should do about this audition?'

'I think it would be a mistake to go. You are all set for university: this is a huge distraction from that.'

'I was looking forward to uni, but I was talking to my friends last night. They say I'd be mad not to go for it.'

'We'll have to talk more about it later.'

'By the way, you know the flute that Grandad gave me–'

'What about it?'

'It's beautiful, but I tried it out last night. I prefer playing the one you gave me. But I don't want to hurt him–'

Catrin was secretly pleased, but said, 'Use it today. Don't say anything to Grandad. Heaven knows what he paid for it.'

'OK, but it won't be my best performance. Still, there won't be many people there, will there? By the way, there is a real 'mare growing about my birthday night out in Cardiff.'

'Sorry?'

'You know, my party; it's getting even more complicated now.'

Catrin smiled at Bethan's wonderful ability to be so completely engrossed in the minutiae of her own life.

'You can tell me about it on the way to the church. I'd better go and change.'

Catrin put on her best skirt and top, brushed her hair, and went downstairs. There was a knock at the door. She was surprised to see David and Anwen. Catrin grinned at Anwen. If David had gone out to choose a new partner who was as unlike his wife Sian as possible, he could not have done more. Anwen exuded warmth and friendliness. Catrin found herself engulfed in a warm, cuddly body, and overpowered by the smell of some type of rose perfume.

'Hiya, it's so lovely to see you again. Oh, happy birthday for yesterday.'

'Thank you.'

'We must go for a drink while you're here, celebrate properly. David and I both have the week off, so we must do something while you are here.'

Anwen had bubbly blonde hair, and a bright red flowery dress. She spoke in a rather loud, slightly harsh, Welsh accent, more Cardiff than Swansea. Then Anwen looked down and noticed Safi, who was angling for attention.

'Oh, God. Aren't you beautiful?' said Anwen. Safi, of course, was delighted to be acknowledged, and sat in front of her, excitedly wagging his tail, looking up expectantly.

'This is Safi,' said Catrin.

Anwen leant down and fussed him. 'Oh, he's gorgeous. I just love animals. If I didn't work, I'd have loads. As it is, we have just the three cats.'

'Are you enjoying living in the village, then?'

'I bloody love it here. I was brought up in a pretty dodgy area of Porthcawl, bloody bikers. It's great here.'

'David said you were at your daughter's?'

155

'Yes, she's getting herself in a mess again. It's always men with her. You know, they never really leave home, do they? In fact, my second one is thinking of moving back in with me and David. They can't afford to buy their own homes, can they, and then the rents mean they can't save.'

'That's true. Well, we'd better get going,' said Catrin.

Lowri and Mark were ready. Bethan, of course, took longer, but eventually, with Bethan clutching her new flute, they all left together. Even as Catrin left the house, she was hoping Gareth's car would come screeching up the driveway, but it didn't.

Catrin didn't feel like talking to anyone on the walk down, but walking with Bethan was easy, as Bethan chatted away. All that was demanded of Catrin was the odd prompt of, 'Oh dear,' or 'That's lovely.'

As they arrived at the church, Catrin heard David say to Lowri, 'Somewhere in this church is a small slit window that the lepers used to watch the mass through.'

'Keep the peasants out,' said Lowri.

'I have no idea if that was enlightened for the times or not,' said David.

There was a surprising number of people arriving, most of whom Catrin did not recognise. Her father seemed to be greeting them all. He looked very smart in a suit and had exactly the right expression of looking welcoming and sombre at the same time. Inside, the organist was playing quiet, inconsequential, rather depressing music. Her father had put various items of Aled's on a table. There were awards for architecture, pictures and designs, and some photographs of him. Catrin noticed David's mother giving out service sheets and went over to her.

'Hi, Aunty Angela.'

'Catrin, good to see you.'

'You look well, Aunty Angela,' she said, although it wasn't quite true, as she thought her aunt looked older, had shrunk down.

'The arthritis is awful, actually, but there we are. It's lovely having David just up the road. You've met Anwen before, haven't you?'

'Yes. She's great, isn't she?'

'Good for David. Terrible cook and gardener. I try not to look around when I go there, but, yes, she's sweet.' Her aunt looked around the church. 'I hope this gives what you young things call closure.'

'We're not all so young, Aunty Angela. But, yes, I hope it helps.'

'You're right. Lloyd needs to let go now.'

'He plans to go to America, permanently.'

'Ah, I wondered when he'd make the move.'

'You expected it?'

'Of course. I've been expecting him to move out there for years, all things considered, but I suppose he kept coming back for Bethan.'

'Do you mind about him selling the house?'

'Not too much. I'd rather it was lived in. It's not right a house being empty like that.'

Suddenly, Catrin thought of something, but wasn't sure how to ask tactfully. 'Um, the house. It was just left to my Mum?'

'No, to both of us. But I already had my house, so your parents paid me my half, 'bought me out', I think, is the expression. Better for me that way: it gave me cash. Actually, it's how I was able to give the house to David and buy my lovely bungalow. You know, David wanted to pay for the house, but I was having none of it. The government will only have my money when I'm gone, so I said, 'No, you have it now'. You must come to

157

the bungalow and have a cup of tea one day. There's something I want to give you.'

'OK. Yes, I'll come soon.'

'I was showing one of your pictures to a guest yesterday.'

'You have one of my paintings?'

'Yes, it's of the downs. Beautiful.'

'How did you get that?'

'Your father gave it to me years ago.'

'My father gave it to you? That's odd.'

'You were very good, you know–'

Catrin looked around. 'More people have come than I expected.'

'Mmm. Oh, I hear my David has been telling you all the family secrets–'

Catrin felt herself blush. Angela added, 'You knew about my father. What a rascal, eh? I never minded too much. Isabel took it hard, though. Never got over it.'

Catrin was aware of people hanging about waiting for service sheets. Her aunt seemed quite oblivious.

'I think I ought to go and sit down. I suppose I have to sit at the front.'

Catrin went to sit next to Lowri. Bethan was further along the pew. She had taken the golden flute out of its case and was holding it close to her. Her music was already on a stand.

Catrin liked the inside of the church: the cold stone walls, the stained glass windows. It was cool and peaceful. She tried to remember the last time she had been to church. Her mother's funeral had been quite a large affair in the church in Cardiff.

After what seemed a long wait, the vicar came in with a depleted choir. Catrin assumed most were on holiday or at work. She recognised the vicar: Idris. She remembered him coming to the house the day they were told about Aled. He had been very good with her mother. She guessed that he must have retired by now. He looked his age, and had put on weight. As he and the choir walked in, the congregation stood up in that self-conscious way people who are not used to church rituals do, everyone checking discretely that they were doing the right thing.

Catrin glanced around during the first hymn. The church was very small. It was possible to see most of the people there. She saw Harri at the back, who gave a quick nod of recognition. There were a few local people in casual clothes, not quite beach clothes but the women wearing light skirts, sundresses, and sandals; the men in shorts and T shirts. There were a few couples more smartly dressed. Catrin assumed they were friends of her father. Then she spied a woman tucked away at the back to her left. She looked extraordinary, and very out of place. It would be like finding some rare exotic queen conch shell on a beach covered in common mussel and limpet shells. Catrin had seen models like her in Bethan's Vogue magazines, where a blouse cost more than her entire wardrobe. What was even odder, though, was the way she caught the woman staring at Bethan. As Catrin was watching, she saw the woman lift one carefully manicured hand and wind a lock of hair around her index finger, a gesture so familiar to her. It revealed tiny pixie ears. Catrin gasped. The resemblance between the woman and Bethan was uncanny. How strange. Was it possible that some relation of Elizabeth had come? The woman seemed to sense Catrin looking at her, and their eyes met briefly. It was a dagger-like glance, nothing casual about it. Catrin, feeling very unnerved, looked away.

Chapter Seventeen

Elizabeth stared at the back of Catrin's head, numb with shock. She had spent the day before preparing herself for meeting Lloyd, rehearsing arguments with him. She had imagined it all: hiding at the back of a crowded church, a swift safe glimpse of Bethan. Then, after the service, she would take Lloyd discretely to one side. She would tell him what she thought: insist he tell Bethan the truth.

It had started well. As planned, she had arrived late to the service. However, the church was smaller than she had imagined, and Angela being on the door had surprised her.

'Oh Elizabeth,' Angela had said too loudly. 'I thought you didn't know the family.'

The corner of Elizabeth's mouth had twitched. She had quickly taken a service sheet and sat as far back as she could. She had tried to remain calm. No-one was going to recognise her. She would be fine. She had glanced down towards the front of the church and looked at the backs of the heads of, presumably, the family. She had had her first glance of the girl she knew had to be Bethan. She was the only family member with jet black hair, and, even sitting, Elizabeth could see that she was tall. She realised that she had been trying to imagine Bethan with blonde hair almost as a defence. It would make Bethan more distant, even though the tiny baby she had held had had black hair. But there was no mistaking that this was Bethan. Nothing had prepared her for the striking similarity. Elizabeth found herself shaking and feeling very sick. She felt completely overwhelmed by her feelings. She wanted to curl up in a ball and cry but, of course, she couldn't. She felt very alone, just like she had in the hospital the night she had given birth to Bethan. She remembered being envious of the mothers with partners, family, all fussing them and looking after them. She had been the only one on her own. There had been one girl, much younger than her, maybe thirteen or fourteen, but she at least had her mother there. Elizabeth's aunt had come, but she had been quite cold. The only warm thing that night had been her baby, who she had held close. Elizabeth could still smell her hair, feel those tiny long fingers, and remembered trying to drink in every last detail, each moment precious, counting down before she had to give her away. Elizabeth blinked quickly: don't think about it, not here. She realised then that everyone was standing up, holding hymn books. She scrabbled for hers, and glanced over at the open book of the person next to her. The woman rather unsubtly showed her the number of the hymn.

Elizabeth distractedly found the page, but she couldn't stop staring at Bethan. It was like looking at herself in her teens. The height, colouring, gestures, were all there. Bethan held herself more confidently than she had ever done. She was pleased about that. She liked the easy smile she saw. My God, that girl really was her daughter: that was the tiny baby who had grown inside her, who she had given birth to, who she had held close. And then given away. Elizabeth felt very hot and sick. She supported herself against the cool stone wall. Emotions darted around her like sparks. This was too much.

It was at that point that she had been aware that an older woman who sat along from Bethan was staring at her. Their eyes had met. There had been a flash of something, and she had felt defensive. The woman herself looked a mess. Elizabeth was amazed that any woman could let herself go like that. No makeup, shapeless dowdy clothes. She wondered if she was Catrin, and decided that, if she was, she hadn't been much of a role model for Bethan.

Although the hymn was still being sung, Elizabeth sat down quickly, not trusting her legs to hold her. She breathed slowly. People would put it down to emotion. She just had to survive the service. She glanced along the pew, and saw that Angela was looking at her thoughtfully. She tried to smile. The church's wall gave her coolness and strength. She needed to focus on why she was here. She had seen Bethan. She may not be dressed very well, but she was healthy and well. That was all she needed to know.

Lloyd stood up. Elizabeth was surprised at how little he had changed. He was well-dressed, and made an impressive figure. She could see where Aled had got his looks from. Of course, he went completely overboard in his eulogy to Aled, but then she guessed that was only natural. Just as Elizabeth was starting to calm down, Bethan stood up and played the flute. The beauty and skill of the playing was staggering. Her daughter could play like that! Elizabeth had enjoyed music, but her parents had thought it was a waste of time and she had concentrated on sport instead. Obviously, Bethan had had different experiences to her. To get to this standard she must have started young, gone for lessons, and passed exams. All those things had happened, and Elizabeth had known nothing about them. They were gone, like all the birthdays and Christmases, riding a bike, first words, first steps, and all the other firsts. They would never happen again. She had missed them all. Elizabeth pressed her lips together hard: she must not cry. Whatever happened, no-one must notice her.

Catrin was sitting nervously, watching Bethan play. She had had years of watching Bethan perform. So many times, Bethan had completely broken down before a performance or an exam. Lloyd had kept paying for things and Bethan did love to play. It was just playing in front of people: it never seemed to get any easier. When Bethan finished, there was that awkward moment when people didn't know if they were meant to clap or not. The consensus seemed not, and the one or two who did quickly stopped. Catrin allowed her mind to wander back to that woman at the back: who was she and why had she been staring at Bethan like that?

Then the vicar stood up.

'Before we go outside, I would like to give a short Bible reading from Ecclesiastes chapter three.

'To everything there is a season, and a time to every purpose under the heaven:

A time to be born and a time to die;

A time to weep, and a time to laugh; a time to mourn, and a time to dance;

A time to keep silence, and a time to speak.'

Idris looked up at the congregation. 'Eighteen years ago, I visited Lloyd and the family. They had just received the devastating news about Aled. It was a terrible day. We were all in shock. This poor family was numb with grief. It was a time of mourning, a time when no words seemed the right ones. It was right to keep silent. To lose a child is beyond words, and we feel beyond comfort. The circumstances around that death can make things even more difficult. The time to talk about things may have to wait.

'However, that does not mean we are never to talk about them. Something I hear a lot of people say at funerals to people deep in grief is, 'Time is a great healer'. Well, shall I tell you something? I don't think

163

the kind of time they are probably talking about does heal things.'

Catrin sat up, hooked.

'You see the kind of time we are usually referring to is what the Greeks called chromos. It's the clock ticking away, and everything we do to get our activities of daily life going. It's planning, working, being busy. Chromos time keeps us moving fast: it gives us little time to think or talk. Now we need routine, daily life, seeing friends. I know that, and they can help us heal from that devastating, numbing, acute pain that comes with loss. However, I believe deep healing happens in karios time. This is when we are ready to slow down and to start to notice what is actually happening inside and outside of ourselves. It is about paying attention, allowing ourselves to be more thoughtful. It is karios time when we stop, think and talk about our past with courage and honesty. We have come to give thanks for the life of Aled, the brilliant young man who so tragically died. He was a son, a brother, and he had fathered a child. Can I just say this? Sometimes there are things we put off talking and thinking about, we keep busy. That can be right at times. However, we must make sure we eventually find the courage to talk, to reflect, about the less comfortable things. If you like, we need to unravel the past, try to understand what has happened. Then, I believe, we really can find that time can be a great healer.'

The church was very quiet. It seemed a very strange talk to give at a memorial. Idris pronounced a blessing, and then asked people to come outside for the dedication of a bench placed in Aled's memory. Catrin saw the seat for the first time. It was plain oak, and beautiful. The plaque on it said:

'Our most loved child Aled

164

"All beautiful you are, my darling; there is no flaw in you."

Song of Solomon Ch4 v 7.'

Out here, Catrin felt happier, more at peace. Her father asked everyone back to the house. There were simple maps provided with the service sheet.

David and Anwen seemed to be leading the way. Bethan was chatting to them. Catrin looked around for her father, but was surprised to see him engrossed in conversation with the strange woman who she had spotted earlier. She then saw him lead the woman round the side of the church, out of sight. She was about to go and see what was going on when she remembered David saying something about her grandfather Hugh's woodwork in the church. She wanted to see if she could find it. Most of the people had left. When she went into the church there were only a few people left tidying up. Idris, the vicar, saw her and came over.

'Catrin, isn't it?'

'Yes. Thank you for the service.'

'I've officially retired now, but your father asked me to do the service today. He's worn a lot better than me, I have to say.'

'You knew about my grandfather Hugh? I came in to find his work.'

'Oh, yes. I'll show you. He made these.'

He showed her two small wooden crosses. Catrin looked at the beautiful crafted wood.

'Apparently, he used reclaimed driftwood, washed up here on the beach. I think it's cedar.'

'They are beautiful.'

'Yes, your Grandmother Beth gave them to the church after the war. She was worried, you know, that my predecessor wouldn't accept them because of–'

Catrin looked at him. 'You know what happened?'

165

'I was told. Most people in the village knew really. Your family is very complicated, isn't it? I think it has seen a lot of hurt.'

'I suppose so. But then, everyone has their share, don't they?'

'You have a point. The reading I gave today must be my favourite passage in the Bible. To accept things instead of always fighting them. I think it is a better way.'

He started to collect abandoned service sheets. Catrin went to sit down. It was peaceful in here. She felt reluctant to leave. She always felt churches were at their best when there were no people in them, when you could sit and think. As she looked around, she noticed a print of a picture she recognised on the wall.

'Your mother used to come and sit just there, looking at that painting,' said Idris.

'Did she? I didn't know she came to church here.'

'Not to services. She used to sit in here. It must have been a few years before Aled died.'

'Ah, she was feeling a bit better. She'd been unwell.'

'I know what happened. She told me.'

'Oh, did she?'

'Yes, and she told me you had looked after her, given up a lot for her. I think she was reassessing things.'

'What do you mean?'

'Aled had always been the favourite, hadn't he? Never did anything wrong. But I think something happened to change her mind.'

'What was that?'

'She wouldn't say, but I think he hurt her, upset her. She said she was starting to appreciate you more, and also felt you had not been treated well by your father. She got upset one day about it.'

166

'How was that?'

'She was sitting looking at this picture and I asked her if she knew what it was.'

'It's a print of Holman Hunt's 'The scapegoat,' painted in eighteen fifty-four, I think,' said Catrin.

'That's right. You know your art history.'

'It's a funny looking goat: very hairy and all on its own. I don't like it. It's disturbing.'

'It's a difficult subject. From the Old Testament, you know. The scapegoat was chosen on the Day of Atonement. It had a red cloth wrapped on its horns, like in the picture, and then it was sent out into the wilderness. The people symbolically put all their sins on it and sent them out into the wilderness with the goat.'

'Seems a bit tough on the goat. It hadn't done anything wrong.'

'That's exactly what your mother said.'

'Really?'

'Yes, and then she broke down, said she felt you had been treated like that, and that she had let it happen.'

'She never said any of this to me.'

'I think she felt too guilty and, you know, she was scared to upset the status quo in your family. Aled was the golden child. You were the scapegoat. It was how your father chose it to be, and she was petrified of losing him.'

Catrin bit her lip. 'All she ever worried about was losing him. It was more important than everything, everybody.'

'I'm sorry.'

Catrin sighed. 'I never did understand it, you know. Why I annoyed father. I tried. I looked after Mum all that time. He'd come home. He never said 'Thank you'. If the house wasn't tidy, he said I was lazy. He told me I was stupid if I didn't get all A's like Aled, but he

167

knew. He knew why I missed school so much.' Catrin stopped, aware her voice was shaking. Then she took a deep breath. 'How do you understand all this?'

'Ah, because it's close to home. It happened with me, but that's another story. The thing is, Catrin, you were told a lie. You were told that you were stupid, lazy, and other things, I expect. But you have to believe deep down that that is a lie.'

Catrin looked up at the picture of the goat, stranded in a wilderness.

'I'm not on my own. I have a lovely family: people who care about me.'

Idris smiled. 'That's good, wonderful. Make sure when they tell you that they love you that you believe them. You have a right to be loved unconditionally for who you are. You're probably not used to it, but start thinking about what you want and need, and ask for it. It's OK. It's allowed.'

Catrin smiled, but Idris wasn't laughing.

'And one more thing–'

'What?'

'Your father. You know, if he couldn't show you unconditional love as a child, well, he probably will still find it pretty hard. So, don't see it as your problem. It's his. You don't need to prove anything to him any more.'

Catrin stood up, rather embarrassed.

'It's very kind of you to say all this, but, you know, I'm fine. You are not to worry about me.'

They started to walk out of the church together.

'I read a funny thing the other day,' said Idris, when they reached the door of the church. 'It said that the three most common lies people say are, firstly, 'I have read the terms and conditions'; secondly, 'I will start my diet tomorrow'; and, finally, 'I'm fine'. Idris gave her a half-smile, but his eyes were sad. He walked away.

Catrin blinked to adjust to the bright sunshine outside. She heard raised voices from the side of the church. She recognised her father's voice, but not the female voice. She walked around the side of the church to find out what was happening.

Chapter Eighteen

Elizabeth had left the church quickly. She had not stood with the group around the bench. She hid around the corner, away from them all, in the shade, and tried to control her feelings. Maybe she should leave, speak to Lloyd another time. She knew how close to emotional breakdown she was: better to wait here and let them all go.

Suddenly, without warning, Lloyd appeared. 'What the hell are you doing here?' he demanded.

'Pardon?' she responded, playing for time.

'It's Elizabeth, isn't it?'

She sighed. 'That's right.'

'I was afraid it was you.' Lloyd was very pale.

'You look like you've seen a ghost,' she said, as her courage returned.

'Why have you come? You promised to keep away.'

'I came to try to see Bethan.'

'But you said–'

'Not to talk to her, just to see her.'

'Now, look. You have no right to come here, causing trouble. You just get off now, before anyone sees you.'

'I intend to leave, but there's something to sort out with you first.'

'You're not talking to Bethan.'

'I haven't come to do that, but I want to know what you've been playing at. Someone has told Bethan that I am dead.'

Lloyd glanced shiftily away.

'Was it you?'

'It doesn't matter.'

'It certainly does. I think it was you. How could you do that?'

'Look, I kept to my side of things. I never told your parents, did I?'

'I realise that and I'm grateful. But you made promises to me. I'm angry that she's been told I'm dead. It's monstrous.'

Lloyd visibly squirmed.

'You didn't want to see her. It was for the best.'

Elizabeth's anger was growing. 'How dare you say that?'

'But it was. You wanted the best for Bethan, and that was it. You clearly weren't bothered. It's not like you've wanted to know anything about her.'

'I was keeping my side of the bargain. I said I would keep away, and I did. You betrayed that trust.'

Lloyd very obviously looked her up and down. 'You look like you've done well for yourself. I'd hardly have recognised you.'

'I'm not nineteen now.'

'No, of course. Have you your own family now?'

'No. I never had any more children.'

'Oh, so you're suddenly going all broody. Is that it? You've decided you'd like a child after all. Miss all the messy stuff; just take her when she's nicely grown up.'

Elizabeth was shocked at the brutality of his allegations.

'Of course not. I don't even want to speak to Bethan. That's not why I came.'

At that moment, Elizabeth saw the scruffy woman from the church appear round the corner.

Catrin glanced quickly between her father and the woman.

'Hello,' she said quietly. 'I'm sorry. I don't think we've met.'

'I'm Elizabeth.'

Catrin felt her heart racing. She looked to her father.

'Sorry, do you mean you're a relation of Elizabeth's?'

'I am Elizabeth. Bethan's mother.'

Catrin frowned. Was the woman drunk? 'That's impossible.'

'No. Your father has been lying to you.'

'But–'

'I did it for the best,' her father said, firmly. 'When that social worker started telling you that you should think in terms of working towards Bethan meeting her mother–'

'I never asked for that,' interrupted Elizabeth.

'I know, but they thought that you might change your mind. I know they told Catrin that one day it might be best for you two to meet; best for Bethan, anyway. I didn't want any of that. It was best for everyone that Catrin was told you were dead.'

'My God. Dad, you had no right to do that.'

'Oh, come off it. Be honest, Catrin. You were pretty relieved when I told you.'

Catrin felt herself going red. 'I don't know, but you had no right to lie to me, to Gareth, and to Bethan.' She turned to Elizabeth, 'I'm so sorry, but you never got in touch or anything–'

'That's what I agreed.'

'I remember Dad said you'd wanted to leave us to bring up Bethan. You were off to university, weren't you?'

172

'That's right. I still think I did the right thing. For me and Bethan. I assumed that, if Bethan ever wanted to, when she was an adult, she may try to find me. We could sit and have a sensible talk about it all. Obviously, I have my own life. She would have understood that. Maybe we could have met on her birthday, or something.'

'You make it sound all very business like,' said Catrin.

'Well, that's what I thought. You know, I'm not sorry I gave Bethan to you. I saw her today.' Catrin noticed her voice soften. 'She has grown into a beautiful and talented woman. Yes, I'm sure I did the right thing. But what Lloyd has done has been a real betrayal of my trust.'

Catrin looked more carefully at Elizabeth. 'I'm dreadfully sorry. It should never have happened. How did you find out?'

'Angela told me. I'm staying at her B & B. She was just chatting. She has no idea who I am, but she let it slip.'

'So you came down here before you knew. You'd come to meet Bethan. I thought you'd agreed not to do that. It's not a good way just to burst into her life.'

'I know it sounds silly. I am seeing now that it was naïve, to say the least. I thought I could come, just look at her, see she was alright. I didn't think anyone would recognise me. I would have slipped quietly away if it hadn't been these lies about me.'

'So you needed to see her, to see Bethan.'

'I just needed to know she was alright, know I'd made the right decision. I wanted to come back here, make peace with the place; finally say goodbye to Aled. And, of course, I guessed she'd be here–'

'I see.'

'I don't believe her,' said Lloyd. 'I reckon she's come to steal Bethan away.'

'Of course I haven't, but I'm shocked that Bethan has been told I'm dead. I'm sure you can understand that.' She directed these words to Catrin.

'Yes, of course.'

'You need to go. You're not wanted here,' demanded Lloyd.

Catrin was surprised at how aggressive he sounded. 'Stop it, Dad.'

'No, I have to say it, Catrin. You're too trusting. She's come to take Bethan away from us. I'm sure of it. Bethan must never be allowed near her.'

'I have no intention of making myself known to Bethan,' said Elizabeth. 'But I do want your assurance that you'll tell her I'm alive. How exactly does Bethan think I died, by the way?'

'An accident, skiing,' said Catrin.

'Well, I suppose there are worse ways to go,' said Elizabeth, dryly.

'Enough. You need to get out of this place now,' insisted Lloyd.

'I will go when I have your assurance that Bethan will be told about me.'

'Of course we'll tell her. Now, just get out of here,' said Lloyd.

'Catrin, I want your word.'

Catrin looked at her father. She knew that he had no intention of telling Bethan and would not want her saying anything either. They were both waiting for an answer. She decided she must think of Bethan. What is right for her? Instantly, she knew.

'Bethan has a right to the truth. Yes. I shall tell her that you are alive.'

Catrin saw the look of relief on Elizabeth's face as she replied, 'Thank you.'

'You're a fool,' her father said. 'This will start Bethan wanting to find her. You'll lose her then. We both will.'

'I don't want to take Bethan away,' said Elizabeth. 'This is quite ridiculous.'

Catrin worried that, although she may say that, there was a very real threat of Bethan leaving her if she was to meet Elizabeth. After all, just looking at Elizabeth, she could see the likeness both in appearance and the way they spoke. However much Catrin might protest that she had done everything bar carry Bethan insider her, there was no doubt who the natural mother of Bethan was.

'I'll go,' said Elizabeth.

'You really don't want to speak to her?' asked Catrin.

'No. I don't think that would be a good idea. To be honest, I would imagine she hates me. I'm the woman who gave her away. Why shouldn't she?'

'If I tell Bethan you're alive, she will be full of questions and I think she will want to meet you.'

'As I said, we can keep it civilised. Maybe she could phone me to start with.'

'There's something you might not have realised. Bethan is Deaf.'

Elizabeth turned white. 'What? I didn't realise. What happened? '

'She was born Deaf.'

'But she was playing the flute? She looked fine.'

'She is fine. She wears hearing aids and signs. She speaks well but is part of the Deaf community as well'

'That's incredible. It must have been so hard.'

'It was at times, but Bethan is very determined. She's very musical. Are you? I mean, she does look like you.'

Elizabeth blinked hard. 'I never did anything with music. We do look alike, don't we? I was surprised when I saw her.'

Catrin nodded.

'You have to go,' said Lloyd, anxiously.

Elizabeth agreed.

'I need to get to the house,' said Lloyd. 'You have your car here?'

'Yes. I shall leave today.'

'Good.'

Catrin was uncomfortable with the arrangement, but could not think what else to suggest. They seemed eager to leave, to get away. However, as they walked around to the front of the church, they were confronted by Bethan, looking very hot and bothered.

'I came back for my phone. I must have dropped it in the church. Mum I've been trying to phone you from the house to pick it up. Why didn't you answer?'

'I'm sorry. I was talking, and my phone was turned off for the service.'

Bethan looked at Elizabeth and frowned.

'Hello?' she said, glancing at Catrin.

'This is Elizabeth,' Catrin said.

'Who?' Bethan looked puzzled. She looked more closely at Elizabeth. 'Have we met before?'

Catrin could see that Elizabeth was close to tears. She looked in a state of complete panic. She wouldn't have been surprised if she had just run off. However, Elizabeth stayed very still.

'No, you've never met,' said Lloyd. 'This woman is leaving.'

'Who are you?' asked Bethan.

Elizabeth didn't seem to know how to answer. But both she and Bethan each started to wrap a lock of hair round their fingers.

Catrin spoke. 'I think you should be introduced. Don't you?'

'No way,' said Lloyd, but nobody was listening to him.

Elizabeth nodded to Catrin, who took a deep breath and said, 'Bethan, I need to talk to you.' She looked back at Elizabeth. 'Could you wait a minute? Don't go. You mustn't just go.'

Catrin led Bethan away.

'This is really hard. You know we've always believed that your mother Elizabeth had died–'

'Of course.' Bethan stopped. She turned to look at Elizabeth.

'Is she related to her?'

'That is Elizabeth, your mother.'

'But–'

'She's not dead. That's Elizabeth.'

'But you told me–'

'I was wrong.'

'You did it on purpose?'

'No. Um, Grandad told me.'

'Grandad made a mistake. But how?'

'That doesn't matter now. Look, she's alive, and she is here.'

Bethan's eyes filled with tears. Catrin reached out to her. 'Listen, you don't have to talk now. I can arrange for you to meet soon if that's what you want.'

Bethan burst into tears. She held Catrin tight. The storm subsided. Bethan wiped her face with her hands. 'God, I must look such a mess, Mum.'

'Not at all. You look beautiful.'

'So has she come to find me?'

Catrin bit her lip. 'She came to say a proper goodbye to Aled, and to see you were alright.'

'She wanted to meet me?'

Catrin cringed. 'She wanted to see you were well. I don't think she really meant to speak to you.'

'Why not?'

'She thought it was best, thought you would contact her if you wanted to. She's only just found out that you thought she was dead.'

'Oh, I see. That must have been a terrible shock.'

'It was.'

'Does Dad know she's here?'

'Oh, no.'

'I wish he was here. He always knows what to do.' Bethan scowled. 'Why doesn't she go if she doesn't want to speak to me?'

'I think now you've met she would like to speak to you. But, of course, you don't have to–'

'Does she know I'm Deaf?'

'Yes. I told her.'

'Does she mind?'

'No. Of course not.'

Bethan stood quietly, looking at Elizabeth. She nodded her head decisively. 'Yes, I'll speak to her now.'

'Are you sure?'

'I think so.'

'Shall I ask her back to The Dragon House? We could talk to her there.'

'Yes, that would be a good idea.'

Bethan looked over at Elizabeth. 'I look like her, don't I?'

'Yes. You do look very like each other.'

'OK. Well, let's go and talk to her.'

They walked back over towards Lloyd and Elizabeth.

'Elizabeth would you like to come back to the house,' said Catrin.

'No way is she coming to our house,' interrupted Lloyd.

'Dad, we have to do this for Bethan.'

He scowled, but seemed to realise he was defeated.

Elizabeth looked at Bethan and, to Catrin's amazement, signed to her, 'Would you like me to come?'

Bethan, equally shocked, signed a simple 'Yes.'

'I shall come.'

Catrin stared at Elizabeth. 'You can sign?'

'Yes. I, um, knew someone who was deaf.'

'Who?'

Elizabeth looked at Bethan. 'My mother was Deaf.'

Bethan gasped, then smiled. 'Your mother? Oh my God. That's wonderful.' Bethan turned to Catrin. 'Isn't it amazing Mum? I'm not the only one.'

Catrin was shocked at the strength of Bethan's reaction: it really did mean that much to her.

Elizabeth seemed rather shy. 'It's why I can sign, but I'm very rusty. I've forgotten a lot.'

'It doesn't matter,' said Bethan, grinning.

Catrin's head was spinning. Everything was falling into place somehow, but it was going so fast. She had read about how social services arranged these things: both sides writing letters, getting to know each other gradually. There was nothing gradual about this, and this woman could so easily hurt Bethan very badly.

'I have a car,' said Elizabeth. Catrin glanced down at the strappy sandals. They would not be up to walking far.

'So have I,' said Lloyd. They walked over to the car park.

Catrin and Bethan started to walk back towards the path.

'Are you OK?' Catrin asked Bethan.

'I think so. God. It's such a shock, Mum.'

'I know.'

'You really didn't know?'

'I promise you. I never knew.'

'And Grandad?'

'No. He didn't either.'

They walked on. 'She's very posh, isn't she? What does she do?'

'I didn't have a chance to talk to her properly, but she looks well off.'

'It's good, Mum, to be able to ask her things. She's very pretty, isn't she?'

'You look very alike.'

'She didn't want to meet me before, though?'

'She didn't want to upset you, that's all.'

'Well, it's a bit odd not wanting to speak to your daughter. Could you imagine not talking to me or Lowri? I mean, your life wouldn't be anything without us, would it?'

Catrin couldn't help smiling. 'Well, no. You're right. It is impossible for me to imagine my life without you, but I was very happily married when I had Lowri and you. We had a home, money, and parents to support us.'

'That doesn't matter. If you really love your baby, you'd find a way, wouldn't you?'

'Everyone is different. Look, we're nearly back at the house. I suggest you go and have a few minutes in your room. Don't spend it texting your friends. Think about whether this is what you really want. We can see Elizabeth in a month or two if you'd rather wait.'

'It would be better if Dad was here.'

'I know.'

'OK. Well, I'll go to my room and have a think.'

'Good idea.'

Elizabeth got into her car. She watched Lloyd driving off. She was badly shaken by all that had happened. First, there had been all the emotion of seeing and meeting Bethan, but then to have Lloyd reacting so badly: he had not been that aggressive in the hospital. He had spoken gently, persuasively, made her see that the only rational thing to do was to give Bethan to Catrin and Gareth. She had not detected the desperation in him to own Bethan, but now she saw how real it was. They had talked briefly about Aled. He had seemed surprised at how little she had known Aled, seemed relieved for some reason. Just now, when she'd mentioned the gallery in New York he had seemed pleased. She wondered why. Well, she would go along with him for now. She had met Bethan, and the least she could do was put her side of the story to Bethan. Elizabeth was glad to sit in the security of her car. She started to wonder now if she was doing the right thing. Of course, she didn't have to go to the house. She could go back to the B & B, and drive back to London. She had not given her phone number or address away, although she guessed that Bethan could find her now if she set her mind to it. Anyway, how could she possibly leave Bethan again? The universe had obviously decided to take over, but what a mess. Bethan was still in shock, but surely soon the anger would spill out? She must hate Elizabeth deep down for leaving her. And she was Deaf. Elizabeth wished she had known. It had brought her even closer. If only her mother had known that she had a granddaughter who was Deaf as well. What would she have thought? It might have helped her, helped Bethan, but she had kept them apart. Guilt that had been there, gently prodding and creeping in, suddenly became a monster threatening to consume her. Maybe she should have told her parents? Now it was too late. They had never known they had had a granddaughter. She had let everyone down. Whatever was she to do?

Chapter Nineteen

Catrin and Bethan arrived back to find the caterers handing out wine and iced orange juice. Catrin grabbed a glass of wine, then remembered that she needed to go and check Safi. Her father looked far more relaxed than she had expected. H was greeting people as if nothing had happened. Bethan had gone straight up to her room. Catrin found Safi lying quietly on his bed.

'You really are a quiet little thing,' she said, stroking him. Safi lay back, his tail wagging, waiting for her to tickle him. 'Come on,' she said, patting her knees. He climbed on to her lap. Catrin cuddled him close. 'Maybe me and you could run away together,' she said, but added, 'Not today, eh? Too many people need us to be here. Come on, we'd better go out and face them.'

She took Safi out through the back door into the crowded back garden. No-one looked her way, so she took Safi around to the front of the house in the shade. The sharp white stones glared in the sunshine, but it was soothing to stand alone in the shade. In the quiet, Catrin thought about the day so far. The service suddenly seemed rather incidental to everything else that had happened. She had not thought about Aled that much. It had all been about her father, Bethan, and Elizabeth. She looked over at the sea, sparkling in the sunshine as if a thousand stars bounced on its surface. It looked idyllic, still. But her emotions were storming around her. Elizabeth was alive, was here. Her father should never have lied about that. Gareth was going to be furious, and poor Bethan must be in shock. If only she could talk to Gareth.

She took out her mobile and tried to call him, but he didn't answer. She left a voicemail and sent texts. She left another message on the home phone, but felt increasingly annoyed with him. It wasn't fair to leave her to deal with all this. Then it occurred to her that maybe he had gone into the surgery, that she might be able to get through to him via the receptionist. She had hardly ever done this, kept it for emergencies, but surely this counted as one? She scrolled through to find the number, and waited, held on through the inevitable 'Your call is important to us,' held on through some jolly music, until finally she heard a real person's voice.

'Hello, Crown Street Surgery. How I can help you?' Catrin's heart sank: oh god, it's Jasmine. Jasmine treated everyone, including the doctors, as if they were rather slow five year olds.

'Hi, it's Catrin, Gareth's wife. I wonder, is he there?'

'Good afternoon, Catrin. No, sorry. I thought he'd gone to some family service?'

'Ah, well. He had to come back.'

'But he hasn't been in today.'

Catrin could hear the bewilderment in her voice and wished she had never tried.

'Never mind, then.'

'Have you tried his mobile?

Catrin gritted her teeth. 'Yes, of course. Look, I'm sorry to bother you, but if you see him, ask him to phone, will you?'

'Of course. I'm sure he'll phone you soon.'

Catrin ended the phone call feeling very embarrassed and humiliated. Where the hell was Gareth?

She took a deep breath and leaned against the wall of the house. She wanted to stay there but, of course, she couldn't.

'Come on Safi, better go back.'

Together they walked out of the cool, back into the garden. She saw that Elizabeth was arriving through a side gate which led directly into the garden. She was surprised to see her father go over to her, smiling.

'Elizabeth,' he said expansively. 'Let me get you a drink. I'm afraid it's all a bit rustic here, but I did order some decent wine.' Elizabeth followed him over to a rather rickety table on which a bottle of Chablis was standing in an ice bucket. He poured her a large glass of wine. Catrin could think of no explanation for his change of heart, but she went over.

'Where's Bethan, then?' asked her father.

'Upstairs.'

'I think I shall go and tell her Elizabeth is here,' he said.

'No, I will.'

'Where's Gareth? I should meet him,' said Elizabeth.

'He's working.'

'He's a doctor, isn't he?'

'That's right.'

'I'm very sorry he's not here.'

'So am I.'

'I'm also sorry things are moving so fast. Obviously, this is not what I had planned.'

She sounded sincere. Catrin realised that, if she had really not been planning to meet Bethan, this would be a lot for her to cope with.

'Yes. It's taken us all by surprise, especially Bethan. She is very sensitive,' said Catrin.

'We may look alike, but, obviously, I don't know Bethan at all.'

Elizabeth looked away. 'You say Bethan is upstairs. Is she upset?'

185

Catrin frowned. 'Well, it's been a big shock for her.'

'Of course. If she hadn't been told I was dead, maybe it wouldn't be so bad.'

'Of course not. Maybe you could tell me a bit about yourself? Then I could chat to Bethan. It would make it easier for her to come down to see you.'

'Of course. I live in London. I own two art galleries: one in London, one in New York.'

Catrin glanced at her father, who was grinning smugly.

'Elizabeth was telling me just now in the car park that she goes to New York several times a year. I was thinking she could talk to Bethan about it, from a younger person's perspective. It might encourage her–'

Catrin sighed, and turned back to Elizabeth. 'Are you married?'

'No. I have no children. Well, you know–'

'And your parents?'

'My parents lived in New York. My father was an architect. It was at his firm, where I went for three months to work, that I met Aled. '

'So, Dad, did you know Elizabeth's father?'

'I did. We worked together on a few projects. Our firms were closely affiliated. But I never met you at work, did I, Elizabeth?'

'No, we didn't–'

Your father died a few years back, didn't he?'

'Yes. My mother first, then my father.'

'And they never knew about Bethan?' asked Catrin.

'Oh, no. Never.'

'The one thing Bethan really wants to know is why you never came to see her or contact her,' said Catrin.

'I told you. I wanted her to live her own life. I didn't want to upset her. And I have my own life, a life where people know nothing about her.'

This shocked Catrin. 'Nobody knows?'

'No, no-one,' said Elizabeth, her voice hard. She added, 'Well, apart from my aunt, the one who came to the hospital after I had Bethan, but she has never mentioned it to anyone. We've never talked about it.'

Again, Catrin was struck by the coldness of Elizabeth's voice.

Catrin looked down at Safi, who had been sitting very patiently waiting for a stroke from Elizabeth. 'Are you OK with dogs? Not allergic or anything?'

'No, but I'm more of a cat person. I have Poppy in my house in London, a stray that sort of adopted me.' Elizabeth suddenly seemed to get impatient. 'I think it's time for Bethan to come down, don't you?'

'I'll go and see what she wants to do. I'm not going to make her come down. If she's changed her mind then we'll arrange this for another time.'

Elizabeth looked put out. 'OK, but if she wants to meet me, it would be easier to do it today.'

Catrin was starting to feel annoyed. 'It depends on Bethan.'

She could see Elizabeth's face harden, and she detected a flash of Bethan.

'I'll do my best,' she said quietly, and walked away.

Safi was not on a lead, but he followed her.

On her way into the house Catrin caught sight of Lowri. She went to explain to her what was happening.

'God, I don't believe it. Is Bethan alright? Shall I go and talk to her?'

'It's OK. I'm going to see her now. I'll come and get you if I think she needs you.'

'I wish Dad was here.'

'We all do, but he's not.'

Lowri looked over at Elizabeth. 'Bethan looks like her, doesn't she? Grandad seems quite happy about it all now. Odd, after lying about her.'

'He thought it was for the best.'

'It suited him, you mean.'

'No point in getting angry now. They all seem to be getting on for now.'

'I'll pop over and chat in a minute.'

'Thanks, love.'

Catrin went quickly into the house and dashed upstairs.

Bethan was sitting on her bed, her arms wrapped close around her body. 'Oh my God. She's here?'

'She's in the garden with Grandad.'

'Mum, I don't think I can do it. What if she hates me?'

'She won't do that.'

'She will. That's why she left me. All this time I thought that if she was alive she'd have come to find me, but, because she was dead, she couldn't. It seemed her let out and now, don't you see, I have to cope with the fact that she chose not to see me or have anything to do with me. Why did she decide to come today? Why not write to you and Dad?'

'She wanted to see you, see you were OK. That's good, isn't it? Not to talk to you, but just to see you.'

'But why not to talk to me?'

'I think she was confused. She wants to see you now.'

Bethan shook her head. 'That's not fair. She can't decide to leave me alone for years and then come and see me. Maybe I won't see her.'

188

Catrin sighed and sat down. 'Oh, Bethan, I'm sorry. It's very hard for you.'

Bethan burst into tears. 'I don't know, Mum. I don't know.'

They sat in the quiet, holding each other. When Bethan stopped crying, Catrin said, 'Listen, I will ask her to go. It's alright. You don't have to see her.'

'What, ever?'

'Well, not now. We can arrange things another time.'

Bethan got up off the bed, and went to look out of the window.

'She's down there with Grandad. Why did he lie, Mum?'

'I think he thought it would be better for you.'

'He had no right to do that.'

'No. No, he didn't.'

Bethan looked out of the window again.

'Elizabeth is very thin, very sophisticated. I never imagined she'd be like that. I suppose she's still very young in my head.'

'I can understand that.'

'What does she do?'

'She owns art galleries, one in London, and one in New York.'

'That's pretty cool.'

'It is.'

'Why didn't she come and see me, Mum?'

'She thought it would unsettle you.'

'It's amazing that her mother was Deaf as well, isn't it? Did she tell you why her mother was Deaf? Was she born Deaf, like me?'

'I have no idea. It's good that she can sign, though.'

Bethan pursed her lips. 'You know, I think I will go and talk to her. I'm nearly eighteen. I'm not a child. Where's Lowri?'

'Out there with Mark.'

'Good.'

'Look, Bethan. I know you want to talk to her, but if you have any worries, want to get away, tell me. I'm here to protect you.'

'OK, Mum. Well, I'd better change. Wait for me, though, Mum won't you? Don't go down without me.'

'I'll wait outside the door.'

Eventually Bethan came out. In her white dress, make up and brushed hair, she looked lovely.

'OK?'

'Of course. Come on.'

They went down together, out into the garden and went to sit with Elizabeth and Lloyd. Bethan seemed pleased to sit back and not talk.

'Elizabeth, tell me about your work, where you live,' asked Catrin, feeling like she was conducting an interview.

'Yes, tell us about New York,' said Lloyd.

Elizabeth ignored him. She turned to Bethan. 'I live in, um, L-o-n-d-o-n. I have two-' she looked at Catrin. 'How do I sign 'art galleries'?'

Catrin showed her, but said, 'If you don't know a sign, Bethan may be able to lip read you. She's also wearing her hearing aids. Just speak clearly, normally.'

Elizabeth turned back to Bethan. 'Sorry, I haven't signed much for years. It'll come back, I hope. There are words I don't know. I have two art galleries.'

'You paint?' asked Bethan.

'No, I studied history of art. My mother and father were quite comfortable and got me started.'

'They're rich?'

'Yes. My father bought my first gallery. It's really hard work, but I love it. You played the flute very well. I'm useless at music.'

Bethan smiled shyly. 'Thank you. I play the flute and the piano. I really love composition more than performing.'

'She's a great performer, though. She might make it big in America,' said Lloyd. 'She has an audition with Zac Freestone on Saturday. I arranged it. It's a fantastic break.'

'Gosh, that's incredible,' said Elizabeth. 'Are you excited, Bethan?'

Bethan grinned, but then looked at Catrin. Catrin knew what had happened. Although Elizabeth had intended to sign 'excited', the sign for which should be two hands held clawed, rubbing up and down her chest, she had used the sign for 'hungry', rubbing her stomach.

Elizabeth saw them look at each other, and interrupted. 'Did I do something wrong?'

'You just signed 'hungry' instead of 'excited'. It's OK. Bethan knew what you meant.'

'Oh, how embarrassing. I'm sorry.'

'It's OK. Bethan gets used to people making mistakes. They do it all the time.'

'Thank you,' said Elizabeth, but she turned to Bethan, 'I'm sorry.'

'It's OK.' Bethan glanced over at Catrin, then turned to Elizabeth. 'Your mother was Deaf. Was she born Deaf? Do they know what caused it?'

Elizabeth sat forward. 'My mother had German Measles when she was five. She became Deaf as a result of that.'

Catrin saw the look of disappointment on Bethan's face, and interrupted. 'We've never known why Bethan

191

was born Deaf. I think she was hoping that maybe that you could have helped.'

Elizabeth shook her head. 'No, I'm sorry. As I say, my Mum lost her hearing because of having German Measles.'

At that moment Lowri and Mark joined them.

'Lowri, this is Elizabeth,' Catrin said, starting to introduce them. Then she stopped and wondered what title or description she should give for Elizabeth. She couldn't bring herself to say mother, but, on the other hand, birth mother sounded a bit official. Elizabeth saved the situation by leaning forward and saying,

'Hi, Lowri. So you are Bethan's sister?'

Catrin envied Elizabeth's confidence. How could anyone appear so calm and in control?

'Did you grow up in London?' asked Bethan.

'My parents sent me over to boarding school.'

Catrin looked over at Bethan. 'Boarding school: you know, where you stay by the week or term.'

Bethan scowled at her. 'I know what boarding school is, Mum,' she replied, irritably.

Catrin cringed. Explaining the odd expression Bethan might not understand was a habit she had got into over the years, but she should have realised it would embarrass Bethan now. She sat back. She was now in that familiar but difficult position of having to be some kind of invisible support for Bethan.

She was surprised when Lloyd said, 'Of course, Aled was outstanding in school. We had to send him to independent school. The state schools just couldn't cope with him.'

'Did you go away to school as well, then?' Elizabeth asked Catrin.

Lloyd laughed. 'Good God, no. That would have been a complete waste of time and money.'

Catrin felt herself blushing, and looked down.

'What do you do, Catrin?' Elizabeth asked.

Catrin, feeling overwhelmed, mumbled, 'Nothing much.'

'So, Elizabeth, tell Bethan about your art galleries. You must lead an incredible life between London and New York,' said Lloyd.

'There are very good shops,' Elizabeth said to Bethan.

Bethan grinned. 'Better than Asda, Mum.'

Lloyd laughed. 'Catrin wouldn't know what to buy in a decent shop.'

Catrin tried to smile, but her mouth was trembling.

'Where do you buy your clothes?' Bethan asked Elizabeth.

'I like Stella McCartney,' Elizabeth said. For the name, she just spoke.

Bethan frowned at her. Lowri said, 'If you finger spell the whole word it would help.'

'Oh, of course' said Elizabeth. She spelled out Stella McCartney's name. Bethan replied, 'Wow, I love her clothes. I have never met someone who actually wears them.'

'You should,' said Elizabeth. 'You would look good in them.'

'What are your galleries like?'

Elizabeth took out her phone, the latest iphone.

'I have photographs of them. Would you like to see them?'

Bethan moved her chair so as to sit next to Elizabeth to look at the photographs.

'Wow, is that Victoria Beckman?'

'Yes.'

'That's amazing.'

Catrin stood up. 'I need a drink. Bethan, do you want one?'

Bethan shook her head, and went back to talking to Elizabeth.

Catrin, close to tears, walked back to the kitchen. There she found Anwen and David.

'Catrin, who's the posh woman over with you all? Looks a bit out of place here,' said Anwen.

Catrin looked at David. 'That's Elizabeth, Bethan's birth mother.'

'Oh, my God. Bethan is adopted?' said Anwen. 'Well, I can see the likeness. Do they get on?'

'This is the first time they've met.'

'Oh, God. What a time to do it. How is it going?'

'They're all getting on very well.'

'She looks very well off. Maybe she's come to give Bethan some money?'

'I don't think she even meant to meet Bethan.'

'What do you mean?'

'Hang on,' interrupted David. 'Let me catch up. I thought Bethan's mother was dead?'

'Dad told us she was–'

'But–'

'David, he thought it was for the best.'

'And she turned up today?'

'She came to say goodbye to Aled. She says she didn't mean to meet Bethan, just wanted to see her, see that she was well.'

'But she must have known she would be here?'

'I think she thought she could pass unnoticed.'

'She's not going to go unnoticed anywhere, is she? Look at her: she's gorgeous, and those clothes–' said Anwen. She looked at Catrin. 'Are you alright about all this?'

'I suppose so.'

'Does Gareth know?' asked David.

'I can't get hold of him. We haven't spoken since he left the meal.'

'He doesn't know Elizabeth is here?'

'No, but what am I meant to do?'

'Bethan seems to be getting on alright. That woman can sign then?' said Anwen, glancing out of the window.

Catrin nodded. 'I think she can do everything. Beautiful, rich, you know, she owns art galleries and things.'

'Your father would be impressed by that.'

'Yes, and so is Bethan.'

Anwen walked over and put her arms around Catrin. 'Hey, it'll be alright, you know. It's natural that Bethan should be excited seeing her birth Mum. It doesn't mean she loves you any less.'

'I know that–'

'You must believe it deep down, Catrin.'

Catrin frowned. 'I don't know what will happen. Elizabeth says that no-one in London knows about Bethan. She never told her parents or anyone. Oh dear. I don't want Bethan to get hurt.'

'What did you make of her?'

'She seems a bit hard, defensive.'

'She's been through a lot on her own,' said David. He looked at Catrin. 'She's been keeping a secret for a long time. It can be very lonely.'

Catrin looked away. 'Look, I've got a stinking headache. I think I'll go and have a break upstairs, alright?'

'Of course.'

Catrin went upstairs, with Safi quietly following her. There was a large window that looked over the back garden, and she looked down on everyone, feeling strangely detached. They were all chatting. Her father was smiling, pouring more wine for Elizabeth. She felt horribly redundant, but also very worried about what was going to happen.

Her phone beeped. She read the text message.

'Hope the service went OK. Gareth.'

Catrin suddenly felt really angry. Why was he never here when she needed him? She picked up her phone and sent a text, 'Something really important has happened. Ring me ASAP.'

Chapter Twenty

Elizabeth left The Dragon House early evening. She felt so full emotion: to think that she had actually met her daughter. They had talked, and got on. Her beautiful daughter who she'd instantly felt a bond with. They'd even laughed at some of the same things. She had never imagined they would have anything in common. But, most of all, she had never expected to feel anything as strongly as this. It was like falling in love. Her emotions were whizzing around. The love hurt her deep down, stabbed at her heart. She hadn't expected this. She had just agreed to spend tomorrow with Bethan, to take her shopping. Bethan was young, naive, easily impressed; she realised that. But then she had had a sheltered life: look at the way Catrin dressed and behaved. For God's sake, didn't the woman have any pride? Bethan deserved to be spoilt, bought nice things. Still, it was all moving so fast. This morning she had had no intention of even speaking to Bethan. But it was too late for regrets. Even if she was to just get in the car and escape to London, she couldn't undo today, pretend it had never happened.

Elizabeth arrived back at the bungalow. She wanted to get to her room quickly. She didn't feel like making polite talk. However, Angela was in the kitchen and rushed out to greet her.

'Hi. Would you like a drink?'

'No thank you. I think I'll go and lie down.'

'I saw you at the service?' Angela made the statement a rather open-ended question.

'Mm.'

'Did you go down to the house as well?'

'Mmm.'

'So, do you know the family?'

Elizabeth stared at Angela. The woman looked so normal, so sane. Didn't she realise the chaos that was going on inside Elizabeth? It was so hard, always trying to look cool and together.

'I have met them, yes.'

'I may be completely wrong here, but is it anything to do with Bethan?'

Elizabeth looked at Angela. She nodded. Her throat felt tight with tears. She couldn't speak.

'The likeness, you know, is uncanny.'

Elizabeth nodded again. 'The thing is, you see, well, I am her mother.' She got the words out, and then she started to cry, huge, heart-wrenching sobs.

'Hey, come and sit down,' said Angela, guiding Elizabeth into the living room.

'I'm so sorry. The thing is we all thought you were, um–'

'Dead. Yes, you all thought that, didn't you? That's what they told everyone: they said I was dead.' Elizabeth started to cry again.

'I'm so sorry.'

'You don't seem as shocked as everyone else.'

'To be honest I've never trusted my brother-in-law. When Isabel told me what he'd said, I wondered.'

'So you guessed it was Lloyd telling the lie?'

'Well, it was, wasn't it?'

'Yes.'

'I thought so. So, how did you meet Aled?'

'I went over to New York for three months to work in my Dad's firm. He was an architect, and his firm was associated with Lloyd's. Aled was there at the same time. We dated a few times. I was a very naive nineteen year old, and very flattered that this handsome older man wanted to date me.'

'He was very good-looking and charming.'

'Exactly, I didn't realise until I came back after Christmas that I was pregnant. In fact, I think I was about six months before I realised.'

'And your parents?'

'My parents were living in New York. I had a flat here, and I was going to uni in September.'

'But surely you told them?'

'No. I couldn't. You see, to them I was this perfect child. They would never have coped with me being pregnant and not married.'

'Were they religious?

'Yes, very religious. They had everything invested in me. I came here, you know, the night Aled died. I knew he'd come back here and someone told me about the party. I thought he might marry me, and then, you see, my parents wouldn't have minded.'

'You loved him?'

'I don't know. I don't think so, but he had seemed very charming and that. I thought, maybe, he would whisk me off my feet and marry me.'

'And you'd live happily ever after?'

'Exactly.'

'And what did he say?'

Elizabeth shook her head. 'It didn't go that way. In the hospital, before I knew he was dead, I knew we wouldn't be getting married. I decided then that I would have the baby adopted.'

'You didn't think, then, to talk to your parents?'

'No, and to be honest I wanted to go to university. I was very young. I wasn't ready to be a mother. I know you must think that's terrible, but it was how I felt.'

'And were you on your own through all this?'

199

'My aunt came and, of course, Lloyd came and talked to me. He was the one who suggested Catrin and Gareth adopt Bethan.'

'You had Bethan about two weeks after Aled died, didn't you?'

'That's right.' Elizabeth looked up for the first time. 'She was beautiful.' As she said the words, she started to cry again, hard hot sobs. She opened her handbag with shaking hands, and took out a photograph, which she handed to Angela. It was the first time she had ever shown it to anyone. It was a small Polaroid photograph, of a young woman holding a tiny baby with a mop of black hair.

'There was another mother in the bed next to me. Her husband brought in a Polaroid camera, and he took the picture for me.'

Angela looked at the photograph, and handed it back.

'I remember the feeling of holding her next to my cheek: so warm and soft. The smell, I can still remember the smell of her. And touching her tiny fingers; her little arms moving around; so vulnerable; her eyes shut tight. Then I remember her suddenly opening her eyes, deep brown eyes. She looked at me so intently, as if soaking in every detail of my face.'

Elizabeth felt tears on her cheeks. She brushed them away. They were hot, and seemed to burn her cheeks. Her throat tightened; it hurt. She put her hands on her throat to try and ease the pain, and gulped in air.

She felt Angela's hand, warm and comforting, on hers.

'I did love her. I did. But I just couldn't keep her. You do understand, don't you?'

Angela nodded. She was close to tears as well. 'I do.'

Elizabeth nodded. 'The social worker tried to talk me out of it, to at least get me to wait, but I talked to my aunt. She said the baby would be much better off with two parents and, to think of it not as giving up my baby, but rather handing her to people who I knew would cherish her. She told me I would forget and move on.'

'Things aren't always as easy as that.'

'No, but I still believe I did the right thing for Bethan and me. Catrin and Gareth sounded a nice couple, and the social worker went to see them, check them out. It being family made it much more straightforward. I thought that was better for Bethan.'

'You were going to university?'

'I had my place. I really wanted to go, you know. I know it sounds selfish, but I was going to do Art History. I loved it. My dream had always been to have my own gallery, buy paintings for people. My parents would invest in that. It was all mapped out.'

Elizabeth put the photograph back in her handbag. Angela handed her a tissue. She wiped her eyes, took a deep breath, and was suddenly embarrassed at her outburst.

'I'm sorry. I don't know what came over me.'

'I think you've been holding all that in for a long time.'

Elizabeth nodded. 'It was a shock, you know, seeing Bethan today. I'd underestimated how hard it would be. It was scary how much she looked like me, and her mannerisms: the way she flicks her hair and tucks it behind her little pixie ear, just like mine, it was spooky. And then she's Deaf.'

'Yes, that must have been a shock.'

'It was at first, but, well, I can sign. My mother, you know, was Deaf'

'No—'

201

'Yes. It's amazing, isn't it?'

'I'm confused. You said you never wanted to meet Bethan. Yet you came here.'

'I thought I would just see Bethan. See she was alright. But I didn't think anyone would recognise me. Then, you told me Bethan thought I was dead. I knew I had to speak to Lloyd about that. While I was talking to him, Catrin found us, and then Bethan came. It all sort of ran away with us.'

'They must all have been very shocked to see you.'

'Lloyd was furious at first. Bethan coped very well, I thought. Difficult to tell with Catrin. She didn't say much. I have to say, Catrin seemed rather weak. She lets Lloyd speak to her quite rudely, and she doesn't stand up for herself.'

'That's how it looks to you?'

'Yes. I mean, she's given up on herself, hasn't she? I guess she's one of those women who want to live her life through her children.'

'Don't be too hard on Catrin. She's not always had it easy.'

'Nobody has it easy, do they? But let's face it; she doesn't have to work like most people. She's got it all: nice home, husband with a good job, the two girls. She's not come out of it all so badly. She needs to get a grip and get on with her own life now.'

'Sometimes life is a bit more complicated than that. Now, would you like that drink?'

Elizabeth shook her head. 'No, thanks. I think I'll go out for a walk, get some fresh air before I turn in.'

'Are you alright?'

'I'm fine now. Just a moment's weakness, really.'

'What will you do?'

'Do you think I could stay? I know I was meant to be going tomorrow–'

'Yes, it's fine. I've no-one else until the weekend.'

'That's great. Thank you. I'm seeing Bethan tomorrow. It'll be fine. I think I'll go and get some fresh air.'

Elizabeth left the house quickly. She didn't want Angela fussing around her. She walked up the street, glancing over at the Dragon House. There were lights on. She kept walking until she reached the pub. Outside, the smokers stood with drinks, some having left family in the pub, others were joined by friends.

Elizabeth went inside, ordered a large vodka and tonic, and came back outside. She found a seat on the edge of the crowd. What was she to do next? She had promised to see Bethan the next day to go shopping. Yes, that would be a good thing: buy her some decent presents, and that would be enough. She should also set some boundaries. She had her own life in London. Bethan was separate from that and had to remain so. Elizabeth thought about Richard. There was no way he would cope with her having given away a baby. All this time she had insisted to him that she would never have children, was not the maternal kind. He would hate her. No, this had to be contained. Difficult, though. She had bonded with Bethan so quickly, really liked her. They had a lot in common. It would need careful handling.

Chapter Twenty One

At The Dragon House, things were quiet. It had been a long, emotional day. Nobody seemed inclined to chat. The caterers had packed up efficiently, and left. There was no need to cook as everyone seemed to be happy finishing up the left-overs.

Catrin found Bethan in the garden.

'How are you, love?'

Bethan spoke breathlessly, smiled over-brightly. 'I'm alright, Mum. It went OK, didn't it?'

'Yes, it seemed to. It was surprising she could sign.'

'I know. Some of the signs are pretty dated, though.'

'Really? They change?'

'God, yes. I only recognised some of hers from the old people who sometimes come to Deaf Club.'

'I'm glad you managed. Do you want to talk about it?'

'Not really. Mum, you're alright, aren't you? You don't mind me meeting Elizabeth do you?'

'Of course not. No, it's fine. I just don't want you to get hurt, and it's very sudden.'

'I know, but, you know, I think everything is going to go really well.'

'Shall we go for a walk, have a chat about things?'

'No,' Bethan replied rather brutally. 'Actually, I'm going for a walk with Lowri. Shall we take Safi?'

Rather surprised, Catrin thanked her and went to find Safi's things. It was a long time since her daughters had spent time together. She was pleased, although, it would have been quite nice to have been invited to go with them. She handed over Safi. 'Watch him on roads, and don't let him off unless it's away from roads and cliff edges. Don't walk too far with him. Take water–'

Lowri smiled reassuringly at her, and the girls left.

Catrin sat out in the garden alone. The whole day had felt surreal, as if she could turn around and find it had all been some bizarre dream. But, of course, it hadn't. She picked up her phone: no reply from Gareth. She went inside, and found her father watching the Olympics.

'Dad, we ought to talk about today.'

Lloyd glanced up, but with one eye on the television. 'Mm, what about it?'

'About Elizabeth. It was huge meeting her, and if you hadn't lied it wouldn't have been quite such a shock.'

'I explained. I did it for your own good. Anyway, it's turned out alright. Elizabeth seems to have done well for herself. No, it's worked out well.'

'I would hardly say that. A meeting between a birth mother and her child should be carefully planned. I've read about it. It's important the meeting is done carefully. It's a massive thing for everyone, and it can easily go wrong.'

'Well, Bethan will always have us, won't she?'

'But she could be very hurt. If it goes wrong, it will be like being rejected all over again.'

'I expect they'll work it out,' her father said, and turned back to the sport. Frustrated, Catrin returned to the kitchen.

The light was fading. It was very quiet. Only the rustle of the late evening summer breeze in the hedges and the distant breaking of waves disturbed the silence. It had been such a warm, sunny weekend. Catrin wondered when the weather would break. Her mind picked at all the things that had happened. She was restless, and unable to concentrate on anything. She went inside, made coffee, and tidied the kitchen. She wanted to go to bed, but years of habit made her stay up to wait for the girls to return. When they came back, they looked tired but happy.

'Good walk?'

'Great.'

Safi came running over to her, tail wagging.

'I'll go on up,' said Bethan. Lowri went to find Mark.

Catrin, feeling redundant again, locked up the back door and went upstairs to her room. From her case, she took a large album. It was a present for Bethan. She opened it and started to look though it. It was an album of photographs of Bethan from a baby right through to the present time. She'd had the idea from the social worker who suggested keeping a life story book for Bethan. It had seemed such a lovely idea she'd made one for Lowri as well and had given it to her on her eighteenth birthday.

Catrin sat flicking through the photographs. She remembered someone saying that if you looked at photographs you would think that all children did was blow out candles on their cake and sit on the beach on holiday. There were certainly lots of those. Then she had an idea: maybe the right thing to do would be to give this to Bethan soon so that she could show the album to Elizabeth. Yes, she would give it to her tomorrow. She stroked Safi, got changed, and got into bed, leaving the windows open. She lay in the darkness, listening to the distant waves, until she fell to sleep.

Tuesday 31st July 2012

The next morning Bethan surprised Catrin by getting up early.

'I just had a text from Elizabeth. She's coming around.'

'Oh, right. Well, I've had an idea. Wait there.'

Catrin returned from her room with the album.

'This was meant to be for your birthday, but I thought you might want to show it to Elizabeth.'

Bethan took it and grinned. 'This is like you did for Lowri? Thanks, Mum. That's a brilliant idea.'

Elizabeth arrived. Bethan took her into the garden. Catrin stayed with them. Catrin was struck again by how alike they were. They walked with the same upright confident stride.

'Mum has given me something to show you,' said Bethan.

They sat at the wonky metal table. Bethan opened the album on it. Catrin had a momentary panic. She hadn't really thought about it before, but would Elizabeth get upset, see it as a catalogue of things she had missed?

'I thought you might like to see some of the things Bethan has done. Um, you don't have to look at it if you don't want to,' she said quickly.

'No, I'd really like that,' said Elizabeth. 'Never having had kids I don't really have much idea, you know, of the stages they go through.'

Bethan excitedly opened the album.

'Of course. There aren't any pictures just after my birth, you know, like there's some of Lowri with Mum in the hospital.'

Elizabeth smiled. 'Hang on.' She opened her handbag, and showed Bethan the Polaroid photograph.

'There you are: you and me.'

Bethan's face lit up. 'Look, Mum.' She handed the Polaroid to Catrin. It was very strange for her, looking at a tinier Bethan than she had ever seen, and Bethan being held by this very young girl. What she had never imagined was the look of wonder she saw in Elizabeth's face as she looked at Bethan. Somehow, she had never thought there had been any bond. She knew it shouldn't, but it hurt.

'You were beautiful,' Catrin said to Bethan. She looked at Elizabeth. 'You were very young.'

'And I was very naive by the standards of today's nineteen year olds.'

Catrin handed the photo back to Elizabeth, and watched her put it carefully back into her bag. When Catrin thought how many pictures she had of Bethan it was moving to see how treasured this single photo was.

Bethan started working though the album, explaining to Elizabeth in great detail the various birthday and holiday pictures. There were also photos of her in fancy dress, standing by Christmas trees, opening presents, and pictures of her with friends who had come and gone, and with Lowri, playing in the garden. As Bethan grew older, the photographs became fewer and more self-conscious: dressed up for parties, playing at concerts, taking part in school plays. Catrin thought Elizabeth might find it boring, but she seemed gripped, and asked a lot of questions.

As they reached the end, Bethan looked up and grinned. 'So, I can add a photo of you now.'

Elizabeth smiled, but it was a sad, wistful look. A tear ran unchecked from the corner of her eye.

'I missed so much,' she said, quietly.

'I'm sorry,' said Catrin. 'I didn't mean to upset you.'

'No, I realise that. Thank you–'

'Yes, let me make coffee.'

When Catrin returned, Bethan and Elizabeth were still talking.

'Bethan was telling me about all the appointments and things when she was little. That must have been difficult.'

'It was. The endless fittings for ear moulds, adjustments of hearing aids. Of course, there are all the embarrassing ones when I had to explain how we lost the latest, most expensive aid down the beach, or dropped it in the bath. Nothing was easy. Some of the teachers were great. Some refused to make any concessions to Bethan at all. She had an assistant, but I would hear that, instead of helping Bethan through a maths lesson, they'd been putting up a display in the hall.'

'No? Really?'

'Yes. It was a matter of fighting.'

'Did they sign in school?'

'Not usually. To start signing with Bethan was a big decision. You see, there were plenty of professionals who said that if I signed with Bethan she would never learn to talk.'

'Really?'

'Yes. The idea is, you see, that she has this tiny bit of hearing, her residual hearing, and she must work hard at using that. They said that if she signed she wouldn't, and so would never learn to talk. The way I saw it, Bethan was getting very frustrated. It didn't seem fair, so I found someone prepared to teach us, and that is the way we went. The expression they used then was 'total communication', when you use speech and signing in parallel. I think it's called something different now.'

Bethan started to get bored.

'Aren't we going shopping?' she asked Elizabeth.

'Oh, yes. If that's alright, Catrin?'

'Well, I suppose so. What for, though?'

'Elizabeth is going to buy me new clothes and things.'

'Oh, I don't know–'

'Please, let me treat her–'

Elizabeth looked so desperate that Catrin agreed. They swopped mobile numbers, and Elizabeth and Bethan left together.

Feeling a bit lost, Catrin took Safi out for a walk. She had returned, and was thinking about starting on some clearing out when her father came down.

'Where's Bethan?'

'She's gone shopping with Elizabeth.'

'What do you mean? We arranged yesterday that Elizabeth would come here.'

'I know, but they've gone out now.'

'Oh. Well, I suppose that is OK.'

'You seemed to change your mind about Elizabeth yesterday.'

'I suppose I think she could be a good influence on Bethan; might encourage her to do this audition, tell her about New York.'

'You're not worried about her coming to take Bethan away any more?'

'Well I wasn't. I didn't expect her to go off with her like this though. I suppose I thought she would encourage Bethan to think about America.'

'I don't want her to go there. In a few years time, maybe, but not now. It's too soon.'

'Well, I disagree. I'd love to have her out there with me.'

Catrin frowned. 'She could come and see you, Dad, but she should go to university. Gareth is right.'

'What's happened to him, anyway? He didn't bother coming to the service yesterday.'

'I don't know, Dad. He was very angry.'

'He was. I don't know why. It's not like him to storm off like that, is it?'

'No, it's not.'

'You two alright, are you?'

'Of course, Dad.'

'Right, good. Well, I know I've always thought he could earn more, but he's alright.'

Catrin realised this was the equivalent of high praise from her father.

'I thought I might do some more tidying upstairs today. By the way, a drawer and the wardrobe in mum's room are locked. Do you know where there are any keys?'

'Have you looked in the dresser? Loads of odds and sods in there.'

Catrin looked, and found a small box full of odd keys.

'Good. I'll take this upstairs, see how I get on.'

Catrin went up, but she didn't go immediately to her mother's room. She started on what they called the games room. What it contained was really more junk, not collectors' items, like an original game of Monopoly, but old games of snakes and ladders with the dice missing and buttons replacing the lost counters. Some of these Catrin designated for recycling, but most for rubbish. Once she started sorting out, she found that the time passed quickly. A lot of the other stuff in the room was the sort of things found in hundreds of charity shops around the country: unbroken but unfashionable glasses, old prints in cheap frames, old recipe books and out of date atlases. Catrin, like so many people, did not have the heart to throw out or recycle any of it, but boxed and labelled the items for the charity shops. Occasionally, she checked her phone, but there were no messages from Gareth or Bethan.

Catrin carried on getting dusty and grubby sorting out the room.

She made herself some lunch. Her father seemed content watching the Olympics. As she sat in garden eating her cheese sandwich, Catrin decided to try contacting Gareth again. There was no answer from his mobile. Then she tried the home phone number. To her surprise, Gareth answered.

'At last, I've got hold of you,' she said. 'I did ask you to call me urgently.'

'Sorry. I haven't looked at my phone. I'm really busy. We've come back to work here. Can't concentrate at the surgery.'

'We?'

Gareth went very quiet.

Chapter Twenty Two

Catrin waited for Gareth to reply. Eventually, he spoke.

'Oh, Carol came back here. We constantly get interrupted at work. So, how are things there?

'A lot has happened since you left on Sunday. I've been trying to get to speak to you.'

'Is something up?

'Yes. I've left you a lot of messages. You should have phoned back.'

'What's happened?'

'It's Bethan.'

'What's that, then?'

As clearly as she could, Catrin told Gareth about Elizabeth.

'I can't believe this. You mean, your father lied to us?'

'Yes. I guess he thought it was for the best. All I can think was that he was frightened of losing Bethan. Something like that.'

'He had no right. For heaven's sake, your father has never understood that we are Bethan's parents. You should have stood up to him years ago.'

As always, Catrin realised that the conversation was veering off to an argument about her father.

'The point is, Bethan has now met Elizabeth.'

'And how did it go?'

'Actually, well. Bethan is with her all day today.'

'Without you?'

'Yes. They went shopping.'

'You should be involved. You can't let Bethan just go off with some stranger.'

'There wasn't much I could do about it. To be honest, Gareth, I don't think you have a right to criticise me. I've had to deal with this all on my own. I decided that Bethan is nearly eighteen, and that she could go. Anyway, it was arranged without me. You know what Bethan's like if she thinks we are confronting her. She'd be a lot worse. At least this way she is telling me what is happening.'

'And what's Elizabeth like?'

'She's very together. Not married. Doesn't have kids. Well off. Her parent sent her to boarding school.'

'Really?'

'Yes. She wears weird clothes, you know, designer. She owns art galleries in London and New York.'

'Well, that will impress Bethan and your father, I should think.'

'It did.'

'So why hasn't Elizabeth been in touch before?'

'She didn't want to interfere. She says she hadn't intended to talk to Bethan at the memorial. She was just going to leave quietly.'

'But they are with each other today–'

'I know. Elizabeth seems to have had a change of heart.'

'And what did you make of her? As a person, I mean?'

'I don't know. She's quite assertive. Likes her own way, I should think.'

'That's where Bethan gets it from, then.'

'And Elizabeth signs.'

'Really? How's that?'

'Her mother was Deaf.'

'Really? Do they know why?'

'She had German Measles as a child.'

'Oh, so that doesn't help Bethan, then.'

'No.'

'It must help that she can sign, though?'

'Yes, Bethan says it's old-fashioned but, of course, it makes it a lot easier for them. They seem to get on well.' Catrin felt her voice break, but Gareth missed it.

'Maybe it could be a good thing; at least she might put this nonsense about America out of Bethan's mind.'

Catrin sniffed. 'Actually, Dad said he was thinking her having a gallery in New York might encourage Bethan.'

'I can imagine from Bethan's point of view that this is good news. You know, she's nearly eighteen. She must have a lot of questions. It's a good thing Elizabeth is alive. Bethan can meet the real person. I've never been comfortable with the way your father has built up Aled into some kind of hero. Meeting her birth mother will perhaps help her.'

'I suppose so, but it's all so sudden, and Bethan has just leapt into it with both feet.'

'That's just the way Bethan is. You watch, there'll be drama soon, and we'll have to pick up the pieces.'

'You think so?'

'Of course. But, on balance, I think it could be a good thing for her to meet her real mother.'

The words shot home like a bullet.

'I'm her real mother,' Catrin said quietly.

'Well–'

The rational tone grated. 'I am her mother' she said more firmly, adding 'And actually, you are her father, but you're not here. You're never here. You shouldn't have just stormed off on Sunday night. You should have answered my calls. It's not fair to leave everything to me.'

'Hey, calm down, now,' said Gareth, in his annoying 'pat on the head' voice. 'Don't worry. It'll work out.'

'You always say that, but maybe this time it won't–'

It went quiet. Catrin heard the sound of his keyboard. She realised Gareth was back working. Mentally, he had 'moved on to the next patient'.

Stifling the scream of frustration, Catrin said, 'I need you here. So does Bethan.'

'I'm sure you're handling it all fine. Tell Bethan to text me if she wants. Try not to worry about it. I really need to get on, try to relax this evening. Right, better go.'

The line went dead.

Catrin sat back in the chair, clenching and unclenching her fists. She felt so much hurt and inner rage but she didn't know what to do. Safi came and sat next to her. She stroked him gently, and started to calm down. Finally, she decided to go back upstairs.

Catrin found the box of keys. This time, she went into her mother's room. She tried various keys in the lock of the wardrobe. Catrin was about to give up when one slipped into the lock. She turned it, and the doors opened.

It was odd to see her mother's clothes hanging up. Very neat and smart. Catrin held a dress to her face; the smell was still there. It shocked her. Her mother had certain perfumes like Chanel Number Five, which she always wore, and the scent lingered on her clothes. For the first time in a long time, Catrin felt an overwhelming sense of loss for her mother. Coming here reminded her of the good times with her. The really awful times, well, they had been in Cardiff. When her mother had died, Catrin was ashamed to admit to an enormous sense of relief. It had been so hard covering up for her mother, rushing around at all times with two young children to look after. All those years of worrying about her mother had come to an end with her death but it had been exhausting. She had hardly cried at the time, just felt numb, but, as she held her mother's clothes, the tears came easily, and they felt healing. It was a relief to know that she really had loved her mother, and missed her.

Catrin started taking the clothes out of the wardrobe. They were clean and in very good condition. She folded them carefully to take to a charity shop, although she wondered whether anybody would want these old styles. The shoes were more worn. She thought they should probably be thrown away. Once the wardrobe was emptied, Catrin noticed a large rectangular package, standing upright at the back. She frowned, leant in, pulled it out, laid it on the floor, and opened it.

Catrin stared at the folder in front of her. It was the art portfolio that she had prepared for her interviews back in the sixth form. What ever was it doing in there? Had her mother brought it here and hidden it? It seemed so odd. Her mother was in pieces at that time from the loss of Nana Beth. Still, maybe she had been petrified of losing Catrin. Was that why she had done it? Catrin started to breathe quickly. Her heart was thumping against her chest. She couldn't breathe. She thought she was going to die. Safi came over and nuzzled her. She started to stroke him, which helped calm her breathing. She sat back. She could hear the television downstairs. She decided she had to speak to her father.

'Dad, guess what I have just found,' she said, her voice shaking.

'What's that, then?'

'My work, all my art. Remember, the stuff they said was lost.'

Lloyd frowned. 'Sorry?'

217

'Remember, the school said they'd lost it, but it's here.'

'Hang on. From years ago, you mean?'

'That's right. When I was in the sixth form. Come and see. You have to come and see it all.'

Her father, bemused and irritated to be dragged away from the sport on television, followed her upstairs. Catrin's work was spread over her mother's bedroom floor. Her father stared down.

'I'd forgotten that was in there.'

'She pounced on the words.'

'Forgotten? You knew.'

He looked sheepish. 'Well, yes.'

'You put it there.'

'It was for the best. Your mother would never have coped with you going away.'

'You had no right to do that.'

'I think I did. Look, you were never one for school. I had to keep working. Aled's school fees didn't come cheap, you know. I could see your mother was going into meltdown again. I had to do something.'

'So you decided to ruin my life?'

'Oh, don't over dramatise, Catrin. I never ruined your life. Just think, you would never have met Gareth if you'd gone to college. You'd have married some penniless artist instead of a doctor.'

Catrin was speechless. Her father really didn't see anything wrong with what he had done.

'You gave one of the pictures to Angela, didn't you?'

'Gosh, yes. I'd forgotten that. She came in when I was putting them away. I offered her one. It was quite good, actually.'

'You thought I was good?'

He looked away. 'Well, yes. Yes, you were, but there we are. No money in art, except for a very select few. Sometimes these things work out for the best. Right, I'd better go.'

Catrin watched as he practically ran out of the room, leaving her alone with Safi. She couldn't believe what she had just heard. She didn't know how she was meant to react. In some way her father had made a good case for his actions. Something niggled as unfair, but she wasn't sure what. She went downstairs to the kitchen. From the fridge she took a bottle of white wine, poured herself a glass, drank it quickly, and poured herself another, to take outside. She felt quite dusty and untidy, but shattered. She read a text from Bethan saying that she was having a great day, and that she and Elizabeth were going to the cinema, then to some late night pizza place. She would be quite late.

Catrin sent a text, 'Don't be too late. Come back after the cinema.'

Bethan replied. 'Don't worry, Elizabeth is giving me a lift. I will be fine. xx.'

Catrin scratched her wrist in frustration. She felt that Elizabeth was taking advantage. It was ridiculous to be out this late. But there was nothing she could do about it. She sat back in the chair and tried to relax. Safi jumped up on to her lap.

'Well, Safi, it's just you and me for this evening.'

Safi looked up in response to his name, then closed his eyes again. Catrin was startled a few minutes later by someone shouting.

'Hi!' she heard. She looked towards the end of the garden. Harri was waving. Catrin smiled.

'Come in. I'm all alone. Bethan's out. Lowri and Mark have gone for a walk, and Dad's inside watching the Olympics, so I'm out here on my own.'

Harri came into the garden.

Catrin told him about Bethan and Elizabeth.

'Was that the woman I saw at the memorial?'

'Very smart.'

'Yes, I saw her at the hotel having coffee on Sunday morning. She's very good-looking. Her clothes are fabulous. Wow. So, she's Bethan's mother?'

'Well, yes.'

'How do you feel about that?'

'Completely lost, actually. Part of me knows I shouldn't mind, but I can't help worrying about her. You know, is this it? Am I just going to lose her now? Elizabeth is, as you saw, so sophisticated, well off. I must seem very dull in comparison.'

'Don't be daft. Elizabeth looks quite a prickly woman. I certainly noticed her at the hotel. She's very striking. I even thought of going to say hello, but there's something about her, like some exotic but very prickly plant that you admire, but don't want to go too near.'

'I don't want Bethan to be unhappy.'

'Of course not. Anyway, what does Gareth think?'

'He seems to think it'll be OK. I wish he was here, though.'

'Of course you do. I can't believe he hasn't come. It's only an hour or two's drive. He can't be that busy, can he?'

'He said they're working on this research.'

'They?'

'Oh, I don't know. People he's doing the research with.'

'Did you have a good birthday?'

Catrin laughed. 'It was great. We went to the pub. Dad gave Bethan an extravagant present and promised her an audition to go to America with some big shot. Gareth stormed off. Perfect.'

'So it seems to me like you could do with being taken out somewhere–'

'Oh, no–'

'Come on. It's a lovely evening. I know just the place to go.'

'But Safi–' Catrin said, starting to weaken.

She can come. It's OK. We can sit outside. It's really special.'

Catrin looked around. Everyone had left her. Why not?

Chapter Twenty Three

'OK, you're on,' Catrin told Harri. 'Give me a few minutes to change, though.'

'That's fine. I'll be here with your dog.'

Catrin ran inside and upstairs. She felt terribly guilty, but also excited. She never did anything like this. Going out for a meal with another man? Well, it may be something more sophisticated people did regularly, but this was something she had never done before. Would Gareth mind? She decided that at the moment she didn't think he would care in the slightest. It wasn't a date, anyway. It was going out for a meal with an old friend. She quickly showered and put on her old skirt. Then she remembered how Harri was dressed. She couldn't go out with him in that old thing. She changed into her new dress and cardigan. Her hair she would just have to give a good brush. She put on a bit of make-up, and hurried back downstairs.

'Good grief, that was quick,' said Harri. 'Francine takes hours to get ready.'

'That's because she looks immaculate, I expect.'

'You look great. Love the dress. Come on, then.'

They walked together though the village to Harri's car. It was much smarter than Catrin's or Gareth's, and left hand drive. There was a safe place for Safi in the back. Catrin felt very nervous. Harri started the car. Somehow, the feeling of leaving the house and everyone behind was irresistible.

'Lovely evening,' said Harri.

'Yes. It feels strange, though, to be going out.'

'Really? My God, Catrin don't you do anything?'

'Of course I do. Just not like this.'

'Well, relax and enjoy the ride.'

Harri leant forward and put on music. It was Mozart, which surprised Catrin. It was the flute concerto which she had watched Bethan play in a concert recently. Catrin looked out of the window, the sun slipping lower in the sky. She saw the ponies on the downs, lazily munching at the grass.

'Gosh, this is so lovely. I feel like, well, I'm on holiday,' she said.

'I think it's time someone looked after you, Catrin.'

'Oh, no–'

'Yes, just this evening. You're going to let someone else look after you for a change.'

They arrived at a small, stony car park. Catrin got out, let Safi out of the back and put him on his lead. In front of her was a small bistro with tables and chairs outside, overlooking a long sandy bay. The waiter, fortunately, smiled at Safi, and showed them to a table at the edge, looking directly over the beach. There was a dog bowl which Safi sniffed at, but refused to drink from. He settled quietly under the table and put his head on Catrin's feet. To Catrin's relief, everyone was in casual clothes, some looking sandy and red from a day's walking or a day on the beach. It was mainly couples and older people, though: no young children. When she glanced at the menu she could understand why. It all looked appetising, but very expensive. Hand-dived scallops; dressed crab; beef fillet. Lobsters and crabs, fresh from Oxwich Bay, were a speciality, also cockles, laver bread, vegetables from the hotel's walled garden, and eggs from their ducks. The wine list was the longest Catrin had ever seen.

Harri grinned. 'Hope you haven't eaten today.'

'No, I've just snacked.'

'Good.'

'It's incredibly expensive–' she whispered.

Harri laughed. 'It's not too bad. Where does Gareth normally takes you for a special night?'

Catrin tried really hard to think when she and Gareth had last been out, just the two of them, for a meal. She could see Harri watching her intently. Quickly she said, 'Oh, the Ritz of course.'

'OK. Well, what shall we have here? I know the chef. She's fantastic.'

Catrin had no idea what to choose.

'I tell you what,' said Harri. 'Let's go for the taster menu.'

Catrin glanced again at the menu. It seemed to her a staggering amount to spend on food.

'Right, what we need is a good bottle of something.'

'Oh, I don't drink much–'

'Well, I'm not buying you a glass. It's a bottle, or nothing. I'll just have the one glass, as I'm driving.'

Harri ordered their meal, with a bottle of rosé, and bottled water.

'So, tell me about your village,' said Catrin.

'Collioure used to be a fishing village, famous for its anchovies, and painters like Matisse. It's getting much more touristy now. I was glad to get away for August. The rest of the time, though, it's lovely. Much warmer than here, real summer.'

'So Francine comes from there?'

'That's right. Her family go back generations there. It's a good life.'

'You enjoy your work?'

'I do.'

'But if you and Francine–'

224

'If we do split up, well, I have plenty of connections now.'

'You wouldn't come back here, then?'

'No. I would never come back here to live now. It's wonderful out there. The summers are warm and exotic; the food rich and sumptuous. It's the most sensuous place to live.'

Catrin was surprised to hear Harri speak like this. She remembered him as being far more down to earth.

'But you said you were thinking of buying property here, at Rhossili. So, could you bear to leave Collioure?'

'I wasn't planning to come back here. I'd have someone else running things. No, I was thinking of it as an investment.'

The waiter brought the first dishes of scallops, then oysters. It was all wonderfully fresh. Catrin felt like she was drowning in beautiful tastes and smells.

'This is incredible food,' she said.

'It is very good. The food around here has improved so much in the last couple of years. It's part of the reason I would like to invest in property here.'

'You mean like our house?'

'I think so. Yes. It's got so much potential here.'

'You didn't speak to Dad yesterday at the memorial?'

'No. He seemed a bit preoccupied. I can see why, now. Anyway, what have you been up to the past eighteen years?'

'I told you. Bringing up the girls really.'

'Tell me about them.'

Catrin started, rather hesitantly, telling Harri about Lowri and Bethan growing up. She wasn't sure he would be that bothered in hearing about them. However, he appeared genuinely interested.

'They're lucky girls to have you spend so much time on them.'

'I think a lot of people think that I spoil them, that I do too much for them.'

'Rubbish. I think it's great.'

They were brought sorbet, then sweet dishes. Catrin looked out to sea. The sun appeared to be resting on the horizon. The sea was a gentle blue. The setting sun gave everything a warm glow.

'It's later than I thought,' Catrin said. 'I don't know where the time has gone.'

'It's only nine. You don't have anything to rush back for, do you?'

'No,' she said thoughtfully. 'I haven't.'

'Good, then there is somewhere else I want to take you.'

'Where do you mean? It's getting dark.'

'Don't worry. It's just the right time to see it.'

Catrin could feel Safi moving on her feet.

'He's been very good.'

'I think he just wants to be with you.'

Catrin laughed. 'I think you're right. It's good that somebody does. Well, OK. Let's go on this adventure.'

Harri paid the bill. They walked up to the car. Catrin felt a thrill of excitement. Where on earth were they going? They drove a relatively short distance, then Harri pulled in.

Catrin got out of the car wide-eyed. The sky was darkening, but there was a bright full moon, and Harri had a torch.

'Where are we?'

'This is Pennard Castle.'

Catrin's eyes adjusted to the darkness. She could make out the outlines of the ruined castle.

'It's an early twelfth century castle. Over there is Three Cliffs Bay. It has the most wonderful views in the daytime, but there is nothing like it for the atmosphere at night. The cliff edge is over there, so be careful.'

'I've never been here. I know what you mean: it's full of atmosphere.'

'That's why I brought you here. There's amazing stories about it.'

'What are they?'

'Well, there's one about it being haunted by the ghost of an old winged witch who bewitches anyone who sleeps there overnight.'

'Well, we don't intend to stay here, do we?'

'You know they talk about the faerie land of Gower?'

'Oh, yes. Nana Beth used to talk about the faeries.'

'Well, the story goes that the faeries cursed the castle. Apparently, the owner of the castle was celebrating his forthcoming marriage to the daughter of the then Prince of Wales. They had a huge feast here, but were disturbed by some lights on the beach. Everybody rushed down to the beach with drawn swords, to find that the revellers were faeries, who were furious about having their dance in the moonlight disturbed by mortals. They cursed the owner of the castle. A sandstorm came, and choked him and his followers to death. The castle was also engulfed by sand.'

'Wow. That's a great story, although I always thought faeries were nicer than that. In this light, I can almost imagine it.'

'You should draw it, or paint it.'

Catrin shrugged. 'I don't think I could, now.'

They sat down looking out into the darkness.

'Catrin, what's happened to you? When you were seventeen, you were so full of excitement, dreams. I remember you talking, saying that life had been difficult, but that your mother was well again and you could make plans. What went wrong?'

'Well my Nana died. Mum needed me. I worked locally in Cardiff. I met Gareth. I don't see that as my life going wrong, just changing direction.'

'And now, what direction are you going in?'

'I don't know. I was thinking of doing some kind of college course.'

'What in?'

'I don't know. I'm not really any good at anything.'

Harri shook his head, frustrated.

'For God's sake, Catrin. You and I are fifty now. Time's precious. We can't fritter it away. What about your drawing, your art?'

Catrin looked down, remembering the work spread across her mother's bedroom floor.

'What is it?' asked Harri.

Slowly, Catrin told him what had happened that day.

'That's so bad. How could your father have done that?'

'I think he thought it was for the best.'

'Good God. You don't believe that, do you?'

'Well, there were things to do. Looking after Mum and stuff.'

'Catrin, he had no right to do that.'

'No, maybe not. I would love to have gone to college. I loved drawing and painting.' Catrin felt tears welling up. 'Look, sorry. I've drunk a lot of wine. I ought to go back now.'

'It's never too late to do the things you love. You should come and visit Collioure. It's full of artists and painters.'

228

'It sounds amazing, but it's not for me.'

'Why not?'

Catrin laughed and stood up. 'I ought to get back to the real world.'

They walked back towards the car. Safi jumped happily in the back. Harri drove back to the house.

'Thanks for a wonderful evening,' she said.

'Don't forget what we talked about. It doesn't have to be a dream. Give me your mobile number.'

Catrin did this, and then got out of the car. She watched Harri drive away.

Catrin met her father in the hallway.

'Where've you been?' he asked

'Just out for a meal.'

'Who with?'

'Harri.'

'Gareth phoned the house phone,' her father said, briskly.

'Oh. What did he say?' Catrin felt consumed with guilt, as if Gareth somehow would know everything that had happened that evening.

'Nothing. I didn't know where you were.'

'OK. I'll try ringing him back now.'

'Don't forget that article for the website. I'd like it up soon. You can mention what I said, and about the bench.'

'Oh, dear. Are you sure you want me to do this?'

'Of course.'

Catrin sighed, heard the sound from the television, and went into the living room. As she expected, Lowri and Mark were in there.

'Hi, Mum. Gosh, you look lovely. Where have you been?'

'Just out for a meal.'

'What? Who with?'

'Just Harri.'

'Oh, Mum. Out on a date?'

'Of course not.'

'Where did you go?'

Catrin told them about the restaurant. 'It was lovely. You and Mark ought to go there. My treat, its pricey.'

Lowri grinned. 'It sounds good.'

'Did you and Mark have a good day?'

'Oh, yes,' said Lowri, glowing. She turned to Mark. 'What was it we saw?'

Mark grinned, took out his phone, and showed Catrin a photograph of an enormous, light, purple-coloured moth.

'Goodness. What's that?'

'It's a Convolvulus Hawk-moth. Quite rare. I was very excited to see it,' said Mark. He gave Lowri that wonderful, warm, intimate smile: exclusive, and private.

'Dad rang, by the way,' said Lowri.

'Grandad said. I'll try calling him back.'

'I think he was having trouble with his mobile.'

'OK, right. I'll try anyway. Do you two have any plans tomorrow?'

Catrin noticed them look quickly at each other. 'Maybe go for a long walk.'

Catrin nodded, but was hurt that they were being so secretive. Then she heard the front door. It was Bethan, carrying handfuls of smart carrier bags.

'You're incredibly late. What on earth have you been doing?' Catrin asked.

'It's been great. Honestly, Mum. We had the most fantastic day, shopping in Swansea shopping centre. There was a lot more there than I expected. Not as good as Cardiff, but pretty good. Then, of course, we went to the cinema.'

'I didn't expect you to be out this late.'

'I sent you a text.'

'I know, but I couldn't do anything about it.'

'Don't fuss. We went to this incredible place for Pizza after, like a cocktail bar.'

'You didn't drink, did you?'

Bethan gave her a kiss on the cheek. 'Of course not.'

'I'm not happy about it. You've only just met Elizabeth.'

'But we get on so well. Honestly, it's great walking around with her. I'd look at our reflection: we really look like mother and daughter.'

Catrin swallowed hard. 'Well, that's good,' she said, trying to smile.

Bethan patted her on the head. 'You're really not to worry about me. It's all going really well. Look at all the clothes we bought. Honestly, Mum. Elizabeth thought nothing of Topshop prices. She thought it was cheap, and we went to some places, you know, where they seem to have only about three outfits for sale, really expensive. You have enormous changing rooms all to yourself, and the assistant just keeps bringing you things to try on.'

'Elizabeth paid for all this?'

'God, yes. Mum, I reckon she's really loaded.'

'My goodness, Bethan. It's more than we spend in a year on clothes.'

'She didn't mind. She seemed to like doing it.'

'Well, I don't want her spending money like this every time you meet. Were you alright at the cinema?'

'To be honest, I didn't have a clue for some of it, but I didn't say anything to Elizabeth.'

'How was her signing?'

'OK. Not as good as she thinks,' said Bethan. 'She made some real bad mistakes, but I didn't tell her. Fortunately, I'm used to crap signing. It was interesting. She was telling me about her mother. She was brought up in England, but when she moved to New York with her husband's work she found it very hard because all the Deaf people out there use American Sign Language.'

'Is it that different?'

'Oh, yes. Really different, and they do it one handed. Her mother found it really hard, felt very isolated. It's amazing her mother was Deaf, isn't it?'

'Yes.'

'I know it's not for the same reason. It doesn't explain my Deafness, but at least there is someone in my family who was Deaf. I'm not the only one. Does that make sense?'

'I think so, yes. I hadn't realised you'd feel like that, but, yes, I can understand that.'

'I do wish I could have met her.'

'It would have been good for you. I can see that.'

'And for her. Elizabeth said she felt isolated. I can understand that. It's hard being different all the time.'

'It was what I was trying to explain to Grandad when I was telling him about Deaf Club.'

'He doesn't get it, does he?'

'No, I'm afraid not. Anyway, are you seeing Elizabeth again soon?' asked Catrin, hesitantly.

'Tomorrow. She would like to give me something special for my birthday.'

'I think she has spent quite enough on you.'

'She loves doing it, Mum. She's very generous, never looks at the price of things. I talked to her all about my music and the world of Deaf musicians. She was really interested. She told me about her art galleries.

Mum, she's amazing. She flies to New York and to loads of places to auctions and things. She knows a lot about art and meets such interesting people.'

'It sounds very interesting.'

'It is, Mum. Wow, who'd have thought my mother would be like that?'

Catrin tried to push the words away, but it was like trying to use a piece of tissue to bat away a ball of fire. The pain was great but, despite it, like many mothers, she forced herself to smile.

Bethan, not completely oblivious to her mother's feelings, stopped and said. 'You don't mind, do you?'

'Of course not. It's lovely that you get on.'

Bethan breathed out, and grinned. 'That's great. Just think. If I was to get the audition and go to New York, I could see her over there. Right, better get off to bed.' Bethan kissed her on the cheek. 'I'm so happy, Mum,' she said, and ran up the stairs.

Catrin knew that she should be pleased for Bethan. The last thing she would have wanted was for her to be hurt, but to have Elizabeth swoop in with her money and sophistication was pretty hard to bear. Everything was moving too fast.

Catrin went upstairs and opened the window wide, allowing the breeze and the soft rhythmic sound of the sea into the room. She tried phoning Gareth on his mobile and on the landline, but got no response. What was she meant to do? Was she really about to lose Bethan? Would she go off to New York? It would be like losing a limb. Of course, Bethan would still come home. They would email and text, but it was a long way and, if she had Elizabeth, would it be her she would turn to? Catrin stared out of the window at the blackness. Suddenly, pictures of sitting drinking rosé on the harbour at Collioure drifted in and out of her mind. She could feel the warmth of sun on her face. At her feet was a half-finished painting. Foolish dreaming, but it didn't hurt, did it? Just for a minute, to escape, to dream?

Chapter Twenty Four

The next day Catrin got out of bed resolved that she would try and get the article for her father's website done. It was one of those things hanging on in her head. She just needed to get it finished. She took Safi outside. Under her arm she carried a notebook and pen. She opened it to a clean page and put the heading: 'Aled, the architect'. Not very inspiring, but she would return to that. She wrote some things about him making models as a child, the drawings he'd done in churches they had visited. It didn't flow because, when she closed her eyes and remembered Aled, he was always running, climbing, playing sport. He wasn't still that often.

She quickly moved on to university. She knew he'd got a first, done very well. He had worked with some firms in London. She would have to get the names of them from her father. Then he had gone to America. Catrin had seen so little of him in those years. But then they had never been that close. She sat staring at the almost-empty page, then she glanced out at Worm's Head. It was very clear this morning. It looked very close. Why had Aled gone there that night? Then she thought about Elizabeth. Of course, she had known him in America, and she knew what was in his mind the night he died. Catrin could ask her now. Maybe if she understood some of these things, she could write this silly article, but more importantly actually understand what had happened.

Catrin went in to make coffee. The front door bell rang. Catrin opened it to find Elizabeth, immaculate as usual, standing on the doorstep.

'Hi, you're early.'

'Yes. I have some exciting plans.'

'Well, come in. Come through to the garden. Bethan is asleep in bed, I'm afraid.'

'That's OK. There's something I want to ask you first, anyway.'

They went out together. Catrin watched Elizabeth sit rather gingerly on the edge of a wobbly metal seat.

'Actually, I have something to ask you as well,' said Catrin.

'Really? OK. Well, you go first,' said Elizabeth.

Catrin felt rather like she was being interviewed, but plunged straight in.

'I hope you don't mind me asking, but could I ask you some things about Aled?'

Elizabeth stiffened, but she replied, 'Of course.'

'I was wondering about his time in America. I mean, what sort of work was he doing? What did people say about him? I have to write something for Dad, you see, and I realise I don't know anything about him at that time. He never came home or phoned or anything.'

'Well, I only knew him for a while. I was a bit star-struck, you know. He was very good-looking, always joking around–'

'But he was outstanding as an architect?'

'I didn't know much about that side of things.'

'Your father would have–'

'Dad didn't talk about work to me much. Actually, I think he didn't quite approve of some of the younger architects at the firm. Aled was part of that group.'

'Why was that?'

'He said they were too busy out partying. You have to realise my father was very religious. He never drank or anything.'

'But you still went out with Aled?'

'Yes. My father thought I was going out with a friend for coffee and suchlike, but actually I was going out with Aled.'

'And what did you do?'

'We'd go out for drinks. He had a flat. I'd go round there sometimes.'

'That doesn't sound that wild.'

'Well, he had another life, apart from me. He went on to other parties later, after I'd gone. They were a bit heavier. They played poker and things.'

'Gosh. I hadn't realised my brother was leading such a colourful life. I assumed it was sport or work.'

'Oh, no. He definitely was involved in more than that.'

'Right. So he was popular?'

'Oh, yes.'

'Do you know how he felt about coming back to England? I mean, it sounds like he was having a good time out there.'

'I was very surprised when I read that he had come back. He told me that he liked being away from the pressure of home.'

'But my father made a lot of trips over there–'

'Yes, but Aled was pretty good at avoiding him.'

'But he came back–'

'Yes. I didn't see him until the party. I heard about it on the grapevine.'

'You hadn't told him you were pregnant?'

'No. I didn't realise for ages and, when I did, I sort of froze. I did try phoning him at the office but got no reply. I gave up hope. I was planning adoption when I heard he was back in the UK. I decided to come and see him.'

'Dad told me he was thrilled about the baby. I'm so sorry. It was tragic that he got killed that night.'

Elizabeth frowned. 'You think Aled wanted the baby?'

'Of course.'

'I'm sorry, but he didn't. He was very upset about it.'

Catrin scowled. 'I think you must be confused. No, he definitely wanted to get married. He'd have been a wonderful father,'

Elizabeth opened her mouth to speak, but stopped herself.

'By the way,' said Catrin, missing the hesitation, 'Did you know that he had a row with my mother? Have you any idea what that was about?'

'Maybe something to do with money.'

'Money?'

'Yes, he said she was, well I won't say his actual words, but he said it was terrible that his own mother wouldn't help him.'

'Help him with what?'

'I don't know.' Elizabeth was looking around, fidgeting.

'What did he say?'

Elizabeth frowned. 'I can't remember. I fell. I blacked out.'

Catrin shook her head with irritation.

'Look, it's not my place to tell you this. Ask your father. He knows.'

Catrin realised Elizabeth wasn't going to tell her anything else.

She sighed and asked, 'So what was it you wanted to ask me?'

'I've been really lucky. I've managed to get tickets for a band I know Bethan would really like to see.'

'Oh, really? When is it for?'

'Tomorrow afternoon, the London Festival Hall. I was hoping it would be alright with you for me to take Bethan up with me tonight to stay at my house, and go to the concert.'

Elizabeth watched Catrin's smile fade into a frown. She had expected Catrin to be nervous. She was, after all, a very clingy woman, but nothing had prepared her for Catrin's reaction.

'No. No way is Bethan going away. You kept her out really late last night. And what were you doing taking her to a cocktail bar?'

'I didn't let her drink. It was fine. And this is only one night.'

'Yesterday, you took her off for the day and spent all that money on her, and now you're proposing to cart her off to London. Well, the answer is 'No'. No way is she going away with you.'

Elizabeth sat up straight. 'Look, Catrin. What harm can it do? Be reasonable. Bethan will love it. You can come as well if you want to, although I've only got two tickets for the concert.'

'Of course I can't come. Bethan would hate that. It's not like she's a child.'

'Exactly. You need to let go a bit, Catrin.'

'It's nothing to do with that. Bethan is my responsibility, and I am saying 'No'.'

'But that's ridiculous.'

'I don't care what you think.'

'So, does Bethan get a say in this?'

Elizabeth saw Catrin cross her arms tightly, her mouth clamped shut, defiant. But there were tears in her eyes.

'Look, Catrin, I haven't come to take Bethan away from you. I mean, I couldn't if I tried. You're her mother, but have you any idea what her birthdays are usually like for me? I spend them crying, grieving. Let me spoil her just this once. I thought Bethan would hate me, but she doesn't. I'll be back in work next week, but at least I can see her a bit before that.'

'But you can't just drop in for a week in her life and then forget about her again. That's not fair. What do you plan after this?'

'Why do we need plans?'

'For God's sake. You sound like Bethan, but you're not eighteen. You're an adult. You should behave like one.'

Elizabeth froze with anger. 'How dare you speak to me like that? How can you be so condescending?'

At this point, Bethan walked into the garden. She was wearing new jeans and a new top.

'Elizabeth, you're here. I didn't know,' she said. Looking at Catrin she asked, 'Is something the matter, Mum?'

Elizabeth waited. She wondered what Catrin was going to do. She was surprised when Catrin explained exactly what Elizabeth had proposed.

'The thing is, Bethan I don't think you should go.'

'But why? Mum, it would be so exciting to see Elizabeth's house, and it would be fantastic to see the band.'

'You've heard of them then?'

'Yes. The lead guitarist is Deaf. The band collaborate and experiment to write songs that are authentically from the perspective of Deaf musicians. They experiment with all kinds of sounds and vibrations. Their aim is to reach both Deaf and hearing audiences. Mum, they are a one off. I really should hear them. I've seen them on YouTube, but they've been sold out for months.'

'Elizabeth, how on earth did you get tickets?'

'We were just lucky. Maybe they were a cancellation.'

'That's amazing. Please Mum. Let me go. Please say 'Yes'.'

Elizabeth could see that Catrin was starting to weaken.

'Look, I have my phone–'

'There's the audition–'

'I'll have her back late Thursday night,' said Elizabeth. 'We'll come straight out of the concert and drive back.'

'Mum. It's one night, please.'

Elizabeth took out her phone. 'This is my house.' She handed the phone to Catrin, who scrolled through the pictures. 'Bethan can text you as often as she wants. As I say, if you, or Lowri, want to come, that would be fine.'

Catrin sat back and sighed. 'Well, I suppose it would be OK.'

Bethan kissed her mother, then ran inside quickly, threw some things in a bag, and was back before Catrin could change her mind.

Lloyd came out into the garden. 'What's all this noise about? Oh, Elizabeth–'

'I'm going to London. We're going to stay away for a night at Elizabeth's,' said Bethan, breathlessly.

'What?' Lloyd looked at Catrin.

'I said she could go, Dad.'

'Really? I don't think that is on. What about the audition?''

'We'll be back tomorrow night,' explained Bethan.

'Now, hang on,' said Lloyd. 'You need to practice for your audition.'

'I think Bethan has a right to spend a day with Elizabeth,' said Catrin. 'I have her phone number and address. Elizabeth, I think it is best if you just go now.'

Elizabeth was surprised, but also impressed, at Catrin standing up to her father.

'Well, OK. Fine. Good. OK, Bethan?'

Bethan hugged Catrin. 'Love you, Mum.'

Elizabeth looked down. It hurt. She knew it shouldn't, but it did nevertheless.

'Love you too,' said Catrin, tears in her eyes.

'But–' began Lloyd.

'No, Dad. Leave it,' shouted Catrin.

He stopped. He looked stunned at her outburst.

'What?'

'I said, leave it, Dad. Bethan is going.'

Elizabeth looked over at Bethan, who grinned.

'Come on, then. We'll have to walk down to the B & B. My car is back there. I'll have to let Angela know I'll be away for a night.'

Catrin watched them leave the garden, then heard the front door slam. Lloyd turned on her, and, grabbing her arm, said, 'If we lose her, you're to blame.'

Catrin shook him off, and sat back down on the chair. Her father stormed into the house. Safi jumped up on to her lap. She sat stroking his ears and he cuddled into her. She was sure there were things Elizabeth wasn't telling her. She was also worried about Bethan going off. Had she made the wrong decision? She hardly knew Elizabeth, but how could she have said 'no'? She turned her phone on and immediately she saw that she had missed a message from Gareth. It read:

'Ring me, it's urgent. Gareth.'

Chapter Twenty Five

Catrin looked at her phone again. The message had been sent at six that morning. She stared at the phone. She tried ringing Gareth back, and sent a text, but he didn't respond. What else could she do?

Lowri appeared from the house.

'Alright, Mum?'

'Fine,' Catrin said automatically, trying to smile.

'I saw Bethan going off with Elizabeth.'

Catrin explained what had happened. 'I hope I did the right thing letting her go. Do you think she's alright?'

'I'm sure she is. She's growing up, you know.'

'She's not eighteen yet.'

'She will be a week Saturday. She'll keep in touch. Bethan and I looked up stuff about Elizabeth online. It's surprising how much is out there when you have a name. We even found pictures of the school she'd been to and everything.'

'Good God. You both know a lot more about her than I do.'

'She seems OK. Very materialistic, though. Still, I don't think that will bother Bethan.'

Catrin was about to go inside to phone Gareth, when Lowri said, awkwardly, 'The thing is, Mum, there's something I need to talk to you about.'

Catrin was torn. She was desperate to know what was the matter with Gareth. On the other hand, Lowri so seldom asked for her time that it didn't feel right to put her off. She sat back in her seat.

'Of course. What's it about?'

Lowri scratched the end of her nose, a nervous habit she'd had since childhood.

'It's OK. You can tell me.'

'OK. Well, I have been thinking of taking a year out of my medical studies.'

'Gosh, really? Are you allowed to do that?'

'Well, it's not encouraged, but I have heard of people doing it. Someone recently went to America. She worked as a phlebotomist for a year.'

'Went abroad? You'd want to do that?'

'Yes.'

'But why take a break? It'll make your training even longer.'

'I know. But the thing is, Mum, I'm really tired. It was full on getting the grades at A levels, and it's been so intense since. I need to stop. I need to know this is the right thing for me.'

'So you could give up?'

'I don't think so, but I need a break from study.'

'Gosh. Have you talked to Dad about this?'

'I have. He seemed to think it was a good idea.'

'And have you talked to the university?'

'Just put out feelers. I think they might let me do it next year.'

'And you'd go abroad?'

'Yes. I'd like to go to a developing country. I could get funding for that from a charity.'

'It's a huge thing and, well, it could be dangerous. Some of these places are unstable. You could get ill.'

'I would be careful, Mum. It's just, if I don't do it now, when will I?'

'What about Mark?'

'I don't know. He might be able to come. He was thinking about it. He has asked if he could have a year's sabbatical.'

244

'You're that serious?'

'I think so, yes.'

Catrin saw her blush.

'It would be exciting, Mum.'

'You'd be gone for a whole year?'

'Yes.'

'You might want to go back again when you've finished training?'

'Possibly. I really don't know. What do you think?'

Catrin looked at her daughter: her face alight. She saw an excitement and a youthfulness she hadn't seen for a long time.

'I think, love, that you should go for it.'

'Are you sure?'

'Lowri, I'd love you to live next door to me for the rest of my life, but that's not right for you, is it? You should go and do this if that is where your heart is.'

Lowri hugged her mother.

'Oh, thank you, Mum. I'll tell Mark. He'll be so pleased.'

At that moment, there was a shout from the pavement outside. It came from David and Anwen. They came into the garden.

'Hi. How are you all?' asked Anwen.

'Come in for coffee,' shouted Lowri. 'I've got some exciting news.'

They came into the garden. David approached Lowri, who started to tell him all about her plans. Anwen, however, hung back. She looked at Catrin, who was looking at her phone.

'Are you OK?'

'It's been a stressful morning, so far.'

'Good to see Lowri looking so happy.'

'Yes. The thing is, I've had a strange message from Gareth.'

Catrin handed her the phone.

'What ever is the matter?'

'I don't know. I wonder if it's his sister, Jill. Maybe she's ill. I can't get through to him.'

'Why didn't he say?'

'I don't know. I have no idea what the matter is. I have so much I need to talk to him about, and he never answers his bloody phone. Look, I'm just going inside. I need to have a bit of space to think.'

Catrin left the others in the garden and went into the house, closely followed by Safi. She took herself upstairs, sat on the edge of her bed, and tried to calm down. She tried ringing Gareth again, but again his phone went through to voicemail. She tried the house, but the same happened there. There was a quiet knock at the door. Anwen came in.

'You don't have to talk, but is there anything I could do to help?'

Catrin shook her head. 'No, it's OK.'

'I don't think it is.'

Catrin sighed and found herself telling Anwen about Bethan, her father, and Gareth.

'God, families eh?' said Anwen. 'Can't live with them, can't live without the beggars.'

Catrin smiled faintly. 'Quite. It's been one thing after another: Bethan and Elizabeth; Lowri going away. In the old days Gareth and I would work together on all this. But lately, I feel like I have to do everything on my own. I don't know what the matter is.'

'You and Gareth need to talk, particularly with this message.'

'I've been trying to, but he won't answer.'

'Maybe you need to talk face to face.'

'I would if he would come back here.'

'Well, you could always go there.'

'Oh, no. I can't leave.'

'Why not?'

'Well, what if Bethan needs me?'

'You said she's gone off with Elizabeth. She has her phone, and we are all here. She can phone you any time. It's really not far to Cardiff, you know.'

'But Safi–'

'Why not leave him here with us? He could even come and stay if you need to be away for the night. It would be lovely to have him,' said Anwen.

Catrin frowned. 'Well–'

'Seriously, I know what I'm doing with dogs. I love them.'

'You have cats–'

'They'll be fine. Really, I'd love it. You can just come and get him when you're back. Give me your mobile number.'

Catrin gave it to her.

'Are you sure?'

'Go on. You go and find Gareth.'

'But Dad, Lowri–'

'I'll sort all them out. You could do with getting dressed,' said Anwen, smiling.

'Oh, God. I'm still in my pyjamas.'

'It's alright, but maybe not for travelling. You just go, OK? We'll all be fine.'

Catrin felt enormously relieved that someone else for once seemed to take over.

'Thank you so much,' she said.

Anwen left her to get ready.

Catrin showered, dressed, and packed a few things in case she needed to stay away for a night, although she hardly needed to as she would be at home. She went downstairs. Anwen looked out of the kitchen window.

'They're all in the garden. I'm making coffee.'

'Will you tell Dad where I've gone?'

'Fine. Off you go.'

Catrin was enormously grateful that she didn't need to speak to anyone. She smiled gratefully at Anwen and left the house.

It was another beautiful morning. As she drove over the downs, the view over Gower was stunning. The sun on the heather highlighted blues and purples. The yellow gorse shone. By the time she reached the major roads they were getting busy. Her mind was trying to sift through the possibilities of the message from Gareth. Maybe he was lying dying in hospital after a car crash? Maybe his sister was ill, or had been in an accident? Why hadn't he said, though? Maybe he was at home in bed ill? What else could it be? Maybe he was leaving her? It was possible. What would she do? She'd be alone, and know he was with someone else, that he'd chosen someone else over her. On a practical level, how would she look after herself? Catrin put the radio on to try and stop her mind building and knocking down Jenga towers of scenarios but, as hard as she tried, she couldn't stop her mind racing.

Elizabeth had driven over the downs out of Gower. Now that she had won the battle, she was nervous. Suddenly, Bethan was her responsibility, and it frightened her. Of course, Bethan wasn't a child but, sitting next to her in the car, she suddenly looked very young. Elizabeth was also growing more aware of the shortcomings in her communication skills. She had guessed that yesterday she had signed some things wrong and had also found it far more tiring than she cared to admit. It was why she had suggested the cinema: at least she could just sit there. Still, it was just going to be the concert. Nothing more. It was also very tempting to show Bethan her life in London, what she had made of herself. She wanted Bethan to be impressed with her. It was only one night: there was no reason they should meet anyone. Then she would take Bethan back to her family. Bethan would understand about not visiting her in London again. She liked Bethan. She was older, more grown up than Elizabeth had expected, and it had been great fun shopping yesterday.

'Mum and Grandad won't mind too much, will they?' Bethan asked.

Elizabeth glanced at her. She suddenly looked younger again, here away from her family.

'Oh, no.'

'I don't want to hurt them.'

'They'll be OK.'

Elizabeth turned on Radio Four. Bethan groaned.

'What's the matter?'

'Well, I can't hear most of what they're saying, and what I understand is boring. But don't worry. I'll listen to my iPod.'

They drove on in silence.

Elizabeth eventually pulled in at one of the services. She ordered them both coffees without asking Bethan. As she put down the drink, Bethan asked, 'Can I have a cold drink?'

'Oh. I got you a skinny cappuccino. It's what you wanted yesterday.'

'I don't fancy it today.'

'Oh, well. Go and get something else.'

She saw Bethan was waiting.

'What's wrong?'

'It's not that. Mum would normally pay.'

249

'Oh, right.'

'It doesn't matter. I've got money. Are you having something to eat?' Bethan asked.

'God, no.'

'Really?'

'You can.'

'Oh, no. I'm fine.'

They sat with their drinks. Elizabeth was aware of people looking at Bethan and her signing to each other. She had noticed it the day before in Swansea. It was disconcerting. She didn't like being stared at.

'It feels weird being away from Mum,' said Bethan. Again, Elizabeth was struck by how young she sounded. It was very confusing: one minute she was so grown up, the next so needy.

'You go to university in September. You have to get used to it.'

'I know, but my parents are saying I have to live at home. I suppose for you, going to boarding school, it was normal. How old were you when you went?' asked Bethan.

'About eight.'

'That's so young. Where were your parents?'

'My parents lived in New York, but Mum was from London. It's why I was sent to school there.'

'So when did you see them?'

'The summer, sometimes Christmas. I had an aunt in Cardiff.'

'Didn't you mind?'

'It was OK. I had lots of friends, and a lot of their parents were abroad. We had loads of clubs and things to do.'

'And on your birthday?'

'The school would let you choose. My parents paid. We went dry slope skiing. Shows and things. It was great.'

'That's amazing. Lowri and I usually had swimming parties, and then we went into the café at the leisure centre for burger and chips. When we were older, I would take a few friends to the cinema and then to Pizza Express after. That kind of thing.'

'You had all your music.'

'Oh, yes. Loads of time spent practising, and then there were lessons and exams. I used to get really nervous, though, and there were all the extra speech lessons.'

'That must have been tiring. Did your parents make you work hard at school?'

'Not really. They didn't mind what we did as long as we were happy. The only pressure was from Grandad. He was paying a lot of money for the extra tuition. He always looked so uptight at concerts, always looked at my marks for exams and things.'

'My parents were strict. They were paying a lot of money. They wanted me to be very good.'

Elizabeth saw the look of surprise on Bethan's face. They had experienced very different upbringings. Elizabeth remembered it was one of the things she and Aled had talked about. It was something they had had in common. So few people went to boarding school that it was a relief sometimes to meet someone else who had. She had had the impression, though, that she had enjoyed it more than Aled, although he had been far more successful. She had wondered why he had never been head boy. He had sounded the sort who would. Looking over at Bethan, Elizabeth could see very little of her father in her, and she was pleased about that.

Catrin arrived back in Cardiff just after lunch. It felt very strange to be back in the city. Gower seemed like another planet, and all the things that had happened some kind of dream. She went home first. As she drove up to the house, Gareth's car wasn't there: obviously he was at work. She went into the silent hallway.

'Gareth,' she shouted, but there was no answer. She walked down to the neat modern kitchen at the back of the house. On the work top were two used dinner plates, two wine glasses, an empty bottle of wine and the rubbish from various takeaways. She frowned and automatically started to tidy up. Looking in the fridge, she noticed nothing, including the lasagne she had left, had been touched. She guessed Gareth had been living on take away. Catrin went upstairs, tidied the bed, put the dirty washing in the basket and went back downstairs. So what was she to do now? She tried his mobile: no answer. Then she thought of Jill, his sister. Gareth wasn't that close to his sister. They seemed silently to compete with each other as to who was busiest, her as a vicar, or him as a doctor. As a result, neither seemed to have the time to see each other. Catrin didn't even have Jill's number on her mobile, but it was stored on the house phone. She tried it.

Gareth's sister answered. 'St Sebastian's vicarage.'

'Hi Jill, its Catrin.'

'Oh, hi. How are you?'

'I'm OK. I'm just checking you're all well?'

'We're fine. Stressed from too much work but, apart from that, all OK.'

'Oh good.' Catrin paused. She wanted to ring off now, but realised that would be rather abrupt.

'I've just come back from Gower. We're sorting The Dragon House out.'

'Oh, that must be a big job.'

'Mm.'

'So, how's my brother?'

'Actually, I'm trying to track him down.'

'He'll be at work, won't he?' Catrin could hear a patient, slight condescension in her sister in law's voice.

'He could be. I was just checking if you'd heard from him.'

'No. Is everything alright?' Jill asked again.

'Yes, fine. I had a strange message from him. That's all.'

'What do you mean?'

'Oh, it's nothing. Look, forget I rang, Jill. I'll go into the surgery. I'm sure he'll be there.'

'OK, but you will phone me if there is anything wrong, won't you?'

'Of course. Right, I'd better go.'

Catrin put the telephone down, wishing she had never made the call. She tried Gareth again on his mobile. No reply. Maybe he was seeing a patient?

Catrin drove to the surgery and parked in the street outside. She could see people entering and leaving. It was always busy, and this was prime time for the elderly and people with young children. She went to the desk, and cringed. Oh, no, it had to be her.

'Morning, Jasmine,' she said, trying to sound casual.

'Good morning, Catrin. How are you? I hope you found your husband the other day. These men, eh? Have to keep them on a tight leash.'

Catrin tried to laugh. 'I just wanted to see Gareth. Maybe when he's finished with his patient?'

'But he's not in this morning. He said he'd be in about three to do paper work, I think.'

Catrin cursed herself for not checking for his car in the car park: now she looked really stupid.

'Oh, right.'

'I can try to phone Gareth's mobile for you,' offered Jasmine.

Catrin was feeling very humiliated.

'No, don't worry. I can do that. I've been to the Gower to see my Dad,' she added, as if that somehow explained things.

'Lovely on a day like this,' said Jasmine.

'Right,' Catrin cringed. She was aware of people tutting behind her, the phones ringing. 'I'd better go. Sorry to bother you. Thanks.'

As quickly as she could manage, she manoeuvred her way through the pushchairs and left the building. Catrin quailed at the embarrassment of confessing to Jasmine that she had no idea where her husband was, and decided that it would be best simply to go back to the house.

Catrin waited there until after three in the afternoon. She kept phoning Gareth, but got no reply. In the end, she summoned up all her courage and rang the surgery, praying that Jasmine didn't answer. Her prayers were not answered.

'Hello again, Catrin. Still trying to track down Gareth?'

'Well, yes,' she had to confess. 'I assumed he'd be there now.'

'We thought so too. He hasn't got a patient list this afternoon. He did say he'd be in to do paper work but, the thing is, he hasn't arrived. He may be up at the hospital, though, now I think about it.'

'Why's that?'

'Well, he's doing this research–'

'Of course. I know about that,' Catrin added, feeling foolish.

'It's a shame Carol isn't in. She'd be able to tell you.'

Catrin gritted her teeth. 'Well, I think I'll have to wait and see. Sorry to have been such a nuisance.'

'That's OK. Hope you track him down. I don't know, these husbands. We need to keep them on a tight leash, don't we?' joked Jasmine again. This was obviously a favourite line of hers.

Catrin put the phone down quickly, glad to get away from Jasmine, and wondered what she was going to do next.

Chapter Twenty Six

Elizabeth and Bethan arrived at the London house at about six in the evening.

'Wow, this is amazing,' said Bethan as they entered. 'It's really cool. It's lovely; so white and clean.'

Elizabeth took Bethan upstairs and showed her the ensuite. On the glass shelf was a row of designer products.

'It's really posh.'

Elizabeth was pleased to see Bethan so impressed with her home. She said 'I'll change, and then we can go out to eat.'

'Oh, what shall I wear?'

'You look fine as you are.'

Elizabeth had been trying to decide where to take Bethan. She didn't want to over-awe her with somewhere too expensive but, on the other hand, she refused to go to some chain restaurant. She remembered a small Italian restaurant she sometimes went to with Richard, phoned, and booked a table. Just before they left the house Bethan asked,

'Are you sure I look OK?'

'Of course.'

'Where's the car?'

'Oh no, not here. We can walk.'

Bethan walked along the hectic streets wide-eyed, 'It's so exciting, so many people.'

'Haven't you been to London before?'

'Once with school. It's not Mum and Dad's sort of place. We used to go to France for trips when I was little.'

They arrived and were shown to a table. The maitre'd knew Elizabeth and greeted her effusively, adding, 'I never knew you had a daughter. She is as beautiful as you.'

Elizabeth gasped. She hadn't expected anyone to jump to that conclusion. She glanced hurriedly around. Elizabeth picked up the menu, then heard a roar of laughter from a table close by. She realised it was a group of people from an auction house she dealt with regularly. Fortunately, they didn't seem to be looking her way.

'Let's order quickly,' she said to Bethan. 'I usually have the Bucatini with Marinara and Ricotta.

Bethan was smiling at her, but she did not reply.

'Is that what you'd like?'

Bethan kept the same fixed smile.

'What's the matter?'

Still the same smile. Elizabeth felt irritated. What was the matter? She realised she had stopped signing. It was quite gloomy, and very noisy, where they were sitting.

'Sorry,' she signed.

'It's OK.'

'I usually have this one,' Elizabeth said pointing to the dish.

Bethan nodded. 'OK. That would be fine'.

The waiter came over to take their order.

'Oh, what would you like to drink?' asked Elizabeth

'I'll have orange and passion fruit,' Bethan said to the waiter.

The waiter looked at her blankly, and then at Elizabeth.

'You know what she said,' Elizabeth told him, angrily.

'Sorry. She's deaf, isn't she?'

'Yes, so?'

He shrugged, and looked back at Bethan, who repeated her order. Elizabeth asked for a glass of red wine. When he had gone, she looked at Bethan.

'How ignorant can you get?'

'I've had worse. One waiter asked me if a needed a menu in Braille.'

'Good grief.'

'You get used to it.'

'It's awful. It can't have been easy growing up.'

'Well, my Mum always supported me. She always said I could do anything I wanted and no one was to stop me. I watched her fight for me. Like, I had lots of problems with ear infections and ear moulds but she kept taking me back to appointments to sort things out. Another time, when I was about ten, I lost my brand new hearing aids when I went ice-skating. At the hospital they threatened to replace those with cheap ones, but Mum wouldn't let them.'

'I'm surprised. She doesn't look the sort.'

'Oh she is. She would fight anyone for me and Lowri.'

'I'm glad she's been such a good mother.'

'Oh, yes. She's amazing. We always come first.'

'Good,' said Elizabeth, moving to more familiar ground. 'I thought tomorrow morning we could hit Oxford Street.'

'Great. There's a huge Topshop there.'

'You want to go there again?'

'Oh, yes. It's meant to be brilliant. We can spend the morning there.'

'Oh, great,' said Elizabeth, with very little enthusiasm.

As they walked back to the house after the meal Elizabeth wondered how she was meant to occupy Bethan. However, once back Bethan was content to mess about on her new phone, buying apps, and talking to friends.

'I'm going to watch this,' said Elizabeth, holding up a boxed set of Sex and the City. 'Is that OK?'

'Great. Can you put on subtitles?'

'Oh, yes. Richard can't stand it.'

'Who?'

'R-i-c-h-a-r-d, a friend, he hates this.'

'Is Richard an art collector like you?'

'No, he's a music agent.'

'Gosh.'

'He's not Zac Freestone. He works with classical musicians.'

'Wow, that amazing. So is your gallery near here?'

'Not far.'

'I'd love to see it.'

Elizabeth hesitated. 'Maybe.'

'I'd better text Mum, tell her I'm OK.'

'You talk to your mother a lot. I never did with mine. I maybe phoned every week or so. I suppose things are different now, with mobiles.'

'I'd hate that. I like to talk to Mum. Sometimes we text while I'm at school during the break or something.'

'Does she expect you to do that?'

'No. I just want to.'

Elizabeth shrugged. 'Well, you'd better text her now.'

'I'll send her some pics of the house as well. She'll be really impressed.'

Elizabeth was feeling her privacy slipping away, but didn't comment. She poured herself a drink. She sat back in her armchair, and looked over at the cat flap. 'I have a cat, you know.'

'Really?'

'She's in the cattery this week, but she's a stray who adopted me.'

'I like cats, but Lowri is allergic, so we can't have one.'

'But you have a dog?'

'Yes. She's OK with them. That's why she got Safi for Mum for her birthday.'

'So, Lowri said she's training to be a doctor like your father?'

'Yes, she's like Dad. Really conscientious. She could become a workaholic like him.'

'Doesn't your mother mind your father always working?'

'She's used to it. She has me and Lowri to think about. And she's had various jobs herself, washing up and things.'

'Hasn't she ever wanted to have a career?'

'She hasn't got many qualifications. She's happy looking after us all.'

Elizabeth frowned. 'She probably thinks I am odd not having a husband and children.'

'She doesn't judge people much.'

'What has she said about me?'

'Not much. She said she hadn't met you, and, well, she didn't know much. Of course, then we thought you were dead.'

Elizabeth blanched at the bluntness of it. 'Were you upset that I was dead?'

Bethan frowned. 'I don't remember ever crying. I didn't know you to miss you. I did wonder what you looked like and things, though, and, of course, I wondered how you could give me away. It's not like you were poor.'

Elizabeth heard the unmistakable tone of accusation. 'It was very difficult. My parents would not have approved of me being pregnant and not married. They were very religious.'

'But even religious people don't mind nowadays, do they?'

'My parents did.'

'Oh. Did you say they are dead now?'

'Yes.'

'You never told them about me; they never knew they had a granddaughter?''

'No.' Elizabeth cringed.

'Why didn't you have an abortion?'

Elizabeth was feeling increasingly like she was being interrogated.

'No. I found out I was pregnant at six months.'

'So you would have had one?' Bethan was sat forward, watching her intently.

'I don't know. I don't think so. My upbringing–'

'So, how didn't you know? You must have been huge.'

'My periods had always been all over the place, and I stayed very small.'

'So, if you'd married Aled, would that have made it alright?'

'I thought so. It's why I went to the party. I'd heard he was back in England. I hadn't been able to tell him I was pregnant.'

'Why not?'

'I tried, but he didn't answer my messages. I'd given up, I suppose, until I heard he was back here.'

'So, what were you thinking of doing with me before the party?'

'I had already decided I was going to have you adopted.'

Bethan sat back, and spoke more quietly, 'So you were never going to keep me?'

Elizabeth shook her head. 'I'm sorry. No, not unless Aled had wanted to marry me.'

'But he did. Mum said. He wanted to marry you. He wanted me. It's so sad he died.'

Elizabeth was torn. She didn't want to hurt Bethan, and shatter her illusions, but she didn't want to lie either.

'I can't talk about this now.'

Bethan looked very frustrated. Then Elizabeth remembered something: maybe it would help. She took the photograph out of her bag, and passed it to Bethan.

'This is the photo I showed you before. I carry it with me all the time. I never wanted to forget you.' She saw Bethan blink back tears. 'You see, it wasn't that I didn't care. I just couldn't keep you.'

'What was I like? You know, when I was born?'

'You were tiny. A few weeks early, but you had black hair and very intense eyes, like you knew exactly what was going on. Your hands were tiny and in fists. You looked quite angry sometimes, but you were lovely. All the nurses used to say what a beautiful baby you were.'

'So, it was hard giving me away?'

'Of course. I can honestly say it was the worst day of my life.'

'You never wrote, never even sent me a card?'

'I thought it was best for you, for both of us to have a fresh start.'

'If I'd known you were alive, I could have contacted you. We could have been seeing each other.'

Elizabeth bit her lip. She liked to think she would be as honest as she could.

'Look, I'm very independent. I haven't married, or had kids, because I'm not that sort.'

'So you haven't missed me?'

'Sometimes, but I've tried not to dwell on it. I have a great life; travelling, no ties. It suits me. I know it sounds selfish, but it's the way I am.'

'I wondered about you a lot. Now you hear them talk about genetic diseases you can inherit, like that breast cancer gene. Well, I just didn't know.'

'Oh God, I never thought of that.'

'I did.'

'Well, my mother didn't have cancer. I have never had any tests or anything, and all my routine check-ups are fine.'

'That's quite a relief, actually. It's a shame you can't tell me anything about why I was born Deaf, but I'm still pleased your mother was Deaf. I'd have liked to have met her.'

'I'm sorry.' Elizabeth looked down, and felt another pang of guilt about her mother. She had only thought about how important it was for her parents not to know about Bethan. She had never thought about how her child would feel about them, or even that they would have been grandparents. It was a shock to be made to think about it now.

Bethan looked back at Elizabeth. 'I'm glad we've found each other, aren't you? We can have lots of times like this. I've put my choices down for uni but, I was thinking, I could try and go through clearing for a London university. I could live here with you. It would be really cool, and Mum wouldn't worry so much if she knew I was living somewhere safe.'

Elizabeth panicked. 'No. I mean, I don't think that would be a good idea. I'm very busy. I work long hours.

You need to share with other students, people your own age.'

She glanced at Bethan who, to her horror, had tears in her eyes.

'You don't want me to live with you, then?'

'It's not personal. I told you: I'm very independent.'

Bethan scowled. 'My Mum would do anything to keep me living back home with her.'

'But you wouldn't want to be with older people. You need to get out and find your own friends.'

'Mum wants me to stay living at home for my first year.'

'What about this audition?'

'I don't know. I'm really torn. It would be a long way to go. Mum doesn't want me to go, but it's a chance in a million. All my friends are so jealous, and it means a lot to Grandad.'

'And what do you want to do?'

Bethan shrugged. 'I don't know. If I came here, I wouldn't have to choose.'

'I don't think that would work. Let's just take things slowly.'

They both sat in an uneasy silence.

'It's a bit late for a DVD, I think I could do with going to bed,' Elizabeth said.

Bethan nodded. Elizabeth could see that she was upset, but couldn't think what to say.

'Can I have a glass of water to take up?' asked Bethan.

'Of course,' Elizabeth replied, then realised that Bethan was waiting for her to get it.

'Oh, right. Hang on.' She got the drink, and added, 'In the morning, if you wake early, come down and get drinks and things. There are cereals in the cupboard, milk in the fridge. I'll probably get up about half seven.'

Bethan went to her room, Elizabeth to hers. As she meticulously removed her make-up, she looked at her reflection in the mirror. This was all becoming very complicated. Bethan was such a strange mixture: one minute she seemed like a young woman. And then, something would be said or happen, and she regressed into a vulnerable young child. It was confusing, and quite exhausting. She would have to watch things with her. It was just tomorrow. They would shop. Yes, she would buy her lots of really good quality presents, go to the concert, and then back to the Gower in the evening. That way there would be no complications. Yes, it should all be fine.

Chapter Twenty Seven

Catrin sat alone in the house in Cardiff. There were so many things she could do while she waited: gardening, ironing; there was always something. However, somehow, she didn't feel she could do anything. It didn't even really feel like her home. When she became hungry she found herself biscuits, cheese and a Mars bar. She put the television on just for some background noise, then phoned Lowri. Catrin told her not to worry, but said that she would be staying the night in Cardiff.

'Is Dad alright?'

'I haven't caught up with him yet, but I'm sure he's fine. Now, there's plenty of food up there. Make sure everybody eats. I'll send David and Anwen a text to hold on to Safi. I think Anwen might rather like that.'

Catrin sent a text message to David and another to Bethan. After this, she sat and stared at the television. The evening dragged on. It was still light. Sometimes she found summer evenings unnerving: they went on so long, when she wanted to close the curtains and settle down. She glanced at the time: only eight o'clock, but it felt so much later. Catrin was watching a programme about embarrassing health problems, wondering what on earth possessed anyone to appear on it, when she heard Gareth's car on the driveway. Her heart raced. It was stupid, but she felt nervous. Catrin went to the front door to let him in. He looked shocked to see her.

'What are you doing here? What's happened?'

'Where have you been? I've been desperately trying to track you down.'

'Why? What's happened?'

266

'I came because of your message.'

'What message?'

'The one that said to come urgently, that we needed to talk.'

'I never sent that.'

'You did. You phoned last night as well.'

'Oh, that. I was simply checking you were OK. You'd sounded upset, but then your Dad said you'd gone out–'

'It was nothing. Just a meal with Harri.'

'Yes, he said. So I figured that you must be alright if you'd gone out.'

'You didn't mind me going out with Harri?'

Gareth looked puzzled. 'Of course not.'

'But you did send the text.' Catrin found her phone to show him and herself that she hadn't been imagining things. Gareth read the message and shook his head. 'I didn't send that. I don't understand.' He looked again at the message. 'When was it sent?'

'Half six this morning.'

'Oh, yes. Ah, I see. Oh, no.'

'What?'

'Nothing,' he said, quickly.

Gareth sat down opposite Catrin.

'Tell me, how are things back at the Gower?'

'Lowri told me this morning about taking a year out–'

'Oh yes, good idea,' he said dismissively. 'So how is Bethan?'

'It's been really hard. I wish you'd been there. I've kept trying to phone you, and you haven't answered.'

'I'm sorry. I have to turn my phone off or I'd get nothing done.'

'I've had to make all the decisions. Now Bethan has gone to London with Elizabeth.'

'What? To live?'

'No, of course not.' Catrin frowned with irritation. 'Just to do some shopping, and go to a concert. She's staying up in Elizabeth's house for one night, then coming back tomorrow night.'

'Are you sure that was the right thing to do?'

'I don't know, but I had to make the decision on my own.'

'Is Bethan alright?'

'So far. But you know Bethan: it could all go wrong very quickly. To be honest, I didn't want her to go, but I felt I had to let her. Elizabeth is spending all this money on her. It's embarrassing. Bethan, of course, loves it all.'

'She shouldn't do that.'

'No, but I can't stop it, can I? Bethan thinks it's great. This woman can do no wrong.'

'You sound jealous.'

'Well, maybe I am a bit. I mean, it's been really hard sometimes with Bethan, yet Elizabeth gets to waltz into her life and take over.'

'I don't think Bethan is like that. She loves you, us.'

'Don't you mind?'

Gareth looked like he really was thinking about this for the first time. 'No, I don't. Of course, it's different for me. It's good for Bethan to meet her birth mother. It'll be alright.'

'But I don't know if I should have let her go to London. Elizabeth had these tickets for some concert. Bethan was so excited. I didn't know how to stop her. It just felt mean. Dad wasn't happy, but I said it was my decision.'

'Well done,' he said. 'You need to do that more often. Like on Sunday with that nonsense about

America. You should have supported me over that, you know.'

'I was confused. I didn't know what to think. You walking out didn't help, though. You should have stayed and talked to Bethan. She still has this audition on Friday, you know. Then you didn't come to the memorial. That was really tough.'

'Again, I'm sorry. God knows, I'm all over the place at the moment. Actually, I was wound up about something from earlier that evening.'

'What do you mean?'

'Something I found in your handbag.'

'What was that, then?'

'I found a packet of cigarettes.'

Catrin panicked. 'They're not mine.'

'Whose are they, then?'

'Um, Mark, Lowri's boyfriend's.'

'Now, that's odd. He said he was glad it wasn't too smoky in the pub. It set off his asthma, he said.'

'Oh, well, He really shouldn't smoke then, should he?'

'It wasn't you?'

'Of course not.'

Gareth reached down and picked up her handbag. Catrin watched, frozen, as he opened it and took out a packet of cigarettes. 'You never gave them back?'

'For God's sake, Gareth. What is this?'

'Why are you lying to me?'

'Oh, OK. They're mine. But they don't mean anything.'

'Firstly, you know it's a damn stupid thing to do–'

'It's only one or two–'

'That doesn't matter. You know how I feel about smoking, and drinking.'

'Look, it was just something to do. Going down there has stirred up all these memories, you know, about Mum and Aled.' Catrin looked away.

'What memories, Catrin?'

'Nothing.'

'What is it about your mother?' he asked, leaping on the words.

'Well, you know–'

'No, I don't do I? I'm a doctor, for goodness sake. I have a sense when people are hiding things. What are you hiding about your mother, and Aled, for that matter? I mean, nothing about the night he died adds up. You know that. I would have gone and looked it all up, found out about the inquest, but you said not to. I hoped you would tell me.'

'I don't know about Aled. Really, I don't.'

'I don't know what you know about him, but your mother. What are you hiding about her? You would slip around to your mother's when I got back from work, no explanation.'

'You really want to know about my mother?'

He nodded.

Catrin suddenly felt calm. She could remember David's words. It was time to talk. She had nothing to be ashamed of. Gareth would understand.

'Well, I'll tell you. My mother was an alcoholic.'

Gareth sat back. His eyes wide. 'She was what?'

'My mother was an alcoholic.'

Catrin saw him glance over at the photograph of his friend who'd died. 'Why didn't you tell me?'

'Because I didn't want you to despise my mother, to despise me.'

'I despise alcohol. You know that–'

'Exactly. And I lived with an alcoholic most of my life, while I was growing up.'

270

'All your life? I thought you were telling me your mother started drinking after Aled. I knew she was devastated. I did wonder what was going on.'

'It was way before that. When you and I met she was in a good patch. She really wanted to be well. She'd just come out of rehab. Not a spa holiday, like I told you. She said she wanted to be a good grandmother. I think she might have made it if hadn't been for Aled.'

'So she'd been drinking when you were a child?'

'In my teens.'

'You never told me. You should have–'

Catrin suddenly felt very angry.

'This isn't about you, Gareth. I'm trying to tell you about me, what happened to me.'

'I know, but I need time to adjust. Don't you see all the lies you told me about your childhood, your mother? You painted a whole picture of her that wasn't true.'

'But she was all the things I told you–'

'Is that why you never went to college?'

'Yes.'

'But you said you didn't want to go.'

'I know but–'

'Don't you see? Over the years, hundreds of little lies?'

Catrin glared at him. 'I'm not the only one who lies in this marriage, though, am I?'

Gareth frowned.

'Who texted me at half six this morning? Who have you been drinking wine with? Eating take away with? Was it Carol? Carol, who, unlike me, apparently, always knows what you are doing, where you are?'

'What are you insinuating? Me and Carol? For God's sake, that's ridiculous.'

'But it's not. You're never home, never want to be with me, never talk to me, didn't notice my new dress or even give me a birthday card. I came in to find two plates, two wine glasses, in the kitchen–'

'This is crazy. How can you be so stupid?'

Catrin glared at him. 'That's what you think, is it? Stupid Catrin, who never even got any A levels, who works in kitchens?'

'I never said that.'

'You don't need to.'

'Catrin, have you been drinking?'

'Don't you dare accuse me of that,' Catrin screamed.

Gareth stood up, but then grimaced. He started to breathe heavily, and seemed to stagger back.

Catrin was alarmed. She stared at him.

Gareth seemed to get his breath back. He spoke quietly. 'I can't do this now. I'm sorry. I have to go back to work.'

'What? At this time? You don't want to talk now?'

He shook his head.

'Work will always come before me, won't it?'

'I'm sorry.'

'Fine. Well, go then.'

Gareth didn't respond. He walked slowly out of the room. Catrin heard the front door close behind him and his car driven away. She looked out of the window. The close was silent. She could see televisions flickering in sitting rooms, windows, open, trying to cool their houses for the hot night ahead. There was no breeze, no distant sounds of the sea. She missed them. It was just dusk back at Gower: the sky would be preparing for another spectacular sunset. Here it was bleak and lonely. Is this how the future would be? Lowri off with Mark; Bethan

272

in New York; Gareth off with some woman, and her alone here.

Catrin looked over at a wedding photograph of herself and Gareth. She was looking nervously happy, he far more assured. She had an expression of someone who couldn't believe this was happening. Sometimes she felt that she had never really lost that feeling. Like her mother, she had often wondered if her husband would leave her. Was that about to happen? Had telling him about her mother been the final straw?

She sat down, exhausted. She was tired of worrying about everything: if only there was a way to make it all go away. Slowly, she got up and went into the kitchen. She knew that, hidden behind the bags of flour and mixed fruit, there was a bottle of vodka. It had been there since Lowri had brought it home a few years ago to use in a chocolate cake recipe. She had managed to talk Lowri out off making the cake until it had been forgotten. She had hidden the bottle at the back of the cupboard. Catrin carried the bottle to the living room and unscrewed the lid. The smell transported her straight back to her mother. The smell on her breath, memories of finding half-empty bottles hidden in cupboards, the laundry basket, behind books: all over the house. Catrin would find them and pour the contents down the sink, knowing it was hopeless. She found a glass and poured the clear liquid into it. She had never drunk vodka before. Her hand shook as she lifted the glass to her mouth. The liquid burnt her lips, made her heave, but she forced it down. She had finished that glass, and poured another. There was no pleasure in it, but she could slowly feel it seeping through her body. It was like going numb. Slowly, nothing mattered. This must have been the sunshine coming out for her mother, when she would smile as if all was right with the world. Then she would have another, and another. Often, then there would be tears. 'Never leave me,' she would say. 'I couldn't bear you to go.' And finally she would collapse.

Catrin lit a cigarette, poured some more vodka into the glass, and got up to put the television back on. As she did, she glanced over at the mirror hanging over the fireplace. What she saw staggered her. In the mirror, she didn't see herself: what she saw was her mother staring back at her.

Chapter Twenty Eight

Thursday 2nd August 2012

Elizabeth woke very early, and decided to go for a run. It was good to be in routine, seeing the familiar faces: smart, fashionable running gear, the latest smart watches. Each jogger nodded in recognition, but no smiles: running was serious business. She was surprised at how noisy it seemed: so much traffic, even at this time, and the air heavy with diesel and exhaust fumes. Still, it was familiar and safe. Elizabeth went back to her home for coffee and realised that she missed Poppy, who would normally come in now after her night's hunting. Cats were so much more straightforward than people. She and Poppy belonged here.

While she was checking her emails, she received a text from Richard. 'How are you?'

Elizabeth replied, 'Still in Gower.'

'When are you coming back?'

'Maybe Sunday.'

Elizabeth glanced at her watch, and tutted. It was nearly ten o'clock. Bethan had still not appeared. Elizabeth liked to get out early. She went to the stairs, and called Bethan quietly, but there was no reply. Then she realised Bethan had probably taken off her hearing aids. To go into Bethan's room would be too pushy, so she had to just wait.

She was trying to occupy her time scrolling through emails when Bethan finally came downstairs.

'Good morning,' Bethan said politely, shyly.

'You slept late.'

'Not really. I was speaking to friends. They all think it's so cool I'm up here. I sent them pictures of my room: they're dead jealous.'

Elizabeth was annoyed that Bethan had been upstairs texting all this time and also rather shocked at pictures of her home flying around Bethan's family and friends. She tried to hide her irritation. 'If you get on and have your breakfast, we could go.'

'OK. I'll just have toast, cereal and orange juice,' said Bethan. Elizabeth watched her sit down and start texting again, and realised Bethan was expecting her to assemble her breakfast.

'You can help yourself,' she said. Bethan looked up.

'What?'

'I said, you can help yourself.'

'Oh, right.'

Bethan got up and walked aimlessly around the kitchen area. Elizabeth gritted her teeth, but resolved that she was not going to help. Eventually, Bethan found the bread bin and asked, 'Don't you have any white bread?'

'No, I have granary.'

'Oh, Yuck. I hate all those bits. What cereals do you have?'

'They're in that cupboard. There's some granola.'

'What?'

Elizabeth heaved herself off the chair, opened the cupboard, and handed Bethan the box of granola.

'Actually, Mum usually gets in those little packets so I can have something different each day.'

'They're all full of sugar. Try the granola: it's good for you.'

Bethan sighed and poured the cereal into the bowl, looking at it as if it was mouse droppings. Elizabeth took the orange juice from the fridge, and handed her the carton. Elizabeth saw Bethan pull a face but watched her pour some into a glass. She guessed that at home everything was laid on exactly to Bethan's taste. She could imagine Catrin scouring the supermarket for particular cereals and juice. Well, she had no time for that.

'When you're ready we should go,' she repeated.

'Great,' Bethan said, then, 'Last night, you didn't want to tell me about Aled. I was thinking about it in bed. I wish you would tell me. Nobody tells me anything. Did Aled really want to marry you?'

Elizabeth saw the eager, trusting expression. She had to tell the truth. 'I'm sorry. Aled didn't want to get married.'

'Mum said he wanted to. He'd have been a great Dad.'

'Your Mum believes what your grandfather has been telling her. He desperately wants to believe Aled was some kind of saint, but he wasn't. No-one is. I'm afraid when I told Aled I was pregnant he was very upset. He said he didn't want to get married.'

'Would he have wanted anything to do with me?'

Elizabeth cringed. 'It was complicated. I don't think he could take it in.'

'So, is that when he ran off?'

'It was a very difficult situation.'

'You were on the ground when Mum found you. She said you fell. Why did he leave you?'

'I don't know.'

'You sound like Mum now. Why won't anyone talk to me properly?'

'This was all a long time ago. If Aled and I had married, it would probably have been a disaster. Look, there are things that your mother should tell you. Ask her about Aled.'

'I'm confused. Surely Aled would have wanted to do the right thing by you?'

Elizabeth was amazed that a modern young girl should express such an old-fashioned sentiment. She felt terrible, as if she had smashed some kind of fairy tale that Bethan had been holding on to.

'I'm so sorry.'

'It's OK. It's not your fault.'

Elizabeth stood up. 'Look, let's go out, go shopping? A bit of retail therapy. Then we have the concert.'

Bethan still looked upset.

'Come on. Let's not let this spoil our day. It was all a long time ago.'

Bethan seemed to weaken.

'Well, OK.'

'We can have a really good day. I want to spoil you rotten.'

Bethan grinned. 'I can cope with that.'

Catrin had woken early, having slept badly on the sofa, and with a terrible headache. After seeing her reflection the night before she had run into the kitchen and been violently sick. She had been pleased that she had wanted to get the vile stuff out of her body. She had washed up the glass and poured the rest of the bottle down the sink. She had washed the saucer she had used as an ashtray, taken the stub and the rest of the packet, put them first in a carrier bag, which she tied up, and this she had put in the bin. She had drunk plenty of water, and watched television mindlessly until she had turned it off, and fallen asleep on the sofa.

Now, she opened the windows and the back door to air the house. She made coffee, and forced herself to eat cereal and toast. She showered, changed, and checked her phone: no message from Gareth. She wondered if he had gone to the surgery. He could have let himself in. After all, he had the code to the alarms. He was the person who was called if there was a suspected break-in. Of course, he could be with Carol. Was it really possible her marriage was ending? Catrin looked around her home. If she and Gareth split up she guessed they would sell this. She realised that wouldn't really bother her. She would have to find a flat, or a smaller house, she supposed. It all seemed surreal; divorce was something that happened to other people, not her. But then, didn't lots of people think that? She was surprised that she wasn't sobbing into the cushion, but she was too tired and numb to feel anything.

She looked at the clock on the mantelpiece. It was only half past four in the morning but it was getting light. She looked around, and knew then that she had to get out of this house. She needed to get back for Bethan, but she also, strangely, wanted to be on Gower, to feel the air, smell the sea, and walk on a long stretch of clean, unspoilt sand.

Catrin went round shutting up the house, then outside to the car. The roads were very quiet; the sky was lightening. In her mirror, she observed a staggeringly beautiful sunrise. She loved the way nature could do its thing, be special and beautiful anywhere. It was like seeing a daisy pushing its way through concrete paving, or urban foxes playing on a rubbish tip. When she reached the downs it was light, but there was a kind of golden hue to it which lit up the heather. She stopped her car and walked over to a large flat rock. Feeling rather like Tess of the d'Urbervilles, she lay down on the stone. But she was in no fear of harm, not here. Here she felt at peace: it was a place she never wanted to leave.

Catrin actually slept on the stone for an hour or so, and woke to the sense that the day had started for the world. She walked stiffly to her car and drove down the road. But she didn't turn left into the village. She drove straight down to the Rhossili car park.

She walked towards the headland. It was very quiet: just her and the sheep, the seagulls above. The long beach lay to her right. Ahead, Worm's Head stretched out to sea. After a few minutes, she reached the coastguard hut. She glanced at the board in front of her. She read that the causeway was open for the next few hours. She could go: she could walk across to Worm's Head. She started to walk down the steep path towards the causeway. Her heart was beating fast and loud. Suddenly, the sun went behind a cloud, and she felt cold. The clouds seemed to darken, and she heard the waves crashing against the rock. 'Aled!' she screamed, but there was no answer. She screamed again, but again her voice was carried away on the wind. She started to cry. She stared down at the causeway. She couldn't do it: she couldn't cross, and she would never be able to do it. She sat down and sobbed.

'Catrin, is that you?'

Catrin turned her head, to see Harri. She quickly wiped her face.

'What's the matter?' He sat down next to her.

'I was thinking of going, over there, to Worm's Head, but I can't. I can't do anything.' She started to cry again.

'Hey, why on earth do you want to go over there anyway? It's an awful climb?'

'But it's where Aled died. I wanted to prove to myself I could do it. I wanted to prove I could face this.'

'What's happened?'

'I went to Cardiff, had a row with Gareth, and the girls, well, they're both leaving me. Life just seems hopeless.'

'Oh, Catrin. That's terrible.'

'I'm sorry. I'm very tired.'

'Yes, I can see that. You look like you could do with a holiday.'

Catrin looked up, and laughed faintly. 'We're here in a place people come for holidays, and you say that.'

'But you're not relaxing, eating ice creams, are you?'

'No.'

'What happened with Gareth?'

Catrin looked away. It seemed disloyal to talk about it.

'The girls, then?'

She told him about Bethan and Elizabeth, and about Lowri's plans.

'They're growing up. It doesn't mean they don't love you, that they won't come back.'

Catrin looked up. She appreciated the gentle way Harri was talking to her. He was also looking at her in a way that was more than a friend, a way that took her back to when they sat together on the beach making plans in their teens. It was as if he read her mind.

'Just because their lives are taking off doesn't mean yours has to end.'

'But Gareth doesn't want to travel.'

'I know, but surely he wouldn't mind you, maybe, having a break?'

'What do you mean?'

'I've been thinking, since we were talking the other evening. In Collioure, I have a friend who runs long term retreats: three, six months: you choose. You could come out, in September maybe, get back in touch with it all.'

Catrin laughed. 'Harri, that is ridiculous. I can't just leave my family.'

'And why not? The girls will be away, and from what I can see Gareth won't even notice. Come over with me. I have property. You could live in one of the flats, be completely independent.'

'I can't afford to do anything like that.'

'But I can. You wouldn't need to pay a thing.'

'I can't be a kept woman.'

'If I talk to my friend he could employ you in the studio. Honestly, he's very busy with students. He's always moaning that he needs help.'

Catrin suddenly saw an image of herself, like the trailer for a Hollywood blockbuster, painting in the studio, drinking rosé in the evening sunshine by the harbour. In the next shot, she was going to the bakery in the early morning. She could smell the fresh baguettes. She would tear off a piece, give it to Safi. Her daydreaming abruptly stopped.

'What about Safi? He at least might miss me, and he's only just met me.'

'You know, you could bring him. Seriously, you should think about it. Me and Francine, we're finished. And, you know, I never got over you—'

Catrin looked away. All that talk by David, about owning your past. Well, she'd tried it with Gareth and it had been a disaster. David said you can't run away from your past. What if he was wrong? What if it was time for her to write her own future story, a story far away from here?

Chapter Twenty Nine

Harri and Catrin started to walk back along the headland. Catrin hadn't answered Harri, but they walked quietly, peacefully together. She left him at the hotel, where he went in for coffee.

'Don't forget, now,' he said.

'I won't,' she replied, 'and thank you for listening.'

As she walked down into the village, Catrin saw David and Safi. She saw Safi pull on the leash to come to her. She knelt down and he licked her face.

'Ah, thank you, David. Thank you for having him.'

'That's fine; we've just been on the downs. Anwen gave him sausages for breakfast.'

'Honestly. I'm amazed he's so pleased to see me.'

'How are things then?'

'I don't know, David. I think I need to go back and shower, have a rest. I'm exhausted.'

'But how is Gareth?'

'He's alright. It was a misunderstanding.'

'And you talked?'

'We did, but I'm not sure it achieved much. Look, I'm shattered. I think I'd better get on home.'

'Of course. Well, I'd better give Safi back before Anwen kidnaps him.'

As Catrin let herself into The Dragon House, she realised that, having avoided this place for eighteen years, she felt more at home here than in her own house in Cardiff. Safi followed her upstairs. There, she opened

283

the window in her room, and let in the fresh breeze. It was cooler today, but not cold.

She lay down on her bed and rested. Pictures of Collioure flitted in and out her mind, but Worm's Head, Aled, and Elizabeth were there as well. Catrin sat up and glanced over at her dressing table. She saw the little box of keys she had brought upstairs, the one containing the key to her mother's wardrobe. Maybe there was a key for that drawer, the locked one? She picked up the box but, as she headed to her mother's room, she met Lowri in the hallway. She looked anxious. 'You're back. How's Dad?'

'It was nothing. False alarm,' Catrin said, trying to look relaxed.

'You look shattered.'

'It was a lot of driving.'

Lowri looked sceptical: Cardiff was not that far away. 'What really happened?'

In an attempt to distract Lowri, Catrin said, 'I'm going to see if I can open a drawer in my mother's room.'

Really? A mystery, you think?'

'Maybe.' Suddenly, it occurred to Catrin what it could be.

'Actually, you know, I won't bother.'

'Oh, come on, Mum. Let's have a look.'

Lowri walked on ahead of Catrin, and pushed open the door.

'What're all these paintings on the floor?' she asked.

Catrin caught her up, Safi close by her side.

'This is the portfolio of work I prepared for my applications for Art College. I thought the school had lost them. I never went for the interviews.'

'But your work was here? How come?'

'It was Grandad. He told me he hid it here. He was worried about me leaving my mother. She was very unhappy at the time.'

'But it was his job to look after her.'

'Oh, he went away a lot. I had always been the one who knew how to handle her.'

'Hang on; what was the matter with her?'

'She had problems.' Catrin sighed. 'Look, let's not talk about it now.'

'But–'

'I promise. I'll tell you about it later but, really, love I'm done in.'

'OK, then,' Lowri said reluctantly. She looked down at the paintings. 'But these are good. I'm really shocked, Mum, that Grandad did this.'

Catrin was about to dismiss what Lowri said, but then she looked down at the paintings. They were a mixture of landscape and portraits. It was the landscapes that she thought were the best. In fact, Catrin found it hard to believe that she had painted them. It was a part of her she had forgotten was there. 'You're right. It wasn't fair. I would have loved to have gone to Art College. I should have been able to go.' Catrin stopped. It felt good actually to say the words, plain and simple. She carefully picked the paintings up and put them on to the bed. Then she picked up the keys and, without saying anything to Lowri, she tried the locked drawer with the keys. Eventually, one fitted. Catrin quickly looked inside, relieved to find no bottles. She opened it properly. Inside, she saw what appeared to be hand written manuscripts.'

'What on earth are these?' She said, taking them out. Lowri sat next to her. Catrin looked at Lowri.

'I don't believe it. They are stories, children's stories.'

285

'Really? Written by your Mum, my Grandma Isabel?'

Catrin flicked thought them. 'Yes, I remember now. When I was very little, she used to make up stories about a dragon. She would tell them to me at bed time. I'd forgotten. And, of course, my Nana Beth had told her all about the history of this place. She used them as the basis for these, I think.'

Lowri took one of the stories out and started to read out loud.

"I can see the dragon,' shouted Catrin. They had arrived at their holiday. To Mummy and Daddy the dragon was just a funny shaped island, but to Aled and Catrin it was the home of a real dragon. The dragon was magical. He would take them back in time for all kinds of exciting fun adventures. Daddy was singing, 'I do love to beside the seaside,' and Mummy was laughing. Catrin and Aled smiled at each other in excitement. They wondered what the holiday held in store. Would it be catching smugglers? Or maybe searching among the wreckage of a ship blown on to the beach one stormy night, finding hoards of jewels and diamonds? Of course, the holiday wouldn't all be dragon adventures. It would also be a time to make enormous sandcastles with Mummy and Daddy, eat candyfloss, and spend evenings in front of a real fire, while Daddy told them stories and Mummy cuddled them on the sofa. Whatever happened it would be the most magical, wonderful times of their lives.'

Catrin swallowed hard. Lowri smiled. 'Ah, that's so lovely.'

Catrin scratched her wrist hard.

'What's the matter, Mum?'

Catrin blinked quickly. 'It's sad, terribly sad.'

'But why?'

286

'Because her life, our life, was nothing like this. It was nothing like a fairy story.' Catrin burst into tears.

'What the matter, Mum? What do you mean?'

'It's nothing. It's just sad that Mum, Nana Isabel, had to make up this perfect world.'

'Don't you do that sometimes? Tell me, what is happening with Dad? And don't tell me things are fine. What's the matter?'

'I don't know. I tried to talk, made a mess of it. He just left the house, wouldn't talk to me.'

'Mum, you don't think he's seeing someone else, do you?'

Catrin looked more closely at Lowri. 'Why do you ask that?'

'You said he's never home and, I don't know, he's changed.'

'I know. And, oh, I don't know. Maybe he is seeing someone. I did wonder about that Carol.'

'The nurse?'

'Yes. He's always with her.'

'Have you asked him about it?'

'I tried, but we don't seem to be able to talk at the moment.'

Catrin looked again at Lowri's anxious, pale face. 'Oh, love. I'm sorry. It's always you I burden with things. It's not fair. You're here stuck with your mother moaning on, while Bethan is probably buying up the Apple store somewhere in London.'

Lowri laughed. 'I wouldn't want to be there, I promise you. I'm very happy as I am.'

'Mark will be wondering where you are.'

'Oh, he took himself off for a morning walk.'

'You and Mark seem close.'

Lowri smiled. 'I'm very lucky. We can talk about anything.'

287

'It's lovely. I'm pleased. Never let that go.'

Catrin heard a knock on the bedroom door.

'Come in,' she called.

Mark looked into the room.

'I thought I heard voices.'

Lowri stood up, smiling. 'Just chatting. Did you enjoy your walk?'

'I did. I'm ready for breakfast now.'

'Fine. Coffee, Mum?'

'Yes. I'll tidy this away, and come down.'

Lowri went out quickly, off into her own world with Mark. Catrin sat reading through the stories. Now that she had got over the surprise of them, she started to enjoy them. Her mother had a gift of making a past come to life. She started to imagine pictures that would go with the stories. She picked them up and took them back to her room. Her phone rang. She received several photos from Bethan of clothes she was buying and food she had eaten. She was relieved to hear from Bethan, and sent back a quick message. After this, Catrin found an old sketch pad and pencils, and took them downstairs. Mark and Lowri were inside, watching the games with her father.

'I made your coffee, Mum,' shouted Lowri.

'Thanks,' Catrin said. She carried it with her drawing things out into the garden, with Safi alongside her. It was a fresh, bright morning. She put the pad and pencils down on the table, wandered over to the border, looked at the sunflowers and poppies, and then again at a patch of ground that was covered, but only thinly. What had been here? She looked at the back of the border. This was completely over-run with thinker greenery and long grass. Then she saw it. She carefully stepped into the border to pick it up. It was heavier than she expected. She stepped back on to the grass and set it down, brushing off the mud and the grass tangled around it. What she was looking at was a stone dragon, about a foot tall. Whilst not cute, it was not frightening. This had been what had been standing in the border. She remembered it so clearly now. Her mother had told her about how her father had given it to her. Of course, she understood why now: Grandad Hugh had given her mother a dragon because Worm's Head had been their special place. It had been there all through Catrin's childhood and teens. She was sure it had been there the night of Aled's party. She remembered Lady sniffing it. So, her mother must have moved it afterwards. The dragon, Worm's Head: her mother had never wanted to think of it again.

Catrin looked down at the statue. If that is what her mother had felt, maybe she should respect that. She picked it up and heaved it back to the back of the border, even covered it with some grass. Then, she picked a sunflower, took it to the table, and began to draw. She remembered her Nana telling her about the sunflower, how it looks like it has petals only on the outside edge but, if you looked closely, you'd see hundreds of tiny flowers across it. Each one of those flowers will turn into a single seed.

Catrin sat in the quiet, drawing. A peace enveloped her with the gentle breeze. There was something almost spiritual in the moment, like finding something deep down inside her that fed her soul. She realised then that she had missed this. She remembered how at school the art room had been her place of retreat, not just from the rest of the school but from her home, and the stress of her mother. In there she could escape. Then she remembered a quote that had been on the wall of her art room at school, 'We have art in order not to die of the truth.' Friedrich Nietzsche, she recalled.

Chapter Thirty

Elizabeth and Bethan were sitting in the garden, recovering from a long busy day shopping and at the concert. Elizabeth had bought salads from a small vegetarian delicatessen. They took them back to the house to eat before the drive back to Gower.

'That concert was amazing,' said Bethan. 'I'm so confused now.'

'Why?'

'Well, I want to compose like that, but there's this audition tomorrow morning. I mean, it's a chance in a million.'

'But is it what you want to do?'

'I don't know.'

'You could go, and decide after.'

'Maybe. I'll talk to Mum when I get back.'

Elizabeth suddenly realised how tired she was.

'Do you think your mother would mind if we stayed here one more night? I promise to leave first thing. I don't like driving when I'm so tired.'

'Sure. I'll send Mum a text.'

Bethan received a reply quickly.

'Mum's OK. Not too happy about me being away another night but, as long as we leave early, she said I can stay.'

They sat quietly, Elizabeth on her laptop, Bethan on her phone. Elizabeth heard the front door open. She panicked. Even if an intruder got past the security guard at the gates, how could anyone get into her house? She froze. She quietly got off her seat, and crept to look through the patio doors. With a cry of relief, she realised it was Richard, who was looking at her in an equally startled way.

'Elizabeth,' he exclaimed. 'I was worried to death when I saw the patio doors open. I thought you'd been burgled.'

'Sorry, we came up to see a concert and decided to come back here before driving down. I'd forgotten about you coming in to water the plants.'

'We?'

'Oh, I brought someone with me,' said Elizabeth, panicking.

Richard walked over to the open patio doors.

Bethan looked up from her phone and gave him a radiant smile. 'Hello, I'm Bethan.'

Richard grinned. 'Bethan, great to meet you. I'm Richard.' Elizabeth saw him glance at her, waiting for a proper introduction. 'Let's go and make a drink,' she said to him. 'Bethan, you stay here just a minute.'

Richard looked puzzled. When they went in, he said,

'You were signing?'

'Bethan is Deaf.'

'She speaks well. So, who is she?'

'Bethan is my–' Elizabeth paused. '–My niece.'

'I thought you were an only child–'

'I don't tend to mention my sister. We don't get on very well at all, but I like her daughter. She's a nice kid, and Deaf, as you noticed. Anyway, my sister had hurt her ankle. She sent me a text and asked me if I could do something with her as she'd split up with her boyfriend and so–' Elizabeth stopped. She was getting very confused. Who was it who said that it was so much easier to tell the truth as there was nothing to remember?

'So you went to see your sister on Gower?'

Elizabeth sighed. 'They are down that way. Anyway, I said I'd take a day out of my holiday to bring Bethan up here for a concert.'

'That's really good of you.'

'I don't mind. She's no trouble.'

'And how did the memorial go?'

'It was OK, thanks.'

'And you survived the B & B?'

'Of course. Look, I think it's best if you leave us to it. Bethan's very shy, and we'll have to get going soon. I'm taking her back to my sister this evening.'

'Fine. I'll let you get on.'

'Thank you.' Elizabeth smiled up at him. 'It's good to see you.'

'I've missed you.'

'Congratulations about the grandad thing.'

Richard laughed. 'That makes me sound old, doesn't it?'

Elizabeth relaxed. She walked towards the front door to see Richard out.

'Don't worry about the plants. Obviously, I can do them now.'

'So, you take Bethan back to your sister. Are you coming back here then?'

'Yes, I think so.'

'Well, let me know when you're back.'

Elizabeth opened the front door, but Richard stopped.

'I ought to say good bye to Bethan.' He headed for the patio doors, with Elizabeth calling out not to bother. But she was too late: he'd reached the patio door. She rushed over. Bethan was still sitting down. She looked up from her phone.

'You're off?'

'Yes, leave you two to chat. It's nice to meet a member of Elizabeth's family at last.'

Bethan beamed. 'It's wonderful to have found each other, isn't it? You know, I thought she was dead.'

Richard frowned. 'Really?'

'It's time you went, Richard,' Elizabeth interrupted.

'Of course. Well, I hope you're mother's ankle is better soon.'

Bethan looked puzzled. 'What do you mean?'

'Your mother. She's hurt her ankle, hasn't she?' Richard repeated, pointing to his ankle.

'You think my mother has hurt her ankle?'

Richard half-laughed. 'Yes, sorry–'

'No, it's OK. My mother's ankles are fine.'

Richard looked confused. 'I thought that's why Elizabeth had brought you up to the concert, to give you a treat. You're lucky to have such a devoted Aunty–'

'Aunty?'

'Yes, Aunty–'

'Elizabeth is my–'

'Aunty,' shouted Elizabeth. She stared at Bethan hard. 'You're my niece, aren't you?'

Elizabeth looked at her, pleading with her to play along, but Bethan refused. She stood up. Her eyes were blazing. 'No, I'm not your niece.'

'Who are you then?' asked a very bemused Richard.

'Tell him,' demanded Bethan. 'Tell him who I am.'

Elizabeth could feel her heart pounding. Her mouth was very dry. She couldn't speak. It was like some nightmare, with Richard and Bethan staring at her like some inquisition, both waiting for her answer.

Bethan pushed past her and went upstairs.

'I think you'd better go,' Elizabeth said to Richard. 'She's an awful mess.'

'Will you be alright? I'm used to hysterical teenagers, you know.'

'No, really. She'll be alright when it's just me and her'.

'OK. Take care. Ring me if you need me. I'll take you out for a lot of red wine when you come back.'

'Thanks.'

Richard left. Elizabeth stood, wondering what to do. She was just about to go upstairs when Bethan appeared, walking down the stairs, carrying her case.

'You don't want me here, do you?'

'Of course I do. Don't be silly.'

'No, you said it. Last night you pretended to be all honest and open. You think you can just spend a load of money on me and everything will be alright.'

'Of course not.'

'You do. Well, it hasn't worked. It's my turn to leave you now.'

Bethan was crying hysterically. Elizabeth looked at her in horror.

'You can't go anywhere. Stop it.'

'I can. I want to go back to Gower.'

Elizabeth was shaking.

'I said we can go first thing in the morning.'

'But I want to go now.'

'I can't drive tonight. Really, I'm exhausted.'

'Well, I'm leaving now. I'll go on the train.'

'Don't be silly. You can't go off getting trains at this time.'

'You brought me here to poison me against Aled.'

'Hang on—'

'Yes, you did. He wanted me. Mum said. He'd have been a great father. He was better than you. He wouldn't have given me away.'

'For God's sake, Bethan.'

'I hate you. Well, you know, I'm glad you gave me away. I wish you really were dead.'

Elizabeth gasped, but Bethan hadn't finished.

'I'm going up to speak to my mother, my real mother.'

Bethan turned, stomped up the stairs and slammed her bedroom door.

Elizabeth went into the kitchen, poured herself a glass of whisky and clutched the glass. She went back to the sofa and sat down, white faced. Tears started to stream down her face.

She was so stupid. Of course she was a hopeless mother. She was a woman who had given her baby away. Of course she would be useless with children. Her baby: she had given her away, and now she had lost her again. She lay on the sofa and sobbed, deep tears that had been stored since the day she had handed her baby to the social worker, the tears she had wanted to shed when she had gone to her parents pretending all was well, that her body was not aching, that her breasts were not crying out for a baby to feed from. She cried, deep painful heart-wrenching sobs, drowning in sorrow and grief.

Chapter Thirty One

Catrin sat in the garden. The sea was a distant cluster of light blue jewels, the horizon a single dark blue line dividing the sea from the sky. It was easy to see why people at one time thought the world was flat. She could easily believe that you could just fall over the edge into an abyss. It was still as beautiful: there was no denying it. Whatever people did, this place stayed as lovely as ever.

Catrin's phone rang. She received two texts: one from Elizabeth, one from Bethan.

Bethan's said, 'I hate her.' Catrin panicked. What had happened? It was her fault; she should never have let Bethan go.

'What has happened?' she replied.

'She lied about me. She never loved me. She's a rich bitch. I hate her.'

'You're coming back tomorrow.'

'Can't wait. Love you Mum xxx.'

Catrin phoned Elizabeth.

Elizabeth sounded very different to her normal assertive self.

'Oh, hello. I was going to ring.'

'I've just received a text from Bethan. What's happened?'

'I've made such a mess of everything.'

'What happened?'

'A friend came round. It was difficult. He wanted to know who Bethan was.'

'And what did you say?'

'I said she was my niece'

'You said that in front of Bethan?'

'Yes. No-one knows about her. How could I tell the man I may be about to live with, 'Oh, by the way, here's my daughter,' could I?'

'But it was a terrible thing to do to Bethan.'

'She not a child–' Catrin could hear a defiance creeping back into Elizabeth's voice.

'She is, and you have failed to look after her.'

'But I've spoiled her rotten all day.'

'Buying things is not always the answer.'

'She should at least appreciate the money I spent. She said terrible things to me. How did she ever learn to speak to someone like that? I never spoke like that to my parents.'

'Bethan can be very dramatic, but she's had a very emotional week.'

'She shouldn't have been so rude. Don't you tell her off when she speaks to you like that?'

'You have no right to criticise how I've brought up Bethan.'

'Look, I've made mistakes, but she was very hurtful. To be honest, I think you have spoilt her. You have made her the centre of the universe.'

'I am her mother. It's what I do. I look after her.'

'Look after her by telling her lies, then–'

'What do you mean?'

'I started to talk to her about Aled.'

'What did you tell her?'

'All I said was that Aled didn't want to marry me.'

'You shouldn't have said that. It's not true, and it's a terrible thing to say to Bethan about her father. She needs to know how much Aled wanted her. He would have been a wonderful father and, of course, he would have married you.'

'Catrin, how can you be so naïve?'

297

'My father told me–'

'Do you believe everything your father says?'

'No, but–'

'Ask him. Ask your father what really happened that night.'

'He's already told me.'

'No he hasn't. Think about it. You found me unconscious. Why did Aled leave me? What do you really think happened? I've made a mess of things with Bethan, but you know, deep down, that what your father has told you isn't true. It's not fair on me or Bethan.'

'What's not fair is you turning up out of the blue, and hurting Bethan like this. You are still bringing her back, aren't you?'

'Of course, first thing in the morning. I am right. Catrin, you need to talk to your father.'

Elizabeth ended the call.

Catrin was breathing very fast. Her heart was thumping in her chest. She started to shake violently. She couldn't breathe. Her throat was getting tighter and tighter. Without warning, she started to heave. Lowri and Mark came out. Lowri rushed over to her.

'Mum, it's alright. Breathe slowly. It's OK. Remember, feel the ground with your feet. Come on, breathe. Now, slowly. It's OK. You're not having a heart attack. It's all going to be fine.'

'What the hell?' said Mark.

'It's a panic attack,' said Lowri.

Slowly, Catrin felt herself calm down, but she was drained.

'What happened?'

'Bethan and Elizabeth have fallen out.'

'Mum, it will be alright. Don't worry. Shall we drive down to Cardiff and get Dad? Or we could go to London now, pick up Bethan?'

'Elizabeth is bringing her back first thing. She'll be alright.'

'Are you sure? Do you want us to go and get Dad, then?'

Catrin looked at Lowri: again, that same concerned, anxious face. That face: it was her own; all those times looking down at her own mother. What was she doing to Lowri? Poor Lowri: always there, always picking up the pieces like Catrin had done, always being responsible. The one thing she had sworn she would never do to her children.

Catrin shook her head and sat up straight. 'No, Lowri. I will ring Dad. We should be sorting this out.'

'But–'

'No, love. That's enough. I'm so sorry. You and Mark can go and watch telly or something. I need to speak to your Dad.'

They returned to the house. Lowri, still looking anxious and confused, went in with Mark. Catrin went upstairs.

She tried phoning Gareth but, yet again, it went through to his voicemail. She tried the home phone: no answer. Catrin felt a wave of anger. How many times had she done this? She was always the one kept waiting, who got cancelled. She looked out of her window. She saw her father going to sit at the old table in the garden. He had put a small hurricane lamp on the table and started to pour himself a glass of whisky. It was time.

She went downstairs, out into the garden.

Lloyd looked up. Catrin glanced at the bottle and the glass.

'What's been going on then?' asked Lloyd.

'Bethan's had a row with Elizabeth.'

'That's good. She's better off away from that woman.'

'I don't know. You should never have lied to us about Elizabeth.'

'We didn't need her in our life. We had to protect Bethan.'

'By lying?'

'Of course. You and me, Catrin. That's how we look after people. We control things to stop people getting hurt. You did a good job with your mother. Nobody guessed, did they? You know, people don't really want the truth. It suited you, didn't it? Thinking Elizabeth was dead. I saw your face the day I told you. You were relieved. It meant Bethan was all yours; you didn't have to share her with anyone.'

The words came out spitefully, like a finger poking hard into her skin, but they hurt, partly because she knew there was a small element of truth, like a sharp stone in her sandal that worried and rubbed away at her foot.

She nodded. 'Yes. Maybe you are partly right. I was relieved, but I didn't ever think you were lying.' She stopped. 'What other lies have you told me, Dad?'

'What do you mean?'

'About Aled. What really happened the night he died? Why did you bring him back from America?'

'You know why. He was going to work on a new project in the firm.'

'But he had changed. I saw him that night. What had happened?'

'Have you been talking to that woman, Elizabeth?'

Catrin saw her father look at her shiftily.

'A bit. She told me that Aled had rowed with Mum about money. She also said Aled didn't want to marry her.'

'Now, that's not true.'

'Isn't it?'

300

'Look, he was too good for her. She should never have come that night. I had it all under control before she came.'

'Had what under control?'

'Nothing.'

'Dad, tell me.'

'It was her fault. Turning up here pregnant. She should have talked to me. Aled was sensitive, needed protecting from the likes of her.'

'She was young.'

'Old enough to know better. She led him on, trapped him. I've met girls like her. Trap a man into marriage, settling down.'

'Like Mum?'

A lightning look shot her way, a look of hate. Catrin stepped back.

'I was going places, you know, only nineteen. I was already marked out as a top student, but I was a married man with a child, trying to pay to keep a roof over our heads. And you, you never slept. I was trying to study, but you kept crying.'

'I was a baby.'

'Always difficult: all the tantrums. No wonder your mother turned to drink.'

'It wasn't my fault,' Catrin shouted, but he wasn't listening to her.

'And then Aled was born.' His voice softened, 'an angel.'

She stood very still. It was very quiet in the garden, as if all of nature was listening to them. Catrin's father said quietly, 'Aled was perfect. I shall never let you or this woman sully his name.' His hand shook as he lifted his glass, drained it, and refilled it.

'I know what you're doing, Dad,' Catrin said gently, just above a whisper. 'I know you're trying to silence the ghosts, but, when you are sober, they will still be there. I know, because I live with them every day.'

She left him in the garden and walked back to the house.

Chapter Thirty Two

Shaken, Catrin went straight up to her room and phoned Gareth's number. At last, he answered.

'We have to talk,' Catrin said, before he had spoken.

'Hang on. What's happened?'

'A lot. To begin with Bethan and Elizabeth have had a row.'

Catrin explained to him what had happened with Richard.

'I can see Bethan would be very hurt.'

'Deep down, I think she's expressing some kind of anger about Elizabeth giving her away.'

'She's coming back?'

'Yes, first thing in the morning. Elizabeth is driving her back. I should never have let her go. It's all been too fast. Now it's such a mess.'

'Don't worry. I'm sure you'll find a way. You're very good at these things.'

His calmness fed Catrin's anger and frustration.

'I thought you might come. Bethan needs you.'

'What, now? I'm sorry, but you know how my work is.'

The universe silently cringed: it was completely the wrong thing to say. But then, most things would have been.

'You and your bloody work.'

'Look, I told you. I just need to get this finished.'

'We need you here. I need you here, but you're not.'

'Not what?'

'Not here. You are never bloody here.'

'But work–'

'Bugger work.'

'Catrin, what is going on? Ever since you've been down there you seem to have gone to pieces and lost all sense of proportion. Before you went you were fine.'

'No. I was never fine,' she shouted. 'I can't cope, everything hurts–'

'Are you ill?'

'No, but I'm fed up with having to carry everything on my own. Are you fed up with me or something? Is there someone else or is it your job, or what?'

'You know how important my work is, and you always say you're fine with that.'

'Well, I lied. I am not fine with it, and you should see that. Your work has become an obsession with you. It's like you're addicted.'

'That's rubbish.'

'It's not,' she shouted. 'I'm right. It's like you can't live without it. It's more important than me and the girls. If I asked you to stop right now, you wouldn't. You couldn't. You are like my mother. You may not have a bottle in your hand but you are just as bad.'

Catrin started to gulp tears. It hurt to talk. Gareth went very quiet before he spoke.

'Catrin, when I've given this in tomorrow, caught up on my paper work, I promise we will talk.'

Catrin started to cry. She couldn't speak. It would be the same tomorrow. She knew it. It always was. She ended the call, put down her phone, sat on her bed and cried silent tears alone.

Catrin couldn't sleep. She sat in bed cuddling Safi. She was waiting for Gareth to phone, for Bethan to come home. Catrin got back out of bed. It was a full moon tonight. Safi looked up sleepily, sighed, and went back to sleep. Catrin knew then what she wanted to do. She crept out of her room, along the hallway, and slipped into Aled's room.

She closed the door quietly but firmly behind her, and switched on the light. Looking around the room, she saw again the faded posters, the drawings of Worm's Head. 'Who were you?' she whispered. Catrin started to open drawers. As in her mother's room, nothing had been sorted out. There were drawers of socks and underwear, comics, books, pebbles collected from the beach. She sat on Aled's bed, and looked around, trying to see the world from Aled's point of view. She looked up, and saw he had put plastic luminous stars on the ceiling. She turned off the light. The moon shining through the window made them shine in the darkness. The moon was so bright that night. It shone on to the carpet. She saw something protruding from under the free-standing, slightly raised wardrobe. It was the edge of an envelope. Catrin pulled it out, opened the envelope, and stared at the contents. Tears rolled down her cheeks. She gasped with deep pain. Not again: she couldn't bear it again.

Elizabeth sat on her sofa alone. It was very quiet. Bethan was not going to come out of her room. What was she going to do? She sat thinking about the row with Bethan. Slowly the words penetrated. 'I hate you. I wish you really were dead.' It was more than a teenage outburst; she knew that. Elizabeth went quietly upstairs, looked in the drawer, and took out the small white book-shaped box wrapped in tissue paper. Carefully, she unwrapped it and took it downstairs. Sitting on the sofa Elizabeth took a deep breath and opened it. She blinked back the tears which burned her eyes and was about to take something out when she heard the front door open. It was Richard. She carefully closed the box and hid it under a cushion. Richard came and sat next to her.

'I thought I'd pop back to see you were alright. You're not used to this stuff.'

He sounded so normal, rational.

'Where's Bethan?'

'Upstairs.' Elizabeth started to cry. Richard started gently to stroke her hair.

'Hey, it's OK.'

'No, it's not. You don't understand.'

'Tell me: what happened after I left?'

'I can't bear you hating me as much as she does.'

'Teenagers say all sorts of stupid things—'

'No, this is different. She'll never forgive me for what I did.'

'What was that?'

'I gave her away. When she was a tiny, helpless, baby. I gave her away.'

Richard sat forward. Elizabeth saw that look of horror she had been dreading.

'You mean—'

Elizabeth looked away. 'I knew you'd hate me for it. She's my daughter, my baby. I gave her away. Now, please go. I can't bear you looking at me, hating me.'

Richard sat back. He was blinking fast, trying to take in what Elizabeth had just said.

'Hang on. Just give me time. Let me think. You mean, you had a child, years ago?'

'I was nineteen.'

'God, you never told me. All that about not wanting children, and you'd had a baby—'

Elizabeth handed him the box she had been clutching. He opened it. Inside, he found a tiny baby's hospital wrist band, and a photograph of a scan. Elizabeth started to cry.

'No-one has ever seen these.'

Richard put his arms around her and hugged her.

'When I gave her away, I vowed I would never have any more children. I didn't deserve it. I was right.'

'Elizabeth, why ever didn't you tell me?'

'Because I knew you'd be like this. It's why I never tell anyone.'

'But you are presuming I judge you for what you did. That's not fair.'

'But everyone does.'

'Not everyone. Some may, I know, but there are lots of women who've been in that position, made the decision you made for good reasons. You know me and my ex-wife fostered children. I know how complicated things can be.'

'You did that?'

'Yes. Fran was a social worker. She was great with these kids.'

'She was some kind of saint, was she?'

'No, of course not. She was the one who went off with someone else. No, that's not what I'm saying.'

Elizabeth looked up. 'You don't hate me?'

'No, of course not. You should have trusted me.'

'It's just something I've always kept to myself. Only my aunt knew. Not even my parents ever knew.'

'You never told your mother and father?'

'No. They were part of the reason I went for adoption.'

'Why?'

'They were very religious. They were older parents. They'd have been mortified at me getting pregnant.'

'But people, even then, were much more accepting of these things.'

'Not them. You see, I was their only daughter, their world. They'd spent a fortune on my education. It would have broken their hearts.'

'Tell me what happened, properly.'

Elizabeth told Richard about Aled. The night she had given birth to Bethan; the day she had handed her to the social worker and gone home to her parents, trying to live as if nothing had happened. As she told him, it was if wounds that had barely healed opened again. She bled tears as she spoke.

'My God. It must have been heartbreaking, having all those emotions, and just keeping them in, hiding them.'

Elizabeth could see the look of intense pain on his face. He was trying to imagine himself in her position, but she had to be truthful.

'Actually, I was quite numb at the time. But, yes, it was terrible. However, and I know you won't like this, I still believe that for Bethan it was a good choice. I wasn't ready to be a mother, and I didn't want to hurt my parents.'

'Your body would have changed. It must have been so hard not telling them.'

'I had my aunt. She was like my mother in this country, but, having said that, we never talked about it after I gave Bethan away.'

'But you did think about keeping Bethan? That's why you went to see Aled?'

'Yes. There was part of me that held on to some kind of fairy tale ending. I thought he might marry me. Then I could have told Mum and Dad. It was ridiculous. I can see that now.'

Elizabeth found a tissue, and wiped her eyes, but she felt cold and empty.

'It sounds awful. I'm sorry you had to go through it all on your own. It must have been a heavy burden to carry alone. What you did doesn't make you a terrible human being. Bethan is happy, well loved. Isn't she?'

'Yes. Catrin and Gareth seem to have been good parents. She's grown into a beautiful, accomplished woman. She is Deaf. Yet she has done exactly what she wants to do. It's so different to how things were for my mother. You see, she was Deaf.'

'I didn't know.'

'Yes, my Dad signed with her, but she was so isolated. I think she was always ashamed of the way she was. They lived a very remote life. I suppose it's why she sent me away to school. You see, she couldn't speak that well. When I phoned home, I only spoke to my Dad, but Mum would write letters to me. She was so proud of me. I think she saw me doing things she believed she couldn't. It's amazing looking at Bethan. She's so confident. Catrin has done well. I'd have never coped like she did.'

'I think you might have, actually.'

'No. I'm not maternal.'

'Now, that's where I think you go too far. Why are you so convinced you would have been a terrible mother?'

'I just know.'

'You did what you thought was best for Bethan, didn't you?'

'I tried to.'

'And how did you feel when you held her as a baby?'

Elizabeth felt herself tremble. She tore at the tissue.

'I felt overwhelmed. I cried. It was like she was the only thing I could see. I kept looking at her. I whispered to her that I loved her, that I was sorry I was giving her away. I kept staring at her and studying every feature of her. I tried to memorise every detail. You know, some of the babies were put in the nursery at night, but I kept Bethan close.'

Richard looked emotional himself now. 'So, you did love her, you see. You did what you thought was right. So did they keep in touch let you know how Bethan was?'

'No. We agreed I would have nothing to do with Bethan. She could find me when she was old enough if she wanted to.'

'It must have been hard not seeing her.'

'I tried not to think about her. I would remember her on her birthday: that was all. I heard about the memorial for Aled. I thought I would go and just look at her, see she was alright. Does that sound mad?'

'Not really.'

'I went, but then I found out things. Well, anyway, we met and talked. It was incredible. I never expected to feel that way about her.'

'You see, you do love her, and you can love a child again.'

Elizabeth felt herself go red. She looked down.

'But I made a vow–'

Richard sat back and whistled. 'My God. You said your parents were religious. Were you brought up Catholic or something?'

'Oh, no.'

'So you've managed to conjure up Catholic guilt all on your own?'

'My parents had very strict principles. I suppose they were pretty judgmental.'

'You don't need to be feeling guilty. That vow you made: it means nothing. It's superstition. Do you think something bad will happen if you break it?'

Elizabeth looked down again.

'That's nonsense, isn't it?' He spoke gently.

'I guess it is. But it doesn't mean I want to have children. You know, I've made a terrible mess of things with Bethan.'

'All parents row with their kids.'

'But she hates me. She won't want to see me again. I said to Catrin that it was over.'

'Listen. You know, you probably broke every rule in the book, the way you and Bethan met up.'

'Really?'

'Of course. This sort of thing should be done very slowly, gradually building up the contact.'

'I was really shocked when I saw her.'

'Yes, and you can imagine what it was like for Bethan. She had no preparation for meeting you. She thought you were dead. And then, there you were.'

'I suppose I hadn't been thinking of it from her point of view that much. That's it. You see, I'm very selfish.'

'It's natural. You also have a confusing mixture of joy, sadness, connection and loss. It must be very hard.

Elizabeth blinked. 'I really did make an awful lot of mistakes, didn't I? Do you think it's too late to make it work?'

'You don't want to give up, do you?

'No, but what do I do? Bethan just wants me to get her back to Gower.'

'That's not such a bad idea, is it?'

'No. I suppose not.'

'Take her back, but it doesn't have to be the end, does it?'

Chapter Thirty Three

Friday 3rd August 2012

Catrin opened the curtains at seven the next morning. She had made her way back to her bed and spent a restless night. It was a murky day: the first time since arriving that they hadn't had brilliant sunshine. Worm's Head was shrouded in mist. The seagulls' screeching was muffled. She felt stiff and her head was thumping. The world was a greyer place in every sense of the word today. Safi looked up. She stroked him. She read somewhere that a dog gives you comfort because he doesn't ask you what's wrong. Well, it worked this morning.

Catrin received a text from Bethan at seven to say that she and Elizabeth had left London. She went downstairs with Safi, took him out for a quick walk and had coffee.

Her father came downstairs. There was so much she wanted say to him, but not yet. Catrin needed time to think, to sort out her thoughts. However, as she watched him make his tea and toast, she saw him through different eyes. She was in a position of power. She knew what he had done. He was no longer in control. He didn't realise it, but last night he had lost a battle, maybe even the war.

'Right, it's the audition at twelve. The Grand in Swansea, and we mustn't be late. Why hasn't Bethan got back yet?'

'She s on her way. Look, it's been a hard time. She might not want to go.'

'She is going. This has taken a lot to set up.'

Catrin stood up. 'No. Bethan decides, not you.'

Her father scowled, tried to speak, but gave up and walked away.

Bethan arrived back at about eleven. Elizabeth stayed in the car. Catrin went out to her.

'Thank you for bringing Bethan back.'

'It's OK. We had a talk.'

'Really?'

'Things are a bit better.'

'Look, what are you doing next?'

'I'm going for coffee up at the hotel. I'm pretty shattered.'

'I want to talk to you, but I have to look after Bethan.'

'She told me she wants to do the audition.'

'Oh, God.'

'I tried to talk her out of it.'

'Really? Is there any way you can wait around until the audition is over?'

'Why?'

'I need to talk to you.'

'OK. I rang Angela. Her next guests aren't coming now, so I'm going to stay another night or two. I'm worn out. I'm going to take a few more days off. There have to be some perks from being the owner of the gallery! I want some time by myself. It's quiet here. I can think. Bethan can see me if she wants, but let's just take it slowly.'

'Fair enough. The thing is, could we meet somewhere on our own to talk?'

'We could go to the hotel for coffee.'

'Yes, good idea. I'll phone you after the audition is over.'

313

'Fine. Hope it goes alright.'

'Thank you. We'll talk later.'

Catrin went into the house. Bethan looked exhausted.

'Love, how are you?' asked Catrin, and gave her a big hug.

'Actually, I'm alright. Elizabeth and I had a talk this morning, not a long one, but I think I understand better about this Richard. She's told him now who I am.'

'Good.'

'Mum, I'm sorry if I upset you, going off like that.'

'It's alright.'

'I don't want to replace you. I mean, she never could. You do know that?'

'I know.'

'She's just part of me, I suppose. I really wanted it to work.' Bethan suddenly started to cry young, child-like tears.

'Hey, I think it will be alright.'

'Do you think so?'

'Yes. I think Elizabeth wants it to work as well, you know.'

'She said she does.'

'Well there we are–'

'You think it's going to be alright?'

'I do.'

Bethan stood back and sniffed. 'Well, I'd better go and shower, then. It's the audition.'

'You don't have to go.'

'I think it would be good for me, got to give it a go. Sabrina wants me to get a selfie with Zac.'

Catrin, yet again, was amazed at her daughter's resilience. She wished that she had some of it. Somehow, through all the dramas that came Bethan's way, it was Catrin who ended up shattered and a wreck.

'Are you sure?'

'Of course. You will come with me, though, won't you?'

Catrin smiled. 'Yes, I'll be there.'

'Good. Right, then. I'd better go and shower.'

Catrin watched Bethan run up the stairs. Her father came into the hallway.

'She's gone to shower. She wants to go,' said Catrin, abruptly.

Her father grinned smugly. 'Good.'

Bethan returned, showered and changed.

'Do I look alright?' Bethan was wearing a long, red, silk skirt with a split at the side. With it she wore a white silk blouse. Her hair hung down like black velvet.

Catrin stared at her. 'You look gorgeous. I've never seen those clothes before. They really suit you.'

'Elizabeth bought them for me the first time we went out. They were really expensive.'

'They look it.'

Lloyd beamed at Bethan. 'Well, you look very nice. Well done.'

Catrin drove them to the audition. In the foyer of the theatre Bethan grabbed her mother's arm. Catrin was familiar with the sudden panics.

'I'm really nervous, Mum.'

'I know, but you'll be alright. Come on.' As much as Catrin didn't want Bethan to be doing this, she also didn't want her to fail, to feel humiliated. She wanted Bethan to be the one making the decisions.

When they got to the front of the theatre, a young man dressed in black came over to them.

'Are you Lloyd and his granddaughter Bethan?'

'That's right.'

'Good. Come with me, then.'

They found themselves guided behind the scenes, down a corridor.

'Mr Freestone is in here.' The young man knocked on the door, waiting until a low American voice told them they could go in.

Catrin could feel Bethan shaking next to her. It helped her conquer her own nerves. She had to look after Bethan. Lloyd was at his most effusive.

'Fantastic to see you again. Thank you so much for giving us your time, Mr Freestone.'

Zac Freestone looked up impatiently from his laptop, but then he saw Bethan and stood up. 'It's Zac,' he said to Lloyd, but his gaze went beyond him to Bethan. Bethan smiled. Catrin signed to her what Zac Freestone had said.

'Ah, of course, you're Deaf. Forgot. Sorry. I can't sign.'

'It's OK,' said Bethan, quietly.

'Well, let's get on. You brought your, um…what do you play?'

'Flute.'

'That's good. Come on, then.'

'Oh, now?'

'Of course.'

'I need to warm up,' said Bethan.

'Well you'd better do that quickly, then.'

They followed him into the theatre. There were people vacuuming and tidying up, ready for the afternoon. Zac had a word with a few young men dressed in black, who spoke to the cleaners. Soon the auditorium was very quiet. Bethan took out her flute and warmed it up as best she could. Catrin could see that her fingers were shaking and she looked very scared.

'I wish I'd brought the flute you and Dad gave me. I brought the one from Grandad because I thought I'd

316

upset him if I didn't, but I don't feel confident with this one.'

'You'll be OK,' said Catrin. 'Imagine you're playing to me in the living room at home.'

It was a line she had used before many exams. It seemed at least to take the edge off Bethan's nerves.

'Come up with me, Mum.'

'I can't come on the stage–'

'Well, stand at the side.'

Catrin saw Zac was sitting by her father, in a row about a third of the way back from the stage. He was looking impatient, like somebody not used to being kept waiting.

'Come on, then. Let's get on with this.'

They went up on to the stage. Catrin stood nervously in the wings. Bethan walked into the centre of the stage. Catrin could hardly bear to watch. Her stomach was churning over.

Bethan raised the gold flute to her lips and started to play. She had no sheet music. It was as if Bethan and the flute were one. She played a piece called 'The Lark'. It was as if a lark was singing above the theatre, its sweet, endless song. The sound filled the theatre. Catrin was moved.

When Bethan had finished it seemed to leave an almost unbearable emptiness. Zac stood up and came up on to the stage.

'This is it,' thought Catrin. 'She'll be going.'

'Right' said Zac. 'That was good, but I expected that. The thing is, we could do with changing your image a bit.'

Bethan scowled at him. He called to Catrin.

'Hey, can you come and sign for me?'

Catrin walked over. She looked at Bethan and started to interpret for Zac. It was as well. He spoke fast

317

and he looked around all over the place, making no concessions to Bethan at all.

'Well, let's face it: the point is, you're a Deaf girl playing. Well, no-one would know, would they? You need to get that hair back off your face, get some bigger hearing aids if you can. We need to scream out that you're a Deaf girl playing a flute. Now, it would be better as well if you could wear something a bit more, you know. Well, you're a pretty girl–' Catrin stopped, horrified at what she was being asked to sign. Bethan glared at her. 'I'm sorry,' Catrin signed. 'His words.'

Bethan turned to Zac and shouted. 'I'm not a freak. I'm a musician who happens to be Deaf, and proud of it.' Tears of anger spilled down her cheek. Catrin thought for a moment that she was going to hit Zac with her flute.

'It's my way or not at all.'

Bethan didn't need that interpreted. 'Piss off,' she sneered at him as she stormed off the stage. Catrin looked at her father, who was looking very embarrassed.

Zac shrugged. 'Your loss,' he said, and headed off, back to his dressing room.

Lloyd went running after him, but Catrin went after Bethan.

She caught up with her in the foyer.

'Are you alright?'

To her amazement, Bethan was smiling. 'Stupid wanker,' she said.

Finally, her father came out, looking very red-faced.

'How could you embarrass me like that?'

'He's a prat.'

'It's not too late. You must go back in and apologise–'

'No, Grandad. I don't think, to be honest, I want to go to America at the moment.'

'But you must–'

Catrin was shocked at the desperation in her father's face.

'Dad, she doesn't have to do this.'

'Typical. This is all about you, isn't it? Not wanting Bethan to leave you, to have her own life,'

'No, Dad. As always, this is all about you.'

Her father turned away from her, and faced Bethan.

'Bethan, is that what you want? To go to some university, come out with a worthless degree, when you could be famous, rich?'

Bethan started to twist her hair around her finger, tighter and tighter.

'Yes, Grandad. I think it is. I was looking though my course again online. It looks really good,' she said quietly.

'I've spent a lot of money on you over the years. I deserve this.'

'Stop it, Dad,' shouted Catrin. 'This is enough. I'm making the decision. Bethan is not going for this and we are going home.'

Catrin saw her father clench his fists in frustration, but she ignored him, and she and Bethan walked back to the car. She heard her father following but didn't dare look round. Once in the car, Bethan sat in the back texting friends. Catrin sat silently in the front with her father. There were light splashes of rain on the windscreen. Initially, when Catrin turned on the windscreen wipers, the screen was smeared with the dust and dirt that had accumulated over the past week. As they drove out of Swansea, the rain became heavier. Catrin increased the speed on the wipers. As they turned into the village the rain was running down the gutters, and only the most determined smokers were huddled under the awning outside the pub. As soon as they parked, Bethan opened the door and ran inside.

Catrin turned to her father, who was sat, ashen faced, staring out of the window. 'I'm sorry, Dad,' Catrin said, 'but it wasn't the right thing for Bethan.'

'I could have given her a good life out there,' he responded bitterly.

'She's not ready to go.'

'I'd always dreamed of a life out there with Aled, you know.'

'Had you?'

'I wanted to take him out there when he was little.'

'Really?'

'Yes. I'd started looking at high schools for him, but your mother wouldn't allow it, and I found out I couldn't legally take him.'

'You were going to take him without Mum?'

'Yes, but the law said I couldn't.'

'And me?'

'You?'

'Yes, me. You would have left me here?'

'Of course. You had to look after your mother.' He spoke very matter of factly.

'How old was I then?'

Lloyd looked puzzled. 'Hang on. It was when you were applying to college. That was it. Your mother was in a good patch. Aled was about twelve.'

'And you hid my pictures to stop me going so that I would look after Mum while you went to America with Aled.'

He nodded as if she was a rather slow child who had just worked out how to do a simple maths problem.

'Did Mum know you were planning that?'

320

'Not too much, but I realised when I checked things out legally that it wasn't on.'

Catrin scowled at him. 'Didn't you feel guilty leaving me with mum?'

'No, you were always alright. You'd always been fine.'

'Actually, I wasn't always.'

'Nonsense.'

'It's true. It was really hard. I missed out on a lot. I was always anxious and worried about Mum.'

'But she wasn't too bad. I would come home and often you said she'd been better.'

'For God's sake, Dad. You just wanted to believe that. It suited you to think I was OK, but you knew I wasn't.'

He opened his mouth to speak, then stopped himself, and looked hard at Catrin.

'Anyway, it all worked out for you, didn't it? You got yourself a doctor and your girls.'

'But inside I'm not alright. It's left scars, Dad–'

'Oh, I don't think so.'

'Stop it,' she shouted. 'You always trivialise my feelings, the things I've been through. It's not fair.'

'You were like her, understood her. I didn't.'

'If you had loved her, you would have tried.'

Lloyd clenched his fists and spat out the words which followed. 'Look, I always came back, didn't I? God knows, I dreaded it, but I came back. You should be grateful. I did the right thing by you all.'

'Did you?'

'Of course I did.' He glared at her. 'I provided for you and your mother. You never went without.'

'We went without love, unconditional, something for nothing, love. That's what we all went without.'

'That's ridiculous.'

321

'No, it's not. I'm actually seeing things clearly for the first time. It's tough, but I understand things now.'

Her father looked away. 'All this bloody talking does more harm than good. No more, that's enough. No more.' He got out of the car, slammed the door, and walked through the rain back into the house.

Chapter Thirty Four

Catrin picked up her phone and rang Elizabeth, then drove straight up to the hotel.

Elizabeth was sat in a comfortable lounge with a pot of coffee. She looked up at Catrin and, without asking, ordered more.

'How did the audition go?'

'Bethan didn't like this chap, Zac. He was a bit of a creep, to be honest. I was proud of the way she stood up for herself.'

'That's good. I'm sure she will be better off going to university.'

'So do I. Dad is really upset, though.'

'Your father, Catrin. He's a difficult man, isn't he? I don't just mean because he lied about me. He doesn't treat you very well, does he?'

'No, he doesn't. I realise that now.'

'I'm sorry for what I said about you and Bethan. Is that what you wanted to talk about?'

'Partly, but also about Aled.'

'Ah–'

'I've never wanted to dig too deeply, you know. I had a sense there were things I didn't know, but I was too scared to look for answers. I could have looked up the inquest findings. I could have done a lot, but I didn't want to know. That's the truth of it. It was like skipping over the bits in a book you don't want to read. I should have, though, if only for Bethan.'

'Did your father tell you?'

'No, I don't think he will never admit it to himself, let alone me'

'So what happened?'

'I found something in Aled's room.'

'What was that?'

'I found a small bag of white powder.'

'Ah–'

'Please, Elizabeth. Tell me what really happened.'

'What, everything?'

'Yes.'

'OK. Like I told you, when I first met Aled, I was absolutely bowled over. He was so charming, good looking, and clever. Everyone liked him. He was very popular.'

Catrin smiled. 'Yes, that was Aled.'

'It was one side of Aled,' corrected Elizabeth. 'I was hugely flattered when he noticed me, and we went out for drinks. He also hung about with a group of other architects. I noticed, though, that Aled was sometimes late into work. Sometimes he wasn't at his desk when he should have been. Then, one day, I was in the ladies when I heard some of the girls talking about Aled. They didn't know I was there. They were talking about me and Aled. They said I was very young, had no idea what he got up to, that they felt sorry for me.'

Catrin frowned. 'What did they mean?'

'Well, at first I thought they were jealous. Then, one evening we went out and he went off to the toilets. When he came back I saw white powder on his nose. Then it all fitted together.'

'You knew what it was.'

'There were girls back at my boarding school who used it. Rich kids, you know, get targeted in the clubs. I knew he was using cocaine.'

'Was it just at parties and things?' Catrin asked, although in her heart she already knew the answer.

324

Elizabeth shook her head. 'I watched him from then on. I realised he was really hooked. He was using it during the day at work, when we were out, all the time.'

'He was using at work. Did your father know?'

Elizabeth twisted a thin strand of hair around her finger. 'My father knew Aled. He didn't know about him using drugs.'

'Did he know you were seeing him?'

'He heard rumours I had been out with Aled.'

'What did he say?'

'He warned me off. He said Aled was a bright star, really good architect, but he was getting in with the wrong crowd. My father told me not to go out with them.'

'But you did.'

'I was nineteen. I thought my father was being over-protective. Crazy. I know he was right now.'

'I know you were young, but did you try to help Aled?'

'I tried to talk to him, but he wouldn't listen. His friends were as bad as him.'

'He needed help.'

Your father knew. He came over to see him. He was trying to stop anyone knowing, I think. I never saw him, but he would take Aled out.'

'Dad knew?'

'Oh, yes. He was worried Aled was getting a reputation. I left at the Christmas before Aled's party at the Dragon House. I didn't know then that I was pregnant, but I was glad to leave. I was looking into adoption when I heard that Aled was coming back to the UK. I hoped then that he had got clean and I mapped out in my head a happy ending.'

'You wanted to marry him. Would your parents have accepted that?'

'I was hoping they would.'

'But your father didn't approve of Aled?'

'No, but I was thinking he might come round if Aled got himself straight. He was a very promising architect. So, as you know, I came to the party. We went to the headland.'

'Was he taking cocaine that night?'

'He was, and he was desperate for money. Cocaine is expensive. He had found someone over here to buy from, but he said it was costing more. He knew he only had enough for a week or two. He was asking your mother for money when they'd had the row.'

'Why was he asking her for money? He had a good job.'

He told me he was in debt. Your mother had been sending him money in America. He'd told her that it was for gambling, but he didn't want his father to find out.'

'He was in a real mess, then?'

'Yes. Cocaine is a very expensive habit.'

'Did Mum find out what the money was really for at the party?'

'Yes. I think she had started to worry about him. In the end he told her, thought she'd feel sorry for him.'

'What did she say?'

'She said she would pay for him to go to rehab but wouldn't give him any more money.'

'So he went storming out with you, took you to the headland?'

'He did. He told me about the problems getting money. He asked me for some. Then I told him about being pregnant.'

Catrin screwed up her eyes, in dread of what was to come. 'What happened?'

'He said that was good. We could get married.'

'He wanted the baby?'

Elizabeth sighed. 'For a moment, I believed that. He grabbed my hand and said he was going to take me to the most magical place to propose.'

'Worm's Head?'

'Yes, he was crazy. He said that he'd never been there. His mother had stopped him going, but tonight he would go there with me.'

'What did you do?'

'I was scared. I was heavily pregnant. He was just wild. Then he said, wasn't it wonderful that in the morning we would open a joint account; all his problems were over. It was then that I realised that all he was thinking about was getting money to buy cocaine. That was all he cared about. I think that was the first time I really realised how badly addicted he was.'

Catrin blinked back tears: to imagine her brother so desperate was terrifying; that a drug could have done that to him.

'I pulled away,' said Elizabeth. 'I said I would never marry him.'

'He said he was going to Worm's Head with or without me. He was just out of it. I said not to go, not to be stupid.'

'And–'

'He said no-one ever called him stupid. He was perfect. I should know that. Then he hit me, really hard. I fell down and blacked out. Then you found me.'

Catrin sat stunned. It was like hearing about someone she had never known, a stranger.

'I'm so sorry, Catrin, but you should've been told.'

'Yes. I should have known this. I am so sorry for what my brother did to you.'

'I don't think it was really him.'

'He hurt you.'

327

'Yes. In the hospital, I was in such a state. My aunt looked after me. Your father came up with the idea of you adopting Bethan.'

'Do you regret it now?'

Elizabeth shook her head. 'No. I wasn't ready for a child. Fate at least made sure Bethan had the best parents she could have wished for.'

'Thank you.'

'I would like to see Bethan sometimes.'

'I know. We will have to work it out properly.'

'I think I might find someone to talk to, a therapist or someone. When I see Bethan, it should be about her, not me.'

'You are very brave.'

'Not really.'

'Bethan told me you talked to Richard. Will it be alright?'

'Yes. He was fine about it. He's a good man.'

'Good.'

'I would like to meet Gareth sometime. It doesn't seem right that I've not met him yet.'

'Gareth and I, we need to sort a few things out but, yes, you must meet him soon.'

'Good.' Elizabeth stood up. Catrin realised she was ending the meeting.

'Thank you for telling me all this.'

'It's not pretty, is it?'

'No, but better an ugly truth than a pretty lie, as they say.'

'Will you tell Bethan?'

'I think I have to. I'm not sure when but, yes, I will tell her.'

'I'm going back to the B & B. When I came down, Richard said it wasn't my sort of place. In some ways he's right but, you know, it is special. I can think here.

328

I'd like to spend some time just to try and make peace with it. Does that make sense? I don't want it to be a place I avoid, but I know it's there.'

'I know exactly what you mean,' said Catrin. 'It's better to face things, isn't it?'

'Yes. I'm glad I have. If I hadn't, I'd have never seen Bethan, would I? Got to see what a remarkable young woman she has grown into. No, I'm glad I came.'

'So am I.'

'We have to keep in touch. You have my mobile number, don't you?'

Catrin nodded. 'Yes. Well, goodbye.'

Catrin drove back to the house. She had a sandwich by herself. Everyone seemed to be keeping themselves to themselves. They all spent the rest of the afternoon fairly quietly, glad of the rain giving them an excuse to stay in.

In the evening, Lowri, Mark and Bethan went to buy fish and chips from Rhossili. Catrin was getting things ready in the kitchen when she realised that it was getting darker, even though it was only seven o'clock. The day hadn't brightened, and it seemed to be getting dark early.

Her father was sitting in the living room, ignoring them all, watching the television.

'Dad, the girls are getting fish and chips. Fancy anything?'

He looked up, scowling. 'OK, but I'll eat in here.'

Sighing, Catrin left him. She went upstairs to check that her bedroom window was closed. She looked out. She couldn't see Worm's Head but, of course, it was still there, and it still filled her with a sense of dread. The past: always there, always something that frightened her. It never left her. She remembered David talking about

329

unravelling the past, how if we didn't do that it would never go, never rest. There was a knock at the door. She ran downstairs, expecting it to be the girls and Mark with the food. However, she opened it to find Gareth, ashen-faced, unable to speak, and clutching his chest.

Chapter Thirty Five

Catrin sat in the ambulance with Gareth. He was conscious, but lying attached to machines, very still. Fortunately, the others had arrived home immediately after Gareth, and Lowri had run in. She had taken one look at her father and called an ambulance. Catrin had been so glad Lowri had been there as she herself had frozen, not sure what to do.

In the ambulance, she held Gareth's hand. Neither of them spoke. She was petrified of making things worse by saying or doing the wrong thing.

At the hospital, he was whisked off for tests. Lowri and Bethan arrived, having followed the ambulance. Lowri was white faced, Bethan crying.

'What's happened, Mum?' asked Bethan.

'Dad has severe heart pains. They're doing tests.'

'Has he had a heart attack?'

'I don't know. We have to wait.'

Bethan started to sob again. Lowri said, 'I'll go and see if I can find out what is going on.'

Catrin sat with her arm around Bethan. So many things had gone through her mind in the past week. Gareth being seriously ill was not one of them. He was never ill. He was the one who kept going through everything. He may not be home much, but in an emergency he was the one they turned to: the rock, the foundation of the family. She had never realised quite how much, until now. What if she lost him, tonight? It happened. People could be gone that quickly.

Lowri returned.

'They're running lots of tests. Apparently, he's been having chest pains for ages. They think its angina.'

'Not a heart attack?'

'They don't think so. They're doing an ECG now. There'll be a few tests yet, Mum, before they can be sure what's going on. I left Mark outside looking for a parking space. I'll go find him and tell him what's happening.'

Catrin stayed with Bethan. They watched nurses and doctors coming and going. She heard one talking about her daughter's wedding, not knowing if she needed to get a hat; another mentioned the name of someone in her ward who had died that afternoon. It was such a strange place, a hospital, where the mundane and extraordinary, life changing events ran in parallel.

Eventually a nurse emerged from Gareth's room. She smiled reassuringly.

'Your husband is comfortable. We have to wait now for some test results, and the consultant has been called.'

'What?' asked Bethan. Catrin repeated to her what the nurse had said.

'Can I go in and see him?'

'Of course, but he needs to rest.'

Catrin could see the nurse glancing at Bethan, who was crying again. Lowri returned. Catrin told her what was going on. Lowri looked at the nurse.

'It's late. Would it be a good idea for some of us to go, or do you think we should stay?'

Catrin and the nurse knew exactly what she was asking.

'It's OK to go home. Are you staying?' This was addressed to Catrin.

'Oh, yes. I want to stay.'

Bethan and Lowri went in very briefly to say goodnight to Gareth. When they came out, Lowri spoke. 'He's fast asleep, Mum.'

'Right. Well, you go.'

'OK. We'll see you in the morning. You must be hungry. We never had the fish and chips.'

Catrin gave a little smile. 'It's alright, love. Not too hungry at the moment.'

'I'll bring you some clean clothes and things in the morning.'

'That's great. Tell Grandad what's happening, won't you?'

'Of course. He had Safi on his lap when I left. See you later, Mum.'

Bethan and Lowri both kissed Catrin and left.

Catrin nervously made her way into Gareth's room. She was surprised to find that he was awake. Various monitors were flashing beside him.

'Hi, love,' she said quietly. 'You gave us all a bit of a scare.'

'I'm sorry.' His voice sounded weak. It held none of its usual self-assurance.

'It's alright. You're here. They'll look after you.'

'It's my own fault.'

'But you didn't go to the doctor?'

'No. I ignored all the advice I'd have given to a patient.'

'You never said anything to me.'

'I know. I suppose I thought it would make more of a thing of it if I said anything about it.'

'Oh, love.'

'I know. The number of times I've heard patients say that. I've been so stupid.'

She was shocked to see tears in his eyes.

'Hey, it's alright. I should have realised. You've not been yourself.'

Gareth didn't speak, but his eyes seemed full of unspoken words. He looked hard at Catrin, but seemed suddenly to run out of energy. He closed his eyes, and soon he was asleep. She sat with him for a while until a nurse came in.

'Would you like a drink? Coffee, tea?'

'Coffee, thank you.'

She was surprised to see that it was midnight. Somehow, in the hospital, she had lost track of time. She curled up on the armchair next to the bed. The nurse arrived with a cup of coffee. Catrin wished she had Safi to curl up on her lap, but she sat alone, watching Gareth sleep. Nurses came in, busily checking things. Gareth was given injections. Catrin felt very helpless. The lights were lowered in his room, but she didn't really like it. It felt rather serious and forbidding. She longed for it to be light.

Saturday 4th August 2012

Catrin was woken at five by the alarm on the drip, and a nurse coming to change it. Gareth seemed to manage to sleep through it all. She was relieved to see chinks of light coming though the window. It seemed an achievement, somehow, to have made it through the night. The daylight brought with it a sense of optimism. She found the toilet. On her way she looked at the nurses who had been on duty all night. They looked pale as they rushed around. These last few hours must seem long. Eventually, there was the racket of the day shift. Breakfasts and baths started. Catrin sat again, helplessly.

Gareth woke up and looked at her blearily, trying to adjust to where he was.

'You're in hospital, love.'

'Oh, crumbs,' he said, remembering. 'Can I go home?'

'Not yet. I think you'll be in a bit longer while they check the results of the tests.'

He sighed. His resignation frightened her.

'Have you been here all night?'

'Oh, yes.'

'You ought to go and have some breakfast.'

'I could do with a coffee. I think Lowri and Bethan will be coming in this morning.'

Gareth looked at her. 'Can you put them off? You and me, we need to talk first.'

Her heart beat faster. What did he have to say?

Catrin found the café. An area was cordoned off for staff. She sat in the other area with toast and coffee, feeling very out of place. She drank and ate as quickly as she could and went out to phone Lowri. She filled her in on the night and suggested she and Bethan come after lunch.

'Is Bethan all right with that? Tell her Dad is OK, won't you?'

Catrin returned to the ward. Gareth was sitting up. The consultant came round early. Soon, he and Gareth were talking in medical jargon. Catrin had little idea what they were talking about. The medical terminology all sounded pretty alarming to her. Seeing the expression on her face, the consultant turned to her.

'Sorry, doctor speak. You're not getting rid of him just yet.'

Catrin tried to smile. The consultant moderated his tone.

'He's not had a heart attack. We know that. We will run some more tests. It appears this has been going on for some time. Your husband appears to have been trying to pretend it will all go away. I don't know, why are doctors some of my worst patients? Anyway, don't you worry too much. I'll see you both later.'

He rushed off. Catrin was left with Gareth. He looked at her, his eyes sad.

'Sorry. You look worse than me.'

'Thanks a lot.' Catrin looked down, and nervously scratched her hand.

'What he was saying was they think I have angina. I kept putting it down to stress, but I knew it was getting worse.'

'And you've been ignoring it?'

He grimaced. 'I know. I could have had a heart attack, or a stroke. You don't need to tell me.'

'You say you put it down to stress. Has it been that bad, then?'

Catrin saw Gareth's eyes welling up. 'I have to tell you something. I'm so sorry.'

Catrin held her breath, waiting for Gareth to speak.

'It's about my work.'

Catrin breathed a sigh of relief. 'What about it?'

'I'm completely done in, Catrin. God, I'm so tired.'

'You're a very good doctor. You know that.'

'The hours are so hard.'

'Why did you take on the research, then?'

'I don't know. I think it's like I always used to say with the families I saw struggling. They were always the ones who would go out and get a giant dog. I think I understand why now. I suppose we think that if we keep covering up problems with bigger ones we won't see the ones at the root, the ones that really frighten us.'

'There's more,' he said. Catrin held her breath again. Gareth looked very awkward now.

'It's about Carol.'

336

'Oh.' Catrin's heart was beating very fast now.

'She wants me to carry on with the research, extend it. She's so ambitious. Her aim is to qualify as a doctor. There's nothing wrong with that. She'll be very good. But she wants to make a name for herself.'

'So you would continue like this?'

'I don't know what to do. You know, I think she was worried I would die on her. She knew about the chest pains. It's why she sent that text to you. She found me in the surgery really early, looking pretty unwell. She said she was going to tell you about me being ill.'

'And you should have told me. It shouldn't have been Carol. You and she seem to have got very close.'

'There's nothing going on. She's not interested in me, just the research.'

'She sees a lot more of you than me.'

He looked at Catrin searchingly. 'You said some things on the phone–'

She squeezed his hand. 'Not now. Soon, but not now.'

Gareth lay back, sighed deeply, and closed his eyes.

Catrin sat looking at him. She was so relieved that he was going to be alright, but it didn't erase the past few months. She couldn't face going back to how it had been: Gareth never home; never doing anything with her; always coming second. She had done that all her life and she wasn't prepared to do it any more.

Chapter Thirty Six

Sunday 5th August 2012

Sunday 5th August 2012

Catrin drove Gareth back to the Dragon House mid morning the next day. She was surprised at how quickly they had allowed him out, but the consultant said that they had done all the tests and now needed his bed for the next person. He was given medication. A letter was written to his general practitioner, and an appointment made for him at the hospital in Cardiff.

'He also gave me a long hard talking to, about stress and lifestyle. I'm not allowed back to work for at least a month. God knows how they will cope at the surgery. I will have to ring John, the practice manager, on his mobile when I get back, maybe arrange to see him on Monday. Could you drive me down? I'm not allowed to drive for a week or two.'

'I think you ought to slow down, Gareth. Let's just get back.'

Gareth made his phone call. Uncharacteristically compliant, he then sat in the living room watching the Olympics, with Safi tucked up next to him on the sofa. Catrin was aware that they still had a lot to talk about, but wanted to wait until he was rested. She did, however, want to tell him what she had learned about Aled. He listened carefully.

'I am so sorry,' he said, at the end.

'I'm stunned. I suppose I guessed there might be something, but never like this. To think he was addicted to something, and that it had changed him so much.'

338

'I know. I watch patients. It's devastating for them and their families.'

'By the way, I found something, a small bag of cocaine, up in his room. I left it there. What do we do with it?'

'I'll sort it out. It must be disposed of properly.'

'Thanks. You must think me a bit of a fool, the way I went on about Aled being so perfect.'

'Not really. Obviously, I knew he couldn't be as wonderful as you and your father made out, but you seemed to need to do that. You were very fond of him. He was your brother. It was very sad that he died so young.'

'I did love him. I really did. He had great charm and was such fun. Mum and Dad might have gone on about how brilliant he was, but he was not big-headed.'

'Do you think your mother's drinking affected him?'

'I think it must have done. I tried to shield him, but he saw how she was. He saw her turn to drink when she was unhappy.'

'I can see that. And what about Bethan? She's had a hell of a lot to cope with, what with hearing new things about her father, as well as meeting Elizabeth. Maybe you should arrange for her to see her social worker back in Cardiff, to talk about it.'

'That's a really good idea. Yes, we must arrange that. She could do with someone outside of it all to talk to. Do you think I should tell her about Aled and the cocaine? Do I tell her now or has she had enough for one week?'

'She should know, but maybe she's had enough for now, unless she asks.'

'Yes, that sounds right. I think I'd better go and get on with some of this sorting out I keep not doing.'

Gareth nodded and said, 'I know we've got more to talk about.'

'Yes. Not yet, but, yes, we will soon. I'll come down later to make lunch. I think Safi has decided his job is to stay next to you. See you later.'

Catrin went up to Aled's room. She took out the brown envelope she had hidden in a drawer. At that moment, Bethan came in.

'Mum, what's wrong with Grandad? He won't speak to me. Is he really upset about the audition?'

Catrin sighed. Her father had built an invisible wall around him, with barbed wire on top. He was not allowing anybody in.

'I'm sorry. He's very mixed up at the moment.'

'I used to think he was wonderful because he spent so much on me, but I've seen a different side of him here. He shouldn't have lied about Elizabeth. At the audition he was really nasty.'

'He's not always that easy.'

'No. I wouldn't want to be living with him out in America.' Bethan looked around the room and, distractedly, said, 'I never realised Aled was into rugby.'

'He was very good.'

'Of course,' Bethan tutted irritably. 'He was good at everything, wasn't he?'

'I suppose so.'

'Come on, Mum. He couldn't have been. Nobody is.'

'Well–'

'Who was he? Elizabeth was keeping things back from me. I know she was. Someone needs to tell me what happened.'

Catrin bit her lip. Was this the time? 'You really want to know?'

'Yes.'

'You've been through so much. Dad suggested we make an appointment for you to see Janet, your social worker.'

'Yes, I'd like that. She'll know about this stuff. There's a girl at Deaf club who is fostered, but she sees her parents. Janet has helped her.'

'Good. We'll arrange it tomorrow.'

'But Mum, about Aled–'

They were interrupted by Lowri. 'Mum, I don't know what to do with half the things in Grandma's room.' She looked down at Catrin and Bethan. 'Something up?'

'I was asking Mum to tell me more about Aled.'

Lowri nodded. 'There must be a lot that Bethan doesn't know. Isn't there, Mum?'

'There are some things–'

'You don't have to hide it all from us. We're not children any more,' said Bethan.

'I want to know about Grandma Isabel as well,' said Lowri.

Catrin screwed up her face. It was agony deciding whether she really should be telling her girls these things. She so wanted them to live in a world that wasn't spoiled by pain and illness but it wasn't like that.

'Maybe it's time I told you two a bit more. To be honest, some of it I've only just found out myself.'

They sat up on Aled's bed, against the backdrop of the faded rugby posters.

'Well, I'll start with my Mum, your Grandma Isabel. What I've never told you about her is that she had a serious drink problem.'

'She was an alcoholic?' asked Lowri.

Catrin flinched at the word. 'Yes. Yes, she was.'

Catrin paused. Lowri looked deep into her eyes as if locking into her pain.

341

'I'm sorry to be telling you this. I don't want you to think badly of your grandmother. I don't want it to be the thing that defined her. She was so much more than that.'

'Was she an alcoholic while you were growing up?' asked Lowri.

Catrin looked down. 'When I was a teenager. I worried about her a lot.'

'That's why you're so concerned that I shouldn't worry about you?'

'That's right. You see, my teenage years were very difficult. I was left to look after my Mum and worry about her when I needed support myself. And I had to protect Aled from it, although he was away at school a lot. I missed school and I never got to go to college.'

'What about Grandad? Didn't he help?'

'Sometimes, but he also went away a lot on business.'

'Grandad should have looked after you,' said Bethan.

'I don't think he wanted to face it.'

'That wasn't fair,' said Bethan, angrily.

'Didn't Grandma get treatment?' asked Lowri.

'She went into rehab a few times. Grandad paid a lot of money out. She went to good places. She tried, but she always relapsed. And then, losing Aled was just dreadful for her.'

'So why was she like it? Whose fault was it?' asked Bethan.

'There were things that caused her great sadness in her past, when she was growing up. It made her very scared about being left alone.'

'Grandad going away all the time didn't help, then?' said Bethan.

'To be honest, no. It didn't. She was very worried about losing him. However, and this is important to remember, ultimately her addiction was nobody's fault, not Grandad's, no-one's. He might have made her unhappy sometimes and caused her pain. To cover that pain she sometimes drank. The addiction itself, though, was an illness. Uncle David has been explaining to me about how the brain changes when you become addicted.'

'You meant it's like a physical illness?'

'Apparently. Some people do manage to get better, but others don't. Grandma Isabel had some good patches. She really wanted to be a good grandmother to you, but then Aled–'

'Did she really die from a heart attack?' asked Lowri.

'She had a heart attack. What we don't talk about is that her body had been wrecked by alcohol. She had liver disease. Her heart problems arose from the drinking. There's a stigma in telling people someone has died because of addiction, so we always just spoke about the heart attack.'

'That's so sad. You know, I remember Grandma Isabel. She used to tell me stories when I was very little. She told me I reminded her of you when you were little,' said Lowri.

'Yes. She was lovely. I miss her.'

'And what about Aled?' asked Bethan. 'What don't we know about him?'

Catrin bit her lip. This was going to be a lot harder.

'I'm really sorry. The thing is, Aled was an addict as well.'

Bethan blinked very hard. She looked at her mother as if she was mad. 'No, not my father.'

'I'm sorry.'

343

'Are you sure?'

'Yes. I've only really found out in the past few days.'

'But how? What happened?'

Bethan started twisting a long strand of hair round her finger very tightly.

'With Aled it was drugs, cocaine.'

Bethan put her hand to her mouth. Catrin wondered if Bethan was going to be sick, but she saw her breathe deeply.

'It's a shock, I know.'

'But I always thought he was so perfect, good at everything. It's why what Elizabeth said about him not wanting to marry her seemed so odd. I assumed she was lying so that I would forgive her for giving me away.'

'No. I don't know everything that happened to her the night of the party, but I do know Aled was in a bad way. He was using cocaine.'

'You know, I have this picture of this ideal man: blond hair, handsome, charming, and clever. To try and imagine him on drugs, it's awful. We were shown photographs about it at school. It's horrible.'

'I know.'

'But surely someone knew? Who told you?'

'Grandad knew, but it was Elizabeth who told me.'

'Elizabeth? When?'

'I met her on my own on Friday, in the afternoon.'

'She didn't come to see me?'

'It wasn't that. I asked to speak to her alone. I wanted to know the truth about Aled, and now I can tell you.'

'Grandad knew? He never said anything, not at the memorial or anything.'

'Grandad still won't talk about it. He has a different Aled he wants to remember.'

'But not the real one?'

'No.'

'How did Aled come to be taking cocaine?'

'At university. He tried it at parties, apparently. He didn't start taking it more seriously until he started working.'

'It's an expensive habit,' said Lowri.

'Exactly. He was asking Grandma Isabel for money.'

'So she knew–'

'Well, he told her he was gambling and had got into debt. But she found out what it was really for at the party.'

'He asked her for money then?'

'Yes, the night of the party they had this row. She offered to pay for rehab but refused to give him money. He was desperate. He was in a bad way. That's when he went to the headland with Elizabeth.'

'Elizabeth knew about him using cocaine?'

'She knew when they were in New York. She was hoping he'd stopped taking it.'

'When they went out, was that when she told him then she was pregnant?'

Catrin took a deep breath. 'She tried to, but he wasn't listening really. He wasn't thinking straight. To be honest, I don't think he really thought about it too much.'

'What happened to Elizabeth?'

'Well, Aled did suggest they get married.'

'So, he did want me.'

'It wasn't that simple. He was really just thinking about money for drugs. When Elizabeth realised that, she decided that she didn't want to marry him. He was very angry. He, um, pushed her.'

'He attacked her?'

'He hit her, and ran off.'

'Oh God, what a scumbag. How could he do such a thing?'

'He wasn't himself.'

Lowri sat forward. 'Bethan, people high on drugs or alcohol aren't really themselves. It's horrible to watch. I've seen it at the hospital, perfectly nice people getting very abusive and violent.'

'I've seen friends a bit pissed, but they tend to be a bit stupid and throw up.'

'This is very different.'

'Poor Elizabeth.'

'It was awful for her,' said Catrin. 'She blacked out. Then me and Dad found her.'

'Thank God you did.'

'It was a good thing, yes.'

Lowri put her arm around her sister.

'Aled was a brilliant, clever, handsome, man,' said Catrin. 'Maybe he could have been a great man, but he got involved with drugs and that was what killed him.'

'The truth: it's not always so nice is it?' said Bethan

'No. I'm sorry. I haven't helped. I know I was always making Aled out to be so perfect. I'm sorry I did that.'

'To die like that: it's terrible.'

'It was tragic. But, Bethan, I know it's a shock. But please don't let the drugs, the addiction, colour everything you know about Aled. I may have exaggerated, but he was wonderful. When he was not gripped by addiction, he was an amazing person. You'd have loved him, I'm sure.'

Bethan looked at her, tears streaming down her face. She didn't use her voice, but used a sign, making a fist over her heart. It was the sign for deep, heartbreaking loss, the sign for the loss of someone greatly loved. Catrin guessed that was how Bethan felt. It was a time to grieve for the loss of someone, a picture of a person who actually had never existed. It was desperately hard to let go of a fairy tale prince, but it had to happen if Bethan was ever to understand her past, the real Aled, and to piece together who she herself was. They sat together and hugged each other.

Chapter Thirty Seven

They went downstairs. Catrin started to get lunch. Mark came back from a walk, and started showing all his finds and photographs to Lowri and Bethan. It brought a sense of normality and provided the right level of distraction.

Catrin took her lunch and sat with Gareth in the living room.

'I talked to the girls about my Mum, and about Aled.'

'So soon?'

'It came up. It seemed the natural thing to do.'

'How is Bethan?'

'OK. She's with Lowri.'

'What's happened to Mark?'

'He's just come back from a walk on his own. He walks miles, that man.'

'Don't blame him escaping the tension here.'

'Bethan was very upset. I did suggest seeing her social worker, like you said, and she wants to do it.'

'Good.'

Catrin looked at Gareth. He was sitting up, looking well, and actually more relaxed then she'd seen him for ages.

'Gareth we have to talk about us sometime. I've been so unhappy. The smoking thing was just a symptom. I shan't be doing it again, but it doesn't mean everything is alright. I was trying to cover up pain, and not just pain from my past. I've been lonely. You've put your work and this research before me. It's no wonder I thought there was someone else. In a sense there has been, but it wasn't a person.'

'I'm sorry.'

'I can't go back to how it's been. I can't come second any more, not to work, or anything.'

'You want me to choose?'

Catrin took a deep breath. 'I suppose I do.'

'But I find it so hard. I find it impossible to do less hours. I do know it's a problem. I'm there far longer than any of the others.'

'And you took on that research.'

'Yes, that was a big mistake.'

'You must know it's not right never to remember my birthday, never to take me out, or go on a proper holiday, always offering to work Christmas, and then this week. Not to be there when the birth mother of our daughter turns up, and not to come to my brother's memorial, however upset you were with my Dad. You should have done all those things without me asking.'

Gareth scratched his forehead in the way he always did when he was nervous.

'When you put it in a list like that–'

'It's not right. Is it?'

'No. No, it's not.'

'Something has to change.'

'I suppose you wish you could to go to France with that Harri,' Gareth said, sulkily.

'No. I don't, but it was very nice to be taken out for a proper meal. He noticed the dress I wore, the one I bought myself for my birthday as a present from you. He listened to me. He was interested in me.'

'You love him?'

'Don't be so stupid. Of course not.'

'I do love you.'

'But how the hell am I meant to know that?'

They sat looking at each other. Who would make the next move?

Gareth touched Catrin's hand. 'I need time to think. It's good we're talking, though, isn't it?' He said it more as a plea.

'Yes. We need to untangle things, but we have to be brave, Gareth, have courage to make changes.'

He smiled weakly.

Bethan came in to the room with Lowri.

Bethan spoke. 'Mum, we've something to ask you. We've been talking. We would like to go out, cross the causeway, and go to Worm's Head.'

Catrin sighed. 'You still want to go there?'

'More than before. I need to, Mum, but I understand why you don't want to go. Lowri said she and Mark would go with me. Mark has been before a few times, so I would be safe.'

Catrin stood up and looked out of the window at Worm's Head in the distance. She had never ventured over there, not even as a child. Was it time, she wondered, to face it, face the dragon? If she didn't go now, would it always be that thing she couldn't do? Would the memory haunt her for ever?

'I think I should come,' she said. 'We need to find out when the causeway is open, though.'

'Mark went that way earlier. He knows the times. We could go this evening at six.'

Catrin took a sharp intake of breath. 'Today?'

'Yes. Why not?'

Catrin looked in amazement at Bethan. The vulnerable little girl had departed. Bethan had courage. She needed to find it as well.

'Well, OK. We can go this evening then. Have you both got decent shoes to wear? It's meant to be a really rough walk.'

Lowri came over and kissed her on the forehead. 'Good old Mum,' she said, laughing, and left the room.

Bethan put her head to one side. 'So, are you going to invite Grandad? I mean, it would be good for him, you know.'

'Gosh. I can try. You're right. I should ask him. Tell you what, I'll go and do it now, before I chicken out.'

'OK. It's a shame Elizabeth isn't here, Mum. I would like to have gone with her.'

'Really?'

'Yes, it would be good.'

'The thing is, she may still be here.'

'Elizabeth is down here?'

'She stayed at the B & B last night. I don't know if she's gone back to London yet.'

'Can I try and phone her, Mum? Ask her to come?'

Catrin nodded 'OK. Yes, of course'

Bethan ran out of the room

'This is really brave of you,' said Gareth.

'I don't feel it.'

'I can't come. I'm sorry.'

'Oh, no. People have told me it's really quite hard. Maybe it'll be too much for Dad.'

'I think your father is physically fit enough. He goes trekking, doesn't he? I'm not sure about emotionally, though.'

'He said some really difficult things on Friday. I know he was angry about the audition, but he can be so insensitive.'

'More than that, he's been so unkind to you. He doesn't deserve a daughter like you. He neglected you, and you suffered. You've a right to be very angry with him. I know I am.'

'I probably have made excuses for him for too long. You know, I sometimes wonder if he even loves

351

me. I know that sounds terrible, but I can't help thinking that.'

'I'm not sure how capable he is of fully loving anybody. But we can't change him.'

Catrin was about to fight back, to defend her father, as she always had, but she couldn't. Instead, she said, 'I think it's time I stopped fighting for something my father can't give me, isn't it?'

'Probably.'

'But he loved Aled.'

'Did he ever love the real Aled? We love Lowri and Bethan whatever they do. But I think your father just saw the parts of Aled he wanted to. He made him into this saint, but Aled must have known that the love he received from your father was dependent upon him living up to all his expectations. It was an impossible task.'

'Never something for nothing with my father,' said Catrin, sadly.

Gareth looked at her earnestly. 'I love you unconditionally. You do know that, don't you? I've failed at showing it, I know, but I do love you with all my heart. I know I can't bear to lose you. I do know that you are more important to me than anything.'

Catrin smiled. 'Thank you. I love you, too.' She kissed him, then sat back. 'Right. I'd better go and ask my father about this expedition.'

Safi wagged his tail. Catrin leant down and stroked him. 'Not you. I don't want you falling or anything. You stay here safe.'

She smiled nervously at Gareth. 'Right, wish me luck. I'm not sure which is worse, talking to my father or the thought of crossing the causeway.'

Catrin found her father in the study.

'Dad, I've been talking to Bethan and Lowri. I've told them about Mum and about Aled.'

'What about Aled?' Lloyd said, turning around. Catrin saw fire flash in his eyes.

'I told them that Aled was using drugs, that the night he died he had been taking cocaine.'

'How dare you make up lies about him?'

'It's not lies.'

'You're just jealous of him. Let's face it. He had everything you never had: looks, ability.'

'Stop it, Dad. Stop putting me down all the time.'

The words never reached him. 'Aled wasn't an addict. You're as bad as the people out there. They were the reason I had to bring him back here, or they'd have ruined him with their lies. Telling me my son had problems: he was just young, trying things out.'

'It was more than that.'

'No way. He wasn't like your mother. He could handle himself.'

'It's not that. You know it. He was ill.'

'No. No, he wasn't.'

Catrin stopped. There seemed no point any more.

'Listen, Dad. We're going to go over to Worm's Head, this evening. It's time we faced it, owned it. Bethan wants to see the place her father died and own the real Aled. I need to do the same. I need to acknowledge what happened to him, and also Mum. I don't want to be like her, to be frightened to go there. I'm tired of carrying all this guilt and shame from the past. Dad, I think you should come as well.'

'No. No way.'

'I know it's not an easy walk–'

'I can manage that. Good God. That's not the reason.'

'Then what is it?'

He stood up. 'I have no interest in all this going over the past.'

'Fine, your decision. I can't make you come. I can't make you face things, but it won't stop me doing it myself.'

Chapter Thirty Eight

It was a lovely fresh evening. The torrential rain the day before seemed to have washed everything clean. Before they left, Catrin packed up a rucksack with drinks and snacks, and a few other things. Elizabeth called at the house for them. Catrin had never seen her dressed so normally. She was wearing jeans and a T shirt. The trainers looked expensive. Before they left, Catrin suggested she come in and be introduced to Gareth.

The first thing Catrin noticed was the look of surprise on Gareth's face when he saw Elizabeth. He got up from the sofa and shook her hand formally.

'It's good to meet you. I should have done so before. I apologise.'

Elizabeth nodded. Catrin observed how much quieter and more subdued she was than when she had first met her.

'It's good to meet. Bethan has had a lovely home with you and Catrin.'

'Thank you. She looks very like you,' said Gareth.

'Yes,' Elizabeth smiled. 'I wasn't expecting that.'

It was a difficult situation. Time was too limited to talk about all the important things that had happened, but idle chit-chat seemed too trivial.

Catrin coughed. 'Maybe we ought to make time to chat properly soon. I think everyone is nearly ready to go.'

'Of course. We'll see each other again I'm sure,' said Gareth, 'but I'm glad to have at least had the chance to say hello.'

'So am I,' said Elizabeth. She seemed to breathe a sigh of relief on leaving the room, another hurdle crossed.

Bethan was running around madly looking for things, but eventually they were able to leave the house. Bethan chose to walk with Lowri and Mark. Catrin walked with Elizabeth.

They walked up through the village, then down the steep road to the headland. Cars passed them going up the hill, taking tired families home to their caravans, bed and breakfasts, and holiday homes. Catrin felt nervous as she pushed open the gate at the start of the headland path, but there were plenty of people around. It seemed quiet normal. Catrin glanced at Bethan, but she was happily talking to Lowri.

'You OK?' Catrin asked Elizabeth.

'I think so. It feels odd being here. It feels so different to that night. I don't have the history with this place that you do.'

'No, but it was very traumatic for you.'

'It was.' She saw Elizabeth's lip tremble. 'I was so scared. It's the smells that take me back more than anything.' She looked at Catrin. 'Thank you. I needed to do this.'

'We both do.'

'Do you ever dream of that night?'

'I dream of the causeway; calling for Aled. Do you?'

Elizabeth nodded, but her lips were closed tight.

'What?' asked Catrin?

'I dream I am up here, looking for my baby–' Tears spilled down her cheeks. Elizabeth wiped them away.

'You have her now. She's not lost anymore,' said Catrin, gently.

They walked on together. They soon reached the coastguard's hut. Mark checked the board for the crossing times again before they all started the steep climb down to the beginning of the causeway.

Catrin's heart started to pound as she followed the path down. It was not slippery, despite the rain from the day before. She glanced around, and wondered which rock she had cut her arm on all those years ago.

They reached the bottom, and stood at the edge of the causeway. Catrin had never been here before. It looked a harder walk than she had imagined. It was a long, difficult clamber over large jagged rocks and pools. It didn't bother Mark, who was already bounding off in front, closely followed by Bethan and Lowri.

Catrin looked back up the slope. There were people sitting eating sandwiches, drinking coffee. She envied them, then realised that she could go back up there, sit with them, and wait for the others to return. No-one would blame her. They would all understand. It was her choice.

'It's not an easy walk, is it?' said Elizabeth.

'No, harder than I expected.'

'And me. I'm not used to this sort of thing.'

'Well, shall we give it a go, then?'

They started together. Ahead, scores of gull screeched. There was a small number of people preparing to cross the causeway. Catrin started to clamber over the rocks. They were still wet, and covered in sharp mussels and other shells. She had never been particularly nimble, and she struggled rather inelegantly across the rocks. She noticed that Elizabeth was finding it even harder, and slowed down to let her catch up. She glanced into a pool, and realised that each rock pool was its own little world. In some there were purple seaweeds floating beneath the rippled clear water, like an oceanic version of the heather on the moors. In one she saw a large crab creeping out from under a rock. The still water of the pools reflected the almost cloudless pale blue sky, and contrasted with the rough grey rocks, with their occasional patches of orange and pink.

As they walked, Catrin felt immersed in sound, with the noise of the wind, the breaking waves, and the calls of birds. She caught up with Mark and Lowri, who were staring into a pool.

'It's amazing that anything thrives here,' Mark was saying. 'It's such a harsh environment. Things here have to cope with blistering heat at low tide, and then the full force of strong current when the sea floods the area again. See that little winkle: it has a particularly hard time, as they find it much harder than the stronger limpet to hold on to the rocks. When the tide comes surging back, most of them will be stripped from the rocks and then be tossed and battered by waves, currents, and flying debris like stones and pebbles.' Catrin thought of the flowers in her garden: the hardy dwarf sunflowers, and thought how Rhossili, for all its beauty, tested the hardiness of its inhabitants.

Eventually, they all reached land on the other side. There was a steep bank to get up. It was Mark who held out a hand to help Catrin up on to the turf. She was relieved to see that he also needed to stop to catch his breath.

'We are standing on the inner head,' Mark said. He took out a map of Worm's Head and explained it to them. She realised Mark was treating them rather like a group of students on a field trip. 'We walk around here, then come to a stone bridge, Devil's Bridge. Around the south side, we bear left of Low Neck. We can't climb to the top of the Outer Head at the moment because of the nesting birds.' Catrin looked ahead, and back at Rhossili.

The isolated white rectory Bethan had asked her about when they had been on the beach looked tiny on the hillside. She couldn't see Bryn Draig, though. It all looked such a long way away. She lifted her head, felt the strong sea breeze on her face, and heard the screeching chorus of hundreds of seabirds overhead. She had been so worried about coming here, but actually it was wonderful, magical.

Lowri came over to her. 'See those sheep. Mark was telling me that the farmers who graze sheep here say that the sheep, once they have been here, always stray back to Worm's Head.' She laughed. Mark joined them. He started pointing out the Pink Thrift and White Sea Campion, and identified the Herring Gulls, Guillemots, Razorbills, and Kittiwakes, adding, 'Sorry, no puffins yet today.'

Feeling quite light hearted, Catrin followed the others. They walked around the side of the inner head. Here, the noise from the guillemots and razorbills was deafening. It felt very wild and remote. Ahead stood the enormous natural stone Devil's bridge. It was then that the sky seemed to darken. It felt cold. Suddenly, Catrin felt fear. Now, she could imagine Aled alone here in the rain and dark. She felt heartbroken at the thought of her brother alone out here. She also felt fury at the drug that had dragged him here, that had killed him, stolen him from her.

They found a sheltered place to sit. It was a bit awkward. They all instinctively knew that something needed to be said or done, but no-one seemed sure what to do. Mark stood up awkwardly. 'I think I'd like to have a wander around, if that's OK.' He set off.

Catrin took control. From her bag she took a photo of Aled, a photo of her mother, and some small bottles of bubbles. She said, 'From now on we must talk, talk about Grandma Isabel, talk about Aled, and tell their whole story, not just parts. I thought we could blow some bubbles to signify letting go, not of our precious memories, but the guilt, the shame, and the stigma we have all suffered. That way, we can grieve for them, because grief is not about forgetting, it's about remembering. We can now remember Mum and Aled properly. We've come here to untangle the past, but we don't have to leave here and pretend it never happened. We grieve for them, but we don't have to be ashamed of them or what happened to them.'

They stood up and started to blow bubbles. There was innocence and beauty in what they did, and soon dozens of bubbles were being blown haphazardly about in the wind. Catrin glanced at the others. They were all looking up, their faces relaxed. Lights and colours bounced off the bubbles and they drifted away or popped noiselessly.

Catrin then held a piece of paper out to Bethan.

'Can you read and sign this? It's an ancient Tibetan Buddhist blessing. It's for each other and for Aled and Grandma Isabel.'

Bethan signed, 'May you be filled with loving kindness. May you be well. May you be peaceful and at ease. May you be happy.' Bethan handed it back to her mother, hugged her and then Elizabeth. Catrin hugged Lowri. Mark returned. They put everything back in the bag.

'We ought to make our way back now,' said Mark. 'We're not the fastest walkers.'

Catrin knew that he was being tactful. He could easily get back in half the time she needed. They all started to make their way back.

As she left Worm's Head she whispered to herself, 'I forgive you. I shall come back.'

Exhausted, but lighter, they began the walk back over the causeway, back to the mainland.

Chapter Thirty Nine

Monday 6th August 2012

The next day Catrin and Gareth took a picnic up on to the downs. Catrin loved it up there. The air was fresh and it was easy to find a place to sit alone. Safi ran, tracking scents, rolling in the bracken. They sat looking down towards the bay and the far off horizon.

'It's an extraordinary place, like reaching the end of the world,' said Gareth.

Catrin smiled. 'That's exactly what it's like. As soon as I reach here, it's like I leave the world behind me and enter somewhere really unique.'

'But you were dreading coming here. Don't you still find it all difficult and painful?'

Catrin looked out at the sparkling sea, and then Worm's Head.

'Not now. I've made peace with it.'

'I'm really glad. The thing is, while you were out yesterday, I did a lot of thinking. You know what we said about changes?'

'We don't have to do anything immediately,' said Catrin, feeling rather alarmed.

'Actually, I think we do. So, firstly, I've been thinking about work. I thought about reducing my hours.'

'Good.'

Gareth shook his head.

'I thought about it, but I realised it wouldn't work. I'd start, say, on three days a week, and soon I'd be there every day. No. I think I need a complete change.'

'What? Stop being a doctor?'

'No. I wouldn't want that. The thing is, there's something I haven't told you. I didn't see the point, because I'd dismissed it, but now I'm starting to think about it seriously.'

'What's that?' Catrin was apprehensive.

'About a month ago I was approached by someone from the hospital in Swansea. He had heard about my work with the students on placement.'

'Well, you do work very hard with them.'

'I know. I love that.'

'What did he say?'

'They want to expand their teaching of general practice at Swansea. He wants it to be more than students doing a placement, for it to be an integral part of the teaching. I think it's a brilliant idea. I've long thought the work of GPs gets underestimated, and yet we are at the sharp end of things. He knows how I feel and, well, he asked me to consider going there to lecture, and to support students out on placement.'

'Gosh, that's amazing. It's like it's tailor-made for you. But it's over here, in Swansea?'

'Yes. I rang the chap who spoke to me. I had his mobile number. Anyway, the job is still open. I told him about my illness, but the job wouldn't start until October. It's perfect. And that leads me to my next thought.'

'What's that?'

'You can say no.'

'What is it?'

'I was thinking of us putting in a bid for The Dragon House.'

Catrin sat back, stunned. 'What, live here?'

'Yes. Sell the place in Cardiff and come here.'

'But Bethan–'

363

Gareth grinned. 'I knew that was the first thing you would say. I was thinking, let's ask again about that room in hall.'

'But–'

'Why not? We should start to let her go. She told me it was all equipped.'

'I know, but it could be gone now.'

'If it has, I was thinking we could rent her our house, with some other students.'

'But how on earth would we afford all this? I'm sorry, but I can't see Dad letting us have this house cheaply.'

'I know, but we have that money from my parents. Listen, don't be cross, but I was emailing Gary, our accountant, last evening. He thinks we could do it. He even offered to draw me up a bid quickly. We have to show we're credible purchasers.'

'Wow. That's really kind of him, to do all this at home.'

'Well, I did a lot of work for him over some claims and, so he didn't mind.'

'And he thinks we could do it?'

'Yes, definitely. If we use the money from my parents–'

'We said that was for the girls, to help them both buy somewhere.'

'We can sort that out when we get to it. What do you think? It could be a new start, me and you.'

Catrin looked around. 'It would be wonderful. I could get some work locally, but I'd like to get back to painting. I was thinking that I would like to illustrate Mum's stories.'

'Interesting.'

'But, the bid. How does it work?'

'I was planning to put a bid in for the guide price. To be honest, the final decision is with your father. He chooses whose bid to accept.'

'I bet Harri will be offering over the asking.'

'I know. We can only try. We can't afford any more than that.'

'Do you want me to talk to Dad? It's not like he's desperate. He'll get a packet for his Cardiff house.'

'No. Definitely not. I don't want you crawling to him. I want this house to be ours, no strings attached.'

'And if he turns us down?'

'Then we look for somewhere else.'

Catrin took a deep breath. 'OK. Let's go for it.' She stroked Safi, who was sitting next to them, 'You'll have another new home, Safi.'

She looked at Gareth. 'It's all very sudden. Don't you want time to think?'

'No. I've been putting everything off too long. Now, I wondered. Could we go down to Cardiff tomorrow?'

'We could. We're not needed for the open house but why do you want to go there?'

'Well, there's a lot to sort out. I'd like to see if I can catch the surgery manager, pick up this bid. Maybe you could go in to see the university accommodation people tomorrow as well.'

'Good gracious, Gareth. Are you sure you can cope with all this? We might not get the house, you know.'

'I realise that, but we want to come here, don't we?'

'Yes. I'd really like that.'

'Good.'

Tuesday 7th August 2012

The next day, Catrin and Gareth drove down to Cardiff. Bethan, on hearing the news about the possibility of going into halls, went with them. She was very excited.

'I can't believe you're letting me do this.'

'We'll have to see if the room is still available.'

'But you said I can stay in our house otherwise.'

'Well, yes, but hall would be better, I think.' Bethan sat in the back of the car, busily texting friends.

The drive that morning down to Cardiff was going well. Catrin had been glad to leave the house, as people interested in it had slowly started to arrive. She dreaded seeing people who might be living in the house she was now desperate to own. Catrin took Gareth to the surgery. As they drove into the car park she saw him clenching his fists, heard him breathing hard. They sat in the parked car. 'Wait, and calm down,' she said. 'You have got your medication, just in case, haven't you?'

'Yes, I've got it.'

'Good. This is really difficult for you, isn't it?'

'You know, sometimes I would sit out here like this before I went into work.'

'You'd sit out here on your own?'

'Yes.'

'I never knew. Do you want me to come in with you now?'

'No. It's OK. I can do it.' Gareth gave her a quick smile and got out.

'I'll go to the university, see about the accommodation then, and pick you up after.'

Catrin and Bethan went to the university office, and found that there was one room equipped for a Deaf

366

student still available. If they would like to, she and Bethan could go and see it that day. Bethan, of course, was very excited. Catrin stifled a rising panic.

They were taken to the halls of residence by an employee from the university. Bethan was communicating very well with the woman. Catrin was left walking behind them. The place all looked so big and imposing. She felt a lot more overwhelmed by it than Bethan appeared to be.

There was another mother and daughter looking around the halls as well. Catrin thought the woman looked as nervous as she felt. The room was small: there was a shared kitchen, but Catrin was reassured to see the adaptations were all there and working.

Bethan started talking to the other girl who was visiting, and they were soon swopping mobile numbers and Facebook details. The other mother introduced herself.

'Hi, I'm Helen. So, your daughter is starting in September?'

'That's right.'

'It's hard, isn't it?' the woman said suddenly. 'I'm dreading Katy going off. She's the last one of my four. I keep crying. My husband says I'm daft. I know from the others that actually they're home a lot: you know, they have very long holidays. I keep reminding myself of that.'

'That helps,' said Catrin. 'I must admit I'm nervous.'

Bethan turned, signed to her, 'Katy's doing music as well, then went back to chatting to Katy.

'Oh my goodness, your daughter is Deaf,' said Helen. 'You look very calm about her going away.'

'I think it's like the swans, you know: gliding along, frantically paddling away under the surface.'

'Ah, but that's what mothers do a lot, isn't it?' said Helen.

Catrin smiled.

'Do you fancy a cup of coffee? There's a café just outside?' asked Helen.

'Actually, that would be really nice,' said Catrin.

The four of them went and had coffee and cake, and chatted. Catrin was surprised to receive a call from Gareth, saying, 'Sorry to keep you waiting. I've finished now. We need to pick up that bid. I rang Gary. He's not in, but he worked last night doing it for us. We can collect it from the desk.'

Catrin and Bethan said their farewells, headed back to the accommodation office to sort out the paperwork, and then picked up Gareth. He looked very relieved.

'Everything went fine,' he said. 'They will have to get in locums, which I feel guilty about. I went in, and saw the waiting room full. It's not right, Catrin. The system is close to collapse.'

'I know, love, but you can't save it all. You've been a more than dedicated GP for well over twenty years.'

'But heaven knows if they'll get a replacement. I worry about my patients.'

'Gareth, you are no good to anyone ill. In this job you will be able to teach good practice to new doctors, won't you? Pass on what you have learned.'

'I guess so.'

'Come on. Let's go and pick up that bid.'

It was a relief to drive back to Gower again. They went via the estate agent, handed in their bid, then returned to the house.

'How did the day go?' Catrin asked her father.

'Well, all things considered, you hadn't done much tidying, had you?'

'No, but then you didn't finish the painting.'

'Well, it didn't seem to bother people.'

'The bids. Do you think they will go up to the asking price?' she asked nervously.

'Easily. Above, I should imagine.'

Catrin's heart sank.

That evening, she and Gareth went to the pub to eat, the rest cooked for themselves. It was hard to sleep that night.

Wednesday 8th August 2012

In the morning, Catrin watched her father drive off to the estate agent, wondering how long it would be before she knew. She was getting increasingly anxious. The deadline for the bids was ten o'clock that morning. Her father had taken an early morning call from someone who had been round the day before, saying that they were putting in a 'very good bid' that morning.

Bethan and Lowri had no idea what their parents were doing. Despite driving with them to the estate agent the day before, Bethan had not realised. She had been in her own world, chatting on Facebook with her new friend Katy, trying to get together a group of people who would be in halls with them.

It was lunch time when Lloyd returned.

Catrin and Gareth were sitting staring at the Olympics, but neither was taking anything in. They heard the front door open, and waited. Her father didn't come straight into them but went into the kitchen first. She heard him pouring a drink. He came into the living room.

'So, you two put in a bid.'

Catrin nodded.

'You should have told me. I felt pretty stupid when I opened it, not knowing my own daughter was trying to buy the house.'

'I'm sorry. We didn't want you to feel obliged. We only thought about it in the last few days.'

'I see.'

'So, Dad. Did you make a decision?'

The wait was agony, but he was not going to make it easy.

'There were more bids than I expected.'

'Over the guide price?'

He nodded. Catrin's heart sank. Her father took a sip of his drink.

'Anyway, I made my decision.'

'And?'

Chapter Forty

Catrin and Gareth sat, holding their breath.

'The house is yours.'

Catrin peered at her father. 'You really mean it?'

'I do. We have to sign contracts, obviously, but, yes, it's yours.'

Catrin gave her father a kiss on the cheek.

'Thank you, Dad. That's amazing.'

'You really want it that much?'

'Yes.' Catrin told him about Gareth's job.

'That makes sense, yes. Still, I'm surprised you want to be here, Catrin.'

'Its OK, Dad. I'm fine with it now.'

'I guessed you must have had a change of heart.'

'I love it here. Really, I can't believe I'll be living in Nana Beth's house.'

Her father sighed. 'You're like your mother. This place: it's in your blood, I think.'

'I know our bid was less than some of the others,' said Gareth. 'It was good of you to give us preference.'

Catrin's father shrugged. 'Well your bid was convincing, money well worked out. You have a good accountant.'

'Yes, we have.'

Lloyd stood up. 'Right, I have a few things to do upstairs.'

When he had gone, Catrin said, 'I think we ought to tell the kids. I think they're in the garden with Mark.'

That was where they found them.

Catrin felt her heart beating fast. The girls looked at her puzzled. She said to Gareth, 'I think you should tell them.'

He grinned at their daughters, and opened his arms. 'Welcome to your new home.'

'What?'

'It's ours. The Dragon House is our new home.'

Lowri stared at him. 'But–'

'We put a bid in. Grandad accepted it. The house is ours.'

'Can you afford it?' asked Lowri.

'We can.'

'But what about the surgery, Dad?'

Gareth explained about the job offer in Swansea. 'I can have long weekends working on the house.'

'So that's why you're letting me go into halls?'

'It is, but it will be good for you. We are only a train ride away, and your mother will be popping down, I'm sure.'

Bethan smiled.

Then Catrin looked over at Lowri, sitting quietly with Mark. 'This will be your home, you know, when ever you want to come.'

Lowri grinned. 'Don't worry about seeing us. I think Mark will probably take up permanent residence.'

'That would be just great.'

Catrin wondered how her father was. She couldn't find him downstairs, so she went up. She glanced into her father's room. She was shocked to see what he was doing.

'Dad. What's going on?'

'I'm leaving.'

'But–'

'I rang up the airline, brought forward my flight. I'm going to America today.'

'You can't just go.'

'I can. Everything is settled. Look, I'll be back to sign things, but I need to get away. Don't worry about the house. I've spoken to my solicitors.'

'I'm not worried about that. I'm worried about you.'

'I'll be fine.'

'You'll miss Bethan's birthday.'

'I don't think she'll be bothered.'

'That's not true.'

'Well, I have friends over there, who want to see me. I have the trust to set up.'

'The article, Dad–'

'I don't think you'd better write that.'

'No, I'll leave it. Dad, you will come back sometimes? I don't like to think of you over there on your own.'

'I won't be on my own. I have a friend over there, Evelyn. She was on about moving in together.'

'Dad, you have a partner?'

'We've been friends for a few years. She's just retired. She lost her husband. He died. Yes, maybe we could live together. We'll see.'

'I'm glad, Dad. I don't want you to be unhappy.'

'Well, no, and I wish you well, Catrin.'

Her father picked up his bags. She followed him down the stairs. Catrin shouted for everyone to come out. She explained to Bethan what was happening.

'I'm sorry you're going so soon, Grandad,' she said, hugging him. 'I can still come and see you, can't I?'

For the first time that day, he smiled. 'Of course. Any time. I'll send you the flight money.'

373

'Great. I'd really like that.'

Lloyd turned to Lowri. 'If you want to make some money as a doctor, you know where to come.'

Lowri was about to say something, but changed her mind. Instead, she said, 'Thank you, Grandad.'

They all accompanied Lloyd to the front door. Only Catrin walked to the car with him.

'Thank you, Dad, for the house.'

'Well, maybe I needed to make amends.'

He put his cases in the back of his car, turned back, and awkwardly hugged her.

Catrin was so surprised that she stepped back.

Her father gave a lopsided grin. 'There you are: something for nothing,' he said.

He got in the car. Catrin, speechless, watched him drive away.

Later that afternoon, Catrin went out with Safi. Their route took them down through the village. She could hardly believe that this place would soon be her home. Up there was the newsagent, the pub. David and Anwen would be close by. She looked down at the bungalows. Aunty Angela would be down there. She started walking that way but, as she did, she spotted Harri sitting on a bench, looking out over the bay. She went over to speak to him.

'So, your husband outbid me–'

'For the house–'

'That as well.' He grinned.

'I went over to Worm's Head, you know.'

'I thought you might.'

'Well, there was no point in running away, was there?'

'No, I guess not.'

'I'm very excited about coming here to live. We have lots of plans.'

'And dreams?'

'Well, yes.'

'You're sure then that this is the place for you?' Harri looked at her closely.

'Yes. This is where I belong, Harri.'

He sighed. 'I think I always knew in my heart you belonged here,' he said quietly.

'What will you do?'

'Go back to Collioure.'

'To Francine?'

'I don't think so, but I have plans, dreams. You know, I'll be fine.'

'Good. I'm popping down to see my Aunty Angela.'

'Ah, family, yes. You really do belong here. Right, I can't sit here all day. People to see, cases to pack.'

'Good luck, then,' she said.

Harri nodded. 'You take care, and don't forget: you're never too old to have dreams.'

Catrin smiled and continued on her way down to her aunt's. As she reached the neat bungalow, Angela was gardening at the front.

'Hi,' called Catrin. Her aunt stood up stiffly.

'Catrin, I heard the news. Wonderful.'

'You know already?'

'Of course. No secrets here. You've been down to Cardiff, then. How did Gareth get on?'

Again, Catrin wondered how she knew.

'Listen. Come in, and have a cup of tea. Remember, there's something I want to give you.'

'Do you mind Safi?'

'Of course not. Come on in.'

Catrin followed her inside. Despite being a newer building, inside was very old-fashioned. Catrin found it impossible to imagine Elizabeth staying there. Having sat down with an enormous scone and cup of tea, she waited patiently as her aunt slowly disappeared to find what she wanted to give her. Angela returned with a package wrapped in a brown paper bag. She handed it Catrin. Catrin opened it carefully.

Inside was a very old book, leather bound. She turned the fine pages. There were beautiful drawing of flowers, insects, butterflies, as well as line drawings of places and buildings in Rhossili.

'What a beautiful old book.'

'It is, worth a bit now. It belonged to my father, your Grandad Hugh, and he gave it to your mother.'

'And then she gave it to you?'

'Well, yes, but she didn't give it to me to keep.'

Catrin looked puzzled.

'In the years leading up to Aled's death your mother gave me a number of things to sell for her. She wanted the money, you see, to send to Aled. I took jewellery to a local jeweller I knew who would give me a decent price. This was one of the things she wanted me to sell.'

'But you didn't?'

'No. I couldn't. It didn't seem right. I just gave her the money.'

'So that's where all the jewellery went.'

'That's right. I didn't mind selling the gaudy stuff from Lloyd, but this was special.'

'Did you know why she needed the money?'

'It was Aled. He was gambling. It was very sad.'

Catrin looked at her aunt. Should she tell her?

'Actually, there was more.'

Quietly, she told her aunt the story of Aled.

'I see. Well, I'm not surprised. It was a very sad business.'

'Dad still denies it.'

'Yes, he would, but then he never did like real life very much did he? He treated my sister badly. Their marriage was a mess. Now, you and Gareth look a lot better suited to me.'

Catrin smiled. 'We are really looking forward to living here.'

'Good. I look forward to having you living close by.'

Her aunt stood up.

'Good. Oh, there's your picture, on the wall.'

Catrin looked at it from a distance. 'I'm glad you have it.'

'You must do some more now.'

'I intend to. Did you know my mother wrote stories?'

'Ah. She always made them up when I was little. She had a gift making up stories. She never kept a diary, though.'

'You know, I've just remembered that journal Bethan gave me. I can suddenly think of lots of things to write in it. Oh, and by the way,' said Catrin, 'On Saturday, we're having a party. It would be lovely if you came.'

'Now that would be lovely. It's a long time since there's been a party at The Dragon House.'

Chapter Forty One

The party for Bethan at the Dragon House was to be a simple buffet in the garden. Bethan of course would be having a far more raucous celebration with her friends back in Cardiff, but today was a relatively calm affair.

Catrin decided to wear her blue silk dress, but today it would be different. Today there would be no cardigan to conceal her scar. There was no need to cover it up. It wasn't ugly. Her father had been wrong about that. If anything, she should be proud of it. It showed that she had been through something difficult and survived. She brushed her hair, which she let hang loose. She wore a new, light pink lipstick and put on her sapphire necklace. She looked at herself in the mirror, gave herself a smile and went downstairs.

Bethan was excited. She was wearing the dramatic outfit which she had worn to the audition. Lowri was sitting in the garden with Mark. She was ethereal, in a long white dress, looking very relaxed. Gareth was sitting with them, chatting.

Catrin had joined them when David, Anwen and Angela arrived. David gave her his usual bear hug, then looked down at her.

'You look different. Your eyes are shining.'

'A lot has happened.'

Safi went running up to Anwen. She knelt down to fuss him. 'Sorry, no sausages today.'

David looked at Catrin. 'Now, I want to know exactly what has been going on.'

When Catrin had finished he grinned at her.

'Wow. I'm so proud of you.'

'Well, thank you. It was so helpful to talk to you.'

'You've been so brave. I can't believe you're going to be living so close to us. It's fantastic.'

'I know. I can't believe this is my home now.'

'You know, one day, when you're ready, you could think about doing something to support the hostel. We have a charity shop, or there are groups that meet there.'

'You think that would be a good idea?'

'Speaking selfishly, we really need the help, but it's not just that. Sometimes, raising awareness of addiction can help people who have been affected by it. It's doing something positive with your experience. I'm not saying you should be doing anything immediately. It's up to you, but think about it.'

'Yes, OK. I will.'

Catrin heard the gate open: Elizabeth was arriving, with a man, who looked a few years older than her. Richard, presumably.

'Great, they've come. Bethan really wanted them to. Elizabeth spoke to me. She seemed really nervous, but she said she'd try to come. I'll go and say hello.'

Catrin could see Elizabeth holding Richard's hand tightly.

'Hi,' she said. 'Come on in. I'll get you each a glass of wine.'

Bethan came straight over.

'Happy birthday,' said Elizabeth. She took a card from her bag. Bethan read it.

'Look, Mum,' she said to Catrin, who had returned with the glasses.

The card was a print of Van Gogh's Sunflowers. Inside it said simply, 'To my daughter Bethan, with love from your mother, Elizabeth xx"

'That's lovely.' Catrin realised there was no stabbing pain. She was really happy for Bethan. Elizabeth slipped her hand into her bag again, took out a photograph, and handed it to Bethan.

'It's the one of me as a baby,' said Bethan, 'but it looks new.'

'I had a copy of mine made. I thought maybe you would like to put it in your album.'

Bethan grinned. 'Thanks. That's really lovely.'

'There's something else.' Elizabeth handed her a small white box, shaped like a book. Bethan opened it. Inside were the scan picture and the tiny hospital band with her name on.

'Oh, my God. You can't give me these.'

'Yes, I think they should go in the album, like Lowri's.'

Catrin blinked. She touched the hospital band. 'That's a lovely thing to do, Elizabeth.'

'You know, they've been hidden away for too long. They should be in the album with the rest of Bethan's story.'

Lowri glanced over and shouted, 'Great, time for presents.' She reached to her side and brought a bag over. From it, Bethan took a card, opened it, and grinned. The card was a montage of photographs of the sisters from when they were very young. Bethan opened her present. It was in a beautiful glittery box. When Bethan opened it, she found a silver pendant on a necklace.

'Oh, it's beautiful,' she said handling the delicate pendant.

'What is it?' asked Catrin.

'It's a Welsh dragon,' said Lowri with a grin. She glanced at Bethan. 'Do you like it?'

'I love it,' replied Bethan. She put it on.

Catrin smiled as she watched her daughters hug each other.

Catrin handed over the card from her and Gareth, a beautiful print of Bethan's favourite painting by Picasso, 'Girl with a Dove'.

'We've put some money into your account,' said Gareth, 'and your Mum has bought you this.' Catrin quickly found some parcels from the kitchen and brought them out. Bethan unwrapped them, but looked puzzled.

'Duvet, covers, pillowcases, mugs, cutlery?'

'They're things you'll need to go into hall.'

Bethan laughed and hugged her parents.

They lit the candles on the birthday cake and, while everyone sat around chatting, Gareth took Catrin to one side.

She looked at him puzzled. He took out a small rectangular box. She opened it, and from it took out a delicate watch. The round face was surrounded by diamonds and sapphires.

'It's beautiful,' she whispered.

'Happy birthday,' said Gareth. He grinned. 'It's a bit late, which is ironic.'

Catrin placed the watch on her wrist and used the delicate clasp to secure it.

He smiled broadly. 'Good, it fits. You have such tiny wrists.'

'It's perfect. Thank you. I've never seen a watch with sapphires before. Where ever did you find it?'

'I talked to Mark. He put me in touch with his father. I met him after I went to the surgery.'

Catrin looked down at the watch.

'Thank you. It means so much. Thank you.'

Elizabeth was sitting with Richard and looked over at Bethan. It felt like a dream. All those years of hiding away on this day, lighting candles, not knowing how to grieve, just crying comfortless tears as she looked at her one photograph of that tiny baby. Today, she was here with that baby, who had grown into a beautiful accomplished woman, a woman she had a future with.

Then she heard someone laugh. It was Catrin. She had never heard her laugh before. It was a lovely laugh, light and full of joy. She also thought Catrin looked different: she was standing more upright, her head held high. Yes, the woman she had first seen at the memorial had changed. Elizabeth went over.

'Thank you so much for inviting me. It means so much to be here.'

'I'm glad you are here, too. It's been a very difficult few weeks, hasn't it? We've both faced some hard things but, you know, I don't regret it.'

'Nor me, not at all. To meet Bethan has been the most extraordinary thing, and today to be with her, to be with you all, is wonderful.' Elizabeth stopped. Her voice broke. To her embarrassment, she realised she was crying.

'Oh no, I'm so sorry,' she said, frantically trying to find a tissue.

Catrin gently wiped away a tear. 'It's alright. You don't have to be ashamed of tears. No more silent tears for us now.'

Elizabeth swallowed hard. Rather self-consciously, she leant forward, gave Catrin a quick kiss on the cheek, and returned to Richard.

Catrin stood alone for a moment. She looked around the garden, and remembered something. She walked over to the border, found the stone dragon, and put it in its place at the front of the border. She looked down and smiled. It didn't hurt to look at it now.

She looked over at Worm's Head, the dragon. After eighteen years, she could look at it, think about it. There were no stabbing pains, no ghosts whispered. She leant down and stroked Safi, who sat faithfully at her feet. She glanced around at everyone. Elizabeth was laughing with Richard. Mark was holding a shell, talking about it to Gareth with his usual intensity. Bethan was signing with Lowri. Catrin watched in awe, struck with the beauty of the signing, understanding again why signing had been described as dancing with words. As Catrin watched, she experienced a deep sense of calm. There were no more ghosts, no more hidden chapters.

I hope you have enjoyed reading "Hidden Chapters". If so, please take the time to post a short review. It really makes a difference in encouraging others to take a look at it. Thank you. To be notified when further books are published please send an email to

marygrand90@yahoo.co.uk

My first novel, "Free to Be Tegan", is available here:

https://amzn.com/B00UC9R1YM

http://www.amazon.co.uk/dp/B00UC9R1YM

A collection of my short stories, "Catching the Light" is available here:

https://amzn.com/B01AGWVQJ0

http://www.amazon.co.uk/dp/B01AGWVQJ0

Find me at https://www.facebook.com/Author-Mary-Grand-1584393925166154/ *or follow me on twitter @authormaryg*

Mary Grand

Acknowledgements

To my husband who continues always to inspire and support me and who spends many hours editing and formatting in the evenings and weekends.

To Janet, Adele and Jess for being fantastic beta readers, for your thorough, encouraging and detailed comments. Of course, all errors and typos are my responsibility.

Thank you to all my lovely family including Anne, Gerald and Ruth, and the many friends who support me through thick and thin, and provide countless cups of coffee and chats. Thank you to Harriet (and Safi!). Also, a big thank you to all the fantastic writers and readers I have met here on the Isle of Wight, on 'the mainland' and online. Every encouraging email, review and comment has helped far more than you can imagine.

Finally thank you to Ryan at Love Your Covers for the inspired covers for my novels.

About the Author

I was born in Cardiff and have retained a deep love for my Welsh roots. I worked as a nursery teacher in London and later taught Deaf children in Croydon and Hastings.

I now live on the beautiful Isle of Wight with my husband, where I walk my cocker spaniel Pepper and write. I have two grown up children.

'Hidden Chapters' is my second novel, after 'Free to Be Tegan' which is available for kindle. I have also published a book of short stories 'Catching the Light' also available for kindle.

J.W

18972976R00216

Printed in Great Britain
by Amazon